TAUNTED
By Choice...

A Jamaican Saga of Living on the Edge

Damali A. Henry

Cover design: Jiann S. Lawrence
Typeset and book layout: Damali A. Henry
Front & Back cover photograph: iStock.com

Printed in the U.S.A   ISBN: 978-0-9866982-0-0

ACKNOWLEDGEMENTS

To Jah Almighty, I exalt all praise and gratitude for the gifts of creativity, expression, and sensibility.

This novel was inspired by my love-hate relationship with life and all his facets. Whether I was soaring with achievements and temporary highs, or sinking low with setbacks and depressing consequences, I had my life. He's always been the blessing. Through thick and thin we've viewed, analysed, and contorted the world together, using the power of words to manifest greatness. I've shared an aspect of those times here, in *TAUNTED By Choice...*

For Mom, Dad, Kathryn, Gianni, Gary, Mark H., Nathan H., Kamali L., Danielle M., Orlando W., Sherriann B., Melanie C., Andrea W., all other foundation family members & friends:
Thank you for your input to my being, my imagination, and for your undying support. I look forward to walking the rest of my path with you, enlightened by our individual lights that we inspire each other to shine.

For Jiann L., Danielle M., and 'The Editors':
I appreciate that you worked and volunteered adamantly to manifest this dream. Much love and thanks!

For my readers:
Through fiction, elements of facts are alighted. Choose wisely; prepare for the consequence; but most importantly, full-joy being *TAUNTED By Choice...!!!*

CHAPTER ONE

*D*amn! *My day just got fucked! It's definitely too damn early in the morning for this shit! Too damn early in the year! Some New Year this is cracked up to be!* Shane cursed inwardly.

"We'll definitely conduct more testing so don't be so pessimistic." The voice continued, interrupting his thoughts.

What the hell is she talking about? How many tests do we need to confirm the same shit? Fool shi tek man fah! With his head still resting on the doctor's desk, Shane refined his sentiments to voice them aloud.

"Listen Doc, I know you're only saying that to make me feel better, and don't get me wrong I definitely appreciate it. But just give it to me real nuh man...once and for all. Test after test and they all show the same thing. Unless new tests and all the machines can perform miracles, why yuh think you'll find sup'm different? Or what, something's gonna disappear?"

"Shane you can't have this attitude already. The individual tests are necessary to isolate the probabilities of what we're dealing with. The findings so far are all preliminary. We *cannot* jump to any conclusions. This is your *life* we're talking about!"

"Or the ending of..." He took a deep drag of air and leaned all the way back in the chair.

The room suddenly fell silent, alerting him to sit upright and look forward. Just as he'd anticipated, she pointedly eyed him, evidently not pleased with his remark. He held her gaze with utmost defiance, and deliberated. *Now that we're all pissed off...*His mental smirk unconsciously graced his lips. *Why are you so mad anyway?*

And looking even sexier while you're at it! I'm not about to retract what I said…suh stay vex!

And that she already was. "Well that's enough for now." The woman offered in a calm tone, prematurely ending their weekly session. "I'll…" She clumsily lingered on the words. "*The office* will contact you to schedule your next appointment. Enjoy the rest of your day Mr. Wright!"

Oh! We're doing surnames now? That's cold Doc! He was somewhat angered by her switch from 'I'll' to 'the office'. *That's the most formal you've ever been. But as you wish…*

"Well until such time then *Natalie…*" He paused to gather his belongings. "Peace!" He stormed out of the office without stopping to look back or close the door.

Shane Wright was through the waiting area and out the building in the blink of an eye.

Though she had avoided eye contact while dismissing her troublesome client, Natalie sat staring in his direction as he left. *What a stubborn…no! I was wrong!* She truthfully reassessed her take on the situation. *Oh my God, did I really expect him to be okay with all this? How could I be so inconsiderate? So unprofessional? I lost my cool. I was too hard on him. Why do I always lose my cool with Shane? He's so damn handsome! Whoa! Where the hell did that come from? Lord, I'd better call my husband.*

"Roxanne, you're either in or yuh out yuh nuh! Every morning is the same routine with you. How many times I have to repeat that I begin work at nine o'clock? Not nine thirty! Not ten! Nine!"

"Lawd Regina, enough of you and yuh misery!" Roxanne hastily retorted. "*You* choose to repeat yourself. Nobody asks you to! Every morning is the same for me too; nagging, nagging, and more nagging. Leave mi if yuh can't wait!" She left it at that, but only on the outside. *Miserable gyal! Stir up mi nerves every friggin' morning. Can't wait fi get ma own place and get out of here! Geesum!*

Regina scrutinised her little sister with disdain. "I'm not even going to respond to you!" She made a quick exit from the kitchen in lieu of breaking her jaw. *Ungrateful little brat! I should make you take the damn bus!*

"You just did!" Roxanne chuckled and provokingly blurted aloud. *Whateva!*

The routine rampage continued. "Babe, I'm asking you *again*, to please come and move your car! I need to get out of here! And why do you insist on parking behind me and you can fit perfectly well beside me?" She deep breathed and audibly exhaled. *Control the temper Regina... you can be calm. Deep breaths...yes...you are calm.*

"Like yuh don't know why him park there? So yuh can't leave unheard at nights. Duh!" The familiar voice escaped from the kitchen.

"Mind your business Roxanne! And didn't I tell you to get your crap in the car?" She made her way into the kitchen for a mini face-off.

"I'm coming down now Regina. A little patience, please babes. It's only eight fifteen. Plus why are we so cranky and we *all* had a good night?" Linton's voice greeted them before his wide grin appeared in the kitchen. "Hmm?" He playfully eyed his woman then winked at her.

Regina instantly melted. *He's right. Last night was more than amazing. It was the best ever! Okay, I say that all the time. But Biology is definitely his specialty! I am going to be late for work again! Only eight fifteen...yeah, 'cause everywhere I'm going is next door to each other!*

"I don't even wanna know what was so good about the night. Y'all disgust me!" Roxanne's voice interrupted her thoughts.

Regina snapped. "Roxanne, pack your stuff in the car! *Please!*" She turned to Linton. "Baby you're right. I'm sorry. I just hate being even a little late. You know I'm up for that promotion? I have to keep everything in tact."

They were all trying to make their way out the door.

"I know baby. And you definitely will be promoted so stop worrying so much. I've seen your competition, or lack there of..." He busted out laughing.

Regina stopped halfway down the driveway. "That wasn't nice! Thanks for the encouragement though." She returned his wink from earlier and giggled.

"Anytime, and every time. Kisses for my misses?" He playfully puckered up.

She planted her lips on his.

"Y'all are so damn corny!" Roxanne loudly exclaimed. *But cute!* She admitted to herself. *I need to find me a mister...see what I'm missing. Yea right! Gina would just kill me!*

She stretched through the window and snatched the car keys from her sister's loose grip. It was time to tune in to the morning's Dancehall music station.

Life can sure be a bitch sometimes! This must really be two thousand and hate! It barely kicked off and this is the shit that it brings? Fuck! You just never know what the hell you're in for with life! Shane was more than irritable as he walked into the Juici Beef restaurant.

"Morning. Gimme a ackee and salt fish with food nuh please...and a Tru Juice too." He ordered as he got to the front counter, skipping the line-up entirely.

"What flavour?" The counter clerk asked indirectly, in her seductively under-toned drawl.

Shane immediately lapsed into flirting mode and turned up 'Mr. Charming'. *Watch dem dreamy eyes deh nuh! That's some big tits yuh have there bway.* He smirked at the thought of having his way with the voluptuous woman, and coyly replied.

"Are we talking about the Tru Juice still? Or sup'm else?" He flashed a flirtatious grin.

The young woman visibly blushed and fumbled to retrieve a Fruit Punch flavour, before handing him his change.

He scribbled the number to his 'bootie line' on the face of the five hundred dollar bill, and slid it back towards her.

"Take care of your-sexy-self! Make sure them *things* call me!" He playfully pointed at her chest and winked, much to the amusement of female patrons admiring him from afar.

A few men lurking outside the restaurant immediately pounced on him as he stepped through the exit. They were undoubtedly Track and Field fanatics.

"Big up yuhself yute!" One of them shouted. "Mek sure yuh dun di place a Australia next mont yuh zimme?" The burly man chuckled heartily.

Shane smiled and offered his usual response. "Nuff respect! Yuh done know!"

Another younger man slowly approached. "My lord, beg yuh a brekfass money nuh?" He grinned, revealing two rows of gold teeth.

Shane consciously avoided a scowl and handed him the rest of his change from the restaurant. *All a part of the growing fame huh?* He tried to coach himself out of annoyance as he learned to cope with his increasing fame and consequently, the diminishing privacy. *Just the price I'll have to pay to put Track back on the minds of Jamaicans worldwide.* He hopped into his Lexus truck and cautiously eased out of Lane Plaza's parking lot, already over-crowded at eight thirty in the morning.

"Ok chic. Remember I can't pick you up today. I have a presentation at class tonight that might run a little late. Call Linton if you can't get a ride okay?"

"Yea sis, I will." Roxanne airily responded as she gathered her belongings from the back seat with little haste. She glanced at her hair for the umpteenth time in the mirror before opening the car door.

Regina gently held unto her arm. "Hey, and as usual, I'm sorry about shouting at you this morning. You know it's nothin' but love right?" She offered an emphasised grin to spice up her renowned sarcasm.

"Hmm! Whatever you seh!" She reflexively rolled her eyes to compliment that thought.

"*What*! Are you kidding me?" Regina made her best sulking face.

"I'm joking Gina. Calm down. Yes I know it's *all* love. See yuh later…and love yuh." She slammed the car door and hastily headed up the front steps of her school.

"Love you too sis." Regina watched her sister until she went out of sight. *You better know that.*

As soon as she was honked by another parent to make her way out of the congested parking lot, her phone began to vibrate somewhere in the car. She quickly scanned the center console then blindly dug through her pocketbook. *This can only be one person…* She pressed the send button before fully retrieving the phone.

"House of tits, may I take your order?" She shouted, smiling as she wrestled the phone out of her bag.

"You *wish* you had tits to serve! Them things start growing yet?"

"Kiss my ass Shane! Was that really necessary? What's up? What do you want?"

"Now *ass*…yes! *That's* what you could definitely serve a lot of! Feeding of the ten thousand…" He always enjoyed teasing his best friend.

"Jokes…but truth. You bringing me breakfast this morning or what?"

"No time for breakfast today hun. Got tonnes of appointments. One of those tight-schedule days yuh nuh?"

Regina manoeuvred her way through the traffic, but was attentive enough to know a lie when Shane uttered it.

"You're such a liar! *You* miss ackee and salt fish on a Monday morning? Spare me Shane! You're probably on your way for some breakfast sex as we speak. But anyway I'll eat from the cafeteria. And I love how yuh call me back last night too. Which *one* of the hoes? Or was it a new groupie? I can't seem to keep up!"

Shane chuckled. *Always so presumptuous, but yet so on point Miss Mitchell. Gotta love you!* "When have you ever kept up Gina? And why yuh sound so jealous? A joke! Hun, you know what the late night talking does to Linton. Can't overdo it and mek the man extra jealous yuh zimme? As a man myself, I'm forced to respect the man hours!"

"This has nothing to do with Linton. Yuh full of it!" She quickly checked him. "Shane, when yuh plan to stop 'hoe-ing'? You're such a dog! *Ruff ruff*!" They both laughed. "Anyways I'm almost at work. You plan to talk about that appointment this morning or it's *another* of your secrets?"

Shane cringed at the undertone of her last remark. "Gina, I don't have any *secrets* with you…don't say that. This doctor just did some more in-depth examinations than the other ones did. Just a waste of my money if yuh ask me. But she seems more knowledgeable overall though. Yuh ever notice how the pain seems to hide as soon as yuh sit in the doctor's chair? It's like it has its own mind to rahtid. But that's all there is to it for now. Nothing new to report."

You're lying again! She knew his half truths too well. *What the hell is going on with you Shane? Lying to me now?* She chastised him inwardly.

Of all the seventeen years she had known Shane, this last year had been the most mysterious of their friendship. She knew he had been having painful stomach cramps, and that he had been going to a series of appointments with different specialists to get his health examined. But all his reports on the visits thus far, were just as nonchalant as the one he had just provided. She had never before experienced such levels of secrecy from him.

You're probably a pro at hiding things from the rest of the world Shane, but not with me. We're like blood! This must be extremely difficult for you...or terrible period! She sighed heavily.

"Gina!" He repeated loudly, jolting her out of a daze.

"Yeah! Shit, you almost made me hit the curb. Well Shane, whatever is in the dark *must* come to light right?"

"Well that's what they say. So we'll just wait and see." His heart weighed heavily. *I'm so sorry for being dishonest with you Gina.* He wanted to add.

You're killing me softly Shane. "I see. Well I'm where I'm at. I'll call you around lunch time. Enjoy your training, and do some crunches for my seriously-bulging tummy. Love yuh bro." She truthfully admitted, her eyes gleaming with tears.

"Love yuh too Gina, and enjoy your day."

They disconnected.

"Thank you for calling Clark and Simmons. This is Antoinette speaking, how may I direct your call?"

"Hi Antoinette, is my husband around?"

The receptionist immediately recognised the voice. "Hey Natalie. Why yuh sounding so stressed? Yuh need to take it easy with that new practice." She chuckled. "Hold on for your hussy okay?"

Before Natalie could respond, the lines were switched.

"Hey baby. How's your day going so far?" Michael picked up with much enthusiasm.

She sighed heavily. "Hun, it's so intense. The training definitely didn't teach me enough about controlling my emotions. I take everything so personal. Like this morning..."

"Hold a sec baby. I'm sorry...emergency line's beeping." He quickly switched over. "This is Michael."

"What a way yuh dash mi weh? How yuh stay so bad baby? Yuh haven't been to *The Club* this long time..."

He recognised the voice and instantly regretted answering the call. "No man, nothing like that. I've been a bit busy with work lately. But I did give you a call a couple days ago and you didn't pick up." He volunteered unnecessarily. *At least I thought about it.*

"Oh okay. I didn't get that call at all, but there's a special show tonight baby. I need yuh to come check it out. Yuh definitely won't be disappointed."

What is definite is that the devil is alive and prowling. Michael loosened his tie. "I'll see about it. But the short notice..."

"C'mon baby, don't disappoint me. I've been missing you. And tell me yuh don't miss my sexiness?"

Goddamn this she-devil! "I'd be lying if I said I... *Oh shit!*" *Natalie...* He looked at the flashing Hold button just as it stopped blinking. "Hey sexy, I have some work to get back to. I'll come by later if anything. Cool?"

"Alright baby. I'm looking forward to seeing yuh. Smooches!" She giggled and hung up.

Regina relinquished her unnoticed post at the office entryway and delved into her co-worker's affairs.

9

"Morning missy! So why yuh *smooching* oh so giggly? And who you're going to see lata? One of your hoes? Spill the deets."

Stacy hastily spun around, not surprised to see Regina lurking behind her, listening in on her conversation as always.

"Yuh too faas! Happy New Year to you too. I didn't even hear when you got in. Yuh tell Linton about the promotion? You had the longest weekend to get it over with!" She successfully diverted the topic, however temporary.

"Did I tell Linton? Of course I did...*not*! I'm still trying to break it into our conversations. Girl, I don't know what to do. But don't remind me, I definitely know I have to do something soon."

"So what yuh going to do if he decides not to move? Dem long distance relationships never work out yuh nuh. Man will love yuh and all, but dem levels a loyalty deh... deep!"

"I know Stacy. I don't even want to think about that option. I don't know what I'd do if we should ever break up. But back to the real issue at hand; where yuh going likkle more with that seductive voice?"

She impulsively rolled her eyes. "You had breakfast? Let's go eat!" She thoroughly disregarded Regina and smirked.

"Funny! Keep your secrets. I'm starting to get used to that treatment. Boss came yet?"

Stacy sulked and negated that fact with a nod.

They both broke into laughter and saddled up to head to the cafeteria.

Right in the middle of my fu...my story, he puts me on hold for eternity! If you're not interested to hear about my day, then why do you even bother to ask? Natalie vented while ignoring her ringing desk phone.

Already sure who would be calling so obsessively, she picked up on what could easily be the tenth call.

"Baby, I'm really sorry about that. You know how Monday mornings can be?" Michael started to apologise before she even said 'Hello'. "Please don't be mad with me." Her prolonged silence made him uncomfortable.

Natalie audibly exhaled. "I'm not mad Michael. Just tense that's all."

"So you were saying about this morning's appointment?" His voice was loaded with relief.

"Oh nothing! I'm over it. I just need to control my emotions more." She left it at that.

"You'll get the hang of it soon babe...it's only been three months. Give yourself some time to get the hang of things. Hey, you wanna do lunch today? I'll even drive."

She knew how much he hated the lunch hour traffic so the gesture warmed her heart. "That would be cool. Where?"

"Baby, that's for you to choose. It's going to be after court though, so that should be around twelve thirty...twelve forty five with the traffic. That's cool?"

"Works for me. See you then. I love you Michael."

"I love you too Natalie. Now take it easy, okay? See you soon." He hung up.

She had to admit she felt a little better. Her husband always had a way to soothe her even while getting on her nerves. As far back as she could remember, he had always been the more composed one in their fourteen year relationship. There was no doubt that she really loved her man; her Michael.

You're always my rock. Natalie smiled from within.

This is way more people than I anticipated. I'm so not in the mood for all this. Shane's mind was made up.

"Coach, please keep this brief for me. I don't feel so well right now."

"No problem Shane, I understand. It's just all the anxiety of the Australian meet. Just do the best you can today. It should be brief."

"Okay Coach."

The two men ascended the podium and the questions instantly barraged them. The incessant camera flashes proved to illuminate the room much better than its intended lighting.

The commotion was almost too overwhelming for Shane, who usually preferred radio interviews until now.

Coach Sullivan spoke first. "People. Please, settle down. Your questions will be addressed in an orderly fashion. The smoother this goes the more we'll get done. Shane…" He stepped aside as the reporters steadily calmed, clearing the way for his star athlete.

Shane moved into the spotlight, took over the mic, and took a couple deep breaths to steady his nerves.

"Good afternoon ladies and gentlemen. To your questions…" He was brief.

"Shane, are there any plans to break your world record in the one hundred meter opener this year?" Glanville, a reporter from the Star newspaper blurted his question above the unsettling raucous.

Shane audibly cleared his throat and tried to adjust to the bright lighting. "Hi Glanville. My main priority at this time is to qualify for the 2008 Olympics. I can definitely say that I am in my best shape ever, so breaking my record may just happen. But it's not my main focus." He flashed his charming grin, and watched as the ladies stage-side shifted uncomfortably.

"Shane, what about the American, Tyson Blake? He's been talking big about the two hundred meter. Is he a threat?" Ian from the Gleaner asked boldly, standing to get a better visual of the athlete.

He chuckled before replying. "Which American doesn't *talk* big Ian? That's what they do *best*. The bark is usually bigger than the bite. I don't foresee a threat at this time." Shane looked toward his coach, signalling the 'wrap up' as the audience erupted with laughter.

Coach Sullivan instructed the reporters accordingly. "Ok, we'll take two more questions here, and the rest in back. Shane has to get back to training. Please also bear in mind there will be other segments scheduled, shortly."

The reporters who had begun to complain were tamed by his last statement. The proceedings continued.

"Shane! Any plans on settling down some time soon?" The question pierced through the otherwise noisy room. "You know, with the gorgeous housewife and kids?"

That could only be one person so fucking irrelevant! He did not hesitate to respond. "Actually I don't."

Everyone turned in their seats to see who had asked such an off-topic question in their tightly-scheduled spot.

Shane mused inwardly. *Dagger! How's that for a response Miss Fox?* He smiled and continued.

"I'm twenty six years old and at the top of my game! There will be time for wife and kids. I'm all about my career and my family right now, and all the other people who *really* love me unconditionally." He knew he went too far, but was too provoked to care.

The crowd was stirred, but not surprised, by the long-standing tension between their star athlete and Amanda Fox of RE TV. Their history was not exactly a private affair.

Shane quickly composed himself. "And the last question will go to?" He was fuming on the inside.

Brent from the Jamaica Observer hastily interjected. "Shane, given that you have dual citizenship with the United States, is there a possibility that you will switch allegiance soon? It's on every tongue in the sports arena…"

"That is not an option Brent! And on that note, I'd like to thank you all for attending. I will make you proud! I will put Jamaica back on the map in a good light! Big up to all my fans worldwide!" He quickly descended the podium and left his coach to 'wrap up' the session.

The recent speculations about him possibly running for the United States made him very uncomfortable. He knew well enough that Jamaicans were unforgiving sports fan with no tolerance for betrayal; switching to the US track team would signify just that. The most annoying part about the buzzing hoopla was that he had never uttered such an intention.

Shane spotted Amanda the instant she made the corner and quickened his steps towards his truck.

Unfortunately for him, she had the clearance to venture into the private parking area and roam the entire premises, given that it belonged to her father.

"Why are you running from me Shane? I won't bite you!" She called out after him.

"Are you sure? That's not what *I* remember!"

Their story could plot an award-winning Hollywood drama series.

Shane fumbled with his keys, avoiding eye contact. "What do you want Amanda? I have to get going. How about you give me a call?" He chuckled teasingly.

"You know you don't take my calls so don't patronize me Shane! All I want to do is talk. You've never given me the opportunity to apologize; to tell you my side of the story."

"Ha! That's funny 'cause there's only one distinct side to two bodies intertwined...well technically there's four!" He laughed scathingly. "But respective of which side *you're* looking at, all that shit just doesn't matter anymore!

14

You get the drift?" He hopped into his truck and slammed the door, opening the window just enough to stare dead into her eyes.

"Please don't do this Shane! I'm begging." Her eyes magically brimmed with tears, as always.

"No! *You* don't do this Amanda! That crying shit! I'm over that with you! For real, you need to get over it too." He was seething inside. *Damn you for trying to play with my emotions! Trying' to jump on my fame train. Musta lost your goddamn mind! Of course…that's old news too!*

"Look, get at me…somehow. Peace!" Shane sped off and left her standing in the dust.

The two had dated for six years spanning high school and college. With Shane mounting the track and field ladder and Amanda enthroned to acquire subsidiaries of her father's companies, they were known as 'the Favourite Couple' in the elite Jamaican uptown societies. Though everything had seemed glamorous on the outside, the walls masked the inner turmoil of jealousy and infidelity.

Amanda had to stand by Shane when he was almost destroyed by a prostitution scandal; and also had to do the public relations to rectify his image. Out of spite she had cheated on him one night three years ago, and to her dismay, it was recorded on tape. That was the first of such occurrences, but the end of 'them' as a couple.

Shane sat in his truck and dialled the only person he could stomach at the moment.

"This is Regina." She discarded the usual courtesies when answering her private line.

"Gina, are you free for lunch? I need some company." He got right to the point.

"Of course! Is everything okay? You sound stressed…angry even. It's kinda early…"

"We'll talk about it when I see you."

"Okay, but what time?"

"I'm already downstairs." He clicked over to the next line before she could reply.

Doc a call me back already! She's so timely with the bad news when shi ready. Jah know! The thought quickly crossed his mind.

"Hello." He answered, not trying to mask the fact that he was already annoyed.

"Mr. Wright, Dr. Simmons would like to speak with you. Is it a good time?" It was the assistant.

"Sure Tameka." *So why didn't she call me herself like she always did? Using Tameka as buffer, so lame...*

"Shane, I wanted to apologize for being so insensitive this morning." Natalie delved into her reason for calling. "It just upset me that...forget it. There's no excuse. I'm truly sorry. I was out of line."

So we're back to first name basis and more apologies. I see..."Doc, it's all good. I shouldn't have been so impatient with you either. You have been nothing but supportive of me, and I'm sorry for my behaviour."

She released an audible sigh. "Thanks Shane...that's nice of you to say." She needed a moment to blush. *Oh boy, awkward silence. What to say? What to say?*

Shane relieved her. "So Doc, would I be forward if I asked you out to dinner, *again*? I mean I know the doctor-patient thing, but it's just food."

She nervously chuckled. "I'm flattered Shane, but I can't do that. I'm a married woman, and yes the doctor-patient thing as you call it."

"It's cool Doc. Know that that was only round one though. I'm known to be persistent." *And I'll definitely keep prying on that thing I do to you...believe that!* "Well thanks for calling. Let me know when I have to *come in* again; cool?"

His insinuation unnerved her and she almost stuttered. "Okay. Okay Shane. Uhm, I'll be in touch. And you enjoy the rest of your day."

He grinned and bid his farewell as Regina hopped into his truck. "Damn girl! Just rip the door off the damn hinge while you're at it. You think this is your granny old minivan? Take it easy man!"

Regina laughed and punched him on the arm. "Shut up Shane! Where to? I'm starving. So glad you called!" She busied herself with the seat belt and adjusting the chair.

Realising the unusual silence, she looked up to find him staring blankly at her. "What? What's that look?"

Shane smiled and shrugged. "Hot Pot or fast food bumble bee?" He backed the Lexus out of the parking lot.

"Hot Pot will do. And I'm ready to listen when you're ready to talk. I know you're keeping secrets Shane." She piercingly stared into his brown eyes, silently daring him to lie to her face. She also felt the onset of a migraine.

"Yea, I know Gina. We'll talk okay." He had to accept that he was out of time. *No more lies.* "By the way, your haircut's real pretty. It looks good on you."

She blushed uncontrollably.

"Roxanne yuh mek up yuh mind yet bout lata? Mi tell yuh seh di bwoy want a introduction. Yea or nay?"

Roxanne knew better than to believe that Cindy indeed wanted to introduce her to a 'bwoy'. After all, her 'bwoyfren' was twenty six years old; eight years her senior.

"Cindy, I done tell yuh areddi. My sister would kill me if she found out that I was hanging with people damn near her age. I can't afford to get caught in any situation right now. She's already stressed out as is."

"So how she ago find out *ediat*? Who ago tell her? Mi done tell yuh the plan areddi. We a leave school roun two before the bell ring and link them up a Half a Tree. The whole ting shouldn't tek longer than three hour or so. Yuh still ago reach home before Regina. Stop gwan like yuh a punk nuh!"

Roxanne caved. "Alright then, I'll follow yuh. But if yuh ever give mi no shit when I seh I ready…that's it fi me and yuh going nowhere again."

"Alright den, that's fair. Mi a guh mek di call den. Sign the attendance roster fi me." Cindy discreetly slipped out the back door of the classroom and headed for the bathroom to use her cell phone; its use was otherwise prohibited during school hours.

CHAPTER TWO

R oxanne looked over at Cindy impatiently tapping her foot and glimpsing at her watch, evidently uninterested in the knowledge the teacher aimed to depart.

Cindy caught her stare. "Roxanne a two a clock yuh nuh? Time fi cut outta dis blasted place. Yuh nuh ready?"

"We have to leave during class change or we'll get caught! Stop gwan like ediat nuh Cindy!"

"Arite a true, but yuh nuh affi a gwan suh!" She re-combed her hair for the hundredth time, added another pound of lip gloss to her already dripping lips, and discreetly slipped off her underwear stuffing it into her school bag.

The school bell sounded the end of the second to last period of the day, and their plan went into motion.

Cindy and Roxanne walked with the crowd through the halls and across the pathway, but snuck away through a large hole in the wall that led to the Patty Shop adjacent to the school yard. They both laughed at their successful getaway.

"Yuh know seh we too bad though? When we ago stop do dem shit yah?"

"*We*?" Roxanne hastily retorted. "No, you're too damn bad! When yuh gonna stop getting me into shit like this? I swear sometimes…"

"Stop gwan like yuh nuh glad fi come. Yuh know yuh like off di bwoy to."

They walked through the shop premises and exited onto Half Way Tree Road, trotting the short distance to the York Pharmacy parking lot. Their 'friends' were already present as arranged.

Cindy spotted her man as soon as she stepped through the main gates, and anxiously called out to him.

"Hey Benji baby! Oonu waiting long?" She hurriedly walked towards him.

Benji waited until she got closer to reply. "No babes, we jus reach." He leaned forward and embraced his 'woman'.

"Where's Andre? I thought you said he was coming?" Cindy murmured within his grasp then quickly pulled away to scan the parking lot.

"Cool nuh babes. Him inna di pharmacy. This is your fren him so anxious to meet? Whe she name again?"

"It's Roxanne." She bluntly interjected before Cindy. *Asking about 'she' like I'm not standing right here! Ediat!*

Before she could append her feisty remarks, Andre exited the pharmacy sporting a wide grin. She immediately blushed, her knees offering little support.

"Whagwan Cindy, I see yuh bring me a present." He focused all his attention on Roxanne. "Hi beautiful. I'm Andre, and you are?"

"I'm Roxanne. Nice to meet you Andre." She nervously shook his hand. *Nice is an understatement! Damn you for being even finer up close!* She smiled uncontrollably.

"So what you girls want to get into?" Andre asked, still holding onto Roxanne's hand.

Cindy spoke up. "I guess we can just guh hang out by the studio for a likkle. Miss Roxanne has to get home soon. Her sistah is a drill sergeant." She chuckled and made a face at her best friend, who eyed her with fury.

"Funny! I simply have a more structured upbringing." Roxanne shot back, rolling her eyes at Cindy. *Yuh just chat too much sometimes! Always have sup'm extra fi seh!*

Andre chuckled. "Alright, oonu tek it easy. We can hang by the studio and orda some food den. Dat cool?"

Roxanne, along with the others, nodded in agreement.

Benji handed over his car keys so he could ride in the back seat with Cindy. Roxanne of course, would sit in the front to accompany Andre.

He turned up the volume on the stereo, blasting the music that was softly spilling from the speakers until now.

"A mi new tune dis." Andre boastfully informed his new passengers. "Tell me if oonu like it."

Roxanne jaws dropped when she recognised the voice 'deejaying' over the beat. She had no idea before now, that 'Andre' was her favourite entertainer 'Biggs'. She didn't remember Cindy mentioning such a fact, and silently damned her friend for 'setting her up'. *Oh Lord! Could this really be happening? This must be a dream! Somebody pinch me!* Her heart began to skip beats with the bass line in the song. The sound of Andre's voice interrupted her trail of thoughts.

"So how you one so pretty Roxanne? Yuh know how long mi tell Cindy fi get the introductions going? What took yuh so long? I'm not your type?" He was surely being modest.

She thought hard on her response. "Well...I can't really roam the streets like Cindy or do my own thing. I live with my sister, and she is very protective of me. School days are the only days I have a little freedom, and even then I have to make my curfew..." She caught herself rambling. *That was way too much information.*

"I know them ways babes. But yuh gonna mek time now to see your Andre right? I mean, that's if yuh like me like I like you..." He flashed a sultry glance.

Oh please! You know damn well that I like yuh already! Hmm. "Well we'll just have to see right? If you play your cards well..." *My sister didn't raise no fool!* She mused inwardly.

Her forward response quickly turned Andre's lingering smile into a wider grin.

"Alright mam. Your rules! Just mek sure when I play ma cards right, yuh nuh start change up the rules." He chuckled as she blushed uncontrollably.

Behind them, Cindy and Benji were heavily engaged in their usual frolicking. He had his tongue buried down her throat and his hand was nestled under her skirt. She moaned softly as his fingers friskily massaged her.

Roxanne began to feel slightly uncomfortable at the mood being set behind her. She didn't want Andre to expect that he was going to get the same play from her, because unlike Cindy, she was a virgin.

Noticing her discomfort, Andre continued to probe. "So Miss Roxanne, yuh like the song or what? Why yuh so quiet? I hope you're thinking about *us*!" He smiled teasingly.

"Can yuh stop calling me Miss Roxanne? And yes, I like the song a lot. It's very clubby." She consciously disregarded his last statement.

"What yuh know about club? Yuh ever been to one?"

"No, but I know what it should be like. I do watch TV!" She feigned a pout.

They both laughed, somewhat breaking the ice.

Biggs drove into the studio parking lot and noticed two other cars parked up on the lawn.

"Benji, who suppose to be here now?"

Benji released his lips from Cindy's and surveyed the parking area to identify the cars. "Oh! Warriah a voice... and a mussi Lorna cyar dat." He temporarily exchanged a quizzical glance with his friend. "Yo oonu straighten up oonuself mek we go in. You two just hold yuh head straight and follow wi, cool?" He sternly instructed them.

They walked through the studio lobby and Lorna quickly acknowledged them, of course noticing the two schoolgirls who were in their company. *Nasty rasshole dem and people gyal pickney. Look how much big ooman deh a road! Slackness!*

Biggs was the only one who replied. "Everything cool Lorna? Come fi do some work..." He playfully winked at her.

Work my ass! "Cool. Don't mind me, I'm outta here shortly." *Damn disgusting!* She kept that thought in her head.

They retreated into the back half of the studio that was specifically reserved for the elite artists. Benji stopped in the general area kitchen to get some sodas from the refrigerator, with Cindy huddling closely behind him.

"Babes hold this!" He handed her two of the cans before they joined the others in the private room.

Cindy seemed to be right at home. She dropped her book bag on the floor in the corner and carelessly plopped herself onto the plush leather sofa.

Roxanne was almost sure she had glimpsed her friend's bush when her skirt had flown up. *You are so nasty Cindy!* She scowled at her unaware friend.

"Where is the bathroom?" She asked indirectly.

"Oh there is one through that door behind you." Biggs was quick to respond.

The back studio came equipped with its own bathroom and kitchen, eliminating the need to go back into the general hall to access the amenities of the studio.

When Roxanne returned to the room, Cindy and Benji were not in immediate sight. She began to feel nervous, but soon spotted them through the glass window, canoodling in the back booth.

Biggs turned on the plasma TV and flipped the channel to RE TV that was currently playing music videos. He turned on the computer systems then looked up and noticed Roxanne awkwardly lounging by his desk.

"Babes, you can sit down yuh nuh. I promise I won't bite yuh." He laughed at her daring stare before obliging his request. "Yuh want mi order the pizza or sup'm else?"

"Okay." Roxanne replied, evidently distracted.

"Okay to which one babes? The pizza or the sup'm else?" He chuckled at his own sarcasm.

Roxanne's face flushed with embarrassment. "The *pizza* please." She purposely avoided eye contact.

"Domino's or Pizza Hut? And what toppings?"

"Pizza Hut; the Chicken and Pineapple special." She turned to face him. *And a bit of your special too! Jokes!* She stifled a smile.

"Okay. Pass me that phone book under the desk. I'll call them now." He lustfully admired her derrière as she bent to locate the telephone directory. *What a fat ass yo! Cya wait fi hit dat!* He straightened up as soon as she turned around.

"Thanks babes. Did I tell yuh how pretty I think you are?" He noticed her sudden tension though she feigned a smile. "I'm just saying babes. Nothing implied." He chuckled and skimmed through the yellow pages.

In the adjacent booth, Benji bent Cindy over the back of a white leather sofa and eased his body in between her legs. He entered her moisture with a merciless thrust, gently massaging her over-developed breasts.

"Clench up di pussy fi mi baby. Yuh love di cocky?" He barked the words closely by her ear without reverence.

"Mmm…of course Benji. Of course mi love it. Fuck mi hard!" She blurted through appreciative moans.

Delving in as deep as naturally possible, he ground her with slow, circular movements. He moaned while enjoying the orifice he professed, was moulded to the shape of his phallus; this he based on the belief that he was her first and only.

Cindy switched positions and boosted herself onto the back of the chair to sit facing him. She possessively wrapped her legs around his bony waist while he swept her up into his arms. She rotated her pelvis in midair with great expertise, as she easily accommodated his unsheathed cock.

With every thrust he forcefully pulled her downward, causing her to feign ecstasy though wincing in pain.

After much stimulation, Benji exploded with a monstrous guttural sound and dropped them onto the couch.

Cindy clung tightly to her man, and he in turn kissed her with the aggressive passion a man shares with his wife.

Roxanne tried to warm up to her companion who was already busy at work. "Andre, I can ask you a question?" She watched him through the corner of her eye.

"Yuh jus did babes." He replied without looking up, and they both laughed. He steadily turned his attention away from the mixing board. "What's on your mind beautiful?"

She began to fidget when he gave her his undivided attention. "Well, Cindy *did* in fact tell me that yuh wanted to meet me...a long time ago. But I just wanted to know why? I mean, I know I'm pretty but so are a lot of other girls...and *women*. Why me?"

"What yuh mean? Babes, yuh not only beautiful but mi spirit did jus tek yuh the first time I see yuh...that's all. And me is a man who move fast when mi see a nice girl that I want. Have to move before the next man yuh zimme?" He smiled and watched as she noticeably blushed.

"I hear yuh. So what yuh want from me though? I'm not like Cindy so if *that's* what's on yuh mind..." She motioned towards the back booth.

He hastily interjected. "Babes, I only want what yuh want to give me…nothing more, nothing less. As I told yuh earlier, you're the boss!" He grinned and winked at her just as the intercom on the desk buzzed.

It was Lorna informing them that the pizza delivery man was in the lobby.

As soon as Andre exited the studio, a laugh involuntarily escaped Roxanne's mouth. *This must be a damn dream! Andre 'Biggs' Jackson likes me? Likes me, Roxanne Mitchell just so? This is crazy! Overwhelming even…* She quickly composed herself as his footsteps thudded back down the corridor.

Within half an hour they devoured half of the large pizza and breadsticks together, leaving the remainder for the other two 'love' birds canoodling in the back room.

Roxanne checked the time and almost choked on a piece of crust. *Where the hell did the time go? I am so screwed!* She jumped up and blurted.

"It's six thirty! I have to go!" She snatched up her bag and made a dash for the door.

Andre glanced at his Rolex and quickly rushed towards her. "Relax babes, I'll drop yuh home. My Range will cut your trip in half…don't worry. I'm really sorry about the time." He checked his pockets for his truck keys and they headed through the door. "I'll carry this for yuh babes." He took her bag and secured the lock on the door.

Benji and Cindy weren't even aware they were leaving.

The Club was packed to capacity as the vibrant announcer tauntingly introduced the headlining dancer. It was evident from the frenzied response that she was the favourite of both male and female patrons alike.

"Ladies and gentlemen, all jokes aside. Welcome on stage…*Caramelllll!*" He shouted into the microphone, before exiting stage left.

The exotically beautiful star made her way center stage, and immediately fell into a one hundred and eighty degree split. She expertly flexed her hip muscles, causing her butt cheeks to perform their reputable, rhythmic choreography.

The crowd erupted with applause and whistles as paper bills flew about the stage while the men - and women alike - drooled and spiralled out of control.

Caramel, always maintaining a seductive grin, stood and bent backwards. Without much effort, she pulled her legs upward to suspend them in mid air. If that wasn't surprising enough for a woman with her voluptuous build, she added her reputable upside down aerobics to the mix sending the crowd into an uproar.

"What a fat ass man!" One man blurted, though not sparing a minute to take his eyes off the magnet.

"All mi woulda gi har is a solid backshot!" Another added, looking on with the same amazement. "Bwoy mi wife need fi learn how fi do dat. Den mi will come home pon time!"

Theatrics after theatrics she stunned her patrons and the money continuously poured in. One of the regulars even found the guts to hop up onto the stage and smother his head in between her ass cheeks. She expertly bobbled his head from side to side before shoving him back into the crowd, causing an eruption of laughter.

"Him cyan manage yuh baby! But gimme a try and yuh see!" One man shouted causing everyone to laugh.

She motioned for him to meet her backstage and wrapped up her set with a few more signature tricks that her fans favoured. By the time she got to her dressing room, the VIP big spenders had already lined-up, waiting to take advantage of her more personal and reputable services.

Money a run tonight! A dat mi like fi see man. She made a quick stride towards her dressing room, but instantly stopped in her tracks when someone special caught her eyes. She smiled from within and quickly tugged him along.

"Ey! Yuh can't do dat yuh nuh! Yuh nuh see me inna di front?" An angered client vented his rights.

Caramel completely ignored his outburst and yanked her fellow in the room, slamming the door behind them.

"I'm glad you made it baby! You liked the show?" She seductively purred at him.

"Loved it! But you know that already. It really made a man start to wonder…"

"What yuh wondering exactly?" She kneeled between his legs, staring daringly into his eyes.

"Just…nothing. I mean…forget it." He wasn't making any sense.

She could sense from his rigidity that he was indeed very nervous. Of all the previous times that she had invited him to see her perform, he had never once ventured into the back room. *Well yuh back here tonight for a reason baby. I'll show yuh more than one!* She foully deliberated.

"It's alright baby. You don't have to explain. I can be yuh everything tonight, and if it pleases you, we can see about other nights; deal?" She expertly massaged his groin.

"Deal." He silently moaned as she playfully caressed his crotch. He tentatively reached for her voluptuous boobs as they sprang free from her bikini. *Why am I here Lord? Why?*

She used her mouth to free his hardened dick from its restraints then continued to wholeheartedly massage his testicles with her tongue.

He reflexively held onto the back of her head moaning appreciatively, writhing in her grip. As he neared his eruption, he held her head firmly into place and wildly pummelled her mouth without hesitation.

Caramel wrestled her head from his grip, not wanting him to release before she felt him within. Grinning at the expression on his face as he watched her saliva glide down his glistening shaft, she stood up to mount him. With one leg on either side of his now limp frame, she enveloped his face with her ample bosom.

Completely warped in the moment, he nibbled and tweaked her nipples as she anxiously buried his unsheathed, turgid manhood deeply within her.

"I can't do this!" The words escaped his mouth almost instantly. "No, I can't!" He gripped her by the thighs and forcefully eased her up and off his lap.

"Wha you mean baby? Yuh already doing dis! *Baby*..." She grew irritable when he didn't back down.

"I'm not your *baby* Caramel! I just can't do *all* this! *I can't do this*!" He commanded his mind. "I don't expect you to understand." He looked down at his feet, trying to mask his humiliation and avoid her watering eyes.

He has got to be fucking kidding! Nutt'n to me like the annoyance of a married coward! Don't lose your cool girl...jus stay focused. Jus school him through it! Her determination went into overdrive.

"Baby, what's wrong? You didn't like the feel of ma fat pussy? Huh? Was it the head that you won't ever forget?" Her tears spilled freely.

"Caramel, don't do this. It's not you at all...it's me. No, it's more than me. It's my wife, my career, and my life as I know it!" He hurriedly dressed himself and searched for his wallet. "I just can't go down this path with you. But don't worry about the money. I'm still paying the full price."

She stared at him through eyes that expertly portrayed pain. "So why did yuh come back here; to tease me? Yuh know how I feel about yuh! *Why*? Huh?" She grew more aggressive.

He moved closer towards the door and removed five thousand dollars from his wallet. "This should cover it." He outstretched the money to her, but rested it on a corner table when she refused to take it. Speaking with more authority, as he had fully regained his composure, he relayed his closing arguments.

"Girl, you know you're sexy as hell! But *I* just can't do this!" He unlocked the door and stormed out the room.

"Michael! *Please*! Don't leave!" She screamed and tried to run after him; but it was too late.

He had already disappeared into the crowd that had assembled outside her door.

She lingered at the doorway in shock, fully naked, until her eyes wandered to the handsome young man leaning by the stage.

The older man who had been standing at the head of the line for the past hour, even after she ditched him for Michael, noticed he wasn't the object of her attention and wasn't about to be overlooked twice.

"Caramel, it look like a my turn yuh nuh." He was quick to exclaim while giving the young man a stare down.

The angered patron's bravery quickly subsided when the man reacted by patting his hand on his waist, signalling the position of his gun. He quickly averted his gaze, mumbling under his breath.

Caramel giggled and backed up into the dressing room, pulling the big spender in with her.

"I see yuh still after those married men huh bitch?" Her guest asked while locking the door.

"What reason, if any, is that your business Biggs?" She sat in the couch, spreading her legs wide apart. "Pussy is your *only* business here! And who yuh calling bitch?"

"Mi soon show yuh!" Biggs smirked sheepishly. *But a wha Michael Simmons a do ya though God? And him wife so tiefish to! What a rass!* He stored that fact mentally.

I can't believe Shane took so long to confide in me. I knew all this secrecy had to mean something bad...but this...it's worse than I thought! This is just too damn crazy! Lord, why my best friend? I don't know what I'd do without him in my life...I shouldn't even be thinking like this already! No wonder he hid it from my ass! Well, Shane always pulls through...he'll be more than okay.

I better get some sort of supper started before Linton gets home. And where the hell is Roxanne? I swear that girl wants me to put her out. Its seven thirty on a Monday evening and she is not in the damn house!

"Hey Regina, I'm so sorry to be late!" The front door swung open and banged on the closet as Roxanne rushed into the house. "Please don't get mad at me! It was an emergency. Cindy..."

"Yuh see the time?" Regina cut her off. "And you know it's a school night right? How many times are we going to go through this for the school year? I'll tell you now; not many!"

"Lawd I said sorry! It was just..."

"That you were born sorry Roxanne?" She harshly offered, and returned her attention to the refrigerator.

Roxanne stormed into her bedroom, though mindful not to slam the door.

"Hey baby, why is the front door open?"

Regina turned to see Linton standing at the kitchen entrance. "Hey hun, miss adult over there just barged in."

"*Oh!*" He gave her a kiss on the cheek and retreated to the upstairs, carefully avoiding any involvement.

Sitting in her bathroom, Roxanne contemplated her sister's remark. *What the hell does she mean I was born sorry? I swear that bitch feels she can say whatever she wants to me because she takes care of me. She can be so hurtful! I wish we had a mother in our lives; then we'd just be more like sisters for once, and I could tell her where to stuff it! What kind of mother could just up and leave her*

31

kids without looking back? She must've been evil...and now Regina is just like her. I swear this shit gets worse with time. She began to cry.

Regina heard her sister's sobs, but disregarded the situation to go find Linton. She found him sitting on the bedroom floor watching one of his old basketball tapes of a Chicago Bulls championship game.

"Baby, I feel so drained. Can a sister get some loving?" She playfully pouted.

Linton already knew where she was headed. "Anytime sweety. What's the matter now?" He refrained from even glancing at the television.

"Well, a little bit of Roxanne and a lot of *other* things. There's so much pressure at work trying to stay on top of this promotion; and this law class is so demanding. And I just feel like I haven't been enough for you lately."

She started to undress, causing Linton to jump up and find his way to the edge of the bed to meet her.

"You know what I'm saying? I mean we haven't had lunch together in like forever...and our love-making just seems so rushed. And I know you'll never complain, but I'm aware." She was fully naked now.

Linton's breathing grew heavy as she lingered between his legs and leaned in to kiss him. He ran his hands over her hips and smiled within. *I am so blessed!* He marvelled inwardly while palming her buttocks, giving them a light squeeze before standing. He hoisted her unto the bed and closely hovered above her.

In one swift motion, he dimmed the lights, put their favourite Sade CD in the rotation, and turned off the television. He undressed with much haste to return all his attention to the love of his life.

Passionately kissing the inside of her legs, he slowly worked his way upwards along her inner thighs. He chuckled as his lips traced her tickle zone, and she giggled.

Regina eagerly wrapped her legs around Linton's waist when he climbed into the bed atop her. She forcefully pulled him closer, yearning to feel his warmth within.

When his sturdy shaft first penetrated her eager pinkness, she tensed as always in anticipation of his overwhelming size. With each stroke, she relaxed and comfortably welcomed half of his ride.

Linton explored his woman with long, sensual strokes that increasingly opened her passage, sending her eroticism into overdrive. He resisted all her mechanisms to force him deeper within, all to maintain control of her orgasm as he teased her inside and out.

Eventually, the tease plan became more unbearable to him and he plunged in all the way. He ground her pinkness to incidentally massage her clitoris, and she moaned and writhed in pleasuring pain. All the while, his hands remained buried beneath her, cupping her well-endowed ass cheeks for leverage to delve deeper.

Regina shrieked in ecstasy, but in some realm wondered if his shaft would pierce her chest. *Lord knows how Linton is blessed!* She bit into his shoulder with all her might, and it fuelled his aggression even more.

"Baby, you're going to kill me?" She pleaded in a whisper. "Mmm...mmm...fuck me baby! Yuh love it?" She moaned almost in a whisper, reflexively.

"Of course! Of course I love it baby!" He lovingly embraced her for the final hoorah and gave her the love that he felt she deserved. "I love you Regina."

After thinking about her family situation, especially realising how she ill-treated her sister, Roxanne decided to go upstairs for a much needed heart to heart.

When she got to the top of the stairs, she could hear warped noises flowing from the direction of their bedroom.

Her curiosity propelled her forward, regardless, especially since the bedroom door was ajar. She peeked into the room and was immediately disgusted by the sight of Linton and Regina in the exact position as Benji had Cindy earlier.

Reflexively, Roxanne backed away from the door and began to cry again.

Shane sieved through his call log and chose his companion for the day. With a tingling groin, he made the call.

"Hello." The raspy voice bluntly spilled through the receiver.

"Wassup sexy Simone? Long time nuh hear from yuh. Yuh rich and switch?" He tried to joke.

"Don't *sexy* me! Yuh a fraud Shane. Yuh galang!" Simone was not amused by his flattery.

The girl's insolence not only amused, but aroused him further.

"Damn sexy! Well it sound like yuh really mad, and I not in the mood to argue. So hear wha, likkle more!"

"*No Shane!*" She shouted, manifesting the reaction he had predicted. "It's just dat yuh treat mi so bad. Yuh only call me when yuh wan fuck! We neva hang out or anyting like yuh promise. Is like yuh shame a me or sup'm!"

He audibly sighed. "Babes, how many times yuh ever open the paper and see me photographed at any party? When last yuh go out and see me? Mi nuh go out again babes. Too much attention! Besides, I'm busy with track. All I do is train and sleep! Why yuh act like yuh don't understand?" *Come on girl, melt!* He mused inwardly.

"Sorry Shane. Mi jus miss yuh dat's all. So wha yuh want mi do? Come ova?"

Now you're being a good girl. He smiled. "Of course sexy! And yuh know I miss yuh too that's why I call yuh as soon as my time free up. You were the first on my list of things to do, sexy." He lied to seal the deal.

Simone giggled, revelling in the attention from a super star. "Alright then. Yuh ago send your taxi man? Or mi fi jus grab a different one?"

"Just take any taxi. I'll pay for it when yuh come. Make sure yuh wear sup'm sexy for me; cool?"

"But nuh mus! Later den!" She quickly hung up.

Shane had met Simone at the Tivoli Gardens weekly street dance *Passa Passa*. Though she was from the ghetto, she was undoubtedly the sexiest being he had seen in a while, with a body to die for and an unimaginable beauty. The fact that she was overly smitten by him had boosted his chances that night. He had bought her a drink, saved her phone number, and made an effort to use it thereon. She had turned out to be a very good cook, and her 'ghetto slam' always had him speaking in tongues.

He went into the bathroom and studied his reflection in the mirror. *What a handsome young man! Hmm, if I were the ladies I'd love him too.* He chuckled. *Well I hope Doc call me for that last appointment soon so we can get all this shit sorted out! Hopefully this test shows something else that I can get rid of without extra effort. Thank God I cleared it up with Regina though. Really hated lying to my best friend.* He carefully examined the tiniest pimple.

Well Miss Ghetto Slam should handle my worries for now. That, I know for a fact! Affi go drink up the Irish moss for this bedroom bully. Oh what a night it'll be! He hopped into the shower, feeling more anxious than triumphant; a rendezvous with Simone always did that to him.

CHAPTER THREE

"**S**o are you going to tell me why you missed dinner last night or are we going to pretend it didn't happen?"

Michael reluctantly plopped onto the counter stool then stared blankly at his wife. "Good morning Natalie. And to the question, let's pretend!"

"Michael, don't get on my nerves you hear me? Where the hell were you last night? And don't even try to tell me work!" She slammed his breakfast unto the counter.

"I guess I was nowhere then Natalie, because I was helping John to resolve some issues with a case at his office...where *we work*!"

"And what, the phones don't work there?"

Her cynicism always irritated him. "For Christ's sake Nat, I got in at eight! I'm a grown ass man. Are you trying to tell me I have a curfew? Or give me one? Huh mother? Can we just extend it to nine please?"

"You're missing what's important as always! This has nothing to do with the time Michael! You had me worried! I spoke to you late in the afternoon and you didn't say anything about meeting with John; then you just disappeared off the radar! I don't know what it is with you and this new attitude, but you'd better shape up and stop igniting unnecessary fights."

"You're the one that's starting fights! I'm not even fighting right now! I'm just being annoyed!" He smiled coyly.

"Oh, this is funny to you? Okay Michael." She got up and headed towards the stairs.

"No! What *is* funny, is always talking about what *you* find important! You never have anything to say when we discuss my issues! I'm not gonna bicker with you over minor details when there are bigger fish to fry Natalie!" He shouted without looking in her direction.

She paused half way up the stairs, and turned back. "And what exactly is the bigger fish Michael? Huh?" Before she could continue, he loudly snapped.

"I'm not happy Natalie! To be honest, I'm bored out of my *fucking* mind! If I don't initiate sex, we don't have any. If I don't say honey lunch, we don't do that. If I don't plan an outing, we come straight home. And on top of all that, you know damn well I want to start having kids, but you prefer to play dumb! All you talk about is your practice and patients, and all that shit that has nothing to do with *us*!"

"We have a good life! A *great fucking* life! We make roughly four hundred thousand dollars per year between us; and that's *after* taxes! I am thirty *fucking* nine years old! When will I become a father? Please great one, do enlighten me!" He loathingly stared at her.

Natalie's eyes widened and her jaws cranked her mouth ajar. "Okay. So that's what this is all about; us having *kids*? You want me to what, quit my job Michael? Is this about me finally having my own practice and excelling at something that you didn't hand down to me? Which one really bothers you the most? Huh?"

Michael wasn't surprised that she had fully dismissed his concerns, but he also wasn't prepared to entertain her any longer. He got up and replied coolly.

"Honestly Natalie, the only thing that's bothering me at this moment is this breakfast fit for a bum. I'm outta here!" He slid the plate of half-eaten food across the counter, and walked past her into the hallway. "Oh, and I might be late tonight again mother! Don't wait up!" He slammed the door behind him.

Natalie began to cry.

Regina and Linton descended the stairs bursting with laughter. Upon entering the kitchen, they were duly surprised to see that Roxanne was not only awake at six o'clock, but had also prepared a surprise breakfast of scrambled eggs, fried bacon, and Belgian waffles. She had even made a fresh pot of coffee, though she personally didn't drink it.

They all sat together at the dining table; something else that hadn't occurred in a while.

Regina made much of Linton, conversing about their pending lunch date and his annoying co-workers, laughing unnecessarily with much fanfare. She was even more interested in discussing his work projects, which she usually found uninteresting. All the while, she thoroughly ignored her sister. When she was finished eating, she got up, kissed him goodbye, and headed towards the door.

"Thanks for the breakfast." She called out indirectly, and disappeared through the door.

Linton looked over at Roxanne and saw the tears welling in her eyes. "Don't pay your sister any mind. You know what you need to do, so just do it from now on. Anyways, thanks a mil for the breakfast; it was delicious." He started to clear the table. "Looks like I'm taking you to school so get your stuff together. I'll pack these away."

He cleared the counter and washed the dishes while Roxanne packed her belongings into the car. He watched her through the kitchen window and genuinely sympathised with her. *I can just imagine how you feel sometimes Roxanne...but I also know what your sister goes through with you. I think we all could use a vacation! Take a break from this hectic lifestyle. I'll look into that on the Net today. Lord knows I could definitely use some recreation...* The thought alone excited him.

Shane awoke feeling jollier than he had felt in weeks. He roamed his apartment in search of Simone, and his nose led him to the kitchen where she was busy preparing his breakfast in the nude. Unable to resist the urge to touch her, he playfully slapped her on the butt.

"Morning sexy." He grinned when she spun around. "I see you're overworking yourself...as always."

"Shane yuh frighten me yuh nuh! Mi neva even hear when yuh get up! Yuh brekfass ready. Mawnin."

She shared his meal and poured his coffee, along with a glass of juice.

"It smells great in here Simone. Wonder if I should just hire yuh full time!" He plopped onto the counter stool and took a sip of his coffee; it was just right.

That was the thing about Simone that kept Shane wanting more. She knew better than any of his uptown women, how to spoil and cater to his every whim.

This morning, as well as all the previous ones she had awoken at his place, she had wasted no time in rising before the sun to prepare a hearty breakfast of steamed Snapper fish with boiled dumplings and bananas. The orange juice was also freshly-squeezed, and the coffee and mint tea were made from scratch.

The scents swirling in the kitchen stimulated Shane's palate and he was eager to devour his feast.

Simone smiled appreciatively. "So what are yuh plans for todeh Shane? I mean, after yuh drop mi home." She walked over to the sink to wash up the dishes.

He quickly acknowledged that her last remark was a reference to the conversation they had the previous night, where she complained about them not spending any time together outside of the bedroom.

"Well..." He spoke between bites. "After I drop yuh home I'm just gonna come back here and sleep I guess. Or maybe go out with the boys." He stuffed another oversized dumpling into his mouth.

"So yuh nah go training todeh?"

"Hmm…" He tried to swallow before continuing. "I'm going right now."

She stared at him, confusion plastered her expression.

Shane helped her out. "So while I'm gone, just make yourself comfortable and miss me 'til I come back. I'll take you somewhere later." He flashed a wide grin.

"Oh *Shane!*" She smiled and shrieked with excitement. "Yuh really mean it? Yuh gonna tek *me* out?" She laughed uncontrollably, covering her face.

"Babes, that's what I said right?"

She finally settled down. "Alright then. So bout wha time yuh normally get back?"

"Well yuh see now…that I can't do; go by a schedule. I'll call yuh when I'm on my way back; cool?"

"Okay. But Shane I neva bring nuh clothes. What a going to wear out?" Her excitement temporarily flat-lined.

"Well, I'll just have to pick up something for yuh don't it?" He made a mental note to get that taken care of.

"Ok." She grinned childishly.

He glanced at the kitchen clock and saw six forty. *Training starts in twenty minutes. Really should be getting out of here…*He stood.

"So Simone, what's that thing yuh did with your tongue earlier? Can yuh show me in slow motion?"

She busted out laughing. "Shane don't start nutt'n yuh can't finish! Yuh affi guh train soon and yuh need all yuh stamina for dat!"

He knew she was right. "Alright then…" He playfully sulked and headed out of the kitchen.

"Shane…" She ran after him and pounced on his back. "Alright, come den!"

He walked them over to the bed and turned on the TV to catch the morning Sports recap. His picture flickered across the screen amidst talks of the Australian track meet. Snippets of his press conference speech regarding Tyson

Blake and the hundred meter race where they last ran together were being replayed and analysed.

Why the hell are they making such an effort to build a story about this 'beef'? This is giving that dude way more props than he deserves. Unbelievable! He was pissed.

When the program went to commercial, Simone crept between his thighs.

"Shane, yuh mad with mi?" She playfully pinched him, jolting him out of his daze.

"Hmm? No man, why yuh seh dat? I was only playing babes."

Without hesitation, she took his entire phallus into her mouth in one complete motion.

Oh shit! Shane's mind caught on. *What a blessed mouth! What the fuck is that pain in my balls though?*

"Sexy, take yuh time nuh! Yuh trying to swallow me whole?" He relaxed as she slowed her pace but continued to do that special *thing* with her tongue that overwhelmed him.

This shit is surreal! Every man should experience this! He eased her head away from his pulsating manhood, and grabbed her off the floor. He bent her over the edge of the bed and slipped on a condom in record speed.

Simone stuck her butt high in the air and bravely welcomed the entire ten inches of his thick shaft without flinching.

"Fuck mi like neva before Shane! Gimme all a wha yuh have pent up inside!"

Her vulgarity sent his eroticism over the edge. "All of it?" He asked sarcastically, though he knew better. "Yuh sure yuh can manage?" He teased her.

Instead of a verbal response, she pushed up on her arms and wrapped her legs backward around his waist, thrusting her groin aggressively unto his turgid cock.

A wha di bloodclaat this man? Shane was caught off guard, and yet again astonished. *She mad fi di cocky!*

"Yea Simmie. Fuck mi hard!   Mi love dem moves ya!" He completely lost track of the time.

"You've reached NCB Business Brokerage. This is Regina Mitchell speaking. How may I assist you?"

"Yes Regina, it's Mr. Mullings. How've you been?"

Shit!   Not the call I was expecting... "Hello Mr. Mullings. I'm fine thanks and yourself?"

"Well just hanging in there; nothing to complain about. I just wanted to do a follow-up to see if you've decided to join us here in Cayman? I know you have two months left to decide, but I just wanted to start with the preparations if your decision was leaning in my favour." He chuckled coolly.

Though she hadn't made her final decision, Regina knew a thing or two about being politically correct.

"Sir, I am definitely excited about the opportunity. I'm in the midst of sorting things out with my family as we speak. Most important is my sister's academic performance for the remainder of the school term. This shall weigh heavily on my response."

"I understand your concerns Regina. And as I told you before, she'll be well provided for here in Cayman too. But I didn't call to pressure you."

"Thank you for understanding Sir. I will definitely be contacting you shortly; but I must say that I am leaning towards moving." *That's all he needed to hear.*

"Well I'm pleased. With that covered then, is Hugh in office as yet?"

Is he ever at nine? She mused inwardly. "Not as yet Sir. Should I have him call you?"

"No. It's not that urgent. I will try him again later. Anyways young lady, it was a pleasure speaking with you as always. You enjoy the rest of your day."

"Thank you Sir and you do the same."

They disconnected.

As soon as she hung up, her private line began to ring. Before she could answer, Stacy sauntered into the office with a disastrous black eye. She reflexively picked up the phone anyway.

"Uhm, this is Regina."

"Baby, I'm calling about the lunch plans." It was Linton.

She stared at Stacy astounded, finding it difficult to play nonchalant.

"Uh, sure hun. But let me call yuh back though." She rested the handset on the desk.

"What the hell happened to your eye?" She went over to Stacy, who casually ignored her. "Oh! You really want to do this? Maybe I should call the police?" She removed her cell phone from her pocket.

Stacy quickly grabbed her hand. "Regina, don't! He didn't mean it. It was my fault this time."

"You mean like the last twenty times? How long are you going to put up with his shit Stacy? I mean, is it love? Cause you sure as hell make enough money to support your family without having to put up with his shit!"

"Girl, what would you know? You're busy living your perfect little existence. You uppity girls don't know what it's like for the rest of us."

"Are you fucking kidding me?" Regina caught herself and lowered her voice. "You, more than anyone, know that my life is far from perfect! And what is that shit about uppity girls. Excuse me, but our pasts are not that distant in nature. You choose to subject yourself to them bruises you obviously desire. Stacy, I don't want to argue with you at a time like this, but this is serious. He is going to kill you!"

Stacy began to cry. *Regina if you only knew what I had to go through to make ends meet. We might share the*

43

same office space but definitely not the same means. You're favoured around here; law student, gorgeous, and well educated. I'm not like you. I have to work twice as hard to support my son and my mother. I'm all they have. I have to do it all!

Regina calmed down and extended her sympathy. "Stacy, do you need somewhere to stay for a while? I mean, seriously…"

"Girl, you're forgetting that I come in threes? I'll be alright. This is the first in a long time, yuh have to agree. I provoked him girl, and I hit him first." She tried to explain in between sobs.

"Well that is no excuse to hit your face like that. Yuh want me to get somebody to kill him?"

Stacy started to grin and then soon, they both laughed hysterically. The pain from Stacy's jaw shot to her head.

Regina saw her flinch. "Girl, you better go home before Hugh gets in. You don't need these nosy people all in your business. I will cover the phones for you. Better yet, go see a doctor to make sure your face aint broken."

"Alright girl. Yuh sure?" She continued when Regina rolled her eyes at her. "Thanks a mil girl."

She picked up her belongings, gave her a hug, and made a dash for the stairs, hoping she didn't pass Hugh or anyone for the matter in the stairwell.

Regina called back Linton.

He picked up on the first ring. "Yes baby, what happened? I heard something in your voice."

"If yuh saw the nasty bruise on Stacy's face; unbelievable how cruel some men are! And how weak the women want to be! Babes, I love yuh; but not that much."

"Regina please. *Nobody* will be bruising my baby; not even me! But what is she gonna do? Although I think I know the answer to that."

"Don't we all know the answer to that? She is crazy; crazy as hell! Anyhow, lunch will definitely be good 'cause there is something I need to discuss with you too. Please don't ask me what right now."

"Ok boss. Pick you up at twelve fifteen."

"Cool. Love you baby."

"Love you too. Later."

They hung up. Her extension rang again.

She checked the time and knew exactly who it was. "A pleasant good morning to the *other* man in my life. How are you feeling?"

"The other? Yuh bright!" Shane laughed. "I'm doing superb my *little* friend. I'm damn content if you ask me."

"*Little*? I see. Is it the stardom?" They laughed. "And why are we so *content*?"

"Let's just say Simone slept over last night."

"Oh God! Let me guess, dinner food for breakfast?"

They doubled up with laughter.

"Regina why yuh hating? Yuh jealous? Would you have preferred to come and make me eggs?"

"Whatever Shane, I make more than eggs when I'm in the mood. Sometimes I add toast!" She laughed heartily.

"Anyhow, so I'm like over two hours late for training and I'm in the parking lot. I just wanted to check on my favourite girl. Yuh undastand?"

"When are you ever early? Anyways, I'm going to tell Linton about the promotion at lunch today. The boss in Cayman called me this morning and gave me a reality check, a real ride or die eye-opener. I just have to lay it on the table and hope for the best Shane."

"Well good luck with that and keep me posted. Gotta run so talk to yuh later sweety. Love you."

"Love you too Shane."

It was nine o'clock.

Natalie was in a complete state of disarray. Arguing with Michael always made her uncomfortable and jittery. She could hardly function or concentrate on anything. *I can't believe he got on me like that this morning. Was he kidding about having kids right now? Right at the beginning of my private practice? I know marriage only works with compromise, but God knows I did all that. Put myself through that strenuous, intensive training schedule so that I could come back to Jamaica to be with him. Now he wants to whine about kids. Unbelievable! Always whining about something or the other...*

It's about time I schedule Shane for his next visit. I should give him a call. Haven't spoken to mom in a while...should give her a call too. God knows I want to have kids one day, but it just can't be right now! And if he thinks he's slicker than a doctor, always trying to time my cycle and ejaculate inside me, well!

On an impulse, she dialled Shane. His voicemail picked up.

"Shane, this is Doctor Simmons calling to schedule your appointment. Please call me back so we can decide on a date. Take care."

She dialled her mother. There was no answer. *Must be out as always mother; guess I'll try back later.*

Her cell phone vibrated somewhere in her drawer.

Roxanne had sneaked through the escape hole leading to the Patty Shop before the lunch bell had sounded. She had arranged with Andre to meet there at twelve and just as planned, he was right on time. She ventured on a solo mission today because Cindy had not shown up to school.

"Whappen Roxie? Bwoy mi glad fi see yuh." Biggs flashed a wide grin.

"You too. I'm glad you came on time." She climbed into his truck and gave him a hug. "So where are we going?"

"Well I wanted to show you where I lived; if you don't mind?" He flashed an entrancing smile.

"Okay, but don't think that means sex!"

"Roxanne jus cool nuh man. Everything is not about sex with me. When yuh gonna get that?" He started the car.

Headed towards Jack's Hill, they travelled most of the journey in silence as Roxanne observed her surroundings and listened to his tracks. Before long, he pulled into his driveway and she was immediately awed.

"Your house is ridiculously huge!" She exclaimed, flabbergasted. "And yuh live here all by yuhself?" She turned to assess his expression.

He grinned. "Yes mam. But of course my family comes over occasionally."

"Oh..." Was all she could manage.

They walked the short distance up the winding stairs leading to the front door and he let her in first.

Roxanne was instantly taken aback by the exquisite décor. Crystal chandeliers lined the high ceilings; French windows spanned the length of the wall, permeated the sun's mid-day glow; and lavish paintings by some of Jamaica's most renowned artists, detailed the walls of the foyer.

This looks like something from MTV Cribs. She mused to herself. *Wow! This is how DJ's live? A girl could really get used to living like this.* She smiled at that thought.

"You want something to drink babes? Juice...water?" Biggs asked, interrupting her meditation.

She spun around, seemingly overwhelmed. "Uhm, yes please. Do you have Coke?"

"I'll check. The chef's supposed to be making lunch now so we'll eat soon. Cool?"

The chef? Excuse the richness! "Okay then." She barely answered as she ventured off to tour his palace.

Regina climbed into the car and greeted her man with a kiss.

"You down here long babe?" She asked as she adjusted the seat and buckled her seatbelt.

"No man got here when I called you. How's it going?" He eased out of the congested parking lot.

"So far so good; except for manning the phones. You know I can't stand the talking." She turned up the radio to hear the new Mavado song that played back to back on every radio station. *On the rock is right!*

"Babe, I wanted to ask you something." Linton casually mentioned. "You think you're being a little too hard on Roxanne? I'm just saying."

"Nope!" She responded without hesitation. "Not at all. Why? She said something?"

"Calm down Regina; she didn't. But she was very broken this morning. I mean you completely ignored her after the effort she made to please you. That wasn't right babe. And the fact that you assumed I could take her to school…"

"I didn't. Did you take her?" She smiled coyly.

"It's not funny Regina. She's only seventeen."

"I wish you'd tell *her* that! I know how old she is; but I also know how *old* she's trying to make me look with all her stress. I aint having it Linton!"

They pulled into the Courtyard parking lot and did their rounds before they found a spot.

"Regina, on a serious note just be cool later. That's all I'm saying. Don't prolong things."

"I hear you Mister."

They walked into the courtyard and of a myriad of choices, decided on Japanese food.

The restaurant wasn't as packed as it usually was during lunch hours so the wait was cut almost in half. After placing their orders, Linton didn't waste any time delving back into their early morning conversation.

"So what is it you said you had to tell me? Forgive me, I'm anxious." The server brought their soups.

Regina wasn't sure she was ready for this conversation, but she planned to give it a try. "Baby, I got the promotion."

Linton exploded with laughter. "What? When? How long have you been hiding this?"

She forced a grin. "Not long. Day and a half…" She smoothed out the lie.

"Well congrats babe. This is definitely a reason to celebrate. I'm so proud of you." He leaned in for a kiss.

"Thank you baby." She smiled and welcomed his lips, before clearing her throat to continue. "Babe, there's something else. The position is at the Cayman branch." She tensed when the smile instantly disappeared from his face.

"Continue…"

Oh boy! This is not going to go well. She steadied her thoughts. "I…we would have to move there. But baby, everything will be set up for us before we get there. I mean the boss there…"

"No. Everything will be set up for *you*! I can't just move like that. What about my family? My job? Or did you forget that *I* work?"

The server brought their food.

"Linton, I did not forget that you work! I researched it, and there are a lot of jobs in Computer Science in Cayman. With your experience…"

"And what about my family? I do have *one*!"

Motherfucker! "That's a harsh implication. I guess I don't! But anyway you'd make enough money to visit them as often as you want. Babe, I don't see why you're just shutting down the whole idea. I've been doing the research, and Cayman is booming right now Linton."

"Oh! You *researched* it. It sounds like you've known about this longer than a *couple of days*!"

What difference does that make? Breathe...don't shout. "Baby, I just didn't know how to tell you before. And for good reason because this conversation is going exactly like I envisioned it. Besides, it's not like we have to do this in a week or two. We're talking about two-three months from now."

"It doesn't matter when it is Regina. How can you make plans *without* me? What did you expect? You'd just what? *Research* it, lay it on me and I'd just tag along like a puppy?" He was evidently agitated.

"You know what, let's just drop it..."

"Yes. We're definitely dropping the conversation and the *entire* idea. Eat your food so we can leave." His lunch date was ruined.

"Shane what yuh saying? Yuh lunching with us or what?" Sean shouted through his car window.

"That sound like a plan. I'll drive behind you guys." Shane packed his overstuffed gym bag into the trunk.

"Cool. Oonu come on nuh man. Man belly a growl yuh nuh." Sean barked at his teammates.

Their little posse piled into Sean's truck and they all headed to their favourite lunch spot; the Courtyard.

Shane knew he spotted Linton's customized Evolution on the way into the restaurant and just hoped he wasn't in for any uncomfortable surprises. He spearheaded the gang, and spotted Regina as soon as they entered the terrace.

"Yes a table for four please." He answered the hostess at the Italian restaurant, though his focus was on Regina. He could tell that something wasn't right with her.

He turned to his friends. "You guys go ahead. I see Gina over there, gonna go say hi real quick."

"The girl's with her man! Leave dem nuh Shane and stop exert yuhself." Nicholas was the talkative one.

Shane completely ignored him and made his way over to the table. As he got closer, he locked eyes with Regina. Though she shook her head displeasingly, he was determined to interrupt anyway.

"What's up Linton? Hey Gina..." He pounded fists with Linton and continued. "All is well with you lovebirds?"

Linton responded dryly. "As far as I know. How yuh been though? I hear you're readying up for Australia?"

Shane knew Linton was not an avid track fan, much less a fan of his. "Yeah man. Nuff training yuh nuh. Anyways I was just saying hi. Y'all enjoy the rest of your lunch. Gina..." He nodded towards her and walked away.

When he rejoined his friends, the server was taking their orders. She quickly acknowledged him as he sat.

"And for you Shane?" The young lady grinned uncontrollably.

He was a regular at the restaurant, and also the most popular athlete of the bunch. "I'll have the shrimp scampi today, with garlic mashed potatoes and a house salad. Oh and lemme get a lemonade."

Nicholas, of course, had to make a comment. "Just waste coach well-planned training while yuh at it. Wha kind of heavy lunch dat?"

"Nicholas, sometimes..." Shane quickly dropped it.

Kendra rolled her eyes at her annoying teammate in agreement with Shane. "So what are your plans for the rest of the day *you*? Checking out Quad tonight?"

Shane glanced in her direction and frowned. "*You*? Sean I think Kendra's asking you a question."

"Funny! Shane a you mi a talk to!" She quickly snarled at him. "What yuh getting into lata?"

"I dunno, maybe your panties." He cynically replied, knowing that would gravely irritate her.

Everyone laughed except for Kendra.

Not wanting to outright blast her in front of the gang, he hastily tried to reconcile his deed.

"I'm only playing with you Kendra. Why you take everything so serious?"

Nicholas thought he should answer on her behalf. "Everybody knows why Shane, including you. Geesh!"

She became more agitated. "This is why I can't stand hanging with you guys. You," she almost stabbed Nicholas with her finger, "just chat too *damn* much! And the rest of yuh jus damn dumb!"

"Ouch! I wasn't even involved in the conversation." Sean spoke up for the first time. "Y'all stop picking on the young lady. No threesomes at lunch time please."

"Okay, let's reconvene at dinner!" Nicholas insisted.

The three men laughed respective of Kendra's visible annoyance.

The waitress brought their orders and as expected, Shane was served first. She catered to his every whim before even removing the others' plates from the tray.

Kendra's disposition reeked of rage while the others hastily devoured their meals in silence.

"Roxanne, where yuh gone?" Biggs called out to his wandering house guest.

Her head appeared over the second floor banister.

"I'm up here." She enthusiastically shouted.

He ascended the stairs and met up with her. "I see you like the paintings huh? You're into art?"

"Yes. I'm an aspiring artist." She replied without looking towards him, fully mesmerised by the wall length piece of a naked, pregnant woman.

"That's all I've wanted to do since I was a kid… paint. But my sis says art's not a real profession."

"That's bullshit babes. Nice to know we're *both* artists though! You should paint me something sometime."

He went into the foyer and opened the sliding doors leading to the balcony. "We can eat out here if you like."

"I'd like that very much." She curtly replied. "You have a very pretty home Andre."

"It's alright I guess. Just need somebody to share it with." He lustfully stared into her wide, bright eyes, causing her to bashfully look away.

"I see. So what about your *women*? Why don't you move one of them in?"

"I don't have any *women*. I've just been working hard these days. My kids' mothers and I don't really get along much so I just take care of the kids and that's that."

"*Kids...mothers...*Is how many yuh have so?" She quizzically eyed him.

"Well I have three baby-mothers and five kids. I won't even lie to yuh."

"Damn Andre! Yuh busy though. How old are you anyway?"

"How old I look?"

"Just tell mi nuh. I don't know, twenty three?"

"Ha! I'm twenty nine. I'll be thirty this year."

Her eyes widened. "Okay. Well yuh definitely don't look your age."

"I could say the same about you. You definitely look like an older woman." He lied and moved closer to her.

Woman? Nobody ever called me that before. She smiled inwardly and it snuck onto her lips.

"Babes, your smile sexy though." He ran his thumb across her chin. "What so funny?" He knew exactly. Calling her a woman pleased her, like it did with all his school girls.

"Nothing." She sat on the patio chair and rested her elbows on the table. An awkward feeling swirled within her.

He sat in the chair beside her and turned her face towards his. "Roxanne, I don't want to scare you or anything, but can I get a little kiss?"

The awkward feeling heightened and now she was nervous. Her hands began to tremble.

Using her body language as her response, he cupped her face in his hands and pecked her on the lips. Her mouth slightly opened, so he went in for another. This time, he slipped his tongue into her mouth. He looked at her with her eyes closed and it turned him on immensely. He got up, held her hand and escorted her back into the foyer towards the oversized sofa.

"Andre, remember what I said right?" She mumbled as they got comfortable in the sofa.

He could feel her resistance in his grip. "Roxanne we're only kissing. You can relax. I promise."

"Okay. But Andre..."

He plugged her mouth with his tongue and patiently trained her to follow his lead. He expertly licked the insides of her mouth, and gently rested his hand on her thigh. When she didn't resist, he slowly slipped his hand under her tunic and softly rubbed her vagina.

What a fat pums! A suh yuh a move Roxie? He revelled in his progress, especially after realising that she was too mesmerised to react. He proceeded to test his luck and slid her panty to the side. When her legs reflexively spread wide, he tested her moisture with one finger and quickly realised the root of her fears.

You're a virgin! Wow! Long time mi nuh feel sup'm so tight. Alright, mi will tek time wid yuh til yuh ready. I'll definitely keep you around for a while. He removed his hand but wasn't done exploring her realms just yet.

"Roxanne, I want to kiss your breasts. Do you want me to babes?"

"Mmm..." She moaned, unable to control or understand the strange feelings swirling within. "Andre..."

"Jus cool babes." He quickly put his finger to her lips. "I'm your man yuh nuh and I promise yuh already."

She accepted his affirmation by removing the shoulder of her tunic, but almost too slowly for his patience. She sat motionless as Biggs hurriedly pulled it down around her waist and opened the buttons of her shirt.

Wow! Now this is flawless skin! You're a virgin in every way eh Roxie? Definitely a keeper!

He opened her bra, allowing her voluptuous breasts to spring free. Reigniting their kissing session, he gently massaged her breasts and slipped a finger into her moisture. His crotch began to form a tent, and he gently stroked it with his free hand.

"Babes, I'm in pain." He gave up attending to her and leaned back in the chair.

With a look of genuine concern, Roxanne moved closer toward him. "What's wrong Andre?"

He patted his turgid erection. "Can you touch it for me please? Just stroke it a little."

She carefully did as he instructed, until he erupted inside his boxers.

Nicholas coyly observed Kendra and figured she was too at ease for his liking.

"So what yuh have planned for the rest of the day Kendra? I mean besides going home *alone*?" He enquired with an obvious smirk.

"Yuh can't shut yuh mouth sometimes?" She irritably snapped. "I dunno. Maybe I'll have you come over and lick the *nani* just the way yuh like."

His boys laughed him to scorn. Nicholas could never live down the day that his ex-girlfriend had barged into the training camp and had blurted out the intricate details of their bedroom activities. The last thing he had wanted the world to know was that he performed oral sex - '*bow-wing*' as it was derogatively labelled in the Jamaican society.

Sean's cell rang, interrupting the taunting. "Hello." He immediately straightened up in his chair.

The others, fully aware now that it was his woman, tried to listen in to get some ammunition on their usually private friend. But Sean knew better; he kept the talking to a minimum.

"Alright, I'll come over and bring you some lunch. Love you too." That he couldn't escape because his girl would chew him out had he not responded sensibly.

"*Love you too.* Oh I'm so whipped for you." Nicholas couldn't resist.

"Shut up!" They all said in a chorus, causing some of the other patrons to look in their direction.

"Yo, I have to go ladies." Sean joked. "Duty calls. Nick, I have a good mind to leave yuh here." He teased.

"Yuh better not!" Shane hastily interjected. "Take him with yuh but leave Kendra. I'll take her."

They all turned to stare at him, then at Nicholas, who surprisingly declined a comment.

Sean only grinned. "Alright, thanks man. See y'all tomorrow. Shane yuh can try coming on time, yuh zimme? No pun intended." He winked at Kendra.

"I'll try." He grinned sheepishly.

The men laughed as they walked away.

Kendra couldn't bear to look Shane in the face now that they were left alone. She occupied herself with re-arranging the condiments in the center of the table.

"Kendra, I hope what I said earlier didn't really hurt your feelings. You know I was just joking. I mean, why do you take everything so serious since...you know?"

"I know you were joking Shane. But what can I say? I fell for you, though I knew better and I seriously tried not to. But not to worry; I know nothing can come of it. I'll figure me out." She averted his gaze once more.

"Look, you should've said something to me before now. I mean, yes it can't really go anywhere with us because we're on the same track team; and I do have a girl. But I'd be more sensitive towards subjects like that, yuh feel me?"

"Yeah. Well now yuh know..." She inspected her fingernails just because.

There was an awkward silence.

Shane watched her as he pondered their situation. *If the circumstances were different, I'd definitely give us a chance. You're a pretty cool chic; smart, athletic, and competitive. Almost like the female version of me. But being in the same club equals too much drama; too much jealousy; too much distraction.*

"Well, I have a couple of errands to run. Yuh wanna ride with me or you ready to go home?"

Kendra looked dead straight into his eyes. "How about I ride *on* you?" She had the attitude to match.

He was hesitant, but wasn't prepared to turn down a good offer. "If it's cool with you, and you can handle it."

"I'm a big girl Shane. I'll have to *handle* it."

That was all he needed to hear. He paid the restaurant tab and they made their way towards the exit.

Shane glistened with sweat as he expertly hoisted Kendra unto his dick, firmly holding her in place.

"Yea sexy, ride it off for mi! Yuh know how I like it! Mmm...Yuh love it?"

"I love it Shane! I want it harder! Mmm...mmm." Kendra grunted appreciatively.

"Harder? Yuh sure?" He shoved her against the front door of her apartment and aggressively pummelled her throbbing flesh. "You mean like that?" He teased with a smirk, as a scream escaped her mouth.

"Oh shit!" She lost complete control in his arms.

CHAPTER FOUR

S hane opened the door to his apartment and the scent of food immediately permeated his nostrils.

"Simone what yuh cooking girl? It sure smells good in here." He called out as he closed the door.

There was no response.

He walked into the kitchen and saw the containers of food, but Simone was nowhere in sight. Eventually he found her lying butt-naked in the middle of his bed, glistening with oil and dutifully awaiting his arrival.

"Hey baby, yuh ready fi yuh bath?" She asked as he got to the bedroom door.

My bath? Haven't had one of those since I was five! "I guess so sexy. What yuh have planned?" He was blushing.

"Jus get naked and lef di rest to me." She commanded.

Shane removed three articles of clothing in less than a second. "Ready!" He complimented that with the widest grin.

Simone crept on the bed towards him then fluidly slid off inches away from his face. She gently held onto his hand and led him to the dimly lit bathroom.

The floor leading from the bed to the bathtub was fully covered in rose petals. There were candles everywhere, releasing scents of vanilla that forced his hormones to react.

"Guh inna di bath baby. Tek time and nuh bun up yuhself wid di cangle."

He stepped into the bath and carefully sat, the water nice and warm scented with lavender.

She retrieved a wash cloth and slowly began to bathe him. Starting with his feet, she wiped each individual toe - being mindful of his blisters - before washing and sensuously massaging them.

Next, Simone used a different cloth to wash and caress his backside from his head to his heels, in a gentle manner that gravely aroused him. She washed his stomach and smiled in admiration as the water rippled down his chiselled abs. When she got to his turgid shaft, she lingered there. Not being able to resist him anymore, she moved the candles to the counter and entered the bath.

Shane was stupefied to the point of not realising that she had straddled him without a condom. He moaned in sheer ecstasy, and even came prematurely.

Simone emptied the Jacuzzi tub and turned on the shower to rinse them both. She dried him from head to feet with an oversized towel and asked nonchalantly.

"Yuh ready fi eat baby? I'll get yuh dinner."

He was dumbfounded, but managed a nod.

She left him in the bathroom and went to share his meal; naked. When she returned to the bedroom with the tray, she set the TV to the sports channel and they both ate in silence.

"Sexy, yuh really got me this time. Thanks a lot for *all* that! I really appreciate it." He urged himself to give her a kiss though he hated being so mushy. "You can get ready when yuh finish. I'm going to take you to the movies; cool?"

"Alright. But yuh got me a outfit?"

"Oh yeah, they are in a shopping bag. I must've left it in the living room or somewhere. Just look for it."

She eagerly wandered off to find the treasure.

Wow! Shane was in bliss. *Of all the years I've been rendezvousing with women, and of all the women I've dated, I've never been given a bath before. Simone is the real deal to rahtid; just a totally different package! She always caring for me; feeding me, and fucking me right. And she*

59

doesn't even nag! What more could any man ask for? Not a damn thing!

She came back into the room wearing the fitted, corseted, dress he had bought. The lavender color perfectly suited her olive skin, and the fit was just right for her dangerous curves.

"Yuh like it on mi Shane? Mi love it bad!" She twirled and smiled. "Oh! And dem shoes are da bomb! Tanks."

"Of course I like it. And yuh know yuh look sexy... so stop show off!"

They both laughed.

She twirled her way to the bathroom and styled her hair the way he usually liked it; half up in a bun, and the other half spilling loosely over her shoulders. She looked glamorous; no make-up and all.

Shane got dressed in his designer linen slacks, cotton shirt, and his loafers. "And we're off?" He slapped her on the butt as she walked past him and curtsied.

Simone was happier than ever.

Michael had broken. He had given up on playing tough guy.

"Natalie, can we talk? How long are we going to do this? I'm sorry for pissing you off."

"What are *we* doing exactly Michael?"

He audibly exhaled. "I've been calling you all day... you haven't taken my calls. I just want to apologise and move on from this. I don't want to fight with you. Why are you punishing me?"

"Maybe I'm just practicing your insensitive and selfish mannerisms." She moved about the kitchen preparing dinner, not once pausing to acknowledge him.

Oh, so you are punishing me... He smirked inwardly.

"Baby, *you* more than anybody know that this man is very sensitive." He moved in closer and groped her butt. *Hmm! No resistance...* "Especially when my baby is sulking, and hiding that beautiful smile." He hugged her from behind and slid his hand under her silk blouse.

Natalie didn't push him away, but she didn't warm up to him either. "You noticed we carried the wrong cell phones this morning?" She asked as if he wouldn't.

A nervous feeling welled within him. "Yes, but since I hardly use mine during the day it didn't matter much." He gently massaged her breasts.

She dropped the knife and vegetables into the sink, and leaned back into his embrace.

"Michael, if you feel the answer to everything..."

He spun her around and sucked on her mouth, purposely trying to avoid her usual lecture. Expertly intertwining his tongue with hers, he evoked appreciative moans with his soft caress. After swiftly removing her blouse and tossing it to the floor, he hoisted her unto the kitchen counter.

"Baby, I don't want you to be hurt. I love you too much. More than I can say with words." He whispered closely by her ear, knowing that alone would greatly arouse her. He eased her legs wide apart and softly bit on her unexposed vagina. "You hear me baby?" He looked up at her with glistening eyes.

"Mmm...hmm." She managed in between moans.

He eagerly exposed her and delicately moved his tongue about her moistened pinkness. As he gently nibbled on her throbbing clitoris, her juices flowed from their warm origins and she reflexively clutched his head.

Michael purposely limited her control while he tongued her until she came. Almost immediately, he impaled her haven with his turgid cock, destined to rock her world.

As tears gingerly cascaded down her cheeks, Natalie mustered the strength to speak. "Michael..." She whispered.

"Who is Caramel?" She groaned as he aggressively plunged deeper within.

"A client of mine baby…Mmm…I love this pussy." The words involuntarily escaped his mouth.

She was fully aware that he never gave clients his cell phone number. Most important right now, she was stunned by his vulgar outburst.

They made love in that position for what seemed like hours. Though it was erotically enjoyable, they both preferred to be somewhere else.

Norman Manley International Airport chaotically stirred with travellers and airport personnel.

"We are now boarding Air Jamaica flight 009 to New York City at Gate number 12…" The voice on the pager was announcing.

Shane dialled Regina and made his way to the gate.

"Hey you. She picked up on the first ring. "I guess you're leaving now?"

"Yea, I'm about to board. Why yuh sound so distressed though? I hope it's not because you love me and I won't give you a chance." He chuckled.

"Shane, seriously…I won't even lie though, I'm a *little* worried about you; but still positive. It's just all the other things I am going through at the same time yuh nuh?"

"I guess Linton didn't take the promotion news too well huh? If that's what set the tone of that lunch date today, Gina you have to give it some time. But I'll remind you that at the end of the day, you have to do what's best for you and Roxie. Dude is a grown man…and if he really loves you… you know."

"Yeah, I know. It's still so stressing though. I always support him one hundred percent, and he just shut me down like that. I just wonder if this is the end for us."

"Well babes, I'm not going to tell you what to do with your relationship. But you'll regret passing up an opportunity like this. It will haunt you forever. This position is something you've dreamed of since the day you got into Finance."

As he spoke, he overheard voices whispering behind him. *'That's Shane Wright! Mommy look! It's really him!'* He tried to continue his conversation.

"And yea, you didn't plan on moving; but when opportunity knocks, you better open the door. That was always our motto right?"

The voices continued as Regina affirmed his philosophy. *'Mommy can we say hi please? Mommy ask him to take a picture with us. Please mommy?'*

"Excuse me, Mr. Wright?" That had to be the mother.

Shane turned and offered a smile.

"I'm sorry to bother you." She seemed sincere. "I see you're on the phone, but would you mind taking a picture with my boys? They are very big fans of yours."

He made it his duty to never disappoint children so he kindly obliged. "Sure...no problem."

He spoke into the phone. "Gina can you hold on or should I call you back?"

"I'll hold...do your thing."

He posed with the boys while their mother snapped more than *'a* picture'.

After posing for a few more pictures with children, women, and one man that also wanted to have a long conversation, he returned to Regina.

"Gina, I can't deal with this...seriously."

They both laughed.

"What can I say my friend, you're everybody's sugar these days." Regina teased. "Enjoy it while it lasts. Yuh better not lose any race before you retire! You know how *patriotic* our people can be!"

They laughed at that underlying fact.

He boarded his flight with ease and greeted a few familiar air hostesses.

"Anyways, so just take it easy and be smart; what is to be shall!"

"Definitely. Shane, you know I love you right?"

"Gina please don't! I know exactly where your emotions are headed. Don't do this to me or yourself. Jus tek it easy...for both of us. Cool?"

"Alright. You're the boss. Call me when you get in before you get locked down." They laughed hysterically.

"Whatever! I love you too my friend. You're the bestest ever!"

Shane couldn't resist smiling as he hung up. *Gina is something else.* He settled into his first class seat and got comfortable.

The hostess offered him a drink while the other passengers boarded.

Destination Lisa Artuso. He took a sip of his ginger ale. *You, I'll definitely make Wright one day soon.* He smiled at the irony. *I should call her fine ass right now and confirm the arrival time.* He dialled his official woman but the phone rang without an answer. *Hmm!* Before he could process another thought, his phone began to vibrate.

"I was just about to say." He spoke softly into the mouth piece and reflexively smiled.

"Say what honey? I was in the shower. Are you on the plane? I'm so excited!" Lisa's tone already revealed that.

"Are you? Well, about that..." He was about to tease but heard the breath she held after inhaling. "I'm joking babe." He laughed. "Yeah, I just boarded."

She giggled nervously.

"You sounded nervous there for a sec. What's up? You miss your number one man *that* much?"

"Shane! You're my *only* man! Don't play with my heart like that. Are we still doing breakfast at your mom's tomorrow? Your brother called me earlier…said I should get you there on time." She laughed.

"We'll see about *on time*. You know I have to make up for lost time with my baby first."

"That we must! But I'm actually anxious to meet your mom too. It would really mean a lot if she likes me."

Shane blew a silent kiss at one of his hostess friends. "Lisa, let me worry about mom. You're *my* girl. Just make sure you get to the airport by nine thirty. I hate to wait."

"I know baby. I'll be there for nine. I really can't wait to see you! I love you so much Shane."

"I love you too babe. Air kisses 'til I see you."

She giggled. "Tonnes of air kisses!"

"Alright then. In a bit." He hung up feeling loved.

"Cho! How the fuck di place so dark? Mi tired fi tell di ediat dem fi leave on a light inna di studio when dem a lock up. Cho bloodclaat!" Biggs cursed aloud as he tried to locate the switch for the patio light.

With his hand firmly positioned on his Glock, he did a thorough walk through of the studio to ensure there were no surprises looming in the dark.

"Guh in deh so and tek off yuh clothes!" He aggressively instructed his guest. "Mi soon come. Yuh want a wata?" He barely waited for the faint response.

Spending the afternoon being teased and titillated by Roxanne had left him yearning to satiate his sexual appetite. He returned to the private booth for his evening rendezvous, with two bottled waters in hand.

"Yuh ready fi di cocky? Cause a nuh whole night ting tonight yuh nuh! Mi affi get somewhere yuh see it?"

Knowing that Biggs preferred doggy style whenever he was in a rush, Jules bent over and assumed the position.

Biggs dropped his pants, freed his fully erect wood, and anxiously moved in between Jules' legs.

"So whappen to the condom Biggs? I know yuh in a hurry but…"

"Wha yuh a worry bout? Yuh can breed? Relax yuhself man and fling it up gimme!"

"A breed alone yuh a worry bout? Yuh so ignorant sometimes."

"Yo don't piss me off tonight yuh nuh! Me nuh inna di mood fi di whole heap a chatting! Yuh a fuck or chat? Time is money and mi nuh like waste mi money." He forcefully shoved his unsheathed cock into his prepaid destination.

The pain swiftly shot through Jules' spine. "Jesus Christ Biggs! Kill yuh wan kill mi?"

"Back it up pon mi and stop chat! Stop run from di cocky to! A whappen to yuh tonight? Yuh want a beat up?"

"Tek it easy wid mi nuh Biggs. It's just been a long night. Why yuh being so miserable? A wha mi do yuh?"

"Wha mi seh 'bout the talking? Yo stop chat!" With that said, the palm of his hand strongly connected with the smooth skin of a jaw already agape. "Yuh undastan now?"

"Yes Biggs…sorry!"

"Alright. So back it up pon mi now and tek all di cocky! Yea, so mi like it. Yea, work yuh waistline for daddy. Bloodclaat, look like mi affi start deal wid yuh face more often. A so mi activate di boom wine. Oy! Nuh badda bruk it off! Tek time! Suck it off fi mi now Jules. Yea, deep throat it! Shit, mi a cum! Fuck!"

He eagerly released into the warm throat that enclosed his throbbing dick. "Yeah! Dat was the best! Mi affi double yuh pay tonight. But don't think a Christmas every time though!" He took out two thousand dollars and threw it onto the mixing board, partially zipped up his pants and headed for the bathroom.

When he returned to the empty booth, he immediately got to work. It didn't bother him one bit that his guest had left without notice. He played a disc with some new tracks he was invited to work on, and would do so for the producer who offered the right price. His phone sounded, agitating him.

"Yo!" He answered irritably from his headset.

"Wha yuh a seh mi dads? Yuh check out di tracks dem yet?" It was his main producer and friend, L.J.

"Whagwan mi link? Yuh know seh a dat mi deh ya a do now. The first two have mi a way star. Whe yuh seh is a medley thing or a single ting?"

"Whatever yuh feel like. Up to you at this point. A you have the airwaves lock ya now so just call it!"

"Alright hear wha, mek mi gwan vibe it and link yuh lata. But wha yuh seh, Quad tonight?"

"Dat can gwan yes. Linkage…"

"Nuh seh nutt'n. Likkle more!"

As he disconnected the line, his phone rang again.

No man, this a get ridiculous now! "Who dis?" He rashly barked into the mouth piece.

"Ah me Biggs…Sonia. Mi can see yuh tonight? Di baby dem need stuff and mi want some fuck."

"A fuck get yuh stuck weh yuh deh ya now! Mi will see and call yuh back. Mi deh a studio!"

"Alright, just come through any time."

"Eeh." He hung up without regards.

He scanned through the tracks again and tried to feel which would work best for his current vibe. He revelled in the opportunity to finally be in total control of his career and be in a position to take the first shot at tracks as they were produced.

There was no doubt that Jamaicans - locally and abroad, paid big money for whatever product he put his name on. Music producers knew it; and so did the stage show promoters.

His cell rang again.

Farin phone dat. Dem call ya mi like! "Hello."

"Hey baby, I'm missing you like crazy! What you gettin' into?" It was Toya, his babe from Boston.

"Is this my favourite woman in the world?" He had to temper the patois for his foreigner.

"You better mean your *only* woman!" She replied testily and giggled.

He laughed. "Of course baby! Your baby's just here at the studio trying to get some work done...wondering if you're calling to give him some good news. Jah know I could use it."

"What's the matter with my baby? Who's stressing you now?"

"Not as much *who*, as it is *what*! But when's my baby coming? That's what I want to discuss."

"Maybe I'm already here." She teased, laughing.

"No you're not. You would already be sittin' on my dick! Am I right?"

"Damn right! I wanted to ask you if Wednesday was okay. This coming Wednesday, that is."

"Woman, any day is okay when my baby's coming home. Come tonight if you want. I done told yuh that yuh don't have to ask!"

"I know baby, but...well, Wednesday it is. What should I bring for you?"

The best part of the entire conversation... Biggs mused inwardly. He sat forward and allowed his mind to flow freely.

"Ahm, well I like that new phone with the touch screen..."

"You mean the Iphone?"

Of course he did. "Yeah, that one if it's not too pricey. And I could use some clothes as usual. You already know your baby's size. Bur definitely bring those Prada and Jordan sneakers that came out last week."

"Of course. Okay, and did you get the windshield motor for the truck?"

"Yes babes. Bought it and installed it already. Oh and one more thing...make sure to bring nuff thongs so yuh can model them for me. You got that?"

She laughed uncontrollably as always when he offered the softer, more comical side of his personality.

"Ok baby, I really want to finish up my work so I can go home and get some sleep. Cool?"

"Okay baby. Call me when you get up later tonight to go out. I should be up."

See it deh. She just undastand di runnings without nag off mi ears. "What you going to be up doing at them hours? Watch yuhself yuh nuh!"

"Andre! What else could I be doing but work?"

"Baby, I'm just joking with you."

"I know, but I don't like when you say those things."

"Okay. I'm sorry ma baby. Yuh know I love yuh right?"

"Yes. And I love you too. Go finish up your work."

"Alright, later baby." They disconnected.

Linton was almost sure that Regina was anxiously awaiting his arrival so she could bombard him with arguments for moving to Cayman. For that reason, he slowly pulled into the driveway and left all his stuff in the car in the event he would have to go to his mother's for the night.

He took a deep breath before opening the front door. Surprisingly, there was no attack. There was no Regina. He could hear the TV blasting in the upstairs bedroom; but downstairs was empty and quiet. He looked in on Roxanne.

Unbelievable! It's damn near eight and Roxanne's not here? She is definitely trying her best to get on Regina's nerves. I'm sure it's working. He went upstairs and blurted and indirect 'good evening', before he disappeared into the bathroom to stall some more.

"Okay. Let's do this." He declared as he shoved the bedroom door open.

He was shocked, and admittedly a little disappointed, to find Regina curled up under the covers sobbing uncontrollably.

This is not exactly how I imagined it...a forfeit? He hesitantly walked over to her.

"Regina…"

Of course, she didn't respond.

He leaned over her limp frame on the bed and slowly peeled the covers away. "Baby, I'm sorry about today." The guilt instantly set in. "If all this is my fault, I'm so sorry Regina. I don't like seeing you like this. I was wrong for shutting you down today at lunch. Yes, it was very selfish of me. I came home to apologize first thing baby. Talk to me…" He instinctively embraced the love of his life.

Hmm, I guess I could've been a little easier on the one person who always stands by me. I really fucked up big this time! "Regina baby, will you please talk to me?"

She slowly turned to face him.

A lump welled in his throat. *Even with your eyes all swollen and your nose all messy, you're still more beautiful than some who try.* His heart was heavy.

"Baby, I was wrong. We'll talk more about Cayman. Just give me some time okay? I'm truly sorry about lunch."

Regina nodded and tried to speak, but her temper overpowered her efforts.

"Baby, take a deep breath." He hugged her tightly.

She broke down even more. This time she held onto him as if her life depended on it. She tried to speak again.

"I just feel…I just feel like everything is falling apart. I'm really trying…I try my best to be everything to everyone. Not that I don't want to, but it feels like too much sometimes. It's after eight and Roxanne's not in the house.

She is seventeen years old...and it's a fucking school night! Maybe I care too much. Maybe I should just live my life selfish like the rest of the world. I'm not a mother or a wife but still I sacrifice so much. I've done so much more for Roxanne than our mother had ever done for the both of us combined. She wouldn't even see the love in what I do and try to be a little grateful. Is it that I expect too much? I'm so many things to so many people but yet I feel so under-appreciated. Twenty five years young but I feel so old. I'm due for a break."

Linton didn't like that idea. "Regina, I hope you're not talking about breaking up." He tried not to panic.

"I don't want to break up Linton. I just need some support. I need a break from all this!" She almost screamed.

He knelt in front of her. "Baby, I will help you get through this. You've never expressed all this to me before now. Give me a chance to fix things. Regina..."

The front door downstairs creaked open then slammed shut. It was eight forty five.

Regina immediately hopped off the bed. "I have to leave this house! I can't sleep here tonight."

"Baby, where are you going? You're not in any shape to drive. It's late. Just go back to bed. I will handle Roxanne."

"No. I want to leave. And if you know you're parked behind me like I've asked you not to *countless* times, I'd suggest you move your car before I get out the bathroom."

He stared at her, temporarily zoning out, but quickly regained his composure when he heard the toilet flushing. He made a quick dash down the stairs to move his car. On his way out the door, he spotted Roxanne lurking in the kitchen.

"I'll deal with you later. You'd better go in your room before your sister gets down here. Not a good night!"

Roxanne moved as quickly as Linton spoke. Before she could close her bedroom door, she saw Regina storm pass with her gym bag in tote. She rushed into the hallway behind her and went to the front door to observe the drama outside. She watched as her sister hopped into her car and immediately began to back out of the driveway.

Luckily for Linton, he had cleared the way in time because she definitely would have slammed his car on this occasion. He pulled back into the driveway and for the first time in years, parked on his side. He noticed Roxanne backing away from the door and called out to her.

"Don't even try it! What the hell is wrong with you? And where have you been? Do you see the time? And had the audacity to slam the door? Are you losing your mind?"

"Let me guess; daddy?" She pointedly eyed him.

"Roxanne, don't get smart with me. You're this close to being sent to your grandmother in Manchester. Why do you insist on disrespecting your sister? She has done nothing but made sacrifices for you. What are you trying to prove?"

Roxanne's innocent eyes glistened with tears.

Linton wasn't moved. "Did she tell you about her promotion that could take us to Cayman? Do you think she is willing to tag along all this baggage overseas? Roxanne, your sister tries her best to ensure that you have a good life. She just wants you to have choices when you get older. When will you see that?" He stepped past her and headed up the stairs.

Roxanne withdrew into her room and cried.

CHAPTER FIVE

After leaving the studio, Biggs drove the short distance up the hill to visit his son's mother Michelle, figuring that she would better fulfill his appetite that Jules had ignited. He dialled her as he neared the top of the hill, and she answered just as he was about to hang up.

"Hello." Her voice sounded irritable.

"What took yuh so long? Open the front door!"

That was the way he usually handled the visits. He never called or checked beforehand to see if it was okay for him to stop by. He stood by his philosophy that she lived under his roof, hence under his rules; she had known better than to complain otherwise. When he finally pulled up in front of the house, the door was open as he had instructed.

"Whagwan sexy? How yuh look so sad? Yuh nuh miss mi?" He slammed the front door behind him.

Michelle sat on the sofa, eyes fixed on a movie. "I'm not sad, just tired. How've you been?" She totally refrained from answering his question.

He was mildly irritated by her demeanour. "You already know how *I've been*. Where's ma boy?"

"In bed. Go in and see him. I'm sure he'd be excited."

"Yuh naffi tell mi seh I can go see ma boy Michelle. A whappen to yuh?" He snarled.

He ventured into the hallway towards the back bedroom where Rashad lay fast asleep. He took a moment to proudly admire how much he'd grown in the short time since he'd last visited him. *Yuh pretty tall for a six year old. Blessed with daddy's genes. Handsome same way too... Hmm! Can't wait 'til yuh get older so we can spar...show yuh the ropes yuh nuh.* He kissed him on the forehead and left the room quietly.

He returned his attention to his unruly woman. "Yo Michelle! Come ya nuh man and lock off di TV. Whappen, yuh nuh see mi?" He went into the master bedroom and got comfortable on the bed.

Michelle rolled her eyes in utter disgust, and ever so slowly got up. She stalled for time by pretending to search for the TV remote.

He grew agitated when he could still hear the sounds emanating from the living room. "Lock off the TV nuh woman! Better yet, leave it and come. Mi horny is a shame."

What's fucking new? That's the only time you show up here! Really not in the mood for you tonight...especially since those rumours. She cursed to herself.

"I said I'm coming!" She called out inadvertently.

"Michelle, mi hope a nuh attitude yuh have tonight yuh nuh." Biggs shouted at the top of his lungs. "Yuh see mi come in a good mood don't it? Don't get mi cross!"

She sauntered into the bedroom and stood silent in front of him. Her stomach churned as he groped her ass, and tried to rip her high cut bikini shorts from her flesh.

Biggs stared into the eyes of the woman that once held his heart. "A whappen to yuh babes? Yuh nuh love mi like yuh used to? Why, because I don't come around? Yuh nuh watch TV and listen to radio and see how yuh man busy? I'm busy babes! A work mi a work fi mine oonuh."

Can yuh just cut to the chase? Who the hell cares about your love? "If you say so Biggs. What you want to do today?"

Her insolence aggravated him. "Take off yuh clothes and dance fi mi. Dance like yuh used to." He knew more than anything that she hated when he regurgitated her past.

He got up, went over to the CD player, and searched through a stack of discs for something he wanted to hear.

"Hmm, no Biggs in here. Is a bad mind ting yuh a deal wid? Alright mam." He settled for the *Get Low* track by Lil John and the Eastside Boys. "This should do it."

"Biggs, I don't feel like dancing right now. If yuh wanted all of that, why didn't you just go to *The Club*?"

He grabbed her by the throat and grinned as the fear rushing through her body, oozed from her defiant eyes.

"Listen to mi Michelle! Yuh a get pon mi fucking nerves! Yuh want mi beat up yuh bloodclaat in ya tonight? Eeh? Tell mi if a dat yuh want yuh nuh. We can work sup'm out. Yuh ago dance, or yuh want mi gwan squeeze yuh bomboclaat troat?" His voice reeked of anger.

She nodded in agreement and he loosened his grip.

"You were dancing at the same club yuh a send mi to all your life 'til I upgrade yuh. So nuh gimme nuh lip now over a likkle dance. Yuh tink a beg mi a beg yuh?"

"No Biggs." She fought back tears.

"And mi nuh wan see nuh tears neither yuh nuh."

Michelle released her hair from its knot and it fell loosely over her shoulders and down into her back. She steadily eased her way out of the shorts that suctioned to her heavy ass and extra wide hips.

Considered by many to have the body of a goddess, her five feet seven frame measured a voluptuous thirty eight - twenty two - forty four. Her black and Indian descent blessed her with a smooth, dark chocolate complexion. Her contrived but exotic features had immensely attracted Biggs when he first saw her performance at his favourite strip joint, *The Club*.

That is where their story had began; and where she sometimes wished it had ended.

She watched as he lit up a blunt and for a second wanted to ask him not to smoke in her house, especially since Rashad was home. When she imagined his probable anger, she decided against it and focused instead on the rhythm spewing through the speakers. Without much thought, she moved to the melody.

Biggs removed his belt and delightfully gave her a couple lashes on the butt; first gently, and then harshly. He lost complete control when she fell into a perfect split, causing his cock to grow solid as a rock.

"Come over here and bless mi up babes!"

She released his fully erect cock from its stifling quarters and used her tongue ring to expertly massage the head. Though Biggs was heavily endowed, she effortlessly accommodated his entire shaft.

He moaned and writhed in her grip, clinging to the back of her head and thrusting his phallus deeper into her mouth.

"Shit! Mi love it Michelle! Mmm…" He released himself in the back of her throat. "Come ride off mi cocky babes! It's been a while since I explored your insides."

He spread her heavy cheeks and slowly entered her from behind. Her moaning fuelled him to thrust harder, and he buried his cock deeply within her. He watched as her butt jiggled to his movements and it further enticed his sexual appetite. In one swift movement, he withdrew his dick from its current haven and slipped the head into her ass.

Michelle quickly clenched up and spoke for the first time since he had chocked her. "Biggs, I can't manage that tonight. Please, anything but that!"

"But that's what I want! If not tonight, then when?"

She tried to put up a fight but he restrained her by her hair and entered her with a firm thrust. She screamed and howled in agony as he mercilessly pleasured himself.

The bedroom door creaked open.

They both turned to see Rashad standing in the doorway, mouth agape, and his eyes welling with tears.

"Daddy, what are you doing to my mommy? Mommy, why are you crying?" He looked back and forth for answers.

Biggs hung his head in shame. "Son, close the door. Mommy is okay and we're busy okay? I soon come and tuck you in baby boy. It's okay, go back to your room."

The door slammed shut.

Roxanne was more depressed than she had ever felt before. The current turmoil with her loved ones and her very own emotions were steadily taking a toll on her.

In her opinion, Regina was fully pissed off at her and probably even hated her. Linton assumed the role of her absentee father overnight; and she was tired of not being able to hang out after school or entertain a social life. She lay awake in bed at one o'clock in the morning, and wished she could be somewhere else. Eventually, she decided to call Andre.

The line went straight to voicemail.

She tossed and turned for twenty minutes and then anxiously called again. She jumped up this time when he picked up on the first ring.

"Hold on deh Roxie; don't hang up!"

She could hear ruffling and loud noises in his background. *What the hell...*She thought to herself but patiently waited for an explanation.

"Yeah babes. Hello?" Biggs was breathing heavily.

"I'm here. What's happening?"

"Crazy gunshots at Quad star, Jah know. A man got shot outside, but I neva stop to find out nutt'n. Hold on babes, one of ma boys calling mi."

He clicked over to the next line, but came back in no time. "Yeah, some crazy shit yo! Jah know. But what yuh doing up so late anyhow?"

"I'm just here...can't sleep. I got into it with my sis tonight and her boyfriend. And now I just feel like crap."

"Eeh? Him trouble yuh Roxie?" He sounded agitated.

"No man, nothing like that." She quickly tried to quell his concerns. "I was calling to see if you could come for me?" She tensed in fear of not hearing the best answer; whatever that was at this ungodly hour.

"Come for yuh? And do what? Tek yuh to my house?"

She was instantly embarrassed for being so presumptuous. "Uhm, just forget it. I guess I'll just call you tomorrow. Good night."

"Slow down nuh Roxie! Why yuh rushing off the phone? I just asked yuh a simple question. I don't mind taking yuh to ma house if that's what yuh thinking. I was just asking to determine the runnings."

"Oh. Then how soon can you get here?"

"In ten minutes. I don't want yuh to wait for me at the foot of the hill again so gimme the directions to yuh house."

"Just come straight up the hill and make the first left, then the next right. It's the second house on the right. I'll meet yuh outside. Oh, and don't call back this number."

"Cool. I'll be there." He hung up.

She got up and neatly padded her pillows under the spread as Cindy had taught her. She got dressed in her matching underwear set that Cindy - again - had bought her; then slipped on a mini dress over it.

She waited ten minutes then climbed out her bedroom window onto the front patio. She snuck down the driveway and sat on the sidewalk behind the bushes, in front of the house. As soon as she began to worry, a pair of headlights dimly approached in her direction. She held her breath and only released when she realised it was Andre.

She hopped into his truck as soon as he pulled up. "That was fast! Thanks for coming so quick."

"Hey baby girl. You okay?" He kissed her on the lips.

"Yeah, better now. Can we get out of here?"

"Of course babes." He smiled and winked at her.

Tonight should be interesting. Biggs mused inwardly. *Bout yuh waan come a big man house...with that sexy little dress too. Look like yuh ready fi give it up. Well I'm very ready to take it!* He chuckled involuntarily.

"What's so funny?" She quizzically eyed him.

"Nothing babes. Just happy to see yuh I guess. I'm not allowed to be happy or smile?"

She blushed. "Of course! You make me happy too Andre. Real happy." She leaned back and closed her eyes. When Roxanne awoke, Biggs was parking in his expansive driveway. "Oh God. Andre I fell asleep?"

He chuckled. "I guess suh babes. Let's go..."

They made their way up the winding front stairs and entered into his grand entryway as before. She found the view more fascinating at night time, now that all the chandeliers were dimly lit. Their light reflected a soft glow off the paintings, and the atmosphere was that of a museum.

Biggs left Roxanne in the upstairs bedroom to watch TV while he took a shower.

As she busied with the channels, fighting the urge to snoop through his stuff, he called out to her.

"Roxanne! Yuh see ma towel out there?"

She looked about the room. "Yes, it's here." She got up to retrieve it and nervously headed for the bathroom.

Standing by the half-opened door, she outstretched her hand behind it. "Here you go." She could hear him laughing.

"Is wha Roxie? Yuh scared a mi? Bring di towel nuh babes. I'm in the bath." He put his plan into action.

Roxanne barely eased the door open and made her way towards the bath, knees trembling.

Biggs had one leg perched on the side of the tub. His *other* leg rested against his thigh. He watched with sheer amusement as her mind stopped her in her tracks.

"Uhm...here." She managed while handing him the towel; her eyes fixated on his shimmering nudity.

"Roxanne why you look like yuh seen a ghost? Breathe babes! Look like yuh waan faint pon mi." He teased.

She followed him closely back into the bedroom, tracing every detail of his back muscles with her inexperienced eyes. *Goddamn! This is what it's all about huh? No wonder Cindy can't do her school work and Regina can easily forgive Linton. God, what is this feeling? My body is aching!*

"So babes, what yuh have planned for your baby?" He sat on the edge of the bed and lustfully eyed her.

"Nothing. I bet you planned something…"

"What's that suppose to mean babes? Come here." He reached for her hand, pulling her closer towards the bed. "Baby, did I tell you how sexy you are?" He spoke softly as he loosened the ties to her dress. "I mean…but wait! Babes, *all* that for me?" He ogled at her matching, lace lingerie set.

She blushed immensely. "I just thought…" Her words warped into the warm air of Biggs' eager mouth.

He slowly eased her onto the bed and undressed her entirely without breaking the link between them.

"Andre…" She came up for air whispered. "Are we going to have sex now?"

He had expected that. "Only if that's what you want baby girl. Yuh feel like yuh ready to try it?"

"Yes, I want to. But I don't want to get hurt Andre."

He gathered the underlying implication. "I won't hurt yuh baby. I won't hurt you at all! Promise…"

Biggs got the once in a lifetime opportunity to explore Roxanne Mitchell's jewel for the first time. He restrained his aggressive alter ego and made sweet love to the newly initiated woman. He even surprised himself when his lips ventured between her thighs, massaging her pinkness with his tongue until she came.

"I love you Roxanne." He whispered out of nowhere.

After leaving the house and driving around in circles, Regina ended up at her office. Since efforts to sleep had proven futile, she decided to get a head start on some paperwork.

With red, swollen eyes from her all-night crying session, she navigated the Internet to research investment opportunities for her next day's appointments. Her private line rang, startling her out of a daze.

Fuck off! She screamed inwardly, knowing exactly who that could be. She continued about her business, tuning out the sound entirely. Her cell phone vibrated for the umpteenth time in her drawer, but she didn't even flinch.

Browsing through her unopened emails, she spotted a new message from her boss.

Shit! I really need to make a final decision. She cursed as she scanned his subtle hints that she had one month left to accept the promotion. *Shane said it best; when opportunity knocks you better open the door quickly. I love my family and everything, but I cannot settle for mediocrity. I refuse to let this opportunity leave me behind...especially since they're willing to pay for the rest of law school. I'd be an idiot to let this chance go...*

She immediately dialled Shane.

"Cayman Airways, how may I direct you?" He picked up on the first ring.

Regina instantly laughed. "You are so dumb Shane!" She enjoyed the amusement. "It's funny you should say that. I just accepted the position. That's why I'm calling..."

"Well I'm glad you came to your senses." He quickly retorted. "Welcome back!"

"What the hell is that supposed to mean?" Regina snapped playfully. "I don't even want to know! How's the trip going? How's Lisa?"

"Trip's going good so far. Lisa is Lisa. You wanna say hi?" He laughed.

She could hear Lisa in the background laughing as well, demanding to know what he meant by 'Lisa is Lisa'.

"Hey Regina, how are you doing?"

"I'm doing fine Lisa, thanks for asking. And yourself?"

"Much better...now that he's here. You wouldn't happen to know what 'Lisa is Lisa' meant right? Shane!" She tried to muffle the phone as she laughed hysterically. "Regina, I'm so sorry. I think he's jealous so I'll pass you back. It was nice talking to you again. Have a great night."

Regina chuckled. "Take care Lisa. Enjoy..."

Shane was on the line before she could finish. "Damn right I'm jealous! I don't like my women talking to each other. That could be cause for some drama." He laughed as Lisa smacked him with a pillow. "So Gina, about that lunch date...I'm listening."

"Lunch date? Oh! Of course I mentioned the promotion and he shut me down two sentences in after the word Cayman. I figured I wouldn't cause a scene in *The Courtyard* of all places so I decided to drop it until later. Couldn't even eat my food the way I was seething inside. Damn Shane!"

"Damn what? You didn't expect otherwise right?"

"I mean no...well, yes and no. At least in my head he would hear me out and then say he'll think about it even if he didn't. Man didn't even hear what I was promoted for."

"No comment. And then later?"

"I'm home at seven thirty, and 'Mr. Five-Thirty' for seven years, is not in. I knew damn well he was stalling me! And to make things worst, Roxanne's not home either! Shane, a sudden depression overcame me and I seriously started to assess my life. It occurred to me that at twenty five years old, I'm a volunteer mom, an *acting* wife, and an educated but complacent student of life! So yuh know I start to bawl? I just lost my composure. You know dem ways?"

"Do I?" He offered a fake laugh. "Just remember those moments are necessary though. They force you to move mountains. Only way from bottom is up!"

Regina chuckled. "God knows you're right. So have you spoken to Lisa about our *little* chat?"

He knew exactly what she was referring to. "Of course not! I will though, in time. So we're having breakfast at mom's tomorrow..." He left it at that knowing Regina would willingly fill in the blanks.

"Ha! Big moves man." She teased, laughing. "So I guess this weekend is the weekend of *all* revelations. Please let *me* know, how *that* goes! Anyhow, I need to leave this office. Just wanted to check in. Love you bro."

"*Office*? I love when my ladies stack my retirement! Love you too sis. And take it easy okay? Don't think I can't sieve through your voice too!" They laughed at that fact.

Shane's cell phone rang immediately after disconnecting with Regina. He glimpsed at the screen and was instantly irritated. He made his way back into the bedroom and plopped down on the bed beside Lisa.

"Hello." He answered unenthusiastically.

"Shane! Why haven't you returned my calls? I've been calling since last night! Didn't you see the calls?"

"Nope." He blatantly lied. "How may I help you Miss Fox?" He looked over at Lisa and winked.

"You're such a liar Shane! I know you got those calls. I thought we were past all the anger. Didn't you say you were over it? Why are you still being such a jerk?"

"Cause I'm Jamaica's famous chicken." He chuckled at his own sarcasm. "I'll ask again, what's up?"

Amanda was undoubtedly infuriated. "I see you're working at your sense of humour, *and* talking in codes. I remember those *lying* days. Are you with someone?"

"Hmm…that I am!   So get to that point!" His patience had run out.

She audibly exhaled. "I want an exclusive interview after your hundred meter race in Australia."

Shane laughed boisterously. "I *dread* to even know you're going to be there!   But no, I can't make any promises." He continued to chuckle.

"I can make my dad force you, Shane!   I'm just asking as a courtesy."

"Well you should try me! I might just have laryngitis that day, who knows?" He mimicked by excessively clearing his throat.

"You can be such an asshole! I can't fathom how I ever loved you!"

"You never did! I have absolutely nothing else to say to you so I'd better go."

Lisa noticed his annoyance and mouthed 'Amanda'.

He rolled his eyes at her, affirming that. Luckily for him, he had been completely honest with her about the events of his life, at least about the things she could possibly hear about. She knew all about Amanda's constant threats to sabotage his relationship with her dad, which would ultimately cost him sponsorship funds and access to events.

"You'd better not hang up on me Shane! I'm not done talking to you!" Amanda was screaming into the phone when he handed it to Lisa.

"Uhm *A-nan-da*!" Lisa purposely aimed to aggravate her. "My baby has to take his bath now okay?"

Amanda's rage overheated when she heard Shane cackling in the background. "It's *A-man-da* bitch! Mind your fucking business and give that idiot back *his* phone!"

Lisa wasn't moved. "I *was* minding *my* business before you called; and I'm minding *my* business right now! I don't know which idiot you're referring to, but the hunk sitting beside me is done speaking with you! We're about to have make-up sex now too. This conversation is over!" With that said, she pressed end.

Shane doubled over in laughter. "Where the hell did that come from? Miss 'I-don't-like-confrontation'? That was funny as hell!" He couldn't control himself.

"Shane, you know I don't like stuff like that..." Lisa restrained a smile. "Seriously!"

"Uhuh! *Make-up sex* huh? Was that real or all talk? Cause you know..." He made his puppy dog face.

"Come here. I'll show you." She left it at that.

CHAPTER SIX

Shane pulled up in front of his mother's house in the opulent area of White Plains, New York.

The entire scenery was a sight to behold. Sitting on forty acres, her house was surrounded by an immaculate landscape that boasted an infinity swimming pool, a basketball court, and a man-made lake that streamed throughout the premises.

The house itself had seven bedrooms, seven and a half bathrooms, two living rooms, a game room, and the biggest, most detailed kitchen any part-time chef could need. Shane's mother loved to cook; and her boys loved to eat.

Lisa felt knots forming in her stomach. She took a few deep breaths and sighed.

Shane grinned. "Why yuh stressing it babe? Whatever happened to relaxing? You're even making *me* feel nervous to see my own mother."

"I'm sorry Shane. It's just that...I know how Caribbean people value their family. I would just die if your mom hates me...and we'd have to break up." She was visibly trembling.

Shane held her hands to steady them. "Lisa, why would my mother hate you? That'd be a pretty strong opinion given that it's the first time she's meeting you; no? Just take it easy. And besides, there is no breaking up going on around here. I love my woman!" He planted a wet one on her cheek.

"Alright then, let's do this! I'm ready to meet your mom!" She jumped out of the truck in one swift motion.

"Well damn!" Shane laughed at her.

They walked up to the large pine doors and pressed the doorbell.

Shane could hear the loud outbursts inside announcing their arrival before anyone came into view.

His youngest brother Simeon opened the door. "Shane!" He rushed to give his brother a hug. "Hey Lisa! Nice to see you." He pecked her on the cheek.

"It's always a pleasure to see you Simeon. How's it going?" Lisa already had a good rapport with him.

They all stepped into the grand entryway and made their way to the kitchen.

Simeon followed closely beside Lisa and continued. "Everything is okay Lisa. I just finished setting the table. Shane, you should see the feast mom prepared! She definitely outdid herself this time. She's such a show-off."

Shane laughed. "Where's mom anyway?"

"Upstairs getting dressed. You should go *talk* to her." He gave his brother a suggestive glance.

Shane understood exactly what it meant.

Lisa did too.

Steven, Shane's second baby brother, walked into the kitchen while towel-drying his shoulder length afro.

"Hey!" Simeon called out to him. "Get that bush away from all this food!"

Steven glared daggers at him, and his younger brother flipped him the finger. He ignored his request and continued.

"What's up bro? Good to see you man...glad you made it." He gave Shane a warm embrace then turned to Lisa.

"And you miss...you're looking lovely as always." He gave her a gentle squeeze and pecked her on the cheek.

It didn't take long for him to shift focus to the counter filled with food.

"Damn! This *is* a lot of food! Who told mom we're trying to feed the 'ten thousand'? Jesus with you?"

Everyone laughed in unison.

"We were just talking about that." Shane commented, and kissed Lisa on the cheek. Leaving her in the safe company of his brothers, he went in search of his mother.

Shane walked through the immaculate hallway, musing at the photographs depicting his childhood. He called out to his first beloved woman at intervals.

"Miss Tina Sinclair! Are thou all finessed or what? Hello! Is anybody up here? An estranged son is trying to find his mother here! Hello!" He already heard her giggling.

He walked past her in the vanity room and looked behind the door, then slowly turned back.

"Excuse me miss, have you seen a fifty year old lady about here? She's olive complexioned like me; well toned… like me; beautiful, and about five feet two inches tall."

"That's not funny Shane! I'm nowhere near fifty!" Tina laughed. "God knows I just celebrated my twenty seventh for your information!" She rushed into the arms of her first born pride and joy, and tightly squeezed him.

"Oh baby, I've missed you so much! How've you been? Are you under pressure? You look tired. Are you nervous about Australia? As long as you do your best right? Where's Lisa? Did you bring her? I've heard so many good things about her from your brothers. I can't wait to meet her. What's going on with you and Amanda? She called me the other day…the boys told me. How's Jamaica? Man I'm due for a trip." She would've continued to babble, but Shane knew better.

"Mother! How many questions are you going to ask me at once? You want answers? Sensible ones?"

They both chuckled, though she gave him the stare-down.

"Shane you know I'm just excited. So go ahead… answer!" She got back to applying her makeup.

"Well, let's see if I remember them in the order of their occurrence. I've been good. I spend my days training and being with *some* of the people I love the most. Am I under pressure? Not really. The media is trying to put me under some though, but so far I'm good at handling it. I look tired because I'm tired, but no biggie. I'm a little nervous about Australia for more reasons than one; but none of them are trivial. Lisa's downstairs with the boys. I haven't seen Sheldon yet though. Well since she's downstairs I definitely brought her." He paused as she began to laugh.

"And as for Amanda…" He continued. "There's *absolutely* nothing going on there! I can't stand that girl and I'd prefer if you stop standing her too. She's crazier than ever before mom, seriously! Anyhow, Jamaica is great and yes you're overdue for a trip. You could definitely use a real tan!" He dodged a slap aimed at his knee. "Hey! I could take you to court for that! Knee's worth millions!"

Tina laughed as she admired her son through the mirror. "Well thanks for the rundown. I see your memory is as sharp as your father's. You didn't miss a thing. Now take me down to meet this '*wife*' of yours. I'm anxious."

He had intended to prep her before she went downstairs, but he thought against it at the last minute.

As Shane got to the bottom of the stairs with his mom in tote, his 'mini-me' Sheldon came through the front door with more grocery bags.

Sheldon grinned as he spotted his mentor. "Bro! That's a nice ride you have out there. I'll be taking a spin with that!" He gave him a fist pound.

Shane looked from the bags to his mother. "Those couldn't possibly be groceries for lunch after what I witnessed in the kitchen."

Tina smiled and walked away. "So, where's Miss Lisa?" She asked, strolling into the kitchen.

Shane stayed closely behind his mother and instantly witnessed the look on Lisa's face that evidently reflected the look on his mother's face.

"*Mother*! Don't *you* look lovely?" His brothers said loudly, as if choreographed.

Tina completely ignored them and turned to face Shane, who was already walking around towards his nervous woman.

"Mom, meet Lisa." He announced with a wide grin.

Lisa stood and walked towards Tina.

"It's nice to finally meet you." They both uttered, almost simultaneously.

"Well let's eat then." Tina curtly wrapped up the introductions, visibly displeased.

The atmosphere in the Wright household redefined the word awkward.

Shane helped his mother to bring the food to the dining table, while his brothers made much of Lisa.

Tina didn't speak another word to her son as they passed each other back and forth. Her previous enthusiasm was entirely depleted.

Shane made the first move to break the silence. "Mom, I wanted to tell you. But at the end, I didn't think it was important mom. You told me that yourself once, that love crossed all borders." She didn't respond. "Mom…"

"*That was before your father left us for her Shane!*" She snapped, talking loudly. "How could you do this? How could you do this to me?"

"How could I do what mom? *Listen*, nobody but dad is to be blamed for what he did. And nobody should have to bear that burden! It could have been any woman mom! What difference would it have made? Would you hate yourself right now if she had looked like you? You're being ridiculous! Lisa's a nice girl...just give her a chance and you'll see." He strained to keep his voice down.

Tina didn't let up. "No, you'll see! I bet if you were broke you wouldn't stand a chance with a girl like that! Just like that wretch, who watched me build my husband so she could sweep him from under my feet! She'll only love you for as long as you're famous and wealthy Shane! Open your eyes! And if not, don't say I didn't warn you!"

"Mom, if you don't stop with that...I'm not going to be very pleased! And I swear, I'll leave!"

She gave him the stare that frightened him as a child.

They dropped the conversation as the others joined them in the dining room. Everyone exchanged the 'are we good' look with each other.

Shane could see the pain in Lisa's eyes but there was nothin he could do for her now. He watched as she lingered, waiting patiently on the seating arrangements.

"I want you to sit beside me Lisa!" Simeon shouted and patted the chair beside his.

"Thanks Simeon." She offered a warm smile.

Everyone else took their places. Shane sat beside his mother for good and predictable reasons.

"Let's say grace." Tina sternly instructed.

They all held hands as she prayed from her soul, carefully dropping hints on her current issues.

"Bon appétit!" She added upon conclusion.

Each person made moves to the dish they were most interested to try. There was a wide selection including ackee and salt fish, callaloo and salt fish, steamed fish and okra, and fried dumplings; boiled dumplings, bananas, and potatoes, honey-smoked ham, scrambled eggs, cream-filled

French toasts, regular wheat toast, fruit salad, crepes, and several different beverages.

The options clearly represented the palate preferences of the occupants of the house, especially Simeon who grew up in the States and wasn't a big fan of Jamaican food. The others lived for that taste of 'home'.

Lisa started out with scrambled eggs, French toasts, and a serving of fruit salad. She carefully poured herself a cup of coffee, and looked about for the cream.

Tina noticed her selection and couldn't resist a comment. "I'm sorry, had I been properly informed I would've catered the selection more to your liking." She crunched on her toast and daringly held her gaze.

The boys noticeably stirred in their seats.

Lisa kept her eyes on her plate. She bit into her French toast to avoid responding.

Shane squeezed his mother's leg. "Lisa loves this food mom, what are you talking about? Don't you baby?" He wanted more to get her attention to ease her.

Lisa looked up, pretending to be unaware that she was the center of attention, and cleared her throat to speak.

"Of course. I'm just starting off." She managed a smile.

Steven tried to help out. "So Shane, are you looking forward to going to Australia man? Are you taking Lisa with you? If not can I come?"

"You wish!" Tina hastily shut down that argument. "You're not going anywhere during the school year and besides…my baby travels alone for his meets so he can concentrate; right baby? You don't need all the *distractions* right?" She casually eyed Lisa then looked at Shane.

"Right mother. *Everybody* knows I travel to meets alone, including you Steven, so I don't know why you bothered! I'm thinking of flying you guys over for the Olympics though…if mom's up for the trip."

His brothers lit up with excitement, and of course the whining ensued.

"Please mom...mom please." Simeon was the headliner and expert. He usually got better results as such.

"Well, I'm grown so I'm definitely down." Sheldon, the twenty two year old, chimed in. "I don't *need* mom's permission to travel."

"Me either...I think." Steven chimed in.

Tina shot him a stare before chewing him out. "At nineteen, the only thing you're grown enough to do is get your grades up and get into college! Try that, and then we can discuss permissions to travel!" She was ever feisty.

Lisa and Shane made subtle eye contact that exchanged love, reassurance, and understanding.

Unfortunately, Tina caught it.

"So Lisa, what do you do for a living?" She enquired without looking in her direction.

Lisa sat upright in her seat. "I'm currently in the final semester to complete my Undergraduate degree in Accounting. I also work part-time as a Junior Accountant at my dad's firm."

"I see. So what are your plans after your Bachelor's? Are you planning to pursue a *professional* designation? You know, Accountants at the *basic* level don't make that much these days."

Lisa visibly flushed. She had honestly not given much thought to immediately pursuing a designation because whether or not she already had a job secured. She sieved through her thoughts to find the best way to explain that to Tina.

"Well, I'm pretty much planning to work full time at my company upon graduation so that I may garner more professional work experience before I pursue a designation."

Good job baby. Shane thought and smiled. He communicated that to Lisa with a glance.

Tina was not entirely satisfied, and it was written all over her face.

"Hey Shane, can we go to the mall after? I mean if you don't have any plans or anything." Simeon enquired.

"Of course he doesn't have any plans baby." Tina answered on his behalf. "The purpose of his trip *is* to spend time with his family; right baby?" She smiled coyly.

Shane deliberately ignored her and addressed Simeon directly. "We'll go to the mall bro. No worries."

Lisa busied herself with another serving of ackee and salt fish and fried dumplings. She could feel Tina staring her down, but she refused to look up from her plate.

"The food is delicious..." She tried to compliment, but hesitated when she stumbled on a reference for the cook, given her current divorce proceedings. She knew for a fact that 'Mom' was definitely not an acceptable option.

"Yea mom, the food is great." Shane interjected on her behalf. "You know I'm taking some of this with me right? I swear you need to travel with me and be my personal chef."

Tina smiled gingerly, though she was not amused.

"What you say about that?" Shane continued to pester her. "Can I hire you?"

"You can't *afford* me!" Tina snapped without looking in his direction.

He laughed, knowing well enough that would've been her response. He kissed her on the cheek and continued with his flattery. "What's that perfume you're wearing? I like it."

Perfume was a subject she was very much interested in. "Oh! It's the one you bought me for Christmas baby, you don't remember it?" She was temporarily distracted from conjuring up questions to breakdown Lisa.

Oh, the one Lisa picked? Shane laughed inside. *Funny, it's one of her favourites too. What the hell was the name again?* He slightly glanced at Lisa for the cue, and she helped him out.

"Gucci something, I can't remember which one." He grinned and playfully stared at Tina. "C'mon I do get credit for the brand right?" He playfully sulked.

Tina smiled. "It's Gucci Rush. My new favourite actually."

Ahh! Two peas in a pod! Shane mused inwardly.

"Lisa, what nationality are you again?" She delved right back into her shenanigans.

"I'm Italian." Lisa replied proudly.

Tina's face lit up. "Oh! If I'd been privy to that, I would've made some pasta." She smiled sheepishly.

Lisa's face immediately reddened, and for an instance she lost her poise.

"*Mom,* Italians don't *only* eat pasta you know? You're so silly." Simeon felt the urge to comment. "That's such an annoying stereotype! Geesh!"

Lisa regained her composure and replied. "You've made enough already Tina, that would've been too much work." She couldn't resist the opportunity to attack, whatever the cost.

Tina stared at her blankly, her face flushing with anger. Surprisingly, she was slow to respond.

Shane, Simeon, Steven, and Sheldon all caught wind of where that last remark would send the already overbearing tension, and everyone felt the urge to avoid it. Sheldon spoke first and took charge of the situation.

"Well, I think it's that time to hit the mall. I'm full to the brim. Steven and Simeon, start packing up these dishes. Lisa yuh done? We could use your help in the kitchen."

They quickly dismissed themselves.

Shane, visibly flustered, stared at his unusually silent mother in disbelief and embarrassment.

"Mom, what the hell was that about the 'pasta'? That was so beneath you! You were being offensive and mean throughout the entire meal! Matter of fact, since she got here! You didn't even properly introduce yourself. She didn't even know what to call you! I am pissed off, I won't lie to you."

"And to make things worse, you're sitting here fixing to have a heart attack because she *rightfully* answered you. What's really going on with you? I know you're mad at dad. God knows he's wrong for what he did. But he didn't just do it to *you* mom; it happened to all of *us*! What he did, is what he *wanted* to do! This is not about *her* and this is definitely not about Lisa. This is about *choices* between individuals with the capacity to choose. You chose your career; dad chose to leave. I chose Lisa; and she chose to come here, knowing damn well that you'd hate her!" He paused to compose himself.

Tina eyes watered up but he continued regardless.

"Were you even aware that she has been to each and every one of Sheldon's NCAA basketball games? Or that she tutored Steven in Math and several other subjects so he could move on to his senior year? Or that she never forgets to get Simeon a gift for his birthday because she knows how much it means to him? No mom, you wouldn't know, because everyone has to lie to you. We all feel the need to protect *your* feelings by hiding all of this from you just because she's white! Listen, I *love* Lisa and she means a lot to me. You mean the *most* to me, and I'd prefer if you could both get along."

Tina broke down and began to sob.

Shane seldom witnessed his mother cry, but he hated it every time. He knew she meant well and that she was hurting tremendously; but he wouldn't allow her to disrespect Lisa as much as he wouldn't allow Lisa to disrespect her. He gently embraced her and she held unto him with all her strength.

"I know you're hurting mom, and you know I'm here for you. This conversation wasn't meant to hurt you, just to notify you. I hope you got the right point."

"I did baby." She whispered through her sobs. "And I'm terribly sorry for my behaviour. I just can't afford to lose you too, you know? I don't know what I'd do without you."

"Mom, you're being silly. You're gonna lose me where? Oh, you can forget about that! The scent of your food will have me sniffing my way right back."

She chuckled in his embrace.

Shane sighed. "Mom, losing me should be the last thing on your mind. You're not losing any of us. The only one that's technically up for grabs is Simeon, being the minor. But we all know he was dad's least favourite. Besides, you're the only one that can afford him!"

They both laughed at that fact.

Lisa stood in the hallway and admired Shane's relations with Tina. She could just imagine the depth of the conversation they were engulfed in, seeing that tears were involved.

The boys watched Lisa as she watched Shane. In their own ways, they empathised with her. They all had great love and appreciation for the way she cared not just their brother, but all of them. Being very protective of Shane, they had always put in overtime to ward off 'the groupies'. When he had introduced them to Lisa, they had felt compelled to accept and trust her, respective of her profile.

Lisa backed up into the kitchen before Shane or Tina could acknowledge her presence as they got up from the table. Some time during her thinking, she had begun to cry.

Shane was laughing at one of Tina's cynical comments when he entered the kitchen. He was eager to console his other woman now that he had his mother straightened out.

He saw Lisa hunched over the counter surrounded by the boys, who immediately cleared the way for him to do his job. He wrapped his arms around her and winked at his overly concerned brothers.

"Oh baby, not you too!" He tried to joke. "This is way too much tears for the *macho* man in one day."

She clung to him tightly.

"Lisa, forgive my mother. She's not *that* bad...trust. I'm so sorry baby. Please don't cry. You know what that does to me. Don't get me started in front of my brothers."

"Oh God, Lisa. Please!" Sheldon quickly interrupted. "We *definitely* don't want to see this idiot cry!"

She giggled under her man's armpit.

Shane slightly eased her away to get a good look at her face. He lovingly kissed her on the forehead after brushing away her unruly locks.

"Does she hate me Shane? Is it that bad?" She whispered, looking to his eyes for any confirmation.

"Not at all! It'll be okay I promise." He tilted her head backwards, grinning from ear to ear.

Lisa teased with a pout.

"Don't start!" He laughed and looked over at his brothers. "Not in front of these guys."

"Yes. Not in front of us!" Steven took this round. "Please and thanks! 'Preciate it!" The two had exhausted his already low tolerance for mushiness.

Tina walked into the kitchen looking refreshed and re-energized. "Are we ready to max out daddy's card while it's still hot?" She confessed with a sly grin.

They all laughed and co-signed on the idea.

"Sounds like a plan to me." Simeon liked the idea the most. "Mom, remember those sneakers that were released last week? And the new Ed Hardy collection has some really cool shirts. It's time I got 'em. And..."

"We'll get to that Simeon." She cut him off. "Who's driving?" She looked around at the eligible drivers.

"Mom, we could all go in your Hummer. And I'm driving." Sheldon was quick to suggest. "Please." He grinned.

"If that's okay with Shane and Lisa." She looked towards the couple.

"That's fine." Shane replied on their behalf.

"Well then, that's the plan. Of course excluding the part where I let Sheldon drive *my* vehicle with *me* in it."

Sheldon was slightly embarrassed. "Whatever mom! Stop showing off 'cause Shane's here. I drive you all the time! Steven tell him!"

"Mom let the man drive!" Shane assisted the cause.

They all laughed.

Sheldon snatched the keys from the hanger in the entrance way and headed towards the door.

His brothers followed suit.

"Lisa, may I speak with you for a minute?" Tina stopped her as she was about to walk pass.

Lisa apprehensively glanced at Shane.

"It's okay." Tina chimed in, nodding Shane away. She continued when the coast was clear.

"Listen, I want to apologize for the way I treated you today. I was wrong to judge you before even knowing you. I should've had more faith in my son to know that he can make good choices. It was even brought to my attention how much you've been there for my other boys when I was too busy working. For that I thank you also. I just hope I haven't caused enough damage to sever a relationship with you.

You're more than welcome in this family; well as long as you take care of my baby." She offered a genuine smile.

Lisa got teary-eyed again. "I'm sorry for my comment too…" She clumsily lingered on an ending.

Tina smiled and offered. "You may call me Tina."

"I'm sorry for my comment to you too Tina and I appreciate the apology. I'll definitely do my best to stand by Shane and to care for him with all that I have. I really love your son and I must say that I do understand your concern. But I'm not that person that you're worried about. Shane's pretty good at seeing through those." She welcomed the woman's warming embrace.

"Well I'm glad we got over that. Let's get out of here." Tina saddled her emotions for their grand exit.

Lisa followed her lead and smiled at Shane when he came into view.

The man of the hour was relieved to see both his women smiling and getting along. *Now that's much better!* Shane mused to himself, smiling. *Only person missing from this perfect pic is Gina. Miss that kid...*

Daddy's credit card swiped from one boutique to the other. The younger Wrights purchased any and everything that the upscale stores offered for sale. They stacked up on sneakers, clothes, video games, and newly-released electronics.

Tina did the signing. Of course, she bought perfume and jewellery of her own and meddled in her sons' tastes in clothing. She also realised that she had way more in common with Lisa than imagined, when she introduced her to a new fragrance that worked for *Gucci Rush* lovers. In return, she had introduced Lisa to one of her favourite boutiques for petite, professional attire.

From the sidelines, Tina had also observed Lisa's humble interactions with her number one son. She admired her unwillingness to take up Shane on his numerous offers to purchase whatever she 'needed'; she felt even worse for presuming that his money was her motive.

Back at the house, Tina pulled out the picture albums and prepared to individually sabotage her boys' reputations. Shane was up first, as always.

They laughed at track and field pictures from his Vaz Prep School days. He was only seven when he won his first major race at the National Stadium, and the photos depicted his rise to fame ever since.

The second set of pictures proved to be tearjerkers. Simeon's car accident when he was six years old provoked the same emotions that were alive on that near fatal day. Tina had sent him on a road trip with a friend of the family and their kids, when a tractor trailer lost control and swiped their vehicle into the highway's guard rails. Simeon and two of the other three kids were the sole survivors. He had been found in a tree overhanging a deep gully, and was in critical condition for over a month. Doctors had even feared he wouldn't survive.

"But like the fighter you are, you pulled through with the grace of God." Tina continued, prophesying between sobs. "And I thank Him with all I have because I don't know what I'd do without my little *jokester*. I don't know what I'd do without any of you."

Everyone straightened up and wiped their eyes, except for Lisa, who evidently needed an extra moment.

"It's okay babe." Shane kissed her on the forehead, and she folded into his arms.

The pack rallied through emotions from the past to the present as captured by photographs.

Shane sat forward when his mom tossed a picture of her training group at the John's Hopkins Hospital on the center table. He tilted the picture towards him and nearly choked.

This cannot be good! His mind raced. "Mom, uhm did you keep in touch with your group members?"

Tina seemed amazed that he was so interested. "Well, we were a pretty large bunch. A few of them stayed on at the hospital so of course we're in touch. But most of the others had left to pursue their private practice. Let me see."

She took the picture from him and raised it to her eyes for closer inspection.

"Put on your glasses mom. You know you're blind as ever." Simeon couldn't resist.

"Be quiet boy! I can see fine." She pointed to the faces of the ones she knew their whereabouts. Shane held his breath, hoping in vain.

"And Natalie, yes, she was my favourite. She went back to Jamaica to be with her hubby. She actually opened the first private oncology practice in Jamaica, and the last time we spoke she discussed interests to open a remedial center for cancer patients as well. She was always so positive and uplifting. We speak occasionally." Tina smiled and continued to go through the group photo.

Shane had heard enough. He stopped listening as his mind drifted altogether. *Mom knows Doc? What are the fucking odds? I'm fucked!*

Lisa noticed him gazing into space, as did his brothers.

"Did you catch that?" Steven mumbled to Sheldon.

"Hmm…" Sheldon replied accordingly.

Tina broke the silence. "Shane, did I miss something?" She furrowed her brows when he ignored her. "Shane!" She spoke louder.

"Mom!" He snapped his head to look at her then lowered his voice when he realised he had shouted. "I'm sorry. Did you say something?"

He steadily noticed that everyone else was staring at him with the identical flabbergasted expression as his mother's.

"What is it? Did I miss something?" He asked, looking around the circle.

"Did *we*?" Tina cynically replied. "You just zoned out there for a minute. Everything's okay?"

"Yeah, I'm sorry. I was just mentally scanning through my agenda for when I get back to JA. You know... the things I have to get done. There's so much to do man and so little time." He caught himself blabbering and stopped.

Everyone slowly peeled their gaze away from him and into their laps, knowing in their own distinct way that he was being dishonest. They all reserved to playing fools.

Shane was uncomfortable. "To be honest, I'm beat. I can't believe it's twelve already." He spoke as he yawned. "We better get going; it's a long ride back. Lisa, can you pack up some of that food so we can feast in the AM?"

His brothers followed her into the kitchen.

He rose from the chair and went to hug his mom. Squeezing her tightly, he kissed her on the forehead.

"I love you Miss Tina. More than you could ever imagine. Don't you ever doubt that!"

"I love you too my son." She held him close. "And remember I'm *always* here for you."

Shane hugged his brothers one by one and gave them sound warning to be supportive of and obedient to their mother. As usual, he handed out pocket money.

Simeon began to cry as he always did when Shane came around and had to leave. To him, his brother was more of the dad than their father had ever been.

Lisa appeared from the kitchen with a shopping bag of food. She hugged Tina and thanked her for the delicious meal, and for tweaking her professional dress style.

Tina in turned thanked her for the perfume recommendations and a lesson in humility.

Steven and Sheldon walked the two to their car, leaving Tina and Simeon at the doorway.

"Alright bro, it was good to see you as always. Make sure you *represent* in Australia! And drive Lisa home safely." Steven gave him a pound, and turned his attention to Lisa.

"Bro you know that I'm always here for you if you need me right?" Sheldon couldn't shake the feeling his intuition triggered earlier regarding his brother.

"Of course my mini-me! You're the main man." Shane gave him a pound then pulled him closer to hug him.

Sheldon smiled. "Alright then. With that said, make sure yuh rip up the tracks in Australia cause I sure could use that trip to the Olympics. International babes yuh nuh!"

They all laughed.

"Alright guys. Take care of mom. And Steven, please give Simeon a break! I love y'all."

He waved them all goodbye and climbed into his car. Feeling the burden of being so secretive with his loved ones, he made his way down the winding pathway and turned unto the main street.

His family stood waving until he cleared the block.

CHAPTER SEVEN

Regina had left work at lunch time to head home and get some studying done before the house grew crowded. She had also decided to prepare a hearty supper, and had stopped at the grocery store on the way.

She unloaded the groceries from the trunk unto the pavement, and made a few trips back and forth to get them all inside. Though feeling exhausted, she seasoned a whole chicken and set it aside to marinate. After that, she prepared the macaroni pie and placed it in the oven; and peeled a variety of vegetables for steaming later on.

When supper was substantially on the way, she ventured upstairs to the study and whipped out her textbooks. The plan had been to practice questions for her upcoming Real Estate law exam. Feeling very productive and overly calmed by her newly resurrected self-motivation, she contemplated.

I can only be me and do me from now on. No more stretching myself thin to be everything to everybody, and nothing to my damn self! That shit just won't cut it!

"Andre I can't hang too long because my sister's boyfriend is coming for me at school today, cool?" Roxanne belted her disclaimer as she climbed into the truck.

"No problem baby girl. Just wanted to see yuh for a little. I just miss yuh all the time. Whe Cindy gone?"

"She went into the pharmacy to get gum. Where's Benji?" She thought to herself, but mentioned aloud.

Oh, Cindy didn't tell her? Biggs shrugged and casually lied. "Must be busy I guess."

So why the hell is Cindy with us? Roxanne deliberated, but responded differently. "I see."

Cindy came out of the pharmacy clapping a wad of gum.

"Whagwan Biggs? Long time nuh see. How tings?" She enquired as she got into the back seat.

"Good yuh nuh Cindy...can't complain. So we ready fi cut?" He asked indirectly.

"Ready!" Cindy spoke more anxiously, causing Roxanne to eye her with disdain.

They travelled the ten-minute distance to Biggs' house in silence, except for his new Dancehall tracks thumping through the speakers.

Michael pulled into the Rib Kage parking lot for his twelve thirty lunch date with his brother, and wasn't surprised to find that he had already arrived. He parked in the space beside his and confidently strutted through the entryway.

Immediately, he spotted him at the bar and made his way over. "We're drinking this early in the day man?" He slapped him on the shoulder as he stepped behind him.

Linton hastily spun around. "Oh! It's you! Just a wonda who the hell so damn nosy, *and* brave!" He chuckled and gave his big brother a hug. "Thanks for coming on time man. Didn't expect that!"

They both laughed at that fact.

"I'm not *always* late bro! But hey, I'm starving! You ordered already?" He snatched the menu from beneath Linton's elbow.

It didn't take long for them to contemplate their choices and Michael eagerly summoned the server.

"So what's going on with you man?" Michael immediately delved into business after he ordered. "What's Regina doing to your brain these days?"

"Bro, you couldn't fathom what I'm coming with. How about she dropped the bomb on me that she got the promotion, but it's all the way in *Cayman*. How yuh like that bro? *Cayman*!" His tone conveyed his annoyance.

"*Cayman*?" Michael repeated aloud. "When did that become an option? And how come she's just telling you that now? And what's the time frame that we're working with?" He didn't make matters any easier.

"I said all that!" Linton lied. "Something like seven months I remember hearing. But it could be two years bro, I'm not moving! Did she think I'd be willing to just up and move away and leave all that I have behind? Whatever happened to being promoted *within* an office?"

"Well I'm not going to pretend that some promotions don't take you above and beyond. But I'm saying she should've mentioned that along with the promotion. She must have known it was in Cayman when she applied. I mean, that's all I'm saying. So what do you plan to do?"

"I just told her we'd talk about it later. But then later came, and next thing I know I'm in the middle of a hot seat. I get home Michael, and Regina's curled up in bed bawling…"

"Ohhhhh! The chic strategy!" Michael chuckled.

"Exactly! Then she's talking about how much she's stressed, and under-appreciated, and needs a break. Now I won't lie and say my heart didn't freeze when I heard '*break*'; 'cause you know I loves me some Regina. Anyways she stormed out of the house in the middle of the night and let's just say that was the last I heard. She won't take my damn calls! I'm in a bad spot bro."

Michael listened attentively. He knew more than anybody that he wasn't in the best position to give advice on broken relationships. He gave it a try anyway.

"Well Linton, I'd suggest you give her the time to cool down, especially since you *definitely* don't want that break. But I'll also tell you that moving should be *your* choice because *you* really want to, and not because you want to keep your girl. 'Cause if you're going to move with her and constantly be a pain in the ass about her *forcing* you to leave home, you're gonna have another thing coming. You don't want to be caught out there in Cayman."

They both laughed then Michael continued.

"On the other side, and yes there is one, you have to understand her position too. If this job means a lot to her, and it's a big step forward, you can't hold her back. And truthfully speaking, you *can* do Computer Programming anywhere in the world and multiply your rewards...trus!"

"Yea, I was looking into that today and that's all good. But my biggest thing is you guys you know...my family and my boys." He looked up at his brother. "I can't be so far from *everyone*."

"Man, Cayman is not that far! You're such a damn kid!" Michael tried to joke to avoid the emotional direction of the conversation. "If that's what's bothering you about leaving, you'd be a fool to stay. Mom and dad got married for the sole reason of being each other's companion at times like this. I got married to compensate for moments like this; and you, need to do you, now that you're at that point. You have to focus on the bigger scheme bro. There's always travelling...add some stamps to that empty passport!"

Michael is right. Linton zoned out and deliberated his predicament. *Regina and Roxanne are my family...my responsibility right now. I'd be a fool to give up my happiness just to be close to my boys and my married bro, and family. It's not like I have to do this tomorrow either! I shouldn't have just shut her down like that. I'd definitely be pissed off at me too!*

Michael smacked him on the shoulder. "You okay there man? I lost you there for a sec."

108

"Yeah, I was just thinking about how I reacted to the whole thing. I just shut her down like I did. Regina has been nothing but supportive of me and my dreams. I think I fucked up man! *Big* time!"

"Well I wouldn't exactly say *fucked* up! You were caught off guard that's all. You'll just have some making up to do. That could be fun." He teasingly winked at him.

"Get your mind out the gutter Michael, seriously."

Roxanne was sitting in the foyer, her favourite place in the house, when Andre and Cindy came into the room. An alarm sounded in her head when she noticed they were both unravelled and seemingly antsy.

"What were you two doing so long?" She asked, her tone heavy with disgust. "And Cindy, why are you here if Benji's not here?"

Cindy shot her a hateful look that could have murdered her had it been a sword. "I can go *wherever* I'm *welcome* Roxanne. Why yuh a act so funny?"

Biggs secretly marvelled at her jealousy. He gingerly walked over and sat beside her on the chair. "Roxie, what's the matter? Is what, you don't trust me with Cindy?"

She passed on a response, holding Cindy's stare.

He leaned over and tried to kiss her.

"Andre! *Not* in front of *her*!" Roxanne pulled away.

"What's the big deal?" He whispered and kissed her more aggressively, this time somewhat pinning her down with his weight.

Forcing the issue, he groped her breasts then swiftly slid his hand under her skirt, slipping one finger then another into her moisture. Reflexively, her legs parted.

Somewhere in her subconscious, Roxanne knew better than to subject herself to his lewd acts; but this instance, she welcomed the attention and sensation.

Cindy sat across from the two, staring as she toyed with her cunt. She had already been turned out by Biggs in the downstairs bedroom, for a whopping four thousand dollars. She got up and slowly walked over to them when she got his signal to join.

Biggs climbed atop a completely subdued Roxanne and lovingly caressed her face with both hands. He built the tempo by continuing to kiss her fervently.

What the hell? The thought immediately raced through Roxanne's head. *If Andre's tongue is in my mouth, then what the...* She slammed her legs shut and forcefully eased Andre's weight off her chest.

"What the hell is this Andre?" She screamed as she jumped up. "I'm not a fucking lesbian! Cindy you nasty *bitch*! Get the *fuck* away from me!"

Cindy clutched the side of her head, wincing in pain.

Biggs rushed towards her as she gathered her belongings. "Babes jus cool it nuh. *I* asked her to do it! Thought you'd want to please your man. You don't have to be a lesbian to please your man, right Cindy?" He turned and winked at her.

Roxanne snapped. "Andre, get away from me! Both of yuh! You damn freaks!" She eyed him with disdain, and then turned to her best friend. "Fuck you!"

Evidently irritated though resisting the urge to punch her face in, Biggs pushed past her and took a seat by the sliding door of the balcony.

"Cindy come ya!" He barked as he undid his pants and unleashed 'biggs'. "Come suck mi hood fi me 'cause right now mi horny and mi nah beg *nuh* pussy!"

Unwilling to forsake the handsome payout she would be rewarded, Cindy obliged him much to the violation of her *best* friend who began to sob. As she expertly devoured his manhood, her silent tears welled as she reflected.

If yuh only understood Roxie. Mi need di money bad. I know what yuh thinking, but pussy is pussy to all these

110

dogs! Benji aint mine alone! And neither is Biggs yours! She silently justified her actions.

Biggs held on to the back of her head and mercilessly thrust his groin. "Yea, dat feel good Cindy!" He looked over at Roxanne who stood motionless. "It's much better than the last time! Yuh a practice?" He ridiculed as he held her stare.

The last time! What the fuck did Cindy get me into? Roxanne screamed in her head. *How long have you two been fucking and planning to set me up?* She silently wished the floor would open up and swallow her.

"Roxie, mi soon bust yuh nuh! Yuh better talk up if yuh want some cocky. Just know seh if yuh nuh tek none, me and yuh done! Mi tell yuh seh mi love yuh areddi!"

Roxanne's jaws reflexively dropped. In an unforeseen move she shuffled towards his chair, though her knees trembled beneath her not offering much for support.

"So I thought..." He remarked, grinning. "Tek off all yuh clothes and jus listen to wha mi seh!"

She did as instructed, somehow.

He eased Cindy's head out of his crotch and instructed her to remove his pants. "Now Roxie, come siddung pon mi cock back way!"

That command froze her in place.

"Move quick nuh babes! Yuh nuh seh yuh affi leave early todeh?"

She willed her body towards him. "So what about the condom Andre?" She asked timidly, stifling tears.

"Yuh love the talking eeh Roxie? Yuh a siddung or mi fi give it to Cindy?"

Roxanne tried to do as he had instructed but the pain was too intense. Tears spilled from her eyes.

"Siddung nuh Roxie! No pain, no gain!" He forcefully pulled her down unto him.

A loud cry reflexively escaped her mouth.

"Cindy, come lick her pussy good and mek sure yuh tongue nuh stop move til mi come. Yuh hear dat?"

This was the side of Andre that Cindy knew too well, but never disclosed to her best friend. She had only learned to tolerate him because he paid her well. For introducing him to Roxanne, she had been paid five thousand dollars because he found her 'pretty and virginal'.

As Cindy played her role, Biggs decided to switch positions with Roxanne, and then to switch girls altogether.

"Come Cindy! Mi want some of the ghetto sweetness that yuh have." He pulled out of Roxanne and entered Cindy with a forceful thrust.

"Fling it up gimme Cindy! You know I love this ass. Yuh want it harder?" He slapped her harshly on the butt and she squirmed beneath his firm grip.

Roxanne's eyes widened and drenched with tears when she witnessed the manner in which Andre handled her friend. She covered her face in utter disgust and sobbed.

Regina jerked awake from the loud chatter funnelling from downstairs. She realised that she must've fallen asleep in between chapters, and jumped up now when she remembered she had left the dinner in the oven.

Before she could take another step, the aroma of her macaroni pie and roasted chicken steadily permeated her consciousness, and she suddenly felt ravenous. She instinctively straightened herself when she heard Linton thudding up the stairs. His first stop was their bedroom. When that door closed, she returned her attention to her textbook knowing the study was his next stop.

"Sorry to bother you baby." Linton peeked in. "I just wanted to tell you thanks for coming home, and for making supper." He lingered by the doorway, seeming nervous.

Regina turned around and looked at him over the frame of her glasses, but remained silent.

He tentatively continued. "Uhm, Roxanne had put the chicken in the oven so everything is pretty much taken care of." He begged for forgiveness with his eyes.

Roxanne is home too? Wow! She stared at him blankly, intentionally delaying a response.

"Well, thanks a lot dear." She managed with much sarcasm. "I'll be down there shortly." With that she turned around, indirectly dismissing him.

He walked backwards out of the room and quietly closed the door behind him.

Linton chilled with Roxanne in the kitchen and cautioned her on the evening's proceedings.

"Your sis seems okay now. We shouldn't have anything to worry about. Just don't provoke her, please! Let's try to eat in peace! It shouldn't be that long."

Another forty minutes had passed before Regina joined them downstairs.

"Good *afternoon*!" She cynically announced her presence, indirectly jabbing at Roxanne.

She noticed that the table had already been set so she proceeded to the kitchen to share the food. She took out the chicken and macaroni from the oven, and sectioned them. Next, she warmed rice in the microwave and shared steamed vegetables for three.

Linton and Roxanne sat in silence as she went back and forth to bring the food to the table. Eventually placing everything in the center, she sat in her usual spot and bowed her head in prayer without a formal announcement.

The others smartly followed suit.

As the trio ate mostly in silence, Regina broke the ice and spoke up first.

"I accepted the Portfolio Wealth Manager position in Cayman. This is an advancing opportunity for me, and it *could be* for this family. I have a target seven months to make preparations and depart. You guys can do your research to determine whether or not this move is right for *you*. The job market there is booming. The schools there are as exceptional as it is here in Jamaica. We wouldn't be that far away, so travelling to see *family* and friends shouldn't be a problem. Now I'm saying *we*, because I would prefer it to be so. However, this train leaves on August thirty first, with or without *all* its intended passengers."

Linton recognised and felt all the jabs concerning family, but declined a comment because he knew from experience she was fishing for an argument.

Roxanne was still in shock at the entire revelation, but kept her mouth shut. She watched as her sister contently resumed eating, evidently revelling in her position of power.

"Natalie, how much longer are you going to be?" Michael called out to his wife, trying to subdue his annoyance. "I made the reservation for six. It's now five forty five." He clenched his fists and pretended to scream.

"Well honey, you didn't exactly tell me that before. I'll be down in a minute. I'm just trying to find one foot of my black shoe."

"Hun just put on one of your many *other* black shoes! Please!" He unlocked the front door.

"No! No! No! I found it anyway so relax." She stormed down the stairs and past him through the front door. "Which restaurant are we going to anyway? You didn't even give me any details to this escapade and now you're rushing me." Natalie whined as she got into the car.

"What difference would details have made? You're *always* late woman."

She completely ignored his remark.

They drove for the next fifteen minutes to the sounds of Sade's *Sweetest Taboo* on repeat, blaring through the speakers. They pulled into the Terra Nova Hotel's parking lot at exactly five minutes past six.

No sooner had they been seated and received the menus, when Michael delved into his agenda.

"So my *wife*..." He began. "Have you given any more thought to starting our family? You know, we're not getting any younger..."

"Oh is that why we're here Michael?" She couldn't resist the rhetoric rebuttal.

In recent times, he had been living on the subject of having kids more often than before. The topic usually resulted in arguments without any meaningful conclusions. It had even begun to plague their marriage, driving a wedge into their usually high-spirited relationship.

"I'm sorry Nat. I didn't mean for it to come out like that." He took a minute to survey the restaurant.

"Michael, why is it so hard for you to accept that I'm just not ready for all that right now? I'm fully aware that we are in our late thirty's and I guess *your* biological clock is ticking away. But I'm really focused on building a respectable practice at this moment. There's just no way I can do all that work and successfully carry a child. I just need a little more support...a little more patience."

They paused their conversation long enough to place their orders with the server.

Michael eagerly persisted when the coast cleared.

"Every time we talk about kids you get so sarcastic and judgemental. Obviously you wouldn't be the *only* one doing work, Natalie. I'm willing and eager to share in the responsibilities seventy-thirty if I have to. I just want to have a kid with my *wife*! We barely have sex any more and I *know* it's because you're scared of becoming pregnant! How far are you willing to take this?" He refused to stifle his anger and disappointment any longer.

"And by *far*, what do you mean exactly? Is that a threat Michael? Being that you stressed having kids with *your* wife, are you trying to tell me you have options?" She stared at him blankly.

"Here we flipping go! You *always* know how to take it far, huh? Is that the *only* thing you heard me say? Don't put words into my mouth! Don't do it! You know what? Let's just drop it! It's no use trying to talk to you about what *I* want!" He flailed his hands and leaned back in his seat.

Natalie snapped. "It's always '*I*' with you Michael! And that's *our* biggest problem!"

He gritted his teeth and snarled. "It wasn't about '*I*' when *you* decided to go away and train for three whole years in the middle of our two year marriage! It wasn't about '*I*' when I passed on opportunities to go away and practice law because *your* parents threw you out on your ass and you needed me!" He lowered his voice now, but maintained the aggressive edge for his closing remarks.

"And it definitely wasn't about '*I*' when *we* got pregnant, and *you* chose to abort it on your own terms! Don't talk to me about selfish! You invented the word!"

Natalie stared at him wide-eyed, mouth aghast, tears welling in her eyes. Hearing the pain in his voice as he mentioned the abortion that occurred almost sixteen years ago moved her.

He defiantly stared at her without remorse.

The server brought their food and they ate in complete silence.

Shane caressed Lisa's back as he intimately penetrated her from behind. He braced her chest against the shower wall and steadily ground her gaping vulva with slow, circular movements.

The mood was set just right with the bathroom dimly lit, smelling of vanilla and jasmine oils, and soft jazz spilling through the ceiling speakers.

With every appreciative moan and pant, steam fogged the shower glass creating an fairytale love scene.

Shane sensually kissed the nape of his woman's neck and effortlessly rotated her on his turgid, unsheathed flank just so he could stare deeply into her eyes. He easily managed her petite frame, hoisting her firmly into position about his waist. Stepping out of the shower with her body still clinging to his wet, muscular frame, he moved them to the bathroom counter.

Lisa seemed entranced by his piercing baby browns as she kissed him fervently and clenched her inner muscles to heighten his sensation into overdrive.

Reflexively and somewhat routinely, he tilted his head backwards and closed his eyes. *Damn Lisa! Keep this up and I'll pop a bun in this oven.* He smiled inwardly. *I know you're onto me like white on rice! Barely said a word since we got in last night. Women and their damn instincts! Well while I got you here...* He released the thought.

"Baby, there is something I have to tell you." The words quietly tumbled from his lips and he slowed his grind. He continued when her stare intensified.

"Baby, I've been seeing a doctor to do some testing..." He fumbled for his next words, tentative of how much 'preliminary' information to disclose.

Lisa urgently leaned into him as her eyes betrayed her inner worries. Still she maintained her silence.

"Please don't be mad with me baby. I just didn't know how to tell you, *or* anyone." He didn't realise it yet, but he was crying. "Based on what they're seeing so far, it looks like cancer babe."

"What!" Her eyes widened and instantly filled with tears. "You cannot be serious Shane! No way! You wouldn't have hidden that from me! No way! You're not that cruel! *Cancer?*" She shrieked. Tears spilled down her cheeks while she shook her head in disagreement.

He lovingly embraced and held her tightly, somehow enjoying the bittersweet sensation of her vaginal motions.

"You want me to stop baby?" He whispered by her ear as he moved them to the bedroom. "I'm so sorry for not telling you before babe. Please forgive me and try to understand." He murmured. "Can you babe?" He eagerly kissed her and she welcomed him.

Shane's thrusts hastened and his breathing grew heavier. With his next breath, he announced. "I'm coming baby. You feel so good to me. Mmm…where yuh want it?"

"Inside…" She whispered. "I love you baby."

Michael drove in circles around the parking lot of the Carib movie theatre, eager to find a spot.

"Maybe we should just do this another time then, I'm kind of tired anyway." Natalie lied.

Maybe I should drop your boring ass home and you can do this another time! He mused to himself, fully annoyed as he finally pulled into a space.

The two had not spoken a word to each other since his outburst at dinner, and now they walked the short distance to the ticketing line one ahead of the other.

A large crowd swarmed the parking area behind them, causing all sorts of raucous.

As he passed the line and walked up to the booth, Michael glanced over his shoulder but instantly turned around when he noticed a familiar face.

"Wait, a Mista Simmons dat?" Biggs stopped beside them, talking at the top of his voice.

Michael unwillingly looked in his direction and plastered a smile. "Hey, how's it going Mr. Jackson?"

"Good yuh nuh, no complaints." He grinned sheepishly, lustfully eyeing Natalie from head to toe. "And is this Misses Simmons?" He asked as his eyes lingered on her rear end, with his hand outstretched for a shake.

Offering no confirmation, Natalie boldly snubbed his gesture without remorse.

"Oh *excuse* me! She's a preppy one, eh? Well on that note, I'll get going. See yuh at *The Club* lata?" He called out over his shoulder as he grinned and walked away.

Michael's face instantly lost color. He tried to avert Natalie's stare, though he knew the heat was coming.

"Who the hell was that *pig* and what *club* was he referring to?" She snapped aloud, totally out of character and heedless of their audience.

"He's a client Natalie." He remained subdued and deliberately ignored the second part of the question.

She audibly exhaled and stepped out of the line. In one glance, she scrutinised him with grave disdain, spun on her heels and stormed away.

Knowing that she would easily use her spare key to take the car and leave him stranded, he relinquished his cool and made a dash after her.

The crowd erupted with laughter as one woman pierced the silence and shouted. "A good fi him! Man too damn lie and wicked! Damn dog dem!"

"This is the *police*! Everybody get flat on the floor!" The voice blasted through the foghorn stemming havoc in the club. "We're here for one thing...so the quicker you comply, the sooner this is over!" The burly man commanded.

The Club was in a state of frenzy. Some male patrons tried to make a dash for the backdoor exit, but were stopped in their tracks by the cold metals of the officers' M-16 rifles.

Caramel lay flat on the stage per the initial orders, but steadily tried to slither towards her dressing area. She knew that Savage occasionally used her closet to stash his drugs, and was unsure whether or not she was in the clear tonight. She successfully made her way into the room, and hastily opened the safe in the closet.

"Don't move another muscle!" The coarse voice of the officer in charge sternly warned her. "*You* are the reason we're here! Back weh from the closet!" He barked at her.

She cowardly moved as instructed with her hands held high in the air.

Still, the man shoved her out of his path though carefully maintaining a visual. He rummaged through the closet and seemed upset that it was clean.

"Where's Savage?" He turned to face her. "And if yuh ever lie!" He snarled with disgust.

She quickly spoke. "Officer, I don't know where he is. He pops up whenever he feels like it. We're not on good terms right now. Haven't seen him since I came."

"When last yuh see him?" His voice was sharp and raspy.

She was visibly terrified. "A couple weeks ago maybe. It could even be a month Sir."

"Hmm, so long? Mi nuh believe dat! So is what yuh run in here looking for?" He piercingly stared into her eyes to deter the lie he was expecting.

"Well he has a key to get in here. And sometimes he'll leave his shit in my closet. I just wanted to check, because I didn't want to get into trouble for him! I would tell you immediately if I found anything."

"Sure!" He paced around her as a means of intimidation, but undoubtedly enjoyed the view as well. "What yuh feel like doing so I don't lock you up tonight?" His voice was lustful as he reached around and firmly grabbed one of her breasts. "Eeh?" He edged her for a response.

Caramel froze. Not many men could resist her naked, but this she hadn't anticipated.

He grew impatient and stuck his pistol into the small of her back. "A wha? Cat's got yuh tongue? Alright then, me affi go book yuh tonight!" He aggressively hand-cuffed her and spun her around to lustfully scrutinise her.

"Yuh sweet eeh? Sure yuh nuh want change ma mind?" He licked her nipple and used his gun to stroke her vagina.

The usually bold woman flinched but remained silent.

"Have it your way then! Maybe next time..." He shoved her through the door and back into the club area.

The accompanying squadron stood their ground and watched wide-eyed as their superior escorted the voluptuous, naked women towards the front exit.

"Sarge..." One of them spoke up. "Yuh nah put something over her at least?"

Sarge paused by the exit and sneered. "Go find mi sup'm nuh Samaritan! A whore yuh nuh! Wha difference it mek if she naked inside or outside the whorehouse?"

Some of the men laughed in agreement.

CHAPTER EIGHT

*S*hit! Roxanne thought to herself, but the word actually escaped her mouth. *Why the hell does this have to happen today? And at school! Four days late and you just pop up unannounced? Unbelievable! How the hell am I going to get outta here without all these boys staring at my backside? Times like this I miss Cindy...fuck!* She saw one of her friends passing by the classroom and called out to her.

"Shari." She spoke firmly, though in a hushed manner. "Come here for a second."

Everyone in the front of the classroom turned around as she had anticipated, and was desperately trying to avoid. *How many Shari's are in here?* She thought to herself, rolling her eyes in annoyance.

Shari worsened the situation when she shouted. "What's doing Roxanne? Yuh cool?"

"Girl I need a favour." She mumbled in response. "Can you walk with me to the bathroom downstairs? I kinda have a situation..." She filled the gap with a gesture.

"Oh, *the* situation! Alright come on nuh. I can do that for yuh. Yuh have any pads? I have if you need."

Roxanne ignored her overly loud question, and carefully stood to leave. "Stay as close as possible, cool?"

"Alright." Shari added a wink.

They left the classroom and headed down the corridor.

Roxanne walked awkwardly slow, and Shari dutifully followed pace behind her as requested.

Regina glanced at the clock on her computer then over at Stacy's empty desk. *It's already ten thirty. Where the hell are you?* She dialled the number to Stacy's house.

"Stacy?" An elderly lady shouted into the phone before the second ring.

"Uhm, no. This is Regina from her office. I was actually calling to see if Stacy was home, but I guess not. When was the last time you spoke to her?" She couldn't fight the feeling that her son's cruel father was to blame.

Stacy's mother explained. "Well I talk to her yestadeh aftanoon to tell her what we need at di supamarkit. She tek dung di list and seh she soon come. Dat was di last I heard. Stacy woulda never sleep out and don't call or check on the baby. Mi nuh like this at all."

Me either! Regina thought, but tried to pacify the woman. "Well I'm sure there's an explanation. If I hear anything I'll call you back okay? And if she comes in, you tell her to call me at the office."

"Alright lady I will."

Regina hung up and leaned back in the chair. *Where the hell are you Stacy? And what the hell is going on? That fucking Savage! I swear if he hurt her...*

She got up and decided to look about Stacy's desk for any clues. Her first stop was the top drawer, but there were only stationeries. Next she tugged on the bottom drawer, but it was much heavier than the first. She wheeled the chair further away and used both hands to pop open the overstuffed cubby.

Damn! What don't you have in this damn place? She flipped through folders, bags of snacks, toiletries, makeup, and novels. A blue planner stuck in the back of the drawer caught her attention. She deliberated her next move, not directly wanting to violate her friend's privacy. She cautiously laid the planner on the desk, and it flipped open on its own turning to the most recent page. It read:

January 27, 2008

Tell Savage I want out! I'm willing to continue to pay him monthly, but I can't do this anymore. I have to live a better life for my son. He's asking too many questions at nights. For God's sake, I need some mercy. Maybe I should take my family and just get out of here. That's the only way out! It's either that or death. Death; maybe I should get him killed! Funny! I'm over-worked and over-sexed! I'm so goddamn tired! Like the loser I am, I write this because I KNOW I won't say it!

Coward!

Regina read the note over and over again trying to piece together the full story. *What could she be paying Savage for? I thought she said he took care of things. She wants out...of what? What the hell did Stacy get herself into this time? Mercy...Death...Coward.* The words appeared brighter to her the more she stared at the paper, sending chills up her spine. She felt the urge to contact the police, but decided to wait.

"Morning Doc!" Shane answered his cell in an upbeat tone. "How are *you* feeling this morning?" He exaggerated, trying to switch their usual tempos.

Natalie chuckled in recognition of his attempt. "I'm doing quite well Shane. I'm glad *you're* in high spirits."

"Only doing what my doctor ordered. What's new?"

"Well, I'm calling to see if you could come in today at four thirty? Sorry it's such short notice but we have things to get done...urgently."

"You and your *urgent* short notices, Doc. Four thirty could work though. Guess I'll see you then if that's it."

"Alright. Take care until I see you." She decided to leave it at that.

"You too Doc. Later." He hung up.

"What did she say?"

He spun around to see Lisa lurking behind him.

"I have an appointment today."

"Yeah, at four thirty." She impatiently interjected. "I heard *that* part. What else?"

The look on her face weighed heavily on his heart. "Lisa that's all she said. Babe, I don't want you to worry too much about this okay? And please don't say anything to my mom or my brothers. I'll tell them in my own way, when I'm ready."

Lisa nodded in agreement then began to cry.

"Baby, please don't do this." Shane rushed to her side and held her close. "You know I hate to see you cry. You have to be strong for me, and for us! If you fall apart, what am I supposed to do?"

Her body trembled as she tried to stifle her sobs. "I know baby…" She whispered in between sniffles. "But it's going to be a little rough. I can't stand not being there with you every step of the way. You don't want me to come to Jamaica, and that's all I want to do right now."

"Lisa, we both know why you have to stay here. You have to keep your focus baby. But don't think for a second I'm going to take this shit sitting down. I'm not quitting track! I'm still going to stay as busy as I can." He eased her away from him and stared into her eyes.

"I'll make you a promise. If I win my hundred meter race next month, send that Simeon packing, you'll be in JA with me for the celebrations. Cool?"

She managed a smile. "I'll start packing then."

"That's my girl! It's going to be okay baby."

She leaned into his embrace and welcomed his lips.

Natalie and her mother Cecile had finally warped their schedules and agreed to meet for lunch. They were seated at their usual booth at the Cabana's Restaurant, catching up on their respective adventurous lives.

"So Sweetheart..." Cecile continued as the server disappeared with their orders. "Talk to me about what's *really* stressing you. Mommy sees sorrow in your eyes." She would often refer to herself in the third person.

"I've been under a lot of pressure these days mom. I mean, I love my new practice and I'm really enjoying what I do. It's just that the art of detachment eludes me, you know? I take everything so personal, and it stresses me."

"Well baby that's just in your nature. When you have a passion for something you've always given it your all. You've always been that way, for as long as I can remember." She chuckled.

"Remember all those sick pets you stashed in my greenhouse as a kid? You practically started your own little clinic! Now you're dealing with human beings at a very vulnerable point in their lives; how could you not take on what they feel? The key is to take everything in strides baby. That's the best thing you can do as one human being." She smiled affectionately at her only offspring.

"Thanks a lot mom. I really needed to hear that. But then there's Michael."

Cecile urgently sat forward as if that would ensure Natalie's every word would land directly on her ear.

Natalie continued without hesitation. "He's getting on my nerves mother! He's really trying my patience these days. All he wants to talk about is having kids and how much he feels unfulfilled because he has no seed, and yadda yadda. I'm trying to explain to him that it's not like I don't want kids, but right now I have to focus on building a reputable career you know? He's been acting up a lot mom! Enough to even say I think he's messing around." Tears welled in her eyes.

Though she had been listening attentively without interruption, this moment had to be seized.

"Now Natalie, you don't jump to such conclusions without facts. And I can't say I disagree with Michael... entirely!" She paused as her daughter's eyes widened then quickly finished her point.

"*But*, I'm not saying he shouldn't support you either. It's just that men at his age long for children baby, and you've been working on your career for almost all of your marriage. Maybe *his* patience has run out darling. He *is* human."

Cecile and her daughter had always disagreed on a woman's role in the relationship. Whereas she was from the dogmatic school that 'a woman's role is in the house', Natalie was more pragmatic, and had always pitied her mother for not standing up to her father to pursue her own career and independence.

"Well mother, I don't know what he's going to do. But whatever it is, he needs to figure it out and make me aware of it. I love Michael mom, but I also love what I do. It's very important what I do! It's not a joke or a hobby."

"Natalie, don't be erratic! You made a vow to stick by that man and when you took his name, you made a promise to merge and become one. You have to compromise! You knew long before marrying Michael that he was eager to have kids. *This* is not a surprise!" She blankly stared at her daughter and continued. "Now, for you to *think* he is stepping out because of this is rather presumptuous. However, if you continue to push him away that could very well be the subject of our next meeting! Let me tell you sweetheart, what *you* won't do for your husband, he will get done!"

Natalie was taken aback by her mother's last statement. *Is she really picking up for him? Or is she just brutally honest? Doesn't anybody understand why I'm not prepared for parenthood? Why is it such a big frigging*

127

deal? Kids just hold you down! She mentally vented her frustration.

The server interrupted to ask if they'd like to order dessert. Surprisingly, Natalie ordered a slice of cheesecake to go, while Cecile passed on the opportunity as always.

"Natalie I can't tell you how to live your marriage. But know that I have lived the experience. I *can* tell you that a man will get what he wants whether it be from his wife or from outside; makes no difference to him. Your brother is the living testament to that fact!"

They sat in silence as the final remark resonated.

Michael confidently stepped through the courthouse and into the jail area. Dressed in a two-piece, well-tailored, navy blue suit with a pin-striped white shirt, he was the perfect contrast to the otherwise revolting atmosphere.

The air reeked of stale urine, rusted metal, and people whose last shower could've easily been three years ago. The waiting hall was filled with worried faces trying to retrieve or inquire about their loved ones; and recent, angry arrestees waiting to be booked.

Usually, he didn't venture downtown personally as his hired bailiff would make all those runs. Today was an exception however because it was personal. He made his way to the release counter and called out to the officer in charge.

"Dalton!" He shouted above the chaos.

The officer behind the desk turned around slowly, his face curled in a snarl. "Oh! A you Mikey!" He instantly grinned. "Mi a wonder who roun here so bright a call *big* man by mi first name."

They both laughed and shook hands.

Dalton continued. "So what yuh doing bout these places man? Yuh nuh have people fa dirty work?"

"Sure do, but he was on another run. You have to get dirty sometimes right?"

"Tell *me* about it! So what can I do you for?" He chuckled at his intentional dyslexia.

"You should have a woman back there, booked last night under Caramel. Check it out for me nuh."

"Caramel? She nuh have a real name boss man?"

"I don't know. That's what she was booked as. Check and you'll see." They both enjoyed a laugh.

Dalton scanned through the paperwork for recent bookings, and soon spotted the file with 'Caramel' scribbled on the label. He instantly chuckled.

"Well, yuh right to rass! The bail is fifty thousand. Yuh going pay it now or on the way out?"

Being trusted, Michael had options. "I'll leave it with Sheila on the way out. Oh, and give this to the young lady for me." He handed a bag to the officer.

Dalton disappeared down the corridor, headed to the back area that housed the jail cells. He immediately acknowledged Caramel, though she wasn't the only woman housed back there.

Oh! That's why she need the clothes. What a round gyal eeh man? I see why yuh name Caramel...with that brown, smooth skin. Is how Mikey meet this one? Wonder if he can hook I up? He thought to himself and smiled.

He called out to the woman sitting balled up in the corner, wearing an extra tight mini-dress that teasingly revealed most of her hefty cleavage and the lower parts of her buttocks. He handed her the package and she hastily dressed herself while she whispered her goodbyes to the others.

"This way mam." Dalton waved his hand in the exit direction and slammed the cell shut. "So Caramel, tell me how a beautiful girl like yourself end up in a profession that get yuh in a place like dis?" He tried to fill the silence between them. "Where is yuh man that supposed to tek care of your needs? Yuh too sexy for hustling and jail yuh nuh! Know yuh worth and get yuh life straight man! Here!" He slipped his business card into her pants pocket and leaned in close. "Gimme a call and mek *me* treat yuh right!"

She smiled and nodded in response.

Dalton winked at her as they neared the front.

"Alright boss man, likkle more." He released her to Michael, nodding approvingly with a wide grin.

Michael chuckled. "Alright Dalton, see you around. Take care of yourself man."

"A dat mi seh so a so it go! Anybody ask, a Biggs seh so!" Biggs voiced the final lyrics to his newest track then quickly headed into the mixing booth to listen to the replay.

"How it sound Cilon? Run it for mi deh! Yo Felicia! Get some water!"

His groupie of the day scurried out of the studio and his producer replayed the track. They both listened in silence, bopping their heads to the beat.

"It a gwan wicked boss! Di riddim bad! Ma flow just gets better every day." Biggs chuckled out of excitement.

"This is yuh next hit for sure! Bank on it!" Cilon commented after pausing the track.

Felicia returned and handed Biggs a bottle of water. He snatched it from her grip and quickly snarled.

"How yuh only bring *one* bottle a water, and *two* big man deh yah? Yuh nuh have nuh mannas?"

Cilon quickly interjected on her behalf. "Biggs me cool yuh nuh." He dreaded the disrespectful and overbearing side of the admittedly talented artist.

Biggs was unsatisfied. "A wha kind a hot water this yuh bring come too? Yuh nuh have nuh sense? Yuh nuh rate man?" He stood up to rage war.

"That's all they had in the kitchen Biggs." The young girl timidly replied as she backed away. "I looked everywhere for a colder one."

He crudely dismissed her to the corner store.

Cilon observed in disbelief, but maintained his silence.

"Yuh believe her Producer? Dem likkle gyal yah nuh use dem head yuh nuh! Dem just upset man sometimes."

Maybe yuh need to leave out the school girls den! Cilon thought to himself, but airily replied. "If big woman gwan dumb, imagine likkle girls?"

"She may be a *schoolas* but she's nineteen! That is not exactly a likkle girl Produca!" Biggs evidently caught on to his insinuation. "Anyhow, mi dun fi di day yuh nuh boss. Call the cellie if anything. Cool?"

"But Biggs whappen to the medley track? Every other artist voice already yuh nuh, we just waiting on you to get it out there. The plan is to release your track first."

"That affi go hold off for right now Ci! Maybe I swing by tonight. Mi tired bredrin. Trust mi!"

Bredrin? Him tink a likkle bway him a chat to? A whappen to Biggs though God? Fame really lick him! Cilon watched him in silence as he made his way to the door.

"So likkle more?" Biggs avoided eye contact and made his way out the studio, leaving the highly demanded producer enraged.

Shane's flight arrived at Norman Manley International Airport at exactly two thirty. By the time he cleared immigration and customs with the help of a VIP escort, it was three forty five.

He exited the terminal and walked briskly through a barrage of people anxiously awaiting their loved ones. Some of them recognised him, but mostly the females eagerly flocked towards his direction.

"Thanks for the support." He continuously repeated to everyone respective of whatever they shouted. He consciously refused to ease his pace as he urgently stepped towards the long-term parking lot to retrieve his Lexus.

He tossed his carry-on into the trunk and hopped into the driver's seat. By the time he got to the exit and paid the attendant, he had called Lisa to notify her that he had arrived safely. As he sped out of the airport headed for his four thirty appointment, some forty minutes away, he eagerly dialled Simone.

"Hey sexy! Missed *big* daddy?"

Biggs had dropped Felicia at the bus stop in Constant Spring, and on an impulse had decided to visit Michelle. He turned up the last stretch of the hill, and parked his truck on the roadway.

He dialled her house phone from his cell as he walked the short distance to the front gate, and demanded that she opened the door.

"Whagwan babes?" He yelled out to Michelle sitting off in the distance, before slamming the door.

She waited until he made his way to the patio to muster a response. "Nothing much. How you?"

He instantly acknowledged the rigidity in her tone. "Michelle, when wi ago stop fight and get along like wi used to? Is wha? Yuh want out? Yuh want to go back to the streets?" He sat in the chair opposite her.

Michelle deeply exhaled before turning her gaze away from the expansive view of Kingston city.

"Biggs, if yuh want to put me back on the street you're free to. At least I wouldn't be cooped up in this house at your disposal. I feel like a *fucking* slave!"

He tried to subdue his anger as she not only swore at him, but raised her voice in doing so.

"Mich, this house has everything that *you* nagged me to put in it. Why yuh nuh use the Internet and do a course online or sup'm? Yuh have a car, who says yuh can't go nowhere? Just as long as yuh carry yuh cell so I can reach yuh. Listen! Don't forget why we had to live all the way up here in the first place. Rememba dat I saved yuh life!"

"Yuh forget how we got to this point? Yuh sure yuh want to go back dere? If a so, yuh can tell mi yuh nuh! But yuh *not* keeping ma son! Forget bout that!"

Michelle hadn't forgotten the circumstances under which she had met Biggs, or why she was living in prison for the past six years. She just knew that right now, things were much different between them. She began to cry.

"Biggs, things aren't the way they used to be. We're not the same, and *you're* definitely not the same. You used to love me, and treat me right. We used to take trips every week to here or there. Yuh used to come home to *me* at nights!" She paused to compose herself.

"Now, I only see yuh when you're horny. Yuh stop answering my phone calls, and yuh beat me up for the smallest things. Sometimes I wonder if yuh really love me, and if yuh don't why yuh don't just leave me alone! Obviously I stick with yuh and take good care of our son because I love you. I still love you Biggs." Her sobs broke down her barrier and she got up and went inside.

Biggs was so deep in thought that she could successfully walk away from an argument, and have the unusual luxury of the last word. *Michelle is so right. I've become a monster. She's never been a bad woman to me. Gave me a son when everybody else sexed me for my money...and dash weh mi belly! No matter what me and her have, she always take good care of him...and me. Don't even nag me all the time like the rest of them investigators! Jah know, she deserve better. Can't be my only girl like the old days, but I can do her better.* He got up and went into the house.

"Babes, is it too late to forgive me?" He found her in the kitchen. "I know what yuh saying, and I promise I will work on it. I just don't want you out there on the streets so you can get hurt, yuh understand?" He walked up behind her and hugged her tightly around the waist.

She nodded in agreement and welcomed the warmth that had been eluding her with time.

"And I promise to take you on a trip soon. Maybe carry you on tour this summer; you and Rashad. Michelle, I need you to know that I appreciate you and what you do for my baby. I love how yuh always look out for me too, even when yuh want to hate me."

There Michelle quickly interjected. "Biggs I *never* hate yuh! I'm just extremely disappointed that's all. I know yuh did a lot for me...you *do* a lot for me. But I'm still a human being and I also have feelings."

"I know babes...and I'm sorry okay?" He kissed her on the nape of her neck.

Almost instantly, his dick hardened against her back.

Michelle smiled, unknowing to him, and willingly unsnapped the front of her shirt. Her voluptuous caramel-toned, thirty-eight D's sprang free.

"Mich, yuh want me inside yuh?" He spoke softly, almost whispering as he sensually massaged her beasts.

"Yes." She whimpered in response.

He used one hand to swipe the counter clean before lifting her petite, but voluptuous frame unto it. Hungrily kissing her eager, full lips, he ripped her skirt from her body exposing her clean-shaved fluff.

Biggs fingers moved expertly to stimulate her pinkness and other known erogenous zones of her body.

She moaned appreciatively and asserted her demands. "Biggs! I want yuh inside! Fuck yuh pussy Biggs!"

His dick grew unbelievably larger at the sound of the filth that seductively rolled off her tongue. He pulled her to the edge of the counter, and in one swift motion freed his manhood from its clothed restraints.

He entered her with an aggressive thrust, amused by the loud cries that instantly escaped her mouth when he buried all ten inches of his wood deep within her.

As her heavy butt cheeks slapped against his thighs, threatening to overload his mind, he leaned in closer and whispered in her ear.

"Mich, can I get some ass baby?" He edged her closer towards him in anticipation.

"Mmm…mmm." She affirmed.

Biggs anxiously pulled his plank out of her vagina and steadily sunk it - unsheathed - into her anus. He impatiently thrust his groin to build his momentum, ignoring her guttural moans that more reflected unpleasant pain. His arousal neared an eruption, and he thoughtlessly gave her more than she could bear.

"Fuck!" They both yelled in unison.

"Fuck, I love this ass!" Biggs groaned. "Mmm… mmm." He vigorously massaged her clit as he firmly bucked his body against her, causing a simultaneous orgasm.

"I really love yuh Michelle." He murmured as he collapsed unto her. "I hope you will forgive me."

"Mmm…of course!" She softly moaned. *At least for now…* She added mentally.

Shane sat in his usual position in the doctor's office and rested his head on the desk. He had arrived ten minutes late for his appointment, and besides being tired from a long flight home, he was anticipating the worse from this meeting.

"Shane, please don't slob on my desk." Doctor Simmons' familiar voice announced her presence.

"Nice to see you too Doc." He cynically replied without looking up.

"Always a pleasure! You know that." She grinned as he raised his head and stared at her through entrancing, baby browns.

He sensed a familiar disposition that instantly played on his paranoia. "So what's up for this meeting? I'm starting to feel like I'm initiating for the Lodge." He smiled when she scowled.

"We need to schedule your last examination and also explain the general procedure etcetera."

"Hmm, well I'll be around so as soon as possible. And I'd prefer if you spare me the details." He added matter-of-factly.

"Would tomorrow be okay for you? And besides you *must* know the details. Tomorrow we'll do a Biopsy. It's, for lack of a better explanation, a little more invasive than the previous tests. You'll be given a general anesthetic because..." She fumbled for the right words. "Well, we're going to remove tissue samples from the lining of your stomach." She had his undivided attention.

"Doc, you can't be serious! How long will it take to recover? How long before I can go back to training? I *do* have a meet coming up!"

She had anticipated that response and was prepared to remain calm. "Shane, I understand track's your priority. But if your health diminishes..."

"Yeah I know, *so does track*!" He quickly interrupted. "But seriously Doc, how long?"

"Anywhere from three days to a week Shane. I mean, you won't be in severe pain but you'll definitely feel a lot of discomfort."

"Discomfort's not the worst! I could just lighten up on the weights and do minimal cardio. Okay, schedule it for tomorrow morning then. And this *is* the last test right?"

Natalie flipped through her agenda as she responded. "Yes. A definite diagnosis will be made after this. Is eleven good for you?"

"Eleven is cool. How long will I be here until?"

"It's a one hour procedure. But what does it matter Shane? You couldn't possibly plan to hit the gym after." She pointedly eyed him.

He offered a plastic smile. "You know me too well Doc! But how are *you* doing otherwise?"

She managed a smile. "I'm content. I can't complain." She lied through her teeth as her face flustered.

Content huh? Haven't heard that word in a while. Bullshitter! He instantly buried that thought. "Good to know! Well if that's all…" He stood and made his way to the door.

"Yes Sir. I'll see you at ten fifty. Oh! No food up to eight hours before your appointment."

"Great Doc! You *ever* have any good news for me? See you at eleven!" He playfully saluted her.

Roxanne lay in her bed and counted the hours since she had last seen or spoken to Biggs. *It's only been one day and fourteen hours, but I miss him already. I can't believe I'm even missing him after what he did to me! And that bitch Cindy, watch me and her! I should tell Benji so he can beat her ass! But then he'd probably kill Andre. He hasn't even called me or nothing! Like him have the right to vex. Maybe I should call him…tell him a piece of my mind.*

She reached for the cordless phone and dialled his number from memory.

I know this asshole didn't just click my call! She impatiently pressed the redial button. *I can't believe this! That's it for me and him!* She hurled the phone at the wall.

"I hate him!" She screamed and slammed her face into the pillow. She immediately broke into sobs.

"Babes I really missed yuh, yuh see. I'm *soooo* glad my baby's home where she belongs!" Biggs exaggerated and leaned in for a kiss from his Boston 'wifey'.

Toya blushed and eagerly welcomed her man's loving.

They were cuddling in bed, fully naked, after four hours of make-up sex.

He had picked her up from the airport after his rendezvous with Michelle, and they had spent every waking minute intertwined in every possible way. At this point, he was more eager to get her suitcases unpacked.

"Babes, wiggle your sexy ass over there and show me what yuh bring for yuh baby. I'm anxious!" He playfully squeezed one of her breasts.

She giggled and tried to move as instructed. "Alright baby. But are you gonna let me go?" She coyly eyed him.

"Hmm! Only if yuh hurry back!" He teased, but quickly loosened his grip around her waist.

She climbed out of the bed and manoeuvred the luggage to make enough room to lay one flat.

Biggs remained in bed, lusting at her voluptuous breasts jiggling to her movements. When they had first met, he was heavily mesmerized by her gold, curly, shoulder length locks that exotically complemented her dark chocolate, unbelievably curvy frame. He slid to the edge of the bed for a better view of all that was about to go down.

Toya pulled out eight pairs of jeans from top of the line men's designers, matching high end sneakers for each pair of specially designed jeans, and more than a dozen designer shirts.

"Babes! Yuh really did some shopping this time man!" He anxiously hopped off the bed and prepped for a mini fashion show.

She giggled and continued to unload. After removing five belts, four bottles of cologne, boxers, socks, and under shirts - everything designer labelled - the first of three suitcases was entirely emptied.

Biggs tried on each item with much enthusiasm. He paraded in front of the wall-length mirror grinning from ear to ear, while she sat back and watched in admiration.

"So?" She solicited his verbal approval.

"So what babes?" He almost shrieked. "I love everything! Trust me!" He hugged and lifted her into the air. "Baby, I'm not even done." She giggled playfully and freed herself from his embrace.

When she reached for her carryon luggage, Biggs struggled to mask the excitement bouncing within him. *And these must be the valuables!* He shrieked inwardly, before he spotted the PlayStation 3, the newly released Mac laptop, and six baseball fitted hats.

"Toya, you overdid it this time!" He truthfully exclaimed. "No babes...a PS3 *and* a laptop?" He feigned disbelief at her eagerness to please.

"Not just any laptop baby, it's a Mac..." She tried to explain amidst his enthusiastic outbursts. "Just call it a studio on wheels!"

That, he already knew. "Jah know babes, I love everything!" He sat on the edge of the bed. "The way you look out for me all the time, I really appreciate it yuh nuh. I just wonder sometimes if you deserve better than me...better than this." This move was expertly calculated.

"Andre, I don't do anything for you that I don't want to do! You're my man, and I'm only doing what I should as your woman. I don't know what you're used to, but I don't give to receive. Your love is sufficient for me babe! Don't let me hear you talk like that!" She lovingly embraced her 'man', smothering his face with her chest. "I didn't even show you everything and you're tearin' up already." She joked.

"Babes, what else could you possibly have? Keep it!" He lied as he almost pushed her away to retrieve whatever she had hidden.

She wiggled her heavy hips over to the loveseat, and out of her pocketbook came an Iphone.

"No babes! Ya gwan wicked now! Yuh couldn't love that much! I wasn't even thinking about that after all of this stuff. Babes..." He carefully opened the box and removed the prized possession. "Thanks a million! I don't know what else to say." He suddenly noticed the dark red leather box on the bed beside him. If he didn't know anything else, he recognised the gold logo before anything else. *Oh hell no!* He eagerly snatched it up.

A diamond encrusted platinum Cartier? This shit costs thirteen thousand US! This chic is crazy 'ballin'...and I know she don't do fake! Playing down his eagerness to immediately touch the road, Biggs offered his best gloomy expression.

"Babes, I can't take this. This watch is just too much. I feel guilty. Toya, I can't lie and tell yuh that I behave myself when you're not here. And yet you save all of yourself for me. You get me all this expensive stuff..." He expertly looked away; the emotional reel in move.

"Andre, I knew what I was getting into when I decided to be with you. You really think I expect you to be a saint when you're surrounded by so much temptation? With these little fast ass girls that'll do anything to be around you? I know it's all a part of the entertainment package Baby, and I love you all the same. Good *and* not so good." She smiled.

With the emotions exposed and the mood set right, he forcefully pulled her on top of him. His now turgid cock beat drums against her stomach. He aggressively kissed and clung to her, as if his life depended on her existence.

"Toya baby, I want yuh to ride off your cocky! *All* of it this time. Don't be afraid baby." He kissed her again. "You want to have my first son baby? I want yuh to..." He whispered meaningless words as he eased her weight unto his plank.

She steadily thrust her groin to adjust and make way for the second half of his blessings. With painful satisfaction, but a lot of determination, she welcomed his entire length like only one other woman could.

"I love you Mich..." Biggs whispered routinely.

CHAPTER NINE

Natalie sat at the kitchen counter, anxiously awaiting her husband's arrival. She had left her office immediately after her last appointment, and had pretty much raced home. As soon as she heard the front door swing open, she immediately sprung into motion.

"What the hell did that hooligan mean by see you at the *club* later Michael? This is the last time I'm asking you! And where the hell have you been all day? I tried calling!"

"Nat, I just walked into the house for Christ's sake. Can a man get some serenity in his own home? Seriously, I know this little attack plan of yours thrilled you and all...but can this wait?" His facial expression conveyed full-bred annoyance.

"Don't you give me that look! What hooligan club have you been going to Michael? Answer me!" She shouted.

"Watch that tone with me Natalie! I don't have time for your bullshit! Why didn't you ask *him* which *club* he was referring to? I don't even know what the hell he was talking about! That fool's crazy!" He tried to leave the kitchen but she blocked his passage.

"Then why did you have that dumb look on your face, huh? You know the one! When you're caught in the middle of something you shouldn't be involved in? I was humiliated Michael! And now you add insult to injury?"

"Once again, I don't know what look you're talking about, and your humiliation is all you. This conversation is pointless! You *never* listen! I'd suggest if you wanna bombard me as I walk through the front door, you do it like a *real* wife should! You know, with candles, vanilla fragrances, nice lingerie, or even nothing. Oh, and a well-cooked meal would do! *Then* we can make passionate love, and I can release my sperms into you like married men do to their wives. After that, we can talk about *whatever* you want! Try that next time. You'll see better results!"

He slammed his briefcase onto the counter and threw his car keys below the key rack. "Now if that's all *woman,* I'll be upstairs!"

Natalie allowed his exit and began to cry; silently. *I need a break from all this shit! I really do!* She thought to herself as her husband's hurtful words reverberated through her brain. *This is utter bullshit! What about what I want?* She unplugged her cell from the charger and stormed out the front door. *How dare him? How fucking dare him! Fuck all of you!* She hit the send button and took a deep breath.

"Hey Doc!" The familiar voice broke the silence on the first ring.

Shane walked through the halls of the Sullivan Health Club, and as always, admired the many trophies and certificates that adorned the walls and glass cases. Some medals were dated as far back as 1964, while many of the more recent ones had his name plastered over them. He got to the back office and knocked on the door.

"Come in Shane." The husky voice called out.

"Hey Coach, thanks for sitting with me in such short notice." He greeted the middle-aged man as he opened and closed the door.

"No worries Shane. You guys are why I'm here so you're always priority. What's going on with you?" Coach Sullivan looked up from his paperwork.

Lawrence Sullivan was the fifth generation seed of the man who first opened the health club. The Sullivan family was a big name in track and field and in the fitness industry in general. He was a serious-looking and well-toned man, but was reputably caring and charismatic.

Shane had spent a great deal of time contemplating the different approaches he could use to disclose his illness. It was now that time, and he settled on the facts.

"Coach, I'll be frank with you. I've been having pain spasms in my abdomen, along with other irregular bodily disturbances." He paused involuntarily, trying to temper his rising emotions.

"Shane…" Coach Sullivan got up from his desk and went over to his number one athlete. He firmly placed his hand on his shoulder.

"Shane, what are you saying? I already knew something was off with you lately; being late for training more than usual these days and always seeming tired. What are the doctors saying? Have you seen one?"

"Yes Coach. I've done blood tests…CT scans…you couldn't even imagine. Basically, the preliminary results are showing a cancerous tumour." Shane's tears flowed freely for the first time. "I have stomach cancer Coach. My doctor won't say it because she's waiting on the results from my Biopsy. But I just know. I see it on her face. I see the pity."

"Shane, you can't think that way. The biopsy will definitely confirm if the cells are cancerous and the stage and grading of it. My brother…" He allowed the words to trail off.

Coach's younger brother Leonard had died of pancreatic cancer in the previous year. He saw the horror spread across Shane's face and continued.

"Stomach cancer isn't the worse that could happen to an athlete. You have to stay positive Shane. This is more about mental healing than you know."

"But Coach, how am I going to cope with this and still compete? With the Olympics coming up…"

"Shane when we're talking about your health, I don't want to hear about competition! I'd suggest you heed the doctor's warning, which I'm sure you've already received. You need to do whatever is required as soon as possible. Don't sit around and let things get worse for you boy!"

Shane sighed audibly. "That's exactly why I didn't want to tell you about this Coach. I knew you'd say that! I knew you'd take their side!" He stood up to leave.

"Shane, *sit down*! Listen to me, the only side here to take is your side! Don't be foolish! We are here to care about you when you're too *stubborn* to care about yourself! The final decision is yours, but don't say Coach should've done this or told you that like Leonard!"

Besides taking heed to the command, Shane was appalled and somewhat embarrassed to hear this usually resilient man mention the name of his brother in anger. He mindfully avoided eye contact with the man who'd been more like a father to him; the one man who had been present for every life-changing event in his life, and had groomed and nurtured him for occasions beyond the track field.

"I know what you're saying Coach and I'll definitely do what's best! But I don't want you to use this against me in the meantime. Don't start treating me any different, and *definitely* don't say anything to anyone!"

Coach Sullivan was saddened by the predicament that had befallen the young man he would easily call his son. He felt deficient in not having the perfect words to console him as he usually did.

"You have my word Shane. You know that."

Regina had taken the morning off from work to sit her law exam. She had stopped at the Burger King for lunch on the go, and had intended to make it into the office before one o'clock.

Upon turning into the main parking garage, she was surprised to find a car in her private spot. Opting not to bicker with the lacklustre parking lot security, she backed into a spot designated for customers. Her cell phone vibrated as soon as she stepped out of the car, and for some reason, startled her enough to send her drink flying into the air.

"Shit!" She yelled, but still answered the call. "Shane! What perfect timing you have!"

"Why so? How was the exam?" He asked nonchalantly.

"It was good." She was alarmed by his lack of a comeback. "But what's going on with you? What's the matter?" She worked to clean the juice from her feet.

"Gina, things aren't so good for me right now. Life's terrible as a matter of fact. I have stomach cancer." Just like that; no sugar coating. He began to sob.

Tears immediately filled her eyes. "*What*!" She leaned against her car for support. "Oh Shane, I'm so sorry this is happening. When did you find out? I would've gone to the appointment with you. *God*! What did they say? How could this be happening?"

"I don't know Gina…didn't want to break your focus. I can't believe this man!"

Their emotions ran free.

Regina's head began to pound. "Shane…you're gonna have to be strong hun. I understand everything you're feeling right now; but you have to stay up. Have you spoken to anyone else? Mommy?"

"Definitely not mommy! And I don't plan to as yet so you shouldn't either. I'll tell her when I'm ready Gina." He paused, allowing sorrow's choir to perform. "I did talk to Coach though…shouldn't have but whateva. Of course he agrees with the docs that I should start treatment right away. I just don't know if I can make that step Gina. My meets? The Olympics? *Everything* I've been bussing my ass for? *Damn*!"

Regina was not surprised that his passion took priority over his health. "Unfortunately…I have to agree with them too bro. I know what track means to you more than anybody...you know this. But Shane, a couple trophies and the hall of fame can't replace you in my life. To even picture my life without you..." She was almost hysterical.

"Regina, I'm not going anywhere that easy! C'mon, who's gonna stick to you like white on rice?" He tried to cheer her up despite his burdened mood.

It worked; she laughed. "You're so dumb Shane. For real though..." She blew her nose, took a deep breath, and sighed. "I'm not going to tell you that this is your decision to make. This is *bigger* than you! You have to make the choice for the people that love you. The people whose lives will be affected *forever*! This is not about glory Shane."

"I know Gina. I know this. I'm going to call you a little later. I have to get back to training. I love you sis..."

"Love you too Shane. And take it easy today. Make sure you eat something. Call me..." She hung up and made her way up the stairs to her office.

She was caught off guard for the second time in one day, when she saw Stacy sitting at her desk. She spared no emotion.

"I cannot believe you came to work and you didn't call me! I know you got my messages! Where the hell have you been Stacy? We were all worried about you!"

Stacy casually looked in her direction. "Listen Regina, I understand. But I'm a grown woman and I'm allowed to take time off to handle my business. And I didn't appreciate you calling my mother and getting her all worked up either...that wasn't necessary."

"Well *excuse* me for caring! I was *only* worried sick about your reckless ass!" She plopped down in her chair and took a deep breath.

That was not exactly how she had planned to approach Stacy about her problems. But with Shane's news, and everything that's going on, she was admittedly wound up tight.

147

"Stacy, I didn't mean to shout at you like that. I'm sorry. And I'm sorry for calling your house. I was scared for you girl, you know with your 'babydaddy' and all. I almost called the police even."

"I know Regina, and I'm sorry for being so inconsiderate. I know it's all in love and I appreciate your concern. You did what you thought was best."

"Girl you know I care about you right? And you know you can talk to me about anything, if there's a problem. If there's anything I can help you with, don't hesitate to ask me okay? You're always there for me when I need you. It's the least I can do."

Stacy's eyes welled with tears.

"For real though Stacy…I mean you're beautiful, ambitious and *strong*. You can do *anything* your heart desires. But if you need help, just let me know. And if we can't do it on our own, you *know* who got the hook-up on the gangstas?" She indirectly danced circles around the contents of the diary.

Stacy laughed, though apprehensive of her friend's concern. *Girl if you only knew the half! I'm not as smart and strong as you think I am. My life is in so much shit right now! So much running around, I'm losing my goddamn self! I must figure a way around all this though! I fucking have to! I need to do this for my son!*

Roxanne's body ached as if she had done a full day's worth of manual labour. Already feeling drowsy and disgruntled, she had spent the earlier part of the morning cuddling the school's toilet bowl.

Before the bell sounded the end of her third-period class, she was bowled over the toilet again. She gagged and heaved uncontrollably, until there was nothing left to eject. She closed the lid and sat on the toilet to catch her breath.

Hurried footsteps came in and out of the bathroom as was customary during classroom changes.

She remained silent however, and waited patiently until she felt she was alone.

Roxanne flushed the toilet and opened the door. She was instantly startled by the sight of someone leaning against the adjacent wall, staring directly at her. She quickly composed herself and made her way to the pipe farthest away from her spectator.

She rinsed her face, mouth, and hands, entirely ignoring the eyes that observed her every move.

"Roxanne, we need to talk! Why yuh vomiting like that? Yuh sick?" Cindy made a step towards her 'best' friend, but sensibly stopped in her tracks.

Roxanne concentrated on tidying her dishevelled image that reflected in the mirror.

"*Roxanne*! How long yuh plan to stay mad at me? Yuh didn't even ask mi my side of the story. Mi life nuh perfect like yours yuh nuh! I have to fend for maself. Yuh know what that's like? Listen, I'm sorry for not telling yuh that I slept with Biggs. He told me not to 'cause he really likes yuh. I shouldn't have listened though. I shouldn't have gotten yuh into this mess to start with. I'm sorry Roxanne. *Very sorry*!" She paused for any signs of a reaction, and started to cry when none came.

"*Roxanne*, please say something to me! Yuh know I can't manage when we fight. It's not like I haven't been trying to tell yuh sorry. But yuh don't take my calls and yuh ignore me all day everyday, just like yuh doing now. I really need yuh to forgive me Roxanne. You're all I have. You're my best friend."

Roxanne straightened her uniform, re-checked her reflection, and stepped to walk wide of Cindy.

Cindy rushed to her and grabbed her arm. "Roxanne, please! Please! I need you!"

She snatched her arm away and spoke firm. "I *was* all you *had* Cindy! We *were best friends*! I'm late for class. Have fun selling your pussy!" With that, she left.

Cindy slumped to the floor and bawled.

Regina quickly placed Shane on hold and answered her work cell. "Regina speaking…" She had given up staying at the office.

"Girl, I was thinking about what you said and I could really use some help Regina. But I want to talk to a professional. Can you recommend anyone?" It was Stacy.

"Yuh mean to take out Savage?" Regina teased.

Stacy chuckled. "No! Not that kind of professional Regina! I meant like a head doctor or so; just someone I can spill my heart to and get some sound advice."

"Damn! I'm insulted."

"Regina…"

"I'm joking Stacy! Well I know a doctor. Head is not necessarily her specialty, but she's good at listening. Her number's written in my planner on the desk. It should be under Doctor Natalie Simmons or maybe just Natalie. Flip through and you'll find it. When you call, ask for her directly and tell her Regina says she's good at listening. She'll take it from there."

Stacy laughed. "Okay I will. Thanks a lot girl and no offence again."

"None taken. We'll talk later."

"Cool. Run back to Shane." She hung up.

Regina laughed at how predictable her phone schedule was as she picked up her personal cell from the passenger seat.

"You sure you don't need another *hour*? Damn!" Shane complained as she said hello.

"Shut up misery! That was like ten seconds!"

They argued their way back into the original conversation.

The house phone rang, jolting Roxanne out of her intense and much needed sleep. She had eventually given into her ailment and had made the trek home from school, unannounced.

The cordless phone sounded again, somewhere nearby. She glanced at the call display and barely recognised the number, but was instantly irritated regardless.

"Hello!" She snapped dryly.

"Hey Roxie, did I wake you?" Biggs could hear the frustration in her voice.

"Hmm. What's up?" She was blunt.

"I just wanted to hear your voice baby. How come yuh haven't called me? Yuh still vex?"

She restrained what she thought would be the most suitable response.

Biggs was surprisingly tolerable of her attitude. "Roxanne, yuh can't be mad with yuh baby. Come on...mi sorry how di other day went down. I was under a lot of pressure yuh nuh. Yuh nuh plan to mash us up for *that*?"

Mash us up? Roxanne was irate. *Is everybody losing their goddamn mind today? What the hell is in the air? The shit must be contagious!* She would have preferred to scream all that aloud.

"Andre, I mean Biggs..." She had never before referred to him by his stage name, but did so now intentionally. "I'm just tired right now. I'm not feeling so well either. Let me call yuh back later please." Her finger was poised to press end.

"Babes, why yuh calling me Biggs? Is break yuh wanna break up? Why yuh being so cold to yuh baby?"

His questioning intensified her headache.

151

She remained calm despite the urge to blow steam. *"Andre*, I'll call you back when I get up, okay?"

"Alright babes." He coolly replied. "Mek sure yuh call mi! I really miss yuh sexy body."

"Ugh!" She groaned and hung up.

Natalie returned home to the delicious smell of food that her husband definitely couldn't cook. She gently pushed in the door and for some instinctive reason, tip-toed through the hallway. She didn't know yet what she expected to find, or why her intuition felt like playing games with her.

She stopped at the kitchen entrance and thoroughly scanned the area; everything seemed in order.

Hmm! She thought to herself, and allowed her nose to lead her to the dining room. She immediately acknowledged the culprit sprawled off on the dining table.

Michael had ordered Chinese from their favourite restaurant, and had extended himself to neatly set the table with wine glasses and their individual wine preferences.

Natalie wasn't immediately sure how to process his unusual gesture, but checked her watch and realised it was Thursday.

Takeout had always been the jump start to their Thursday night routine for over thirteen years, followed by their over indulgence in wine sipping, and love making. That hadn't been the case in the last two months however, as they would often eat in silence; and the nights would end with her falling asleep upstairs, leaving her husband to watch sports or politics downstairs.

She could hear the TV blasting in the upstairs bedroom. As soon as she got to the stairs, the toilet upstairs flushed, and Michael's heavy footsteps thudded on the ceiling. She listened for another set of steps, just because.

"Hey, I'm back." She called out from the base of the stairs. "Did you eat? Or were you waiting?"

"I *was* waiting!" He shouted down at her. "But I stopped three hours ago. It didn't look like you were planning to come home." He was evidently pissed.

"Whatever Michael!" She airily replied more to herself than to him.

She helped herself to a hefty plate of food, poured a glass of red wine, and brought supper over to the den. She turned on the TIVO to catch up on *Sex and the City*, and got comfortable in the couch.

While she ate, sipped, and laughed at the never-ending drama-filled lives of her favourite Hollywood girls, Michael thudded down the stairs mumbling under his breath.

Her shoulders reflexively tensed in anticipation of the impending drama, and she purposefully avoided looking up in his direction.

"How long am I supposed to wait on you upstairs, while you sit and watch this stupid show? How about you come *sex* me in Kingston *City*?" He spoke sternly, his voice taunting.

"I'm sorry. Like you weren't expecting me to come home, I wasn't expecting you to wait up for me." She slowly turned her head away from the TV and eyed him defiantly. That's when she realised he was naked; handsomely so.

"Natalie, don't start with your *shit*! How long you plan to carry on arguing like this? I already answered all your goddamn questions! You plan to go back to being my wife, and stop being so damn selfish and spiteful? Or..." He purposely left the sentence hanging.

"Or what Michael? You might have to head out to the *club*? Hmm? Don't think I don't know about this *Club* of yours you've been frequenting! I'm on to you *husband*! You'd better get your act together and fast!"

As she eyed him with disdain, she turned off the tube and slammed the remote unto the sofa. She stormed up the stairs to lock herself in her haven; the bathroom.

By the time she returned to the bedroom, her eyes caught sight of him splayed across the bed, gently stroking himself to the tune of moans from the stereo system.

"At least you showered." He uttered without looking at her, fixated on the Latinas frolicking on the screen.

She impulsively rolled her eyes. "Showered for *what*? You wish!" Her tone was filled with ridicule.

Sitting on the edge of the bed, she pretended not to be bothered by his bedroom antics. While moisturizing her feet, her towel fell, incidentally exposing her bare back and the folds of her butt.

In one sudden motion, Michael whisked over to her and slid his tongue along her lower back, lingering by her butt crack.

"What the hell?" Natalie jumped up and screamed. "I already told you. Don't even think about it!" She fought to push back a smile.

"What the hell what? I'm getting my loving tonight Baby, whether or not you want to participate. Right junior?" He looked down at his erect, throbbing cock.

"Michael, I'm so not in the mood for you right now." She started to protest, though her mind led her to do otherwise. "Don't feel like this is going to be another one of your recent fuck sessions though! You're going to make love to your *wife* tonight!" She climbed into bed.

Michael climbed atop her for one of his award-winning sessions, as she held his gaze without emotion. He slid his hand down the side of her face, raised her head by her chin, and passionately kissed her mouth.

While expertly licking and kissing his way down her stomach, he gently massaged her perky nipples with his hand. When he got to her mid-section, he nestled in between her thighs and firmly restrained her.

With his 'no hands' policy in full effect, he used his tongue to spread the lips of her vulva, before using the tip to massage her inner folds. He made love circles around her hidden jewel, sometimes lightly grazing it with his teeth just the way that it pleased her.

"Mmm...mmm." Natalie moaned appreciatively, trying to work her way out of his hold.

Michael held onto her thighs firmly, not relinquishing any control of the intensity.

"I'm coming baby! Oh that feels so good! Don't stop!" She shrieked then whispered repeatedly in between deep breaths. Her body began to shudder.

"You're not getting away that easy baby." He professed while steadily penetrating her, mindful that she couldn't manage his entire length.

"Ahh!" The groan escaped her, signalling the cut off point. "No more baby..."

He ground her pinkness with slow, circular motions, while he adored her beautiful frame. *If you only knew how much I love you Natalie Carey-Simmons, you wouldn't act up over the dumb shit ignorant people say. I don't know how else to tell you or show you.*

"I'm coming!" Her loud outbursts interrupted his thoughts. "Oh fuck me Michael! I'm coming..."

He picked up the pace and leaned in closer for the climax. With every stroke and the clenching of her inner muscles, his own explosion neared the surface.

"Oh shit!" They both yelled, almost simultaneously.

Their heated, sweat-filled bodies tangled and tugged at each other in ecstasy.

Natalie collapsed first as gratification was duly achieved, and their love juices mingled.

"Fuck me Biggs! Give it to mi hard! Yeah, just like that!" Jules boisterously encouraged him.

Biggs pummelled mercilessly with each word of provocation. "So fling it up then nuh man! Yeah, spread it wide for mi! Just like dat! Yuh love the pressure?"

"Mi love it! Gimme the monster! Fuck mi Biggs!"

As his eruption neared, Biggs lost complete control and buried his entire manhood deep with a dreadful force.

"Yea, mi want come! Mi a come! Tek it inna yuh mouth fi mi baby." He transferred his dick from one dark cocoon to another, exploding with a loud guttural groan.

He plopped down onto the leather sofa and pulled his wallet out of his back pocket. He looked up at Jules, whose eyes were fixated on the wall-mounted flat screen televising the headline news.

His eyes strayed and landed on the ticker displaying at the bottom of the screen:

Body of 18 y.o. Ardenne High School female found dismantled in the Grant's Pen gully by local residents. Identity still unknown.

Biggs' jaws dropped as the student's ID picture was plastered at the top of the screen.

The reporter commented further that the victim, whose name was being withheld, had been raped, bludgeoned, and stabbed several times. The police were asking the public for any assistance with their investigation.

"Bloodclaat star...this can't be real!" He yelled aloud. "What the fuck!"

Jules turned around to catch Biggs entranced by the image on the screen. "What's wrong with you? Yuh know her? I was thinking she looks kinda familiar."

Biggs didn't reply for more reasons than one.

CHAPTER TEN

The classroom was in a raucous as Roxanne sauntered through the back door. Her classmates were seated atop desks in groups, and were heavily attuned to the morning's juiciest gossip. This unruly setting wasn't unfamiliar, but it was unusual given the time of day. It was already ten minutes into the first period class, and neither the homeroom nor the first period teacher was present.

One of the students seated in the middle of the large group acknowledged Roxanne's arrival as she walked towards her seat. She whispered something to the other students that made everyone abruptly quiet down and turn to look in her direction. The room was dead silent before she realised she had an audience.

"Is what?" Roxanne asked, staring at them defiantly. "What the hell oonu staring at me like that?" She mustered her defence in anticipation of the next move or response.

The headliner of the large group spoke first. "How are you feeling Roxanne? We didn't expect you to show up today that's all."

"Why wouldn't I show up? What, there's no school?" She began to wonder if Cindy had broadcasted to the entire school that she was hurling her intestines in the bathroom the day before.

"She doesn't seem to know." The words escaped from an unsuccessful whisper.

"I don't know what? What the hell is going on?" She dropped her book bag and prepared to fight.

The headliner got up and walked towards her.

"Roxanne, Cindy was murdered yesterday. It was all over the news last night."

Before Roxanne could realise it, her vision blurred and the room fell pitch black.

"Come in Shane." Natalie called out from the other side of the closed door. "I *am* expecting you, you know."

Shane walked in with a playful grin. "It doesn't matter. My momma told me to always knock at closed doors. What can I say? I'm a man with manners."

They both laughed, appreciating the ice breaker before he immediately cut to the chase.

"So Doc, this *is* the meeting you get real with me huh? Tell me that life as I *want* it is fuc...screwed, I mean." He made a quick adjustment.

"I don't concur with that, but yes I do have the results of the biopsy. I will need you to *listen* to me keenly though, without making up any theories of your own." She fidgeted with her pen while trying to match his piercing stare.

"Shane, there are cancerous cells in the innermost layer of your stomach lining. *However*, there is good news. You're only at stage one out of five, which is technically zero, known as carcinoma *in situ*. Diagnosis of this type of cancer also involves assigning a grade to describe the appearance and behaviour of the cells. In this area too, you are fortunate that the cells are merely *intestinal*, signifying that they grow much more slowly than other grades...where progression is concerned."

She paused to allow him to soak in all the details. "Now as for the treatment, like I've previously mentioned..."

Shane automatically tuned her out. *Better than I thought! Hmm, I'm definitely not starting any treatment right now! I have to go to qualifications and I'm definitely running at the Olympics. Whatever the worst that can happen from all this will just have to be! If the cells grow slow I should be good for the next six to seven months. I have to finish my career with a win in Beijing! I have to make my country proud. Fuck man! Fuck all this shit!*

"Shane!" Natalie spoke more loudly than she had intended after realising she had lost him.

He jolted out of his stupor. "Why the hell are you shouting? I heard you! I just don't need to hear all this! Your mouth is going at a mile per minute! My ears need a breather!" He stared blankly into her piercing eyes, defiantly ignoring her irritation.

"Doc, you *cannot* expect me to begin any form of treatment right now! As *I* discussed, that's not an option. I'm going to compete in the rest of my meets to close out the 2008 season. I'm going to Beijing! Now I'd much prefer to do that in my best shape ever, and *not* as a half dead puppy!"

"Well that it is exactly what you'll be if you wait this out!" She regretted the words the instant they escaped her mouth. "Shane..."

He rose to his feet and restrained his agitation. "Look, we'll talk treatment options when I'm done competing. Right now, I've got to run. Thanks *a lot*!"

She lost her composure. "You will *sit down*, and *listen to me* Shane! Where the hell are you going? If you walk out on me, you can find yourself another doctor!" She spoke sternly and aggressively.

He was appalled at the manner in which she commanded him. For some reason, he sat but avoided eye contact.

She continued regardless. "*I have had it* with your stubbornness in regards to this *very* serious situation!" She took a deep breath and composed herself.

"I know that you're horrified Shane, and I'd be lying if I said I knew *exactly* how you feel. But you have to allow me to help you decide what's best for you. Don't sleep on the fact that the cancer isn't the worst it could be. These things work with their own rhythm, Shane. We all know that

159

track is very important to you, and yes you want to make the country very proud. But what's more important to you? Your *life*? Or trophies and fame on a timeline? You go home and ask your family that question! Then you make the decision to disregard commencing immediate treatment!"

She reclined in her chair and stared at the ceiling as tears welled in her eyes. Overwhelmed with her personal problems and emotionally distraught at the present situation, it was the most natural reaction for the moment.

Shane reached across the desk to comfort her, not expecting that she'd pull away.

"Okay then. Listen, I'm sorry for upsetting you like this Natalie." He hardly ever referred to her by her fist name in public. "But like you said, you'll never understand what I'm going through." With that, he rose and left.

Biggs sat beside Benji on the trunk of his car. The two were heavily immersed in a serious 'reasoning'. He lit up a spliff, took a drag, and then passed it to his friend.

"Jah know Benji star, mi feel it for yuh boss. Just gwan hold a meditation and easy mi bredda. Dem pussy yah nuh sure wha dem start."

"Trust mi yuh nuh Biggs! Dem ago pay fi wha dem do to Cindy! Mi ago mek sure a it *miself*! Mi thugs a look 'bout it now as we speak!" Benji took a deep drag off the joint and handed it over.

"I hear dat boss. Don't know what I'd do if it was Roxie. Some pussy woulda definitely feel it! Trust dat." He audibly exhaled. "Mi a try find Roxie too but I can't hear from her. She mussi still vex with mi to rass."

Benji zoned out and shook his head. "Yo mi did check for deh daughter deh bad yuh nuh...nah go lie to yuh. I did promise her seh *any* pussy that *fuck* wid her ago feel my wrath! Without regards to who! A just di odda day she a tell mi seh some fool a try tek her fi punk too yuh nuh, and mi tell her mi will handle it. Bloodclaat star! Yo mi a cut out yuh nuh Biggs! Need fi go tek care a some tings." He hopped off the trunk and dug into his pockets for his keys.

Biggs didn't hesitate to get off his car. "Alright big man. Tek it easy out there yuh hear that? Don't hesitate to link mi if yuh need mi." He knocked fist with Benji.

"Nuh watch nutt'n Biggs." He hopped into his car and reversed out of the parking lot with lightening speed.

Roxanne's eyes lightly fluttered as she steadily regained consciousness. Almost instinctively, she looked about her surroundings for any indication of where she was or what had happened. She tried to brace herself into a seating position on the bed, but quickly closed her eyes as her vision blurred to each throbbing pain in her head.

On her second attempt to sit forward, she began to realise that she was in the school nurse's office on one of the many twin beds. Not noticing any familiar face around her, she swung her legs over the edge of the bed to stand.

"I wouldn't do that if I were you." The voice softly pierced the otherwise silent atmosphere.

Roxanne cautiously spun around and saw Shari sitting at the head of the bed. "Hey girl, what the hell happened to me? I got hit by a truck?" She tried to smile.

"Well you passed out in class and bumped your head on the way down too! Nurse said you'll have that headache and some dizziness for a little while. Your sis is coming to get you. How yuh feeling?"

"Like crap! I can hear my heartbeat in my head."

"That I can imagine. But I meant more about the whole incident and all. You guys were best friends. You were even crying in your sleep, and saying stuff."

As the events leading up to her black out slowly tingled her consciousness, her eyes immediately welled with tears. She momentarily grew nauseous.

"Is it really true Shari? Did Cindy really die?" The haggard look on her friend's face along with her unusually frazzled hair confirmed her deepest fear. She began to sob.

Shari's cheeks gleamed with tears as she got up and went over to comfort her friend. She lovingly embraced her, held her tightly, and allowed her to grieve.

"I'm so sorry Roxanne. I can't imagine how hard this must be for you. It'll be okay though honey; you'll be okay. Cindy's in a better place now is all. They'll get the murderers that did this to her. God will fix this. I know he will. We have to leave it to Him now."

Regina walked into the nurse's station and followed the sobbing sounds toward her baby sister. She stepped with such urgency that she hadn't heard the nurse calling out to her at the entryway.

"Oh Roxanne! I'm here sweetie. Let's go home." She quickly gathered her sister's belongings.

Nurse Willis joined them, briefly introduced herself to Regina, and handed her a paper bag containing pain killers. After explaining the dosage, she reminded her to take Roxanne to the doctor as soon as possible for a more in-depth analysis of her head injury.

Shari helped Roxanne to her feet and followed behind Regina into the staff parking lot. She assisted her into the back seat, and encouraged her to lie down.

"Get some rest Rox, and call me later if you need to talk." She hugged her once more before closing the door and waving goodbye.

"Thanks a lot for staying with her." Regina indirectly mentioned. "I didn't get your name." She looked in the young girl's direction.

"It's Shari; Shari Davis."

Regina smiled. "Well thanks a million Shari. It was really nice of you to sit with her."

"No prob Regina. You know, you two look a lot alike."

"Yeah, so we've heard." She grinned. "Thanks again Shari." She climbed into the car and saddled up for the journey ahead.

Stacy had left the doctor's office with a bittersweet sensation. She had confided a wide array of her problems to Natalie, who in turn had listened attentively and offered sound advice. If anyone would ask, she would have to admit that she liked the woman. She respected her for being someone in the position to snob or critique her life, but treated her without an air of judgement or disdain.

Still, she couldn't deny that she was jealous of Natalie. She was extremely jealous of what she had. In her opinion, she had the perfect life, living out her dreams to the most intricate detail with which she had planned it. She seemed extremely happy and confident in her perfect, protected world. When she had learned that they were the same age, it had only heightened the resentment.

Maybe it's the age thing. She sat at her desk and quietly seethed inside. *Yes, it's definitely her accomplishments. If I had only kept my life in order and finished up school...I could've been the woman with the career. I was smart enough...I had the brains! But no, I preferred to roam the damn streets and make money the easy way! In the name of nice clothes and jewellery, I dropped out of school and became a nobody! Then came crassis Savage, and the next thing I know I'm pregnant! God knows I always hated that invalid! But the money, I loved spending every dollar! Now I'm stuck with fucking Savage while Doc gets to be happily married to the man of my fucking dreams. The one man any woman in the world would be lucky enough to spend the rest of her life with. My Michael Simmons! I deserve him!*

Regina walked out of ear shot before continuing her phone conversation with Shane.

"Roxanne's asleep right now. I gave her two of those pain killers and she knocked out completely. This situation is so unfortunate Shane. What business could anyone have to murder an eighteen year old like that? And throw her in the gutter? Like seriously…"

"I don't know Gina. I mean who knows what she was involved in? These young girls nowadays nuh easy yuh nuh. Yuh can't swear for them. But it's sad all the same."

"Definitely! I asked Roxanne if she wanted to go to the doctor but she insisted she was okay. What you think?"

"Well, you can't rope her up and force her. If the pain gets too intense she'll change her mind. She'll let you know when it's necessary."

"I guess. So what yuh were saying about the doctor visit this morning now?" She sat at the kitchen counter and plugged her cell onto the charger.

"Gina, tell me why mom called my doctor this morning and straight up quizzed her! I don't know if I told you that I found out they knew each other from NY."

Her jaws dropped. "No! You didn't give me much of the New York trip details. What happened though?" She silently rejoiced that his mom was in the know.

"Well apparently mom was in charge of her training hours at the hospital. So the night we were at the house looking at pics in the album and I spotted Doc's face. I nearly shit! The fam tried to make a big deal out of my weirdness but I played it cool. Cool enough for everyone *except* Tina! She must've known that Natalie is an oncologist now so she couldn't leave it alone. So *of course* she decided to investigate!"

"I bet! That must've been really awkward trying to play that off. So I guess you confessed about the cancer?"

"Gina, please don't start with the nagging!"

"So you *didn't* confess? I swear Shane..."

"No need to swear Gina! I'm going to tell her, don't worry. Just trying to think of the best way and the right time. Anyways, yuh planning to go back to work today?"

"I didn't plan to, but I'm going to. I have some files to attend to." She got up to prepare lunch for Roxanne.

"I see. Well I'll take you for a late lunch. I'll call you back with the details and the time though."

"Alright just call me then."

"Okay hun. Talk to you later...love you."

"Love you too Shane." She hung up.

She wrote a note for her sister with instructions about the medication and placed it beside the sandwiches she had prepared. On her way out, she stopped to check in on Roxanne; she was fast asleep. Regina left the house and dialled Linton.

Biggs sat in his truck and contemplated the dilemma surrounding Cindy. He repeatedly replayed the scenario with Benji at the studio earlier, and each time he was more certain of the air of awkwardness between them.

For some reason, his friend had avoided all eye contact with him and had behaved more aloof than usual. Not to mention the way he'd dryly disregarded his offer of assistance and sped out of the parking lot. The thought made him uncomfortable, and more so, suspicious.

His cell phone vibrated somewhere and he quickly tussled to find it.

"Hello." He answered before the final ring.

"Hey Andre! You were calling me? Yuh heard what happened to Cindy?" Roxanne was in a frenzy.

"Yes babes. I've been trying to find you. I found out last night. How yuh feeling?" He knew that was a dumb question the minute it escaped his mouth.

She began to sob. "It really hurts you know... especially since we weren't talking. I just feel really bad that I didn't forgive her. She tried..."

He listened without interruption as guilt seeped into his consciousness.

"I shouldn't have let you come between us! I should've forgiven her when she tried to apologise." She cried freely and spoke her mind.

Biggs wasn't much for emotions and he didn't know what she expected him to say to her. "Roxanne, you want me to come and get you? You shouldn't be alone right now babes." He eagerly awaited her response because he didn't want to be alone right now.

"I guess you can do that. Bring me some Burger King too I'm starving." She muttered in between sobs.

"Alright babes. I'll be there in half an hour."

He hung up and hurriedly backed his Range out of the parking lot, speeding off to please his Roxie.

"So how was the visit?" Regina asked Stacy as soon as she strolled into the office.

"It was real cool Regina. Natalie's really nice like you said, and extremely patient. Thanks a lot!"

"I'm glad. If anybody can sort you out, it'll be her. She's nice, but she'll keep it real with you."

"I gathered that. How's Roxanne doing by the way?" She was eager to change the topic.

"She's okay I guess. I left her at home sleeping. This is going to be really rough for her, a first hand experience with death. But she'll be okay. Is Hugh coming back after his meeting?"

"Girl, it's Friday." Stacy quizzically eyed her.

"Yeah, dumb question!"

They both laughed.

Stacy went against her own will and decided to test the waters. "Regina, do you know Natalie's husband?"

Regina turned to face her, instinctively wondering why she would ask such an irrelevant question. Instantly, she remembered that she had intended to ask her why Michael's name was scribbled in her diary. She opted to play coy and subtly responded.

"Yes, his name is Michael Simmons. Why you ask? You met him there?"

"No!" Stacy quickly replied. "He just came up in *all* our conversations. Natalie was so happy and excited when she spoke of him. I was just wondering what kind of man he was."

"He's pretty chill. He's a lawyer. A man for all seasons, I guess. He loves his wife and takes good care of her. They've been together for centuries against *all* odds!" She smiled at Stacy, who was visibly flustered.

"Nice." She left it at that.

Regina saw more than 'nice' in her eyes, and heard a lot more in her tone. *Whatever you're thinking or planning get over it honey! You don't stand a chance with this one! Plus you'd have to go through me!* She picked up some files and headed to the door.

"Anyhow darling, I have a lunch date with my BFF. Don't think I'm coming back today either so enjoy your weekend." She winked at her.

"Enjoy your weekend too girl, and thanks again for the reference." Stacy was eager to be alone.

"Oh no sweat." Regina airily replied, but secretly eyed her until she bent the corner.

Roxanne slowly climbed into Biggs' truck. "Hey, thanks for coming so quickly." She spoke in a whisper.

He immediately switched off the radio. "I told you I was nearby babes." He gave her a gentle, but prolonged hug. "I really missed yuh Roxie. How's your head?" He handed her the Burger King and pointed to her soda in the cup holder.

"A little better. Thanks for the food." She buckled into the seat.

"No prob babes. All with that bruise yuh still beautiful eeh…" He tensed in anticipation of her response.

"Funny! But I really missed you too. Where we going anyway?"

"Over to the Hilton to chill out for a bit. I have to get something from someone there so I just got a room." He hoped to avoid an interview.

It didn't work. "Why yuh getting a room at the Hilton? What happen to your house?"

"Doing some work on it so a lot of workmen and noise over there. It'll be too much for you." He didn't even flinch.

What-ever! Roxanne mentally snapped, but calmly replied. "I hear yuh." She turned to look out the window to avoid looking in his direction.

His cell phone vibrated on the dash board and he hastily snatched it up to look at the number.

"Hello." He spoke as if he was annoyed.

Roxanne had already glimpsed the screen. *Home huh?* She listened to the one-sided conversation and seethed inside as the female voice drilled him.

"I'm on the road handling some stuff. You know how it goes…" He tried to sound casual. "So just call and order something. Easy thing that; one, two, three." He shifted in his seat. "Of course, you know that." He peeked in Roxanne's direction. "What? Alright…just go easy wid. No time for dem argument deh ya now. Hmm…*anything*!

Likkle more." He hung up as he pulled up to the valet parking at the Hilton Kingston Hotel, feeling overwhelmed.

He felt threatened by his best friend, despised by his girlfriend, and disgusted with his woman at home. He was fervently greeted by the young valet driver, who willingly accepted the keys to his Range.

"Tek yuh time with the ride yuh nuh. Yuh can't afford it!" He sternly warned him before walking away.

Roxanne followed him closely into the wide-spaced lobby, and to the front desk for check in. She tried to control her temper as the attendant offered Biggs *complimentary* extras with much fanfare, evidently uncaring that he had walked in with someone. She had told herself that the woman was merely doing her job, until she looked over in her direction and subtly rolled her eyes.

She forcefully elbowed Biggs and stepped closer. "Yuh going to stand there and let that bitch disrespect me like that Andre?" She spoke sternly, looking from his face to the woman's.

"What yuh talking about babes? What she did?" He looked from his unruly woman to the clerk.

"You didn't see that nasty look she gave me? And flirting with yuh the whole time? Nobody get so many *complimentary* shit in one stay!"

"Babes yuh being ridiculous." His face flushed with embarrassment. "Terriann was just doing her job! I *am* a celebrity you know? I do get a lot of free *shit*. It's all a part of the business babes." He was about to return his attention to checking-in, when Roxanne blurted.

"Whatever! Yuh just saying that cause you fucking her!" She crossed her arms and reflexively rolled her eyes.

The situation suddenly became a scene. All eyes were now fixed in their direction and everyone was on alert.

Roxanne knew better than to embarrass Biggs in front of an audience, and he knew better than to slap her solid across the jaw.

He held her firmly by her upper arm, pulled her closer, and plunged his tongue down her throat. Slightly pulling back, he spoke closely by her face.

"Yuh happy now? You're *my* girl! Don't matter what no other bitch wanna do or not do! Jus cool yuhself!"

Terriann was noticeably shocked and displeased; that pleased Roxanne entirely.

"Alright *baby*." She whispered in her sexiest voice, as she played up her role. "I'm sorry about that Miss *Toni*-ann. As you were..." She smiled her most devious smile, revelling in the fact that Biggs just claimed her in view of some of Kingston's nosiest and finest residents.

He snatched the room key from the woman's rigid grip and hauled Roxanne away.

"Yuh really tripping Roxie. Don't feel like cause yuh get weh while ago yuh can do that shit again!" He scolded her as they headed towards the elevators. "Don't *ever* disrespect me like that again! Ever! *Especially* in public!"

When the elevator doors slid open, Roxanne's eyes widened and her jaw instantly dropped.

Linton stepped out of the elevator, leaving Michael behind. He was about to continue their prior argument, but stopped in his tracks when his eyes absorbed the image before him.

"Roxanne, what the hell are you doing at the Hilton? Your sister called and said you were home sick. And who is this grown ass *man*?" He had more questions but no time.

Biggs looked up and interjected. "Question is, who the hell are you? And why yuh asking ma woman so many *damn* questions?" He stepped in between the two.

Linton chuckled. "You don't need to know who I am! *Your woman*? That girl is seventeen years old! I'd shut the fuck up if I were you! She's jailbait!" He stood his ground and tried to quell the anger rising within.

Biggs stepped closer towards him, but Roxanne moved quicker and held unto him.

"Andre just relax! He's my sister's boyfriend, Linton." She looked back and forth between the men that were ready to throw down and knock each other out.

Biggs took two steps backwards and laughed. "Fool, regardless of who yuh *think* yuh are, yuh need fi watch how yuh a talk to people yuh nuh! Know yuh place in society yuh hear dat?" He patted his waist as he spoke, aiming to intimidate.

Linton mirrored his action, smiled, and spoke. "My place set inna stone 'hurrycome'! A nuh never see, come see dis! Roxanne, let's go!" He firmly held unto her arm and pulled her towards him.

Biggs hastily clutched her other arm. "She not going nowhere but upstairs yuh nuh big man! Take yuh hand off ma girl before yuh cause a scene." He pulled her back towards him.

Linton stared into Roxanne's eyes and silently dared her to make a wrong move. "Regina's not gonna like this. I can *assure* you of that!"

Biggs chuckled. "Funny thing is, she won't even find out!" He spoke with much certainty.

Roxanne looked up at her man, wondering what exactly he had planned. She personally couldn't think of a better decision than to leave with Linton.

He looked beyond Linton and towards his companion. "Isn't that right Mister Simmons?" He asked, chuckling mischievously. "The sis wont find out right?"

All eyes were now on Michael.

"Right..." He grimaced as he airily replied, avoiding his brother's stare while rubbing his head nervously.

Linton turned back to look at Biggs, who was already positioned for their eyes to meet.

"You see, *little* brother?" Biggs pulled Roxanne closer. "It's already taken care of."

Forcing a laugh, he stepped into the second elevator that had just popped open in front of them. He winked at Linton as the door closed.

"What the hell was that about?" Linton shouted. "What the hell Michael? And how the fuck you just lean back there the whole time this fool was stepping to me? *Fuck*!"

Some guests turned to look in their direction as Michael wilted like a rose under the pressure.

"Man, you know I don't get into the heat like you… can't take it!" He tried to pacify his hot-tempered brother.

"You're this close to getting into some!" Linton demonstrated with his fingers. "Roxanne is seventeen! Gimme one reason!" He looked to see which floor the elevator would stop on, and moved towards the door.

Michael quickly clutched his arm. "Alright man! I'll tell you two! Let's walk…please?" He hurriedly stepped ahead, but ensured that he was being closely followed.

The two exited the lobby under heavy surveillance.

In the parking lot, Michael's cell rang as they got to his car. He checked the name display and reflexively put his hand to his forehead. *Great timing!* He mused.

"Hello." He spoke irritably, and watched as Linton impatiently hopped into the passenger seat. "*What*? And what the hell do you expect *me* to do exactly?" He barked into the phone. "That's not *exactly* my line of work!"

He turned his back to the car and leaned on the door. "You're crazy! Nuts if you ask me! Call the police then… *call my what*?" Michael shrieked. "And how do you propose to do that? *What*? For *what*?" He stomped the driver door with his heel and massaged his throbbing head.

"Listen, I'm sorry for shouting." He channelled his zen. "It's been a terrible day for me. I'll make some calls and get it done. Just take it easy 'til I call you back." He hung up and exhaled with an obnoxious growl.

Linton straightened up in his seat as soon as his brother spun around. He purposely re-plastered his previous scowl, and readied to execute his verbal attack.

"You're really into some shit aren't you?" He asked as Michael opened the driver door and climbed into the car.

"You wouldn't believe it bro. I don't even know where to begin…" He shook his head in distress. "I guess what happened back there is a good start…"

CHAPTER ELEVEN

*C*lap! The sound of the bullet exiting the barrel echoed throughout the air. The commentator revved up the full-to-capacity stadium with the famous 'And they're off', turning the attention now to the matter at hand.

The top seven male sprinters of the world exited the blocks at lightening speeds, commencing the one hundred meter dash at the Melbourne Grand Prix in Australia.

Shane competed from lane three to affirm his title as 'The Fastest Man in the World'. In lane two to his left was his main rival, the American Tyson Blake.

Fifty meters into the race, the two champions seemed to be the only competitors, running side by side, in a race of eight. Ten meters away from the finish, Shane, with a jolt of seemingly superhuman energy, bolted ahead to cross the finish line. He clocked the world's fastest time of 9.75 seconds and set a new world record. The title was duly his.

Jamaicans all across the world were watching the televised races and celebrating their number one athlete. In the heart of the Half Way Tree square in Kingston, residents lined the streets and shouted cries of appreciation and approval.

"A my runner dat man! The American dem need fi know dem place roun here." One lady shouted at the camera crew from a corner shop.

"All the 'steriles' dem a swallow and still can't stop my Shane! Mad!" Another man shouted from a bus window.

Back in Australia, Shane was busy conducting his second and most important interview with Jamaica's own network CVM TV. He was still trying to catch his breath as he tried to explain to Grace, the reporter, his inner thoughts at the mind-blowing fifty-meter mark.

"I knew I had him at that point..." He was breathless. "I knew if he couldn't pass me then, he wouldn't pass...at all! I know his race real well. It was over for him at that point." He smiled and waved into the camera at the well-wishers.

"Anything else you'd like to say at this time Shane?" Grace asked him sporting a wide grin.

"*Big up* Jamaica! We're *back* on top!" He mustered enough energy to shout into the mic. "Mom, this one's for you..." His sentence involuntarily trailed off.

The images within the next few seconds were chaotic and unexpected. The live broadcast immediately ended.

Due to the delays in dropping the live telecast, viewers observed as Shane Wright collapsed on national TV.

In Jamaica, everybody who was anybody was on their cell phones frantically notifying the next person. Some women were even seen crying as they speculated on the causes, and evidently came up with nothing positive.

In New York, Tina's proud smile had immediately disappeared from her face. Her tears of joy were recruited by sorrow. The Wright household was in a state of disarray.

Sheldon frantically dialled his brother's cell number on impulse, to avoid feeling anything but helpless. He tried to maintain his composure, and pacify his restless siblings.

Lisa cried silent tears of fear and guilt. She whispered a silent prayer begging God to spare her man.

Tina clutched her heart and by sheer intuition, dialled the number she had stored to speed dial.

Natalie watched from her living room couch as her deepest fears manifested right before her eyes. She stared, open-mouthed, at what she had just witnessed on her television screen. Her cell phone vibrated beside her, and impulsively, she picked up. She opened her mouth to speak, but the words didn't come. Her eyes immediately welled with tears.

Tina's sobs flooded the line as she blurted rampant questions like a court trial gone wrong.

"Please!" She pleaded between sobs. "Please tell me the truth! Tell me what's going on with Shane! I'm begging you Natalie, as my friend."

Natalie's heart weighed heavily. "Tina, I'm so sorry…" She paused to contemplate her next words.

"Natalie, I know all about the doctor-patient privileges. I just want to know what's wrong with my baby." She was sobbing more loudly.

Natalie began to sob, much to the keen observation of her husband. "It's cancer Tina…in his stomach. I told him to start the treatment. I told him competing was risky…" She caught herself rambling. "He told me he'd tell you. That's what he promised…" She fumbled for the right words as her friend wailed uncontrollably.

"Hello! Who's this? Tell me what you said to my mother." Tina was done for the moment.

*Not the brothers too. This is too much…*Natalie thought to herself. "This is Doctor Natalie…" She subtly replied.

"Hi Natalie! I'm Sheldon, Shane's brother. What's wrong with him? He's sick aint he?"

"Yes Sheldon, your brother's ill. He has…" She caught herself and stopped. "Listen hun, I'm really sorry about all this. I'd prefer your mom explain things to you. Please tell her I'm here when she needs me. I have to go." She hung up and made a dash past Michael towards the upstairs bathroom.

Inside the Mitchell household, devastation had blown through like a mid-June hurricane; chaos had settled in its aftermath.

Regina curled up like a foetus in the living room chair, channelling her fears and guilt through tears. After witnessing her best friend take a heart-wrenching tumble on live TV, she had relayed his eventful week to Linton in between sobs. Eventually, she had broken down beyond comprehension.

Linton on the other hand had held her the entire time, staying close by. He made an effort to not only console, but motivate her to remain positive during such an ordeal.

Roxanne had initially gotten emotional as a natural reflex in response to her sister's meltdown. However when she realized and understood Shane's true predicament, she empathised and sobbed as well. Her tears held mixed emotions however.

Her personal life was a mess, starting with her relationship with Linton. It had been strained since running into him at the hotel, and the tension between them in the house was noticeably awkward. She was fully aware of his scornful glances, and his desperate attempts to avoid unnecessary contact and conversations with her.

Unfortunately, the current discomfort at home was about to amplify.

With Shari's insistence and assistance, she had taken a pregnancy test and to her dismay, it was positive. By her calculation she was about two months pregnant though she had been 'spotting'; per her friend's calculation, an abortion must be scheduled immediately.

'Biggs don't want no more baby-mothers!' Shari had concluded. That's more drama for him! Everything is gonna change. Don't be stupid Roxanne! Think smart, and *fast*!'

She had also mentioned that *everyone* was having abortions these days, and that she shouldn't be ashamed.

Roxanne sat on the edge of her bed and cried the last of her silent tears. *What the hell am I going to do now? Regina would kill me if she found out. I really messed up this time...really wasn't smart. I wish I had Cindy to talk to right now...she'd know exactly how to get through this. Cindy, if you can hear me please tell me what to do. I'm so sorry for not listening to you that day in the bathroom... sorry for not being a true friend and forgiving you. God please help me! Abortion? I know that's a one way pass to hell...no detours...no limbo. But then what? Shari was probably right that Andre would never treat me the same! I'd just be another baby-mother that he throws to the side.*

All the pondering couldn't save her, and only served to intensify her paranoia. She began to sob again. *What am I going to do? I'm too young for this! I'm so lost!*

"Jules, how man a call yuh phone and a get bare voicemail? A dat me a pay yuh bill for?" Biggs barked irritably.

"Sorry Biggs, I was in class! I got here as soon as I could after I checked the messages."

"As soon as yuh could? Mi shouldn't affi lef nuh message! Ansa as I call, yuh hear dat? Dat mi seh!"

"Yes Biggs."

"Drop yuh clothes inna di meantime nuh! A nuh whole day affair yuh nuh!" Biggs hurriedly walked out of the studio and headed into the main hall.

When he returned, his dick immediately sprung forward at first sight of the nude enticement; Jules had already assumed the position.

He slammed the door and hastily unbuckled his pants, slipping on a condom in the same swift motion.

"Bloodclaat Jules! Mi just love fuck yuh!" He spared no time. "No matta how much u get pon mi nerves! Fling up di ass for daddy! Take all a di cocky inna yuh bloodclaat!" He forcefully pummelled his way.

Jules rocked back and forth to easily welcome his ten-inch penetration. "Fuck mi Biggs! Fuck mi hard!"

Biggs relinquished complete control and did as instructed. "Yea, yuh love hot fuck? Tek stab!" He quickened and strengthened his strokes, ruthlessly ruffling the inner walls of the exit-only cocoon.

The studio was unusually busy for a Thursday night, but Biggs couldn't resist the sexual urge for some ghetto loving. He listened to the footsteps going up and down the corridors, revelling in the excitement of his daring actions.

Suddenly, there was a firm knock on the door.

"Biggs yuh in there?" The male voice on the opposite side called out. "Big man, I see yuh truck parked in the front!"

Biggs motioned to Jules to remain quiet as he delivered slow, long strokes and continued to ignore the demanding intruder. He swiftly spun around when the knob noisily turned and the door creaked open.

Only then he realised that he had forgotten to lock it. Before he could react, the door swung wide open and he was standing face to face with Cilon.

"Big man, I have the finished tracks for yuh." Cilon instinctively surveyed the room for a glimpse of Biggs' prolific bouts with the *schoolas*. "Why yuh never just shout out seh yuh *busy* boss?" He teased and tossed the CDs unto the desk, but wasn't exiting the room fast enough for Biggs.

"Whappen?" Biggs barked. "Watch yuh a watch mi ass boss? Come out nuh man! Yuh nuh see mi naked?" He continued with grave disdain. "If yuh knock the door and nuh get a 'come in', dat nuh mean mi busy? It mean let yuhself in?"

Cilon was not moved by the artists' rashness, but was keen to his unusual discomfort. He had been a witness to too many of Biggs' sexual encounters for him to be so angered on this occasion. He steadily walked backwards out of the room, but continued to scrutinise his immediate surroundings.

Khaki uniform...a which girl school dat? He pondered as he exited and closed the door.

Linton enjoyed some alone time in his Evolution, shining the interior with Armor-All. He had ventured outside to wash his car when the emotions in the house became overwhelming. He had decided to call his brother not only to compare notes, but to reinforce that he tie up his loose ends.

"But Linton..." Michael was saying. "Why doesn't she want to have my baby, man? I'm beginning to take this shit personal. We have assets, a sturdy cash flow, and everything we could possibly need! I don't see the need for the hold up."

"Maybe it *is* personal!" Linton jabbed. "With all those late nights you be telling me about...you fooling around that strip club...it's only a matter of time before Nat catches up to you. And don't have her call my house and stir up Regina either! I'm not going down with you for this!"

"What you saying bro? You gonna snitch on me? Leave me hanging like that?" Michael laughed.

"Yeah! That's exactly what I'm saying. Remember how you left me at the Hilton? Just like that!" He couldn't forego the opportunity.

"You still on that man? That's almost three weeks ago."

"Don't matter stupid! The shit continues to spill over. I can't even look Roxanne in the face without wanting to slap her, and I'm lying to Regina for every day I don't say something to her! All because of you! Like I don't have my own shit going on over here with this moving to Cayman bullshit! Fuck man!"

180

"I'm sorry bro. I know what you're saying. So you decided if you're going to move yet? I think you should man…Regina's a great woman."

"Oh! You're giving advice on *great women* now? Tell me, how do *you* treat those, big brother?"

"Whoa! I'm trying to help *you* out! I'm just saying you should go. Especially since she's busy making plans to go with or *without* your sorry ass! Don't miss that boat bro, you'll regret it later."

"I regret *a lot* of things! I'm just trying to weigh out *when* I would have to go there."

"Hmm…" The conversation went silent.

Linton bridged the gap. "How's Natalie doing anyhow? I heard earlier she's the superstar's doctor."

They both chuckled at his cynicism.

"Yeah…she's *his* doctor alright!" Michael sarcastically remarked, still laughing.

"Whoa! What the hell is *that* suppose to mean? She's *his* doctor? You jealous of that guy man? That sounded kinda personal." He laughed at his brother.

"Nope! Not as jealous as you. Just the way she's up there bawling and carrying on though…didn't sit well with me. It's funny 'cause she's always talking about this athlete patient, so young and yadda yadda much more than she talks about any other one. Now I know who he is, and it doesn't help that he's a handsome brother…is all I'm saying."

"You see why men shouldn't mess around man? You know where I'm going with this right? *Do you see why you should keep your dumb ass quiet*? Now you got trust issues building within you. You're crazy man! Not Natalie! *Anybody* but her!" He switched the disc in his stereo player to a Dancehall mix.

Michael audibly exhaled. "Whatever…I'm not stressed. Bro, I'm going to see if she needs anything, cool? We'll talk later if anything."

"Alright man, and get your shit fixed!" He hung up.

Biggs' voice suddenly spilled over the track that blasted through his speakers.

Linton immediately lost his cool. *"Pussy ass mothafucka! Talk shit yuh nuh know nutt'n about!"* He hastily ejected the disc and snapped it in two.

Stacy had spent over an hour on the phone with Regina while she frantically blabbered and sobbed. Because she had already made enough attempts to calm her down to no avail, she had resolved to let her vent until she had been relinquished.

No sooner had she hung up from Regina, when her cell phone buzzed again. She looked at the name display and a knot instantly formed in her stomach.

"Hello." She answered with little enthusiasm.

"Is wha? Yuh nuh happy to hear from mi?" Savage began to argue before even saying hello.

"Ecstatic! What's up?" She audibly exhaled.

"Hmm, yuh gwan man! Who over the house wid yuh? I want to see my son! And of course mi want some pum pum. And nuh worry, mi will pay yuh!"

"Everybody who lives here is here, Savage. And what makes yuh think I'm going to make yuh see Marlon after the stunt you pulled the last time? You're crazy!"

"He's my son! I can take him for the weekend without permission from no one!" He was forever ignorant. "Mi outside anyhow so open the door before me kick it dung!"

Stacy jumped up off the couch and hastily instructed her mother to disappear, while covering the mouthpiece of the phone. She welcomed the lady's tight embrace, and promised her not to worry before she retreated to the back.

Savage was in her ear counting down from ten, when she swung the front door open as he got to three.

"Oh! Yuh lucky!" He teased, and grabbed her by the waist to suck her face. "Mek mi seh hi to ma boy before I deal wid yuh. Marlon!" He shouted without regards to the hour.

Marlon came running out of his room and jumped unto his father. No matter how much Stacy and her mother hated Savage, she couldn't deny that he was a good father to his son, and that his son - their son, loved his father.

"Him handsome eh man? Look just like yuh madda!" Savage made much of his youngest. He put two thousand dollars in his pocket and kissed him on the cheek. "Gwan back to yuh room now yuh hear boy? Daddy love yuh whole heap!"

"Love you too daddy." He replied softly, and innocently glanced at his mother to see if she was displeased.

Marlon, at the tender age of three, was already very protective of his mother.

Savage turned to Stacy and licked his lips. "Gyal, yuh know how long mi want come check yuh? Yuh pussy been on ma mind like crazy! Bend ova and show mi it!"

Stacy stood her ground and stared at him with much disdain, but quickly started to undo her shorts when his smile instantly curled into a snare. She knew better than to upset him or flare his merciless temper.

"Yeah, see di fattest pussy deh! But hold on, weh yuh panty deh? A fuck yuh did a fuck before mi come?" He grabbed her by the arm and shoved her unto the couch, tearing away the rest of her shorts.

When he began to sniff her vagina, she instinctively began to protest. "Savage I wasn't doing anything. I just took a shower and was talking to my friend on the phone. My friend Regina from work…that runner that fainted is her best friend…she was crying and stuff." Though she was being honest, her body reflexively tensed knowing he would believe whatever suited him.

"Mek sure yuh nuh! Cause whoever a fuck yuh better a pay! Money in the bank, yuh hear dat?" He loudly commanded.

"Of course Savage." She hastily replied.

He eagerly kissed her vagina lips and sloppily moisturized her pinkness with his entire mouth.

She reflexively rolled her eyes whenever his face was buried then feigned ecstasy whenever he looked up.

In one hurried motion, he stood, dropped his pants, and motioned for her to return the favour.

As she moved closer towards him, the scent of stale cunt slowly penetrated her nostrils. Though repelled, she knew better than to even suggest to Savage that he had been with someone else before he got to her house.

Stacy held her breath, tucked away her pride, and took his four-inch dick inside her mouth. She worked her usual magic as he moaned and slowly pumped his groin, clinging to the back of her head.

He quickly pulled out of her mouth and barked. "Bend over di chair mek me mash yuh up bitch! Yeah, yuh feel deh sturdy cocky ya?" He was usually overconfident.

Savage anxiously wiggled his half swollen *boy*hood as Stacy assumed his favourite position. He marvelled at the way her heavy set cheeks, the size of two basketballs, enveloped his entire length as she groaned in feigned pain.

"Yeah! Fuck mi Savage! Gimme it real hard!" She vulgarly enticed him.

"A hard fuck yuh love? Alright then...tek stab! Tek stab!" He barked as he aggressively pummelled her.

"Yeah...like that." She whispered, smiling in private.

"Fling it up gimme den nuh man, and stop run from di cocky!" He slapped her on the butt and watched in amazement as it jiggled in response.

She steadily thumped harder against him, though careful not to seem as if she was trying to outdo him.

He pulled out of her vagina in one swift motion, as his eruption bypassed its target and shot over her shoulder. He bit down on her ass cheek, whimpering like a puppy.

Stacy felt dirty and cheap. *This should be the time when I tell you I'm out! The moment when I declare I'm done with all this shit! Ha! You'd just punch my head in and maybe even kill me! I have to find my own way out of this shit! I'm too old and so tired! Too much to lose now.*

"That was better than ever!" He blurted the exact words he'd used after their last session. "Yuh love this cocky huh?" He looked over at her lying on the couch.

She smiled and nodded in agreement.

"Yuh need money or yuh straight?"

"I'm straight." She lied.

"So what's wrong with yuh? Why yuh look so sad? Yuh nuh want mi leave? Yuh want come with mi?" He tooted his own horn.

She smiled inwardly. "I'm good babe...just tired I guess. It's been a long day."

He leaned in and kissed her mouth, covering her entire face with his huge, wet lips. He immediately proceeded to suck on her erect nipples, signalling he was ready for round two.

A small crowd gathered on the sidewalk watching a car filled with men speeding wildly up and down the middle of the street, stirring dust and causing a raucous.

"Yo see di fassy deh!" One man shouted through the window from the front seat and hopped from the vehicle before it screeched to a complete halt.

The back doors simultaneously swung open and three other men quickly ran off in the same direction as their companion. The driver remained in the car.

A group of teenaged boys stood idling by the street vendors in front of the school gates, until now. Upon noticing the commotion, one of them bolted away from the pack and made a dash across the school lawn, headed towards Emmett Park.

"Grab di pussy Craig! Don't mek him get weh!" One of the three men shouted to his comrade in the lead.

Craig was steadily gaining on the young man. But with all his effort, he still couldn't manage to outrun or grab a hold of him. His cronies were almost on his tail when the boy climbed and jumped over a fence, landing badly on his feet. He scaled the fence more expertly than his bait, and landed right on top of him - knee first.

The boy tussled with his opponent and finally stood up to run, but his legs wobbled beneath him offering little for support. Just then, a hard blow landed on the back of his neck. That's all he would remember, if ever.

"Dat him fi get man! Fuck up di bway!" One of the other men cheered on the assailant.

"Yuh think yuh coulda run foreva?" Craig blurted, as he forcefully sunk his foot into the boy's stomach. "Fire fi yuh battybway! Yuh can tek cock so tek kick!"

The trio laughed in unison.

Natalie shrieked at the top of her lungs as she emerged from her private bathroom, firmly gripping two pregnancy tests. The chemicals in her body had somehow reacted favourably with the indicator, and her worst fear had been confirmed.

There is no fucking way this can be happening! She screamed within, and stormed to her desk to gather her thoughts. *This is impossible! "Completely unbelievable!"* She screamed aloud.

On pulling her top drawer all the way out, she noticed that her diary was positioned different than the way she had placed it for over two years. She tried to remember the last time she had used it, but her memory served no use presently. She instantly paged Tameka and demanded her presence.

The soft tap came at the door as Tameka's head appeared into view. "Doc..."

"Tameka, did you go into this top drawer?" Natalie failed at keeping a neutral tone.

"Doc, you know I don't have business in your desk drawer. What's wrong? Is something missing?"

Of course she didn't! "No!" Natalie feigned a smile. "It's nothing. Don't worry about it. Thanks." She attempted an apology as she dismissed her assistant.

Your name is written all over this Michael 'Conniving' Simmons! You're the only other person with a key...and a motive! She was so immersed in the thought of someone being privy to her most intimate thoughts, that she had forgotten why she was initially angry.

"*Motherfucker!*" She screamed aloud as she felt around in the back of the drawer for her birth control pills.

She had ultimately decided to hide them at work to avoid confrontations with her desperate husband. She pulled out the strip of pills, and for the first time in months, carefully inspected the package. Everything seemed in order; that being the name on the package, and the number of missing and remaining pills.

Then how the fuck could I be pregnant? She was beginning to panic. She tossed the strip of pills unto the desk and the solution was instantly revealed.

The three remaining pills flew out of the pack and scattered about her desk. *What!* She seethed, scrutinising the back of the package. That's when she noticed that all the foils were already punctured.

That selfish motherfucker switched my pills! Tears reflexively welled in her eyes. *My own husband set me up? I'm pregnant with a setup child!* She began to sob. *I can't believe this! This is so embarrassing! This is not the life I chose for my firstborn! With all your late nights and philandering activities...this is the best plan you came up with? You don't dictate my life! I'll show you! I'll definitely show you again Mr. Simmons!*

Michael hastily answered his cell on the first ring, riding on his high from the previous evening.

"Hey hun, I was just thinking about you. You just left before I woke up. How are you this morning?"

"Nauseous! I'm sick to my *fucking* stomach! How are *you* feeling, my *husband*?"

He was immediately on edge. "Natalie, what's wrong? What have I done now?" He tried to remain calm but mentally prepared for what may come next.

"What's *right* would be a question with a shorter answer! Why the *fuck* did you switch my pills Michael?" She started to cry. "How could you be so fucking selfish?"

He leaned back in his chair, filled with relief that this wasn't about his extra-marital activities. "Are you saying you're pregnant?" He spoke calmly, while smiling.

"Don't patronize me Michael! You know that's *exactly what the fuck I'm saying*!" She lost complete control. "But you know what? It *definitely* won't be for long! *Us too*, may not be for much longer!" She was sobbing now. "I can't ever trust you after this! Don't come home tonight! You *disgust* me! Sleep at the *Club*! Ugh!"

"Hello! Hello!" Michael shouted into the phone before realising the phone line was dead.

He frantically tried to call her back but she refused to answer her cell or her private office line. She had even instructed her assistant to screen his calls.

He angrily slammed his fist unto the desk and without thought, swatted a few folders to the floor.

"I must've died and gone to hell!" He commented aloud. *First Linton's ready to squeal me out to Regina and move on with his life...then mom calls me to promise her that Linton will remain in Jamaica...and now Natalie? Lord knows she can fuck me from so many angles! And what the hell did 'not for long' mean? She wouldn't dare abort my seed a second time! She definitely wouldn't have to divorce me...I'd forfeit!* His cell phone sounded, startling him.

"Natalie!" He answered on impulse.

A female voice chuckled on the other line, causing him to check the call display.

Shit! The Devil... He thought to himself and spoke more sternly. "What do you want?"

"Why the sudden change in your tone baby? You're not happy to hear from me?" She giggled again.

"Caramel, I'm not in the mood for the games right now. Having a rough day actually. How may I help you?"

"I'm getting there baby, just gimme a minute. What's wrong? Problems with the *wife*?"

The undertone of that question ruffled him. "Not your business! Get to the point."

"I want to see yuh tonight. Come by the club around closing time. I got something for you."

"I can't...not tonight. What could you have for me anyhow?" He was still curious.

"When I see you I'll show you. I *need* to see you tonight! I wasn't asking!" She was overly feisty.

"Excuse me?" He chuckled. "You're getting way ahead of yourself there. Who the fuck do you think you are? And who are you talking to?"

"I'd say it's pretty late in the game to be asking about who I am! What I'm *willing* to do, should be a greater concern! My pussy been longing for you Michael Simmons. You always take me half way then bail. I want that dick to put me to bed tonight. Heard a lot about your love-making skills Mister *Chocolate Thunder...*" The last words rolled seductively off her tongue.

His jaw reflexively dropped. "What! What did you just call me?" He fumbled for words knowing well he had heard her use his wife's nickname.

"Oh I think you heard me perfectly. Tonight, see you around twelve. Don't keep me waiting!" She hung up.

You have got to be fucking kidding me! The phone slid from his grip and dissembled upon hitting the ground.

CHAPTER TWELVE

N atalie hung up from the realtor and leaned back in her chair feeling accomplished.

It had been two days since she had seen or spoken to Michael, though his efforts to contact her were rampant. She had to admit it was awkward sleeping in their bed without him, but the peace of mind was priceless.

She focused her energy on plans of realising her dream to open Kingston's first cancer treatment and support facility. Her realtor had just called to confirm that he had set up five appointments to meet with sellers in prime locations.

The decorating project that lay ahead had also become a guilty obsession of hers. She had even recruited Tameka - an Interior Decorating major - to join in on her frivolous expenditures and planning.

As she picked up the phone to dial her mom, Tameka burst through the door.

"Doc! Shane just called! Said he's coming over and he's in pain...a lot of pain!" She was breathless.

Natalie was too petrified to immediately react.

Shane's arrival at the airport was a media circus. Everyone wanted a piece of him, whether to solicit answers about their concerns or voice their appreciation.

The cameras snapped incessantly, and his track fans struggled to be captured in the moment. Of course, the questions surrounding his health bombarded him the most.

How are you feeling? What the hell happened? Good job kicking that fool's ass Shane! Are you ill? Shane mentally processed bits and pieces of their remarks as he smiled and waved in every direction. He shook the hands of the children who successfully penetrated his bodyguard-barrier. Never slowing his pace, he made it to his truck without commenting.

He hopped into the driver's side and took no time to prep his music and exit the parking lot, third in line with the police convoy. Though Coach had insisted on the security, he had personally requested that no sirens were used to avoid the unnecessary attention.

The police drove with him all the way to Constant Spring Golf Club, where they turned in the opposite direction with his dismissal.

Shane pulled into the Crown Plaza Business Center and parked in the 'No Parking' zone in front of the main building. He climbed out of the truck and put his best public face forward, and made his way to the doctor's office.

A few people recognized him on the way in, but they merely waved in his direction.

As soon as he got inside the lobby and cautiously scanned the room, he dropped all his guards.

"She's expecting you..." Tameka immediately pointed him towards Natalie's office. "And Shane, congrats on your win." Her smile weighed heavily with sympathy.

"Thanks Tameka." He offered a faint smile.

He opened the door to the office and was grieved to find Natalie in a seemingly worse condition than himself.

"Hey Doc, you look a mess." He tried to joke. "Hope that's not my fault. Not asking for a lecture though...please. Those pills you gave me..."

"Don't last forever." She interjected and looked up at him for the first time since he had entered.

Her heart was softened by the terror in his eyes, but she tried hard to mask that fact.

"Where's the bulk of the pain?" She asked, and scribbled notes in her file. "And how long have you had it?" She looked more to his body than his face for any indication.

Shane motioned over the middle, and to the left side of his abdomen. "At first I thought it was just indigestion from some late night junk so I had two Tums. But the pain was still there when I woke up the morning and it lulled around throughout the day. After that race man, the shit just intensified! It felt like my ribs were trying to take a bite out of my stomach!" He illustrated with his hands.

Natalie remained stoic, seemingly void of any emotions.

"Well your system has obviously adjusted to the Vicodin you're taking. Right now I can give you an injection of Morphine, a *stronger* pain killer. With the dosage that you *evidently* require at this *stage*, it's going to put you out. After this instance however, I don't know what you're going to do. I will not be injecting you on a daily basis, and this medication is not readily available in Jamaica. I'm sure you *could* make the necessary provisions though." She barely looked in his direction.

"Is there someone you may call to pick you up?" She continued when he didn't comment.

"Damn Natalie...I know you're upset with me. I get it! I guess you could call Regina for me...can you do that?"

She looked over at him and firmly held his stare. Her eyes involuntarily glistened with tears as she carefully structured her next words.

"Shane, are you willing to trade your life for track and field?" Her tears flowed freely.

He could no longer resist the urge to embrace her, even in his moment of pain.

"That's exactly what will happen to you Shane. That's what you're setting yourself up for. Chemotherapy is a long process, and the sooner you get started, the more effective it will be." She rambled in between sobs. "Your mother called me too. She knows everything. I'm sorry…"

That didn't surprise him at this point. He continued to hold her close, gently stroking the nape of her neck.

"You did what you had to Natalie. But can you pull it together and gimme that shot? I'm desperate here."

She gently pulled away and re-composed herself. "Okay, lie down on the couch." She had already prepared the dosage, and now carefully removed the plastic protector.

"You need to take this more seriously Shane. You really do! You should be out before you know it." She leaned over to check his vitals, but somehow their lips met.

Shane lovingly massaged her tongue with his.

Natalie didn't pull away; nor did she panic.

"So Lisa…I still have to say welcome to Jamaica respective of the circumstances." Tina tried to lighten the mood between them as they stood in line to go through immigration at Norman Manley airport.

Lisa smiled faintly. "Yeah, I know right." She kept her response to a minimum, observing her surroundings.

The two had barely spoken much to each other for the duration of their four-hour flight from New York. In their own way, each reflected on the days ahead or cried silent tears. Now they were both puffy-eyed and exhausted, waiting anxiously in the longest line.

Tina took two steps forward and continued.

"Well my dear, I'm sure we'll find time to do some sightseeing here and there…so not to worry. Of course that's if this line shortens by tonight, and we ever get the hell out of this wretched place."

They both chuckled at her usual cynicism, as Tina's cell phone rang.

"Hey Regina, how's it going darling?"

"Hey mom, everything is just going. You told me to call you when I got word from Shane. I'm about to pick him up from the doctor's office. Apparently he got an injection and he's knocked out."

"Okay, must be morphine. Well I'm actually here in Jamaica as we speak. We're waiting to get processed by immigration...*Lisa* and I." She added as a matter of fact.

"*Really*?" Regina was genuinely surprised. "That's the best news I've heard all day! I was dreading the thought of catering to Shane's every whim all by *myself*!" She joked and laughed. "Seriously, I'm glad. Do you have the directions to his new apartment?"

Tina repeated the instructions aloud as Lisa scribbled on a store receipt. "Perfect! I'll see you soon then Regina. You drive carefully now." She hung up and instantly offered. "That was Shane's *best* friend! You *must* know her, right?" She smiled at Lisa. *After all, she was my pick!*

Regina pulled into the parking lot and hurriedly ran towards Natalie's office ahead of Linton. She greeted Tameka as she stepped past her and into the private office.

Natalie stood as soon as she entered and eagerly welcomed her warm embrace.

"You alright girl?" Regina asked as she gently pulled away. "You don't look your best...everything okay?"

"I'm doing the best I can Regina. That's the most we can do right?" She smiled half-heartedly in an attempt to divert her friend's concern.

"So they say...whoever *they* are!" Regina joked, but got back to the issue at hand. "So how long is he gonna be out Nat?" She walked over to Shane and sat beside him.

"I hate seeing him like this." She reflexively wiped the drool from his cheek; and then the tear that had seeped from her eye. "Damn! He must be really *out*! Shane would never be caught drooling! Definitely not in public! He must really trust you!" She couldn't resist laughing.

Natalie smiled. "He could be out for another three hours or more. But you should wake him at one hour intervals...whether or not he goes right back to sleep. Try to get him to ingest something about four hours from now; a shake or something maybe. He told me he had lunch."

"Anything *else* I need to know? His mom's here anyhow, she'll definitely be calling you."

"*Tina's in Jamaica*!" Natalie almost shrieked.

"Yeah, she arrived with his girl today. They're at the airport as we speak."

"I see..." Natalie was caught off guard and it showed. "Well that's it then! Just get him home I guess."

Regina looked toward the door and noticed that Linton was nowhere in sight. "Can you call that dud outside for me?" She motioned to Tameka while retrieving Shane's truck keys from his pocket.

Linton strolled into the office looking fidgety and out of place. "Hi Natalie, how's it going? You ready babe?" He said all that without a breath.

"Hi Linton. I'm doing well, thanks for asking." Natalie airily responded.

"I've been ready!" Regina irritably blurted, tossing the keys in his direction. "You plan to help me carry him or you think I can manage?" They were always at odds whenever Shane was in the picture.

He purposely ignored her sarcasm and walked over to the chair, avoiding any proximity with Natalie.

Regina gently shook Shane by the shoulder, and pulled him into an upright seating position. "You're going home..."

Linton took over from there, lifting him to his feet and gripping him firmly around his waist.

"Alright Natalie, I'll keep you posted." She hugged her sister-in-law goodbye.

"You do that; and take good care of him. Tell Tina to call me when she gets a chance."

"I will. And Natalie, I know how you are with your secrecy but you *can* talk to me, whatever it is. You look like crap and I'm saying that with all my love."

"I know Regina. Thanks." Her eyes welled with tears. "Thanks for noticing..." She walked with them through the lobby and into the parking lot.

Roxanne sat beside Biggs on the over-sized suede couch in the hotel room that had recently become their meeting place. She was annoyed that he had demanded to see her without much notice, and she grew even more irritable when they had driven in the direction of the hotel.

She was more convinced now than before that he was lying about the renovation at his house.

"Andre, so what have the workmen done so far?" She asked casually.

"Which workmen?" He asked with a quizzical look as he flipped through the channels.

"The ones yuh claim fixing up your house! Those workmen!" She almost shouted at him.

"Oh! So why yuh never seh dat?" He tried to play it off. "They changed a couple of the bedroom doors, installed new ceiling fans, painted two of the rooms and some other crap like that. Why yuh ask? Yuh still pissed bout coming to the hotel? Yuh worried bout sup'm?"

"Not at all! But next time we meet up, I wanna go check out the renovations! My headache is long gone!"

"Okay then Roxie. There's no problem in that."

She was amazed by his insistent and emotionless responses. She knew he was playing games because her friend at school had spotted him at Fiction - a popular nightclub - earlier in the week dancing with this 'girl that

197

was definitely not Jamaican given her limited dancing skills'; she had said.

Though she never mentioned it to him, it constantly ruffled her feathers. "What's the real deal between us Andre?" The question came out of nowhere.

"What yuh mean Roxie? Wha yuh ago trip bout now? Why yuh so miserable lately?" He muted the TV and gave her his undivided attention.

"Can you just answer the question? What are the future plans for us?"

"Look in your crystal ball and tell me nuh! Sounds like yuh have the future in your palms." He smiled at her, though he saw that she wasn't amused. "Roxie right now, all I know is I really care about yuh and I'm trying my best to please yuh. That's as far into the future as my mind sees it. What exactly…"

"I'm pregnant." She impulsively blurted.

Biggs jumped up off the chair and stood directly in front of her. "Seh dat again!"

Roxanne deliberately avoided looking up at him. "I'm pregnant. I'm telling you just because. I don't expect anything from you." She added in defence.

"Roxie, yuh wouldn't understand how that statement just hurt mi a while ago. What yuh mean *you don't expect anything*?" He knelt in front of her and turned her face towards his. "How far is it?"

"About two months, plus or minus a week." She blushed involuntarily.

"So yuh happy to keep it right? I mean there *is no* other option! Yuh done tell mi already!" He tried to pull her closer and grew angry at her resistance. "What exactly yuh not telling mi Roxie? Sup'm not right wid yuh! A nuh my baby?" He firmly held her away from him, staring deeply into her eyes.

"*Of course* it's yours Andre! You're the only man I've ever been with. It's just…"

"Just what Roxie? Yuh nah dash weh mi belly! So if a dat yuh a tink bout, forget it!" He got up and went to the balcony to light up a spliff.

Roxanne sat motionless and observed him, his reactions giving her a bittersweet sensation. On one hand, she was glad to hear that he was more supportive than Shari had presumed; but on the other, Regina's expected reaction and his womanizing ways unsettled her mind.

She walked over to the screen door. "Andre, it's not that I want to get rid of the baby. It's just...I didn't picture myself bringing a child into the world into an unstable home. I want to offer my child a better life than my mother ever provided for me. Some form of stability, you know?"

He took a drag on his joint and spoke without facing her. "Roxanne, how yuh baby wid me must have an unstable life? Who better than me can tek care of a child right now?"

"It's not always about money, Andre. There's more to raising a child than paying for everything. Starting with a healthy environment, I mean your lifestyle..."

"Whappen to my lifestyle Roxie?" He jumped up as if ready to attack. "A criticize time now? Lifestyle good enough for you but not for your baby?"

"And that attitude won't help." She was not afraid.

"Roxanne nuh mek mi rude to yuh yuh nuh!" He interjected with a roar. "I always maintain a level of respect for yuh but don't push it! Yuh attacking ma lifestyle and nuh expect mi fi have an attitude? Who yuh think yuh are? God?"

She continued unnerved. "Andre, let's stop pretending for a second that I'm your *only* girl...and that your priority right now isn't your career...and I wouldn't just become one of your many baby-mothers. Oh, and that I'm as important to you as you'd like me to believe...and that your *only* concern, at the beginning *and* end of each God-given day, isn't *you*?"

Andre Jackson sat in silence; Biggs roared in his place. "*Roxanne*! Mi nah go siddung yah so and mek yuh disrespect life as I know it yuh nuh. What the *fuck* yo? Yuh pass your place now. No matter how much woman or babymadda yuh think mi have, betta know seh none a dem nuh want fi nothing! All my kids are well taken care of! If yuh want dash weh yuh belly, mi can't stop yuh. But just mek sure yuh know seh me and yuh done! And trust mi, a nuh the last yuh ago hear of it!"

"Andre can you just calm down? I wasn't trying to upset yuh." Roxanne started to back away from the patio.

"Don't tell me fi calm down Roxie! Yuh a mi madda?" He jumped up off the chair and leaped towards her, stopping mere inches away from her face.

She froze in her place as her eyes glistened with tears. "I'm just scared Andre. I really didn't mean to disrespect or hurt yuh." The tears flowed freely. "There's just so much going on in my world right now. My household is a mess with the whole thing with Linton and you at the hotel. And the tension between him and my sister over this Cayman move…and then Cindy…" She started to sob now.

Biggs rushed to embrace her, rocking her slowly. "Babes, I know seh things aren't so smooth right now. But like I told you before, I'm here for you if you need me. You *never* call me before to seh this or that. If I don't call yuh, I don't hear from yuh. Roxanne, I really love yuh." The message came direct from his subconscious; he even surprised himself.

She pulled away from him slightly to look up at his face. "You really mean that Andre?" Her bright brown eyes stared straight into his soul.

He had to admit he did, without further thought.

Tina and Lisa relaxed in the back of the rented JUTA bus, in front of Shane's apartment. They anxiously awaited Regina's arrival, passing the time in their own way.

Tina caught up on Kingston's happenings with the driver Milton, who'd made sure to warn her that the city wasn't the same as it had been ten years ago when she had last visited.

Lisa sat staring out the window, and was the first to notice Shane's Lexus pulling up behind them.

"They're here!" She exclaimed, and hopped out the bus through the side door.

Tina hastily followed suit, asking Milton to back out of the parking space to give Regina closer access.

As Milton moved as instructed, Regina carefully pulled into the space, mindful of the two women following closely beside the wheels.

"Regina darling!" Tina happily greeted her as she opened the door. "Always taking care of my baby. I'm so grateful for you." She hugged her tightly.

"Of course Tina. Did you find the place okay?" She welcomed the embrace from her unofficial mother.

"Yeah, Milton had the directions down pat."

Regina wasn't amazed to hear that Tina had already gotten to first-name basis with the bus driver.

"And you must be Lisa..." Regina gave her a welcoming hug.

"Yes. Regina, it's so nice to finally meet you. I feel like I've known you forever." Lisa spoke with a warming smile. "I'm so glad you're here for Shane. I'm happy he has someone like you in these times."

Tina anxiously opened the back door of the truck to see her son. "Oh Shane!" She cried out, clutching her mouth and chest in fear and disbelief.

Lisa ran around to the opposite door. The minute she saw Shane sprawled out on the back seat, completely out of it, she immediately broke into tears.

Regina walked over to Linton who was patiently waiting in her car. He had been reluctant to drive Shane's truck from the doctor's office as she had originally intended.

"I'm gonna need your help to get him inside please. I know you have to get back to work so you can take my car. I'll come and pick it up at your office later."

Wanting nothing to do with her showing up at his office unannounced, he quickly offered. "Regina, that's too much up and down for you right now. I'll just catch a ride with the JUTA."

"Sounds good." She replied without hesitation.

After the men brought Shane into the downstairs guest room and left, the women settled about the house trying to overcome the emotional roller coaster.

Tina vigilantly monitored her son's vitals and nursed his recuperating process. Periodically, she woke him to stabilize his shallow breathing as was customary with deep sedation. She was keen on being at his side - alone - at this crucial moment of his life, though she was disappointed that he had hidden such important details from her.

The words of Natalie's heart wrenching conversation constantly replayed in her mind. She found solace in reminiscing on his growing years, somehow reasoning with Shane telepathically.

You were always such a good kid my son...always striving to make your mom proud. Lord knows I lived through you for most of my life...you were always my foundation. You are my foundation! Always a kind boy... with the widest, most charismatic grin...laughing your way out of discipline. You always knew I had a soft spot for you. And then you are so protective of me and your brothers... they think so highly of you. You're the best big brother in the world.

But your stubbornness and fight for control is something else. Got that from your dad! Alright, maybe a little from me, but this is not the best time for it baby. You'll have to let your guards down for this one. Can't always be in complete control of everything that life throws at you. Sometimes you have to ride in the back seat and just let go and let God. Just let God, my son.

Regina kept Lisa's company in the living room, trying to make small talk over a large pepperoni pizza. She offered a few details about Shane's condition to his woman, while mindful not to drive her into insecurity nor overstep his boundaries.

Lisa listened attentively, keeping her words to a minimum as always. More than anything, she was anxious to spend some quality time with her man – alone. She wondered if his mother had a completely different agenda.

"Are you okay Lisa?" Regina stopped talking long enough to realise that she had lost her.

"Yeah...I'm sorry Regina." She smiled. "I just want to hold him. I've been missing him so much...been so worried about him daily. I felt so guilty around his family all this time. You know I wanted to come with him to JA the last time? But he was adamant that I focus on my priorities. Like, what is he?"

"Well that's Shane alright. He doesn't like people going out of their way for him."

"Yeah, I guess. Do you know if there's any Tums or other antacid in this place? That pizza is working on me..."

Regina was caught off guard by the far-fetched question, and silently wondered if it had an underlying judgement.

"Not sure at all." She firmly responded. "I guess you can check the kitchen cupboards or the bathrooms most likely."

"Thanks." Lisa got up and checked the kitchen and downstairs bathroom, then headed up the stairs.

Regina suddenly jumped up when she remembered that she hadn't checked Shane's bedroom to ensure it was 'wife proof'. *Shit!* She quickly rummaged through her purse.

"I found some!" She called out to Lisa. "Forgot I had some in my bag." She felt relieved. *Thank you Lord! Thank you Lord!* She screamed on the inside. *Hopefully I wasn't too late.* She could hear Lisa trekking back towards the staircase.

"You said you found?" She asked innocently.

"Yeah!" Regina smiled and handed her the coil of Rolaids. "Your lucky day…"

Shane stirred in the bed, and almost instinctively, tried to sit up. He was sure he heard his mother's voice in his subconscious before his vision cleared.

"Mom…" He slurred, and paused for his mind to catch up. "You're here?"

"Baby! You're up!" Tina jumped up from the side chair. "I'm right here. How do you feel? What can I get you? Oh Shane!" She carefully leaned him against the headboard.

"Mom…" He tried to smile.

"I'm here son! You need to potty?" She laughed.

Shane barely smiled. "I need to pee…I think. No potty…" He managed a full sentence.

"Okay baby. I'll help you to stand and you tell me if you can take it from there."

He swung his feet over the edge of the bed and turned to sit forward. Gently passing his hand over his face, he looked up at his mother.

"Mom…how long before…this drug wears off? I feel so retarded. I look retarded?" His tongue felt foreign.

"Not at all baby. The effect should start wearing off in another hour or two. You've already been out for three hours. Maybe you should eat something...that would help."

He held her hand and slowly stood as the ground seemingly danced beneath him. His mind coordinated a few steps with his body, and he made it to the door with assistance.

Tina opened the bedroom door and held it in place. She felt an ounce of guilt as she noticed Lisa gazing off into space, looking quite detached and worried.

"I'm out...for a couple hours...and that's when y'all keep a party? That's foul..." Shane tried to joke.

Regina and Lisa both jumped up, startled by his voice. Following that was the awkward moment where both stood their ground, each anticipating the other to move forward.

Shane outstretched his free arm to Lisa, who hurriedly rushed into his warm embrace. He kissed her on the forehead and squeezed her with the strength he could muster.

"Baby!" Lisa shrieked. "I'm so glad you're finally up. I'm scared baby. How are you feeling?" She clung to him as if her life depended on it.

"I know baby. Feel better than I presume I look..." He snickered and winked at Regina.

"Shane sweety, you *were* going to the bathroom." Tina dutifully reminded him.

"Yeah...I didn't go on myself...did I?" Everyone giggled. "Hook me up with about five slices of that pizza babe. I'll be back..." He flashed a cheesy grin.

After two full days of successfully avoiding her husband, Natalie curled up in the couch and contemplated calling him.

She finally decided to put her pride aside and reached for the house phone.

"Hey baby! I'm so glad you called." Michael answered on the first ring.

"Hey, I'm glad I called." She couldn't deny it.

"How've you been? We need to talk Natalie. I need to talk to you. I'm ready to tell you everything. Baby, I don't want to lose you and I know what I did was wrong. It was deceitful. I'm terribly sorry baby, and I hope you can find it in your heart to forgive me. I'm willing to accept whatever you decide…except a divorce!"

He was saying all the right things that she was longing to hear, but all she could do was cry.

"Just come home Michael. I need you here." She gently placed the phone in its cradle.

The reality of the situation was that she owned up to her selfishness. After giving a lot of thought to the life growing inside her, she had fairly concluded that she was in the best position as a woman to have a child and start a family. She accepted that she had been using her career to put off something that was so important to her husband. She acknowledged that her decision was merely out of spite for his recent incognito activities, and nothing else.

Her cell phone rang somewhere in the adjacent room, and she scrambled to locate it.

"Hello!" She almost shouted into the phone.

"Natalie, it's Regina. I'm just checking in. Shane's up and moving around and he seems okay. Tina wanted to speak with you though, are you busy?"

"No, not at all. Where is she?"

"Right here. Hold on, I'll pass you."

Natalie turned on the ceiling fan as her anxiety zoomed her natural body temperature into overdrive.

"Natalie darling, how are you doing?" Tina's raspy voice flowed through the line.

"I'm doing okay Tina, thanks for asking. Regina said Shane's up and around..."

"Yes, duty had called. But then he saw the gang, and pizza, and he's been up since."

They enjoyed a laugh.

Tina continued. "I wanted to thank you though for letting me in on this *situation*. My son is notably a piece of work. I hope this is not on your conscience."

"Oh Tina, you know me well. But I merely did what I felt I had to; for both sides. I presume Regina gave you my notes on the details of what I administered to him?"

"Yes, she did indeed. That's what I needed to talk to you about..." Her voice trailed off.

Natalie was immediately on edge for reasons she couldn't readily determine. She was also caught off guard when the front door swung open. Seeing Michael so soon unexpectedly took her breath away.

Noticing that she was on the phone, Michael tightly embraced her from behind and expressed his gratitude and remorse through whispers.

Tina came back on the line. "I'm so sorry about that Natalie. I had to put my baby donkey in line like old times. Talking about some club tonight. Where were we?"

Natalie laughed at Tina's reference to her son. "You wanted to talk about the medication I'm guessing."

"Yes! Well, you gave him the morphine and it works for now. But what happens from here? And how may I assist? In your professional opinion of course." She was ready for the breakdown.

"Well, as I explained to Shane...it's either he starts the chemotherapy or *get by* on morphine. There aren't many other options available."

"I see. Well, he has been asking questions and I'm trying to quell his deepest fears. I know I'm getting through to him, but in the meantime he'll need the drugs. Between us

Nat, he's *going* to start that chemo. Especially when Lisa tells him she's pregnant!"

Natalie's jaws involuntarily dropped, and her mind simultaneously blanked. "I see…" She airily offered.

"So I'd like to come down to your place and chat with you some more. I'll get the particulars from Shane and give you a call. Enjoy the rest of your evening."

"Thanks Tina. And you the same."

They disconnected.

Roxanne lounged at the cordless phone in the middle of her bed and answered it before the second ring.

"Hello!" She was almost out of breath.

"Hey Roxie. Come outside for a quick sec?" Biggs had paid her a surprise visit.

"Okay. But I hope you're not parked in front of the house." She wrestled on her pyjama bottoms before she headed outside with the phone still attached to her ear.

When she got to the end of the driveway, she heard his engine running behind the bushes and went over to where he had parked.

"Hey, what you doing up here unannounced? Yuh stalking me now?" She asked jokingly though blushing.

Biggs laughed. "I brought yuh something." He reached into the back seat and pulled out a life-sized, well-dressed teddy bear that could barely fit through his window.

"Oh my God!" She exclaimed louder than intended then covered her mouth and giggled. "I love it Andre! It's huge!" She hugged the bear tightly.

Biggs smiled and welcomed her peck on his cheek. "There's more where that came from." He boastfully added. "Come closer and turn around."

Roxanne did as instructed, smiling uncontrollably. She saw his hands come over her head with something glistening in between them. She got a better look at her necklace as it rested against her bare chest while he carefully fastened it in place.

"What you know about diamonds and white gold sexy?" He bragged from behind her.

She turned around, eyes locked on her gift, speechless.

"You can blink now." He teased, and flicked her on the arm with his finger.

"Ouch! That hurt Andre! Yuh so rough. I'm allowed to be in shock! How much a thing like this cost? This is beautiful!" She ran her fingers over each stone that was snugly set in place in each link.

"Yuh can't ask mi how much ma gift cost babes! Just tell mi if yuh like it...and thanks." He laughed.

"I love it! And thanks..." She joked. "I don't know what else to say." She finally raised her head to look at him.

He smiled and pulled her closer. "Yuh said it all baby girl. Just take care of it. Take care of it like I will take care of you *and* our baby."

Her eyes lingered on his full, pink lips with lust, as she hung on to his every word. "I will definitely do that Andre." She eagerly leaned in and kissed him, hypnotized by the sensation that swirled throughout her body.

When she pulled away, though unwilling, she audibly exhaled. "Thanks again baby." The words lingered on her lips. "We'll pick this up tomorrow." Her confidence was booming.

He licked his lips and winked at her. "Definitely sexy! I love you. I love you both...and I mean that."

"Love you too Andre. Good night."

Linton seethed inside as he observed Roxanne from the upstairs bedroom window. He had picked up the house phone at the same time she had answered, and had overheard the man on the phone telling her to meet him outside. The thought had crossed his mind to go out there after her, but his brother's predicament paralysed him.

Nine years her fucking senior! And right in front of my fucking house! This pussy really come up here, ten o'clock a night? Biggest disrespect ting that to bloodclaat! Cause a fucking Michael I have to put up with this bullshit! What di fuck mi ago do if Regina just pull up right now? Fuck man! Fuck this shit! He slammed his fist into the pillow.

CHAPTER THIRTEEN

Toya stormed down the winding staircase and thudded into the foyer towards Biggs. Though he was fast asleep, she was not about to back down from her attack.

"I can't believe you!" She shrieked at the top of her voice. "You really strolled in here after hours *and* slept downstairs Andre? What the *fuck*!" She screamed.

Biggs jumped out of his sleep with an instant headache. Frustrated, but wanting to remain calm, he massaged his face and spoke in a monotonous tone.

"Wha yuh seh?" He slowly looked up in her direction, eyeing her with sheer disgust.

"You heard me Biggs! If I wanted to sleep alone I could've stayed in Boston. I've been here for almost a *week*! I can count the amount of times I've either fell asleep beside you, or woken up and you were right there beside me. What's your deal? Seriously!"

He was awake now, and extremely agitated. "*Listen*! Yuh know from day one how my line a work guh. I don't clock hours Toya! I do what I have to do until I get it done, *whenever* that may be! I done told yuh, if yuh can't handle the ride, give it up!"

"Everytime you come Jamaica we have the same problem. The same *fucking argument dem*! The shit nah go change yo! So better yuh gwan yuh ways now and low mi in peace!"

"And mek mi tell yuh dis to, if mi want sleep downstairs or *anywhere* else on dis property for that matter, I can. *It's all mine*! Now before yuh come downstairs and wake up man with a hot plate of food, yuh start with the fuckry!" He looked at his watch - her gift to him - and continued.

"Yuh start with the whole heap a talking seven thirty inna the mawnin! Toya *leave* me yah man! *Don't* annoy me!" He got up off the couch and stepped around her.

Though it would have been to her betterment to let the argument slide, Toya felt the need to be persistent. She proceeded to follow him up the stairs into the bedroom.

"Then why the *fuck* didn't you tell me all that before I came? Huh? If you couldn't find the time to spend with me, why didn't you tell me to keep my ass where I was? What, you just wanted your stuff? Is that all I am to you? Designer clothes and shopping sprees?" She stayed closely on his heels, screaming loudly in the side of his head.

Biggs was unusually calm as he took off his overnight clothes and threw them on the sofa by the closet.

"*Answer me when I'm talking to you!*" She trailed him to the bathroom and screamed at him.

He immediately rid her of her miscalculated control with a firm fist to the face.

Reflexively, Toya clutched her jaw in disbelief as tears spilled down her cheeks. She stood motionless as he pushed her into the wall to get by, and back into the bedroom.

Without a care in the world, Biggs hopped into his bed and sprawled out in the middle - butt naked.

Toya began to sob. She stormed across the bedroom and grabbed her luggage out of the closet. She wailed and cursed under her breath, emptying all the drawers and tossing anything familiar into her bags.

In one swift motion she swatted all his items off the dresser, of course breaking a few.

"Fuck you Biggs! *Fuck you!*" She screamed repeatedly.

He lay on his back and watched her without interference, until her eyes connected with the three thousand dollar laptop. Only then did he jump up and lounge at her.

"Where yuh think yuh going with that?" He firmly squeezed her hand and yanked her towards him. "That's a gift! You bought it, but now it's mine! Count your losses and move on!" He flashed her hand out of his and sat on the edge of the bed.

"Matter of fact, seems like yuh have everything that you *can* leave with! Need a cab?" He was ever callous and provoking.

She lost complete control and broke down, slumping to the floor. She knew if she walked out of that house, it would be the last time she had anything to do with Biggs. The last thing she had really planned on was breaking up their relationship.

"Why are you being like this to me Biggs? I've been nothing but good to you. Why won't you love me like I do you, huh? You won't even try to stop me from leaving. Is that what you really want?" She stared at him through innocent, swollen eyes. "You don't want me Biggs?"

He sighed in frustration. "Now yuh want to ask me what *I* want?" He wouldn't deny the feeling of empowerment. "*After* yuh packed all your stuff?" He looked over at her, showing no signs of emotions.

"Yuh come downstairs this morning with your loudness like yuh know everything, after we *done* talk bout you and these assumptions. Mi nah go siddung and mek yuh drive me nuts, Toya! What yuh really want from mi? Hmm? Cause nothing is going to change. *Nothing*!"

"Biggs, you know what I want." Her voice was almost a whisper. "Just some attention when I'm here. Is that too much to ask? We haven't even been out much. It's like you're ashamed of me or something."

He chuckled. "All my life I could neva undastand why you pretty women *always* have so many insecurities? Shame a yuh for what Toya? If I was ashamed of yuh, we would be together? Yuh see any gyal a Jamaica better looking dan yuh from yuh come? Come here man!" His voice roared.

She was on her feet in an instant, but tentatively walked closer to him, folding her arms defensively across her chest.

He firmly gripped her where both arms intersected and pulled her inches away from his face. "A whappen to yuh babes? Is a fuck you want? That's what's bothering yuh? You feel like what? Mi outta road a give weh *yuh* cocky?" He seriously held her gaze.

Toya became almost child-like. "I didn't say all that Biggs…" She eagerly welcomed his aggressive lips, trying to keep pace with his forceful tongue.

Biggs stood, towering over her petite frame, and moved in closer towards her. He instantly grew excited when her dark chocolate breasts spilled from the shirt he ripped from her body. In an expert motion he had her on the bed, on her back, using his fingers to stimulate her pinkness.

"Damn! How yuh so wet already babes?" He smirked as he toyed with her swollen clit. "If a cocky yuh want yuh coulda just ask!" He yanked her closer to the edge of the bed and looked deeply into her eyes.

"Don't expect me to make love to yuh right now either…cause mi still vex!"

Something about his approach sent Toya's hormones into overdrive, spreading her legs wide apart. She took a deep breath and tried not to panic as her eyes frisked the anaconda dangling from his groin.

Biggs firmly gripped her thighs and navigated his grand entry. He could feel the tension in her legs as he impaled her orifice with a firm and steady thrust.

"Yuh need fi breathe baby. Betta yuh relax cause yuh a get the full ten inches todeh. No mercy!" He offered his disclaimer with a smirk.

Shane burst through the door of Coach Sullivan's office uninvited, almost ripping it off the hinges.

"Coach, what the hell is going on?" He frantically enquired, failing at his attempt not to shout.

"Besides you losing your manners you mean?" Coach responded nonchalantly.

"Sir with all due respect, why the hell did the security refuse to let me into the gym like I don't belong here? He told me to talk to you about it!"

The middle-aged man looked up over his glasses at the raging athlete, and spoke with authority.

"Have a seat Shane...and calm yourself."

"I'd prefer to stand thank you very much." He hastily retorted and stood his ground.

"Suit yourself. Listen, I'm forced to prohibit you from training until further notice. You need to get some rest and attend to your *other* priorities."

"What! Where is this coming from? And what do you mean by *forced*? Coach, why would you make a decision like this without consulting me first? I was humiliated out there! Does the team know about this?" He turned to storm out.

"*Shane*! S*it down*!" Coach rose to his feet with that command. "You listen to me, and you listen clearly! It's been ten days since you've fainted on national television, and in case you live in a cave, the media is running wild with this story. The speculations are piling high. And believe me when I tell you they're not in your favour at this stage, especially since I have yet to release an official statement."

"The sponsors are calling relentlessly; your teammates are worried sick; not to mention the entire Jamaica and her people all across the globe. Until you or I come up with a resolution to all this, my hands are tied. I can't have you prancing in and around Sullivan acting as if nothing happened."

"Then what do you propose I do Coach? Are we forgetting that Penn Relays is six weeks away? *I sure haven't*; and I need to train!"

"You're missing the point Shane. Forget about Penn Relays. It's not happening." Coach Sullivan massaged his forehead and took a deep breath before he continued. "Son, this is getting extremely political. The entire situation is spiralling out of control right before my eyes. And why is this Shane? Because a grown man like me has to keep secrets. *Secrets* Shane, because I refuse to lie!"

Shane's cheeks glossed with tears as he slumped unto the desk. "You *betrayed* me Coach. You promised not to use what I told you in private against me. And now you tell me I'm out? How can you?"

Coach slammed his hand on the desk and roared. "*I betrayed you*?" He paced the walkway. "It's funny, those were the *exact words* your mother used to me after she failed to trick me into a confession the exact minute after I vowed silence to you! Not only did she express that I tried to deceive her, she added that I, Lawrence Sullivan the fifth, was 'so *addicted to glory*' that I put her son's precious life in jeopardy when *I* whisked him all the way to Australia, knowing '*damn well*' that he was ill!" The man paused and held Shane's worried gaze.

"I won't even get into the words *your father* had for me! Now I'm not telling you what to do, or how to do it… but public figures don't have private lives Shane. You know that. And you know that I have your best interest at heart."

"Then I'll make a statement." Shane didn't hesitate. "Yeah, I'll confess to being ill, and to the fact that I won't let it deter me. That's what bravery is, right? Sustaining, persevering, and overcoming! I'm *all* about that Coach. Call a press conference. Invite the who-is-who." He leaned back in his chair and outstretched his legs. "I'm handling this today."

"Are you sure about this Shane? Don't jump on this because of pressure." Coach slipped into protective mode.

"Coach, there's no time for PR right now. Call the conference so I can go back in the gym." He would not be deterred.

Lawrence Sullivan chuckled to himself. "Who do you propose I call first?"

"CVM, since their camera guy broke my fall. Then call Amanda, she'll *definitely* get the word to the rest."

They both appreciated the humour.

"That one is *definitely* a keeper babes! Jah know, yuh look sexier than ever!" Biggs relaxed in the plush store couch, ogling at his private star model who was now show-casing a body-hugging mini dress.

Roxanne blushed as she had done when he commented on all the previous outfits. She pranced around the dressing room, pretending to not be irritated by the store clerk who had been eyeing her with disdain. She was learning to adapt to the hatred that came with the 'high-profile' boyfriend package, and subsequently refrained from her usual commentary.

"Babes, put that on the 'buy' pile and try another one! Mad! How yuh a guh so hard?" He called out to her as she disappeared into the changing room.

She re-emerged in a royal blue, laced-back, mini corset BCBG dress. It fully emphasized her curvy thirty-two D's, twenty-three, twenty-eight-inched frame.

"This one is my favourite Andre! Straight superstar! Oh my God...yuh think?"

"Babes mi know! Yuh look like one!" He turned to the young clerk who was lurking around impatiently, and snapped. "Yuh have that dress in other colours?"

If she had intended to hide that she was star-struck, she failed miserably. "Yes...yes sir. We ahm...we do have it in purple, red...I think."

"I get what yuh trying to seh! My baby skin pretty and flawless so she can wear any colour. Bring one of each in her size for mi!" He turned back to his woman. "Roxie, I have to *have yuh* inna deh dress deh tonight! Bloodclaat! Yuh have mi cocky a tingle a way. Come here babes!"

"Andre!" She exclaimed, before she giggled and walked over to him. "Why yuh so loud?" She asked as he hugged her around the waist and slipped his hands under the dress. She tried to pull away with little effort, as the girl hastily made her way towards them.

"Well you could've left them at the register." Biggs remarked as he saw her burdening with the load. "She already tried one so they obviously fit right?"

"But..." The woman flushed with embarrassment and bee-lined back to the front of the store.

"Andre you don't have to be so mean all the time." Roxanne commented as she disappeared into the stall.

"But babes, common sense. Wha she feel? Yuh need fi try on every colour of the same dress that yuh know fit yuh already? I mean, seriously!"

"Babes common sense not so *common*." She replied when she opened the door, all set to go.

"I guess yuh right babes. Obviously! Yuh done model already?" He gestured for her to come close.

"Yeah. I'm starving. Let's go eat." She wrapped her arm around his waist and snuggled close.

"Alright cool. Can your baby get some sugar for planning a good day?" He faked a sad face.

Roxanne smiled. "Of course." She tilted her head and pouted her lips.

Biggs dropped two hundred thousand dollars on the check-out counter. "Hold dat and keep the change." He snickered as the clerk still made an attempt to count each thousand dollar bill manually.

"My girl, a betta yuh just trust mi seh it's all there... and some! Can't be here all day with yuh." He laughed and turned to Roxanne. "But babe, we shop in the wrong store! Yuh can't fit these dresses much longer."

She playfully smacked him on the arm. "Yuh not funny Andre! What yuh trying to say?" She pouted.

"Nuh watch nutt'n babes! Nah seh nutt'n man. No matter what, I'll love yuh same way!" He put his arms around her and tried to kiss her as she playfully resisted.

The store attendant was noticeably repulsed by their shenanigans, but nonetheless keen to the gossip.

Coach Sullivan confidently ascended the podium as he did on numerous occasions before. He took his place center-stage and looked over his notes while the reporters tried to settle down.

"Good evening ladies and gentlemen." He began. "Thank you all for being here at such short notice. As everyone witnessed, Shane Wright collapsed at the Melbourne Grand Prix ten days ago." He paused as everyone stirred and commented amongst themselves.

"As the Head Coach and Business Director of the Jamaica national team, I humbly accept that I should've acted sooner to quell the fears of the Jamaican public. I should've urgently addressed the media speculations and the nation's concerns. I thank each and every one of you for your patience and understanding during those very critical days. I will also say thank you, on behalf of Shane, to Jamaicans and non-Jamaicans spread wide across the globe for their numerous phone calls offering well wishes and undying support. Once again *we*, your team, thank you." He looked over at Shane who offered a nod.

"Shane is here today, to personally address your concerns and impart details surrounding the event. It would be greatly appreciated if he is allowed to speak without interruption at this moment, assuring you that your questions will be answered orderly at the end of the session. Thank you *all* for your cooperation. Shane..." He stepped away from the microphone and moved to the back of the podium.

Shane had no second thoughts when he tightly gripped Lisa's hand and led the way into the spotlight. He flashed his reputable charismatic grin and positioned himself behind the mic. As usual, he briefly acknowledged his closest associates of media, seated stage-side.

After audibly clearing his throat, he went in for the kill. "Good evening ladies and gentlemen." He paused for the seemingly orchestrated response.

"First, I'd like to thank all my fans, all over the world, for their undying support and prayers. I deeply regret all the pain and anxiety I may have caused because of *my* delayed response to your concerns. As for that *pathetic* race, all I have to say, is I told you so!" He smiled and pointed at the cameras as the crowd erupted with laughter.

"I don't know how many times they want us to prove that Jamaicans are born champions! Our bite *is* as loud as our bark no matter how many drug tests they take!" The room drowned in laughter and applause.

Shane's anxiety subsided as the crowd warmed up with his ice breakers. He felt better prepared to 'make his private life public', though unwilling.

"After I won that race, my only regret was collapsing on national TV. With that said, I want to say a big thank you to Eddie, CVM's Camera Tech, whose equipment and apparatus broke my fall. Don't know what I would've done without you my brotha." He clutched his fist to his heart, chuckled, and pointed to the man.

Laughter could be heard throughout the room though less gregarious than before. The people were ready for the big news, all jokes aside, and they hung tightly to their star athlete's every word.

Shane continued. "On a more serious note, is the reason behind my collapse; the reason we are all here today. I had been training intensively for the months leading up to the Grand Prix, and including the day of, as this meet was my 2008 season debut. On the day of the race, I hadn't eaten anything substantial as I usually didn't before any big event." He continued amidst the murmurs growing in the room.

"The difference this time, though I didn't take it into consideration before, was that I was on medication." He maintained his focus though the audience busily stirred.

"I have been taking heavy doses of prescribed pain killers since I was recently diagnosed with stomach cancer..."

The silence shattered as the eager reporters spewed their opinions and moved about the room. Chairs were screeching against the tiled flooring while voices competed for the sound waves. It was official that everyone was instantly ready for the questioning session.

Shane looked back at his Coach, who he'd figured would be heading his way for damage control, and motioned that he could manage. He bravely re-composed himself, mentally blocked the questions and flashing lights, and proceeded.

"I was diagnosed with stage one stomach cancer. The experts are confident that with treatment, and a structured healthy diet, this whole ordeal will be behind me in no time. It will be behind *us*!"

"As for my schedule for the rest of oh eight, I am presently in discussions to determine my ability to compete. We will periodically inform you of the updates as they develop. At this time, I just want to ask the Jamaican public to think only positive things on my behalf, and continue to support the movement to make history in Track and Field.

Continue to support my teammates as they continue to do big things for Jamaica this year. They have a lot in store for you; *trust me*! *We* will get through this people. And don't worry, I'm in good hands. Now I'll take your questions, and I'll do my best to get to all of them." He smiled warmly, re-coating the eager audience with another dosage of charisma.

Grace - CVM's correspondent, offered a genuine sympathetic smile as she stood and accepted the first slot.

"Shane, first I'd like to say that we at CVM are deeply sorry to hear of this obstacle in your course, and we *know* you will overcome. I wanted to know if the doctors have indicated how long it will be before you're back in top form." She signalled the now-famous Eddie to zoom in for his response.

Shane smiled and thanked her for her positive outlook then explained that his 'down time' was presently indeterminate.

"The recovery is relative to how well my body responds to the course of treatment." He concluded, and pointed to Brent of The Jamaica Observer.

"Shane, how did your family respond to the news of your illness? And are they the primary reason you kept it a secret for so long?"

Shane looked over at Lisa and returned her warming smile. "Technically, I wasn't keeping it a secret Brent. Are you trying to get me in trouble?" He paused for the chuckles. "I'd say it was more private. And how are they taking it? Well, my family members are pretty strong people. Like any family would be at this point, they are doing what they can to be supportive and encouraging." He raised the hand that Lisa tightly clutched, and winked.

"And who's the *bitch*?" The outburst rattled the room, emerging from the opposite direction than that of the RJR crew who were positioned to speak next.

Everyone looked about the room in awe, as they tried to identify the culprit; Shane already knew.

Natalie muted the television in her office and looked around at Tina who was as awe-struck as she was.

"My goodness! Whoever that was, was *so* out of line! Did you just hear that Tina?"

"Oh I heard alright. That's the ex, Amanda. She's a tough cookie! But he handled things well overall."

Natalie laughed at her friend's comical expression.

"Seriously. Vulgarity and disgust aside it was a great press conference, no? I mean, my boy was looking so dapper and sounding so smart. I couldn't ask for anything else as a mom! Anyhow, back to what you were saying about these alternative therapies. Shane can handle his own drama." She got comfortable.

"Yes, alternative medicine. So like I said, I've been in discussions with some of our local medical dignitaries regarding the use of alternative therapies along with the medicinal approaches to effectively treat cancer; cancer or any illness for that matter. I firmly believe that such a combination will better stabilize not only the body, but also the mind. And as we both agree, the mind is the center of *dis-ease*!"

"Yes, of course. I mean a disease is just as the name implies; the body is *not-eased*. Therefore it is subsequently vulnerable to malicious energies."

"Exactly! But you try explaining this 'new-age' phenomenon to the old-schooled professionals. It's *definitely* not highly favoured! So, from the belly of this struggle, births my recuperation center. I want to offer an array of alternative treatments and generally provide psychological support for individuals of all ages. Anyone who needs us will be welcomed without all the hoopla."

"I'm in love with the idea! You most definitely have my support Nat. Our hospital too has been moving along the alternative medicine path in recent times. Funny, a lot of the doctors and med students from your alma mater have also taken this route."

"Really?" Natalie was pleasantly surprised. "Like whom? Give me names."

"Well Jordan DeVoe is a Naturopathic Doctor. Roula Saifi is an Ayurvedic Physician. And though Robin Stone is a Medical Doctor, she also works with Acupuncture and Homeopathic remedies. There were a few others who've spread their wings from the traditional path and are doing quite well in fact. The reality is that patients are always willing to try something new Nat; at least the ones who are *truly* suffering."

Natalie leaned back in her chair and appreciated the positive news. "I guess we should all touch base and get the ball rolling then. We'll see what advice or input they'd be willing to provide."

"Let's get the ball rolling then." Tina smiled.

Sheldon Wright powered on his cell phone as soon as the aircraft touched the tarmac in Kingston, Jamaica.

"Hey mom! You told us to call as soon as we landed. We landed!" He added sarcastically.

"Hey baby. It's good to know you still follow my orders! Where are you guys now?" Tina eagerly enquired of her second in line to Shane.

"Well if we *just* landed, I would think we're on the runway mother. What's your guess?" He remarked without hesitation.

"Don't get smart with me Sheldon!" She snapped but continued. "Just for that, you guys will be stuck in there for a while." She teasingly chuckled. "Your vacation starts with Immigration; but don't be discouraged."

"Ha! Ha! Ha!" He teased. "And remind me why you couldn't make the trip with this *Milton*? Damn mom, you know I don't dig strangers!" He spoke softly, trying to offset the rudeness factor.

"Watch your mouth…and you don't have to *dig* anything! Milton is not that much of a stranger, Sheldon. He was very kind to us with the whole Shane saga plus he volunteered to do the pick up. You'd better be nice to him now." Truthfully, she wanted the personal time to unwind before the boys bombarded the house. "Where's my Simeon?"

"You'll see him soon! None of y'all paying my phone bill and we're about to get off. They both send their love though…peace!" He disconnected the line.

Tina chuckled at her son's witticisms.

Biggs slowly pulled into his driveway, distracted as he searched for his cell that was loudly ringing somewhere in the center console. *What the fuck?* He thought to himself, before his hand finally landed on it.

"Yo!" He barked into the mouth piece, without much concern for the person on the opposite end.

"Whagwan big man? Wha yuh up to?"

"Who dis?" Biggs asked irritably while he checked the name display.

"A Cilon dis big man. What yuh mean who dis?"

If I had known. Biggs sighed inwardly. "Oh! Didn't check the number bredrin. What's up?"

Cilon chuckled. "So you gwan man. Mi want talk to yuh bout the other day at the studio."

"Which other day that?" Biggs asked more anxiously than he had intended.

"*Yuh know which day me a talk man*!" Cilon spoke more abrasively. "Is what yuh really up to yute?"

Though Biggs was surprisingly taken aback by Cilon's bluntness, he matched it with his own aggression. "What *the fuck* yuh mean bredrin? *Get to yuh point* and *don't yute* mi!"

"*Pussy*! Mi a talk 'bout the day when mi catch yuh with yuh hood in a *batty*! Yuh memba now? Who the *fuck* yuh think yuh a talk to Biggs? Yuh think man a likkle boy? Yo! Watch yuhself yuh nuh battybway!"

"*Battybway unda yuh mumma bombohole*! A me yuh a try bad up? Yuh a fool? *Suck yuh madda, pussy*!" Biggs disconnected the line.

A wha deh pussy deh really a try though? He thought to himself as he gathered his belongings from the back seat. *Grudge him really a carry gainst man? War him really want with me, Andre Biggs Jackson? Cause mi never use him tired beats dem? A must fuck him want me fuck him up! Like him tek bad man ting for dolly house! Rage the war then nuh bombohole!* He looked up and noticed Toya lurking in the distance by his front door.

You is another one! Why yuh still deh a mi rass yawd...much less Jamaica? Get pon mi fucking nerves! I going fix the whole of oonu bomboclaat!

Toya eagerly lingered in the grand mahogany doorway, and watched as her man carelessly ignored her. She had already made up her mind in the fifteen minutes that had passed, that he was on the phone with a woman.

You're such a damn whore Andre! And those stupid little bitches who don't respect another woman's territory! Sell their ass for fame and money...actually thinking they mean something to him! She smiled inwardly. *Y'all aint shit! You come a dime a dozen! Titts and ass...that's all!* Her smile disappeared as quickly as it had appeared. *I bet that's the same shit they say about me.* She stormed inside.

"I hate you Andre Jackson!" She screamed at the top of her lungs, her words reverberating against the high ceiling. "I need to get the fuck out of here! Fuck out of Jamaica!" She wiped her tears and proceeded up the stairs.

CHAPTER FOURTEEN

A fter three months of fruitless meetings and one week of sale negotiations, Natalie finally found the building of her dreams to house the Hope and Cope Remedial Cancer Center.

With Michael offering legal and spousal support, the purchase was finalised in two days and the vision ensued.

The highlight of the property was the expansive garden that encircled it, which boasted two man-made fish ponds and stone-carved water fountains that lightened the ambience of the sturdy, dark red brick architecture.

Behind the stunning mahogany double doors of the main entrance, an unbelievable foyer welcomed the entrants giving way to a floating mahogany staircase that would urge anyone to venture to the second floor. The interior ceilings were dramatically high at twenty feet on each tier, and the French windows lined each wall half way to the ceiling, on each of the three floors.

Natalie's excitement funnelled her creativity as she moved through the rooms on each floor making recommendations to the renovating contractor.

"I want this wall removed to expand this area…" She pointed out to Mr. Morris. "I find it confining, and it detracts from the ambience." She worked with a mental map of how she had originally envisioned the end product.

Michael sat behind an old desk in one of the first floor offices of Hope and Cope. He worked to refine a summation on a brief he had to deliver in court in three hours.

One of his high-paying clients had called him at six thirty in the morning to seek his representation in a small dispute matter, and he had felt coerced to oblige.

He had spent the better part of the morning revelling in Natalie's re-modelling endeavours, but had politely excused himself to focus on his more pressing matter.

It had taken over an hour to perfect his arguments, but he added the final dot and ran through it mentally. As he geared up to practice aloud and leaned back in the squeaking chair, his cell phone vibrated on his hip. He checked the display then screamed inwardly.

"Michael Simmons." He answered rather politely.

"Hey baby. Long time no see or hear from yuh."

I saw you two days ago goddamn it! And we spoke just yesterday! Michael pondered inwardly, but replied. "I've been busy with work. You know how it goes..." He spoke casually.

"I know baby. But I want to see yuh tonight. I miss that dick! What time will you come?" She purred.

Never o'clock! He screamed in his head. "I can't tonight. I have prior arrangements." He lied.

"Then come to*day* then! I can make arrangements to meet you somewhere."

"Caramel, I've got court *all day*." He lied again.

"Why yuh being so difficult Michael?" Her tone reflected her agitation. "It's either today or tonight yuh nuh so take your pick! You always get me so angry when all I want is to please you! Don't I take good care of you Michael? Hmm? Who can deep throat that dick like I do? Or make you feel good like I do? Why the denial?"

I'm fucking married! What the hell do you expect? "Listen, I'll give you a call back when I flip through my schedule. Cool?" He tried to bargain.

"Not cool! Don't play games with me Michael! You're so fucking bad at lying. I don't know why you bother. I need that dick, *Chocolate Thunder*! I need it deep inside, like no *other* woman can take it! Last time when you entered me from behind...and exploded inside me...and told me *you loved* me...it meant so much to me baby. But that dose already expired. I need a refill."

Michael was irate. Not only was she coyly threatening him by using his marital bedroom name, but her version of their last encounter was irritatingly blasphemous. *Love you? I didn't say that you crazy bitch! Exploded in you? What the fuck is this bitch talking about? This shit is getting out of hand! Caramel has really lost her fucking mind! This is too much for me! It's time for Linton to take over this mess!*

Contradictory to his mental venting, a tent monstrously formed in his crotch. He caved.

"Okay sexy. You win. I'll see yuh tonight, okay?"

"And don't try to be slick either Michael. You should know I have an appointment with your *wife* today too." She lingered on the line then hung up.

Regina urgently clicked her heels into the office, pretending as though she had just arrived to work.

"Morning girl." She called out to Stacy, purposely startling her out of her pensive state.

"Hey Regina!" Stacy replied with strained enthusiasm, her intuition suddenly twisting her insides.

"You sure sound excited to see me." Regina teased as she held her gaze. "What's the matter? Everything cool?" She pointedly eyed her.

"Yeah! Everything's cool girl." She audibly cleared her throat and feigned a smile.

You're not cool! You're up to no good! It's written all over your sorry face! Regina silently chastised her.

"Is Hugh in yet?" She airily asked for her boss.

"No. I haven't seen him all morning. He's supposed to come in though. He has three appointments."

"I see. You better call him on his cell and remind him. You know how he does."

"You're right." Stacy gladly welcomed the opportunity to compose herself and dialled her boss.

Regina sat motionless, pondering her next move while discreetly observing the nervous woman. *First you have Michael's name and number in your little planner... then you're quizzing me about his marriage! Now you're threatening someone about having an appointment with their wife...and acting stupid as hell when I come in. This makes too much sense to be nothing!*

"Hey Stacy, you wanna go shopping after lunch today? There's a big sale." She asked without looking up.

"I can't Regina. I have an appointment with Doc." The words escaped her mouth faster than she could realise the trap.

Regina smiled. "I see."

Natalie locked the main doors behind the contractor and headed off to find her husband. She walked into the office where she had last seen him working, just in time to catch him adjusting his erect penis inside his cotton slacks.

"Where did *that* come from?" She seductively purred, evidently startling him.

"Hey baby!" He replied. "All set upstairs?" He tried to muster a straight face as she neared him.

"You're just going to avoid my question?" She asked sternly. "Or should I repeat myself?"

"Baby, I'm sure you can imagine where *that* came from! Did you see the skirt you're wearing? You know what happens to me when you wear red. I just got a little excited." He stopped one word shy of blabbering.

"Really now? You got hard just thinking about me... in my red skirt?" She started to unbutton her shirt. "Well since it's mine, bring it here then!" She commanded and positioned her stiletto-clad leg on the edge of the desk.

Michael's eyes widened with excitement as her partially exposed fluff peeped from under her skirt.

"Are we alone baby?" He asked, though hastily unbuttoning his pants.

"Does it matter?" She spoke airily, and unsnapped the front of her bra.

Wheeling the chair closer to his unusually risqué wife, he positioned directly between her legs and pushed her skirt up over her waist. Roughly groping her ass cheeks and nuzzling his face into her crotch, Michael handled the work.

Natalie clutched her man's head firmly as he graciously used his tongue to massage her aching pinkness. She reflexively rotated her groin in sync with the fluid motion of his tongue, yearning for the moment he would enter her.

As soon as her legs began to tremble in hi grip, Michael swept her off her feet and laid her on the desk. He expertly rid his body of all clothing and plunged his turgid erection into her eager orifice. He was surprised, yet aroused, when she welcomed all nine inches of it.

"Fuck me *Chocolate Thunder*!" She screamed between moans. "Give me everything!"

Shane frowned as his mother motioned him to the phone to speak with the naturopath, Doctor Vincent LeFranc.

"Get your ass over here!" Tina covered the mouthpiece and sternly whispered. "When the hell do you plan to grow up?" She outstretched the phone.

He laughed and snatched the phone. "Doctor LeFranc, it's a pleasure..." He greeted with much sarcasm.

"The pleasure is mine Shane. Congrats on all your outstanding achievements. I just wanted to affirm that healing is a mental process. The more you remain positive, the better your chances will be to overcome this illness."

"I've been trying to stay positive Sir, though I still have my bad days."

"Well that is expected. My intention is to teach you to be positive naturally, minimizing the need for conscious effort. I look forward to meeting with you for your consultation."

"Same here Doc. But tell me, roughly how many people have you cured of cancer?" Shane obliged the urge to voice his pessimism on the benefits of alternative medicine.

Dr. LeFranc chuckled. "You'll get to understand when we meet Shane, that what I do for people wouldn't exactly classify as a cure. So in that sense, zero. However, I will inform you that thousands of people who were diagnosed, had no signs of cancer after working with me."

His scepticism heightened. "I see. Well until such time then, enjoy the rest of your evening Sir."

"Please, call me Vincent. Tell your mother to keep me posted. And you both have a great evening as well."

"I will. We will. Take care." Shane hung up and turned to his mother.

"You can be a real pain in the you-know-where sometimes. You know that?" Tina pointedly eyed him.

Shane grinned as he casually responded. "I know that mother! You've taught me well."

She was not amused. "Shane, I know all this alternative stuff is new to you, and you're under a lot of pressure. But did you have to ask such an insulting question? And is scepticism going to be your full-time approach?"

"What insulting question mom? Because I asked him if he cured anyone? He didn't seem insulted. What's the big deal?" He knelt beside her on the couch and firmly held both her hands with one of his.

"I'm not playing with you Shane! I'm not in the mood to be tickled! I'm serious." She giggled like a four year old as he disregarded her demands. "Shane, stop! Please..."

He eased up and kissed her on the forehead before releasing her. "I will *try* not to ask any *insulting* questions *mother*. And I'm not sceptic; just cautious."

Roxanne placed her reef atop Cindy's grave, sobbing uncontrollably in Shari's arms.

"I didn't even get to say goodbye...I should've listened to her...I should've forgiven her Shari...and now she's gone...she's gone...she's gone!" She screamed between sobs. "Cindy, why yuh leave me like this? Why her God? Why? It's not fair! She was so young...she didn't trouble anybody!" She wailed and vented.

Shari hugged her friend and held her close, while crying her own silent tears. She observed as the other schoolmates bade their farewell and offered their words of encouragement to Roxanne.

Roxanne peeked up at her friend and whispered. "Did you see her face Shari? Didn't even look like Cindy. Look at what they buried her in...Shari, it's not right! It's not right at all! Oh Cindy! Oh God! Come back to me!" She nuzzled her face in her friend's lap and screamed.

"That's not Cindy, Roxanne." Shari tried to console her, as well as herself. "Cindy as we know her has already transcended. She's long gone to a better place...she's in our hearts now. That's not our friend girl...that's not Cindy." She hushed her friend and smiled to herself.

"You're right Shari." She spoke as her temper subdued. "Cindy's probably looking at us like 'why them fools crying?'" They giggled.

"Buggin'!" They unintentionally blurted Cindy's favourite quote in unison, and laughed even harder.

Biggs leaned back in his truck and concluded he was out of options. He had weighed the pros and cons on the decision he was about to make, that once done, could not be reversed. He had to put an end to the circus that lurked in the shadows, promising nothing but doom.

He parked at the foot of the hill at Cindy's burial site, waiting for Roxanne while he dialled Benji.

"Whagwan big man?" Benji picked up on the first ring.

"Deya yuh nuh Benji. How tings wid you?"

"Just a hold firm yuh zimme? Couldn't even go di daughter funeral star…it have me a way Biggs, Jah know!"

"I know dem ways boss. Just keep her in your heart and pray…leave all else to time."

"True. So wha yuh deh pon?" Benji was never the biggest fan of small talk.

Biggs got down to business. "Bway, mi inna a little situation ya now and mi need some *work* done! But if that's too heavy for yuh right now…I'd understand." He verbally toyed with him.

"Now a di *right* time to *work*! Big ting or wha?"

"One man show…no threat!"

"When and where?"

"Sooner than later. Where? You'll decide. Jus a consult you first. Wha di damage?"

"Well, if it's wha yuh seh, two should cover *everything*."

"*Everything?*" Biggs almost shrieked. "Yuh sure?"

"Why, that too little for yuh? We can double it if yuh like!" Benji snapped.

"Just cool big man. It's been a while. Alright! I'll shout yuh back with the specifics. Nuh seh nutt'n more." He hung up and exhaled.

Two hundred thousand for a cleanup? He felt relieved. *That's chump change in the midst of disaster. A pussy shoulda think twice before him decide fi fuck wid me! Thank God for Benji and the links! Get this shit over and done with in no time! Gotta be sharp like an eagle from now on...tighten up on my loose lifestyle!* He re-dialled Roxanne as he made his way through the grounds of the cemetery. He spotted her walking in his direction and pulled over to the side of the street.

"Babes, there's too much traffic on the bend." He asserted when she answered. "Please just walk down. I'm going to turn around here. Yeah, in the black car. I'll explain later." He mentally prepared for Roxanne's enquiries about his missing truck.

Biggs reached across the passenger seat and pushed the door open for her. "How's my baby doing?" He lovingly embraced Roxanne and stole a kiss before Shari climbed in.

"I'm sorry I couldn't be there with you babe..."

"Me too. What happened to your truck? Whose car is this?" She was more concerned about that explanation. "Oh, and that's Shari by the way." She vaguely introduced the two.

He looked around at their quiet passenger. "Oh, I know Shari. Weren't you the girl I spoke to at Ardenne?"

"When was that?" Roxanne hastily interjected, looking back and forth between the two.

Biggs responded. "The day when I found out about Cindy, and I came to get you. Shari told me you had left with your sis. Babes..." He was embarrassed.

"Just wanted to know." She remarked defiantly, though feeling guilty for being so defensive.

"Lisa, what else do we need? Where's the list you made?" Shane called out as they strolled through the supermarket aisle aimlessly.

He had just driven his mom and brothers to the airport, partook in an emotional farewell, and attended to Lisa's jealous concerns over a friendly flight attendant. He was definitely not in the mood to walk around in circles.

"Don't be mad, but I left it at the house. The same place I wrote it." Lisa playfully frowned when Shane finished her sentence with her.

"You're something special, you know that? Next time, ask me to write a note to remind you to bring the list. Cool?" He pretended to be upset.

"Ha! Ha! You're not funny!" She feigned a smile and pouted.

"This is not a joke!" He shot back then noticed Lisa was looking beyond him.

"Who do we have here?"

The familiar voice chilled every bone in his body.

"Can't return my phone calls?"

"Hello Amanda!" Shane spoke as he coolly turned to face her. "I've been *busy*. What can I say?"

"Oh! *She* wouldn't have anything to do with that now, would *she*?" Amanda smiled mockingly.

Lisa grabbed the reigns and stepped forward. "I'm sorry. I don't think we've met…personally. I'm Lisa Artuso; and of course you need no introduction."

Shane was appalled by Lisa's attempt to take control of the situation. His amusement didn't last long.

"How long will this one be around Shane? I'm so sick of your games! Aren't you?" The princess from hell boldly dismissed his woman and teased.

Shane clutched Lisa's hand and pulled her closer. "Lisa baby, don't pay much attention to Amanda Fox. Remember what we spoke about?" He grinned and winked at her.

Amanda - not one to be ridiculed - lost her composure and loudly snapped. "Remember *what* Shane? That I helped to *make you*? That I bent over backwards to *let you shine*? How *we* made love in private jets flying over the Mediterranean? How you *used* me to get to the top and then dropped me? Wait! Maybe you reminded her that you were busy *fucking* every bitch that happened to know your name? Or that we've *been* broken up for going on four years, but we've *fucked* more times since than the previous years combined? Is that what you've been reminding her? Don't be discussing me with your pay-back hoes, Shane! Not unless you tell them every detail!"

She smirked at Lisa and used her cart to push theirs out of the way. "You look thirsty Blondie." She sneered, and tossed a bottle of water into their cart.

Shane quickly held Lisa as he felt her melt into his arms. "Baby, don't listen to her. Amanda's crazy! I already told you that. Remember? Lisa…"

Lisa sobbed in utter embarrassment.

Cilon sprawled off in the plush suede couch, enjoying his private showcase of other people's property.

"Backside! A so yuh a gwan gyal? Yuh bad sah!" He chuckled. "Do the split again! Yeah, and mek it jiggle! Bloodclaat! Babes, yuh need fi mek daddy get yuh back to work man. Worth yuh weight in diamonds! Come closer and show mi yuh fat pum pum. But how it so sexy and yuh have son? Murda! Babes, I want yuh to kiss it for me…"

Michelle, already positioned on all fours, crept towards him as she teasingly licked her lips. She had already stripped him naked when he first entered the house, and his now turgid cock flailed wildly. Without using her hands, she easily devoured his manhood in its entirety.

"Bloodclaat Michelle! Tek yuh time! Tek time please babes! Hmm...yeah...just like that!" He remarked between groans. "Alright, enough! Come siddung pon it sexy!" He eased out of her mouth and eagerly motioned her closer.

"Where did you put the condoms?" She asked while scanning their surrounding.

"No time baby! Gimme di pussy now! Yuh nuh seh yuh on the pill?" He reached out and gripped her arm.

"Yeah, but there is more to condoms than babies you know?" She retorted cynically.

He grew agitated. "Now mi see why Biggs slap yuh up yuh nuh! Yuh full a too much argument! Come siddung before yuh mek mi get up!" He barked.

She thought about standing her ground, but quickly re-assessed her situation and obliged him. She climbed atop him and slowly straddled his dick.

He aggressively groped her ass, revelling in the warmth of her cushion. Almost instinctively, he smothered his face in her ample bust as she expertly massaged his entire length.

"Yeah! Gimme all a Biggs pussy! Yuh love mi cocky babes? How it mek yuh feel? It's the best eva don't it?"

"It a monster Cilon! It's the best! I love it!" She shrieked at the top of her lungs and tilted her head backwards.

Michelle discreetly rolled her eyes and contemplated. *Anything that makes you feel better Cilon...whatever you need to hear. Your cocky is definitely not the best. It aint half of what Biggs is working with! Don't get carried away thinking this is about comparing you to Biggs or about me and you. This is all about me, and after yuh done with Biggs, me and yuh done! I can't believe Biggs...*

Cilon pinched her vagina, jolting her back to reality. "Look inna mi face when yuh ride mi babes! Tell mi more bout mi cocky!"

Her sensations heightened as her body grew warmer. "I'm coming...I'm coming! Fuck me! Fuck me Biggs!"

Cilon forcefully connected his palm with her jaw.

Regina arrived home at six o'clock in the evening, surprised to find the place in complete darkness. She called out for Linton and Roxanne, but neither seemed to be home.

"What the hell!" She screamed aloud, as she dropped her bags onto the kitchen floor.

Linton, I couldn't care less about...he's a grown ass man! But that Roxanne Alicia Mitchell...she's a piece of work! A fucking masterpiece if you ask me! What do I have to do or say to get through to that child? This is not even my burden, God...seriously! No hanging out on school nights! What the hell is so hard to understand? I scold her...she shapes up...then the shit wears off! She tried the knob to Roxanne's room door and realised it was locked. That sent her over the hedge.

"Locking doors in my fucking house? Now she's definitely lost her mind!" She stormed up the stairs to retrieve the spare key from her bedroom and returned with a vengeance.

When she unlocked the door and shoved it open, she was instantly agitated by the mess that greeted her. After flicking on the light, she begun to realise that what she thought was mess was more like Santa's enchanted forest.

"Where the hell did Roxanne get all this stuff?" She asked her shadow, apparently.

She walked around the room, examining her sister's interesting belongings. *That's a huge teddy bear! When, where, and whom? How the hell did I miss that? All these clothes…BCBG…Bebe…XOXO? And where the hell did she get Dior shoes? That's like forty-five thousand dollars!* Her eyes moved from item to item in sheer amazement, fear, and guilt. *When the hell did she get a Motorola cell phone? Roxanne better not be shoplifting! I'd kill her!*

She noticed a light green jewellery box on the dresser that was reputably indicative of what it held inside. *A diamond-fucking necklace! This shit better be fake! I'm going to kill Roxanne!* Her eyes brimmed with tears as the dark cloud of failure lingered over her head.

Her inspection eventually led her into Roxanne's bathroom, where the cloud burst and failure drenched her soul. *How did I not know Roxanne's navel was pierced?* The thoughts flooded her as she cried, carefully avoiding any acknowledgement of the used pregnancy test that sat bare-faced on the base of the medicine chest.

Where did I go wrong God? I'm just like her! Just like mother! A failure…this cannot be happening to me! When? When, oh God? When did Roxanne find time to have sex? And get pregnant? How did I miss the signs? How did I not foresee all this? It's all my fault… She began to wail.

She cursed her mother for abandoning them at such a fragile age. She damned her father with much hatred for disappearing on her mother the minute she was conceived. She slumped to the bathroom floor and clutched herself tightly as grief overwhelmed her.

All I wanted to do is provide her a little stability…I sacrificed everything! Regina vented mentally. *My youth! My career goals! My entire life revolves around Roxanne! I gave her everything I didn't have! And this is the pay I get? I can't do this anymore…I give up!* She felt defeated.

"Glad you made it baby." Caramel teased Michael as she let him into her apartment.

Like I had much of a choice! He mused inwardly, but airily replied. "Yeah, me too...so what you have planned?"

He couldn't deny the feeling that overcame him when he got a full view of her getup.

She rocked a black sheer bra that strained to cup her forty-two inched double D jugs, and the matching thong that was visible at her waist line but disappeared halfway down. The lace garter that clipped unto the thong did more than complement her enticing outfit; it defined the outline of her heavy rump that enforced her forty-seven inched hips. Her patent leather, peep-toe stilettos was the magnet on top.

The sensations rippling throughout Michael's body sent his mind into overdrive. He tried to appear unenthused, but only his emotions cooperated.

"Is that for me?" She purred confidently as she groped his crotch, fondling his pulsating rod.

"I guess." He confessed with a slight grin.

"You guess? I'd say you're more positive than AIDS." She giggled mockingly.

Her choice of words did an instant number on his already overactive mind. *AIDS? Why'd you have to bring that up? That wasn't funny! Maybe you have AIDS...is that what you're trying to tell me? What the hell am I doing here with this woman? I already made love to my wife today!*

But that goddamn outfit...fuck! Natalie would never wear something like that for me...too old-fashioned. Just stop it right there! Don't bring Natalie into this! This has nothing to do with her! It's all about you and your whoring ways! You're getting what you deserve for stepping out on your wife! His conscience worked its way into the closing arguments as her warm mouth enveloped his already exposed thunder.

Caramel moved her hands and head with skilful coordination, forcing an explosion with two minutes. She welcomed every drop of his love into her eager mouth.

Staring into his eyes, she swallowed. "Go lie down." She instructed, pointing at the king-sized bed robed in silk.

He dutifully obeyed her, but stopped to remove his dress shirt before he plopped down onto the bed.

"You're gonna love what I have in store for you baby. It's gonna *blow your mind*!" She teased.

Blow my mind? Is this bitch going to kill me? I should've known! Got caught with my pants down...or off! He was more nervous than usual.

"What's that supposed to mean?" He sat up.

"Relax baby! Why you so uptight? Good things come to those who wait. You ever heard that one?"

"I've heard a lot of things girl, but is that what you brought me here for a lecture? I don't have all day!"

"Now you're being rude! You'll be here as long as it takes. Relax baby." She pointedly eyed him.

Michael was about to respond when a second woman emerged through the adjoining door and joined them. He made a mental note that she was twice as good-looking as Caramel, and as if it was possible, three times as sexy.

"Hey girl, you ready?" Caramel purred to the female.

"As ready as I'll ever be baby." The woman replied, daringly eyeing Michael.

"Chocolate Thunder, meet *Anne-Gina*...pronounced like *vagina*." Caramel introduced them and giggled at her witticism.

Michael looked over at *Anne-Gina* with her forty-two Double D's protruding firmly from a patent leather, crotch-less body garter, fully exposing her clean-shaven fluff. Her daringly red stilettos capped his mesmerising journey down her slim waist, over her graciously wide hips, and along her well-toned legs.

Anne-Gina walked up behind Caramel and kissed her on the neck, her smile never fading as she daringly held his gaze. When her hands emerged, enveloping the breasts of the once sexiest woman alive to him, Michael observed with wide-eyed enthusiasm. The temptress sensually massaged the impossibly perfect mounds in her grip, tweaking the perky nipples before venturing down to the exposed crotch.

Caramel moaned in sheer delight as her body's sensations responded to the undivided attention. She perched one leg on the edge of the bed to give her playmate more access. While licking her lips, she too held Michael's gaze. Her arousal was increasingly fuelled by his intense concentration, and sheer look of confusion.

"You're gonna just lie there and watch baby? Or you wanna join us?" Anne-Gina purred, grinning.

"Ahm...ahh...yeah!" Michael fumbled for the words, hypnotised by Anne's big, bright, brown eyes.

He moved towards the foot of the bed. *You must be a Goddess! Princess Jasmine even! Shit! God help me!* He was almost salivating.

"You want to taste this pussy Michael?" The *Goddess* teased him with every word she purred.

"Michael's not that type..." Caramel stopped short when his head eagerly nestled in her friend's crotch. She was immediately infuriated but decided to remain calm.

You little cunt! You've never done that to me before! I should've never brought this bitch here! You owe me one Michael Simmons! I will get mine! She climbed into the bed and buried every inch of his throbbing dick in her mouth. She worked at it with much aggression, with every intention to upset him.

Contrary to what she expected, Michael didn't take a breath to complain or even come up for air. He slobbered Anne-Gina's pinkness as if it held the body's necessary nutrients and he hadn't eaten for days.

Anne-Gina enjoyed every minute of her moment; Caramel's jealousy was the added cherry on top. *You should've known better bitch! Don't talk about a good dick to your girlfriends...they gonna get curious.* She mused inwardly. *Especially if he's paid! What the hell else did you*

243

expect? I'll have him...with or without you! She mentally chastised her friend. Michael bit too hard on her clit and she shrieked and jumped back.

"Are you trying to detach it baby?" She giggled, trying to ease his obvious embarrassment. "Caramel, what's up with *your* man?" She noticed his annoyance and winked.

"Newbie!" Caramel replied. "He just needs the practice. He'll get it!" She sheepishly eyed him and smiled.

Michael caught wind of her silent rage and rolled his eyes at her. *You wanted a threesome? You got one! This woman is a goddess! You are too...but too fucking crazy!*

"Anne-Gina, *beautiful*, come back to me...please!" He whined, smiling on the inside.

Caramel bit down on the tip of his shaft and he jumped up, nearly pelting her over the edge of the bed.

"Hey *Newbie!*" He barked. "It's not edible!"

She was officially irate.

Anne-Gina laughed coyly and walked over to him. This time she climbed into the bed and confidently straddled his face, turning her back to her friend.

"Oh, that feels *too* good. You're definitely a fast learner *Chocolate Thunder*. Hmm! Just like that! I'm coming baby...yeah just like that! Fuck! Mmm...mmm... mmm." She whimpered as she came, flexibly rotating her pelvis.

"Who's ready to fuck?" She mentioned dryly as she laid on her side on the over-sized pillows. "I know I am..." She added, winking at her jealous friend.

Caramel was visibly flustered. Her insides churned with every moment she lost more control of the situation.

"Anne-Gina, you're my bitch and all, but *Chocolate Thunder*...don't speak that name again! Cool?"

Her friend gestured a zipper across her lips.

"Michael, I want to feel your dick inside me!" She continued. "Bring it here!" She purred seductively.

"After Anne-Gina!" He replied bluntly. "I'm anxious to try that new pussy!" He spoke without looking in her direction, knowing the exact effect of his actions.

"*I want you first*!" She snapped. "This is *my* treat remember? What *the fuck* are you trying to prove?"

"Caramel, the treat was for *him*! Calm down baby... you're still the boss!" Anne-Gina smiled and playfully slapped her friend's ass. "How do you want me 'Your Highness'?" She looked into Michael's lustful eyes.

Alone! Is that an option? He thought. "To be honest, the thought of giving you a 'backshot' has my mind frantic. You're so sexy!" He licked his lips and spoke feverishly.

Anne-Gina responded by assuming the position.

Michael marvelled at the way her ass cheeks naturally leaned to the sides, revealing the perfectly pink opening to her slit. He slid on his magnum and wasted no time in exploring the new seas.

While accommodating every inch of his sturdy manhood, Anne-Gina motioned Caramel closer to complete the chain link. She smothered her face between her friend's thighs and worked her slit orally.

Michael was in pussy haven as he slowed his pace to the tune of making love. He enjoyed the way Anne-Gina's orifice expertly clamped his thunder.

You're the fucking best! He mused in amazement.

Caramel's eyes were plastered on him. *Don't seem too worried about the wife now huh Mr. Michael? Fucking Jamaicans and their love for foreign pussy!*

When they switched positions, he ruthlessly pummelled Caramel as she struggled to return Anne-Gina's oral favour. In no time, he exploded on her face and leaned back unto Anne-Gina.

"You, I definitely need to see again..." He whispered in her ear, causing her to smile.

Caramel looked over at the teddy bear angled towards them. *Mission accomplished!* She giggled inwardly.

CHAPTER FIFTEEN

"Come inna di cyar!" Cilon barked at Jules through his slightly ajar car window. He had gotten the contact information from Michelle, who had stolen it from Biggs.

Jules walked around to the passenger side of the vehicle and opened the front door.

"Get your rass inna di back! A wha yuh feel like?" Cilon shouted irritably, getting an immediate response.

He closely observed his passenger through the rear view mirror and grimaced in disgust. "Whappen to yuh face? Yuh get a fixing man?"

"Yeah, I was rushed by three men a couple weeks ago…if you must know."

"Nuh dat yuh like man? Dat fi happen to your kind still. You *chose* the dark side! Nah get no pity from me so straight to business! Biggs want yuh dead." He dangled the words to marinate the air. "Him a offer *big* bucks for yuh head. So here's my offer…side with me and I'll get rid of the orders. I'll protect yuh from now on!"

"And what's in it for you? Why would *you* want to help me?" Julian asked, evidently shaken by the news.

"We will get back to that! Right now, I jus want yuh decision…life or death?"

"But how I know I can trust *you*? What are my guarantees? How I know *you* won't kill me?"

"Cause yuh woulda dead already battybway!" Cilon snapped. "Learn fast eh, mi no have the patience fi ediat questions. Come outta mi car too! Mi will keep in touch! Lay low!" He barked and hastily sped off.

Yuh get whatever yuh deserve pussy! Benji chilled in his living room and mulled over the events leading up to his decision to double cross Biggs. *Yuh can get any fucking woman inna Jamaica...inna di entire world...but yuh still fuck my girl. Yuh fuck my Cindy! Yuh violate her...so you violate me! How yuh can call yuhself a friend and fuck yuh bredrin girl? The amount of things I do for yuh over the years...yuh diss mi yute. Diss mi big time!*

Now yuh affi suffer the consequence! Yuh fuck mi gyal and breed her! Yuh put a bun inna mi oven! Breed mi Cindy and mek mi flip pon her. I going blow off yuh fucking head! Just wait til Cilon done wid yuh. Bout yuh a shack up yuh foreign gyal a yuh yard and a stroll round town with Roxanne a play lover boy. Yuh fucking batty fucker!

Shoulda know seh yuh woulda fuck man one day! Yuh fuck too much! Seventeen years we've been friends... and after all we've been through, this is how you repay me. I never ask yuh for shit like the other pussies yuh call friends. All them do is suck out yuh pockets! But me, the one true friend you have, is the one yuh fuck over? You really fuck over Benjamin Barkley? Alright pussy hole...if a so a so. Yuh start the war, and mi will finish it.

His cell phone rang, interrupting his thoughts. *Speaking of the fucking devil...* He took a deep breath and answered.

"Whagwan Biggs?" He smiled inwardly.

Linton hurriedly made his way downstairs to the parking lot to meet Regina. Confident that he was in the clear, he was eager to find out why she had went to bed so early the night before and had left the house in the morning unannounced.

What's going on babe? What happened to you this morning?" He asked as he climbed into the passenger seat and leaned in to kiss her.

"Had to do some thinking." She airily replied.

He hated when she did that. "What about babe? Did something happen?" That fact was already clear from her dishevelled appearance.

"More like what's right these days Linton..." Her eyes welled with tears.

He didn't like the sound of that response, nor wanted to go in the direction he thought she was heading. "Regina, if it's the Cayman thing, I've been..."

"Roxanne's pregnant!" She was crying now. "Can you believe it? Did you know about this?"

Linton was awestruck. "Regina, I...I wouldn't have kept something like that from you. Are you *sure*?" His conscience made him uneasy.

Regina was already in a temper. "I searched her room yesterday..." She fought to control her sobs. "Found all kinds of shit! All sorts of shit that Roxanne cannot possibly afford! And then there was this pregnancy test...and it was positive. I can't believe this *shit* Linton. What did I do wrong, huh?" She was losing all control. "Am I such a bad person?"

"*Baby*...you can't blame yourself for this. Roxanne's a big girl now. She'll do whatever she decides...whether or not you agree to it." He held her tightly. "Regina, you do your best! Don't ever doubt that! You've done for Roxanne what a lot of women your age wouldn't have. Don't for another second blame yourself. It's just life baby. People make choices."

Though Linton spoke words of encouragement, his conscience riddled him with guilt and regret.

This is entirely my fault! I should've left Michael to fight his own damn battle! He's a grown ass man! Now the shit has hit the fucking fan. Nothing but downhill from here! Regina would kill me if she found out that I knew about Roxanne on top of everything else I'm hiding. Roxanne's pregnant! Damn that stupid little girl! How could she?

"Regina baby, we'll figure things out. Let's just take it a day at a time okay?"

"Okay. I'm just still in shock you know? She's only seventeen Linton. I didn't even know she was having sex. At least we could've talked..." Her sobs had subdued.

"Things like this happen everyday baby. Young, good girls make dumb decisions and are forced to pay the price. We'll just have to talk to her and figure this out. Take it in strides as a team."

"Too late for strides...but I hear you. Anyhow, I have to get back to the office. I'll see you later. And don't say anything to Roxanne before I get there."

"I won't. Take it easy okay? Remember, you did and continue to do your best!"

She smiled and nodded in response.

Linton kissed her passionately, and then pecked her on the cheek. "Later baby. Call me if anything."

"Okay, I will. And sorry for the disturbance."

"Anything for my baby." He offered a wide grin.

Shane snatched Lisa from behind and swung her high in the air. "Hey beautiful."

"*Baby*..." She whined, laughing uncontrollably. "I'm fragile you know. Put me down!"

He laughed and eyed her with a faux scowl. "When since? You're the one who attacked me!" He quickly side-stepped a flying pillow.

"I did no such thing! You just love to assault me." Lisa concluded and looked away pretending to be upset.

"Don't give me that face either or I'll show you *assault*!" He hopped into the bed and pinned her down before she had time to react. "Now, assault would be me, Shane Wright, tearing your sexiness apart with my now erect monster." He laughed at her infectious giggle as she writhed beneath him. "But I can't have you crying like a baby."

"*Ha*! How can that lil' thing make me cry? Don't kid yourself *little* boy. I'm *all* woman." She made a desperate attempt to free herself from his grip.

"Then why you running? Ahhhh..." He unleashed his Chinese alter ego. "Wise man say you seem scared of *sometin*. I nuh know, but I tink I know the awnsah."

Lisa laughed heartily. "You're so silly Shane! Get off me! I'm serious!"

"I nuh tink so my fren." He continued, though he loosened his grip on her limbs.

"Do something while you're there then. At least pin me down for *something*!" She mocked him.

"Oh? Wise man sense you can't resist the chawm... and he likey!" Shane released her legs so he could use his freely, but maintained his grip on her arms.

He slid his lower body down along hers and manoeuvred his groin to steer his throbbing shaft. Steadily penetrating her, he inhaled deeply as her walls fit perfectly to his extended muscle.

"You love it baby?" He whispered by her ear before kissing her perky nipples.

"Mmm...mmm" She moaned and flexed to his firm, deep strokes. "I love it Shane! I love it too much!"

He smiled at her uncharacteristic response. "Yeah? Well come all over it for me baby...can you do that?

"Uh-huh. I can definitely...mmm..." She caved under the pressure. "I'm coming Shane! I'm coming! Mmm...mmm..."

He held her tightly, rocking her body back and forth as her muscles pulsated welcoming every inch of his wood.

"That was the best!" Lisa exclaimed, falling back unto the pillows. "I know I say that all the time...but seriously."

Shane revelled in the feedback. "The pleasure was *all* mine. But we're not done here. It's daddy's turn!"

He moved her into doggy-style position without breaking the connection between them.

"Baby?" Lisa whispered beneath him.

"Can't talk right now baby...can't think. Heavens Lisa...this position...I'm coming!"

"I'm pregnant!" She blurted as he bucked inside her with much fanfare.

He collapsed beside her. "Are you *serious*?" He almost shrieked, and reflexively pulled her closer.

"Yeah, like nine weeks serious." She asserted.

Shane laughed. "Why didn't you tell me this before?"

"I wanted to wait until you sorted out your business. You had enough going on."

"Baby, that *is my business*! Ha! I'm going to be a dad. I hope it's a boy." He didn't know what else to say so he kissed her on the forehead and laughed some more. "Wait until mom hears this. But wait..."

"She already knows." Lisa chimed in.

"So that's what the whispering and all that necking was about at the airport. Wise man say y'all are sneaky. He nuh likey! He nuh like being in da dawk!"

Lisa laughed and nudged him in the side. She was content, but also keen to his unspoken reaction.

Shane reasoned with his conscience. *I guess chemo is no longer an option...it's the option! Lisa's pregnant? Wow! Always thought I would be thrown off by some news like that; the end of my womanizing days. Funny how life just threw me under the humble bus. My girl's pregnant! That's crazy!*

What the fuck am I thinking? I can't be a daddy! Alright slow your roll, you're getting paranoid! Breathe! Breathe! That's it...take it easy. This might not turn out to be so bad. I'll just have to make it right...do it like my dad did. I'll give him credit for that; he honoured my mother and made her a wife before she gave birth to me. That's the least I can do for Lisa. Though she'd never complain, it's the right thing.

He kissed her forehead again and hugged her tightly. "I love you mucho Shane Junior's mother."

She giggled. "Love you too Shania's father."

"My sperms are strong baby...I'd accept the facts *now* and avoid the disappointment later." He slapped her on the butt when she plucked one of his chest hairs.

"Oh yeah?" She got up and gave him her wrestler's grimace. "Ready for *another* ass whooping?"

He jumped up prepared for the war. "Alright, my bad. I don't want to wrestle. Lisa, Shane junior..."

She hopped unto his back, knee first, knocking the wind out of him completely.

Shane howled, but laughed uncontrollably as they tussled like school children.

"A wha di *bloodclaat* him a do ya?" Biggs blurted, instantly slowing his Range at the top of Michelle's street.

He spotted Cilon's candy red Mercedes in his driveway, and instinctively parked behind the neighbour's shrubs to scan the area for anything else out of order.

"Shit! Mi son!" He grabbed his gun from under the driver's seat and hastily unbuckled the seatbelt.

As soon as he opened his door, the automatic gates to his expansive property slowly swung open, and the eye soar slowly backed out unto the roadway.

His paralysis wouldn't allow him to react, but he grew more irate with each second. He watched as the driver lingered until the gates closed as if obligated, then sped off down the hill in the opposite direction.

"A Michelle set mi up to bloodclaat!" The realisation instantly hit him. "How the fuck Cilon have remote to my bloodclaat gate? A Michelle really a carry news 'bout mi to people? A she really a violate mi ting so? She better nah fuck deh pussyhole deh round mi son! Mi ago kill yuh Michelle! Not even God can save yuh bloodclaat when I hold yuh!" He cursed aloud as he marched through the bushes and over the back wall unto his property.

Biggs climbed over the first floor balcony and entered the house through Rashad's bedroom window. He frantically scanned the room for any sign of his son's whereabouts or school belongings.

This betta mean one ting! Michelle, if yuh jeopardise mi son life...yuh corna dark todeh! He opened the bedroom door and peeked into the hallway. There was no motion, and no other sounds but the ones emanating form the master bedroom. He tip-toed down the hallway and rest his head against the door; he could only hear Michelle's voice as she gleefully sang in the shower.

After trying the knob and it didn't budge, he stepped back and slammed the heel of his boot into the lock area; his access was immediately granted.

What the bomboclaat! He exclaimed inwardly as he stepped past the door, barely dangling off its hinge. *Where the fuck so much money come from? What the hell Michelle really up to when mi nuh come bout? A cya fi har money alla this!* He surveyed the rest of the bedroom and spotted four tightly packed Louis Vuitton luggage huddled together by the closet.

Bags all a overflow with the shit that I buy. Looks like somebody taking a trip! Sneaky likkle bitch! So yuh betray mi...and collect yuh money...and jus feel like wha? Yuh just tek mi son and lef out? Not a bloodclaat! He emptied one of the cases and hurriedly packed the stacks of money into it.

Michelle was so busy washing her hair and humming her favourite tune, that she only heard Biggs when his hand gripped her firmly around the neck.

"What a way yuh sound happy?" He barked. "Yuh all a hum and bare tings! Yuh hype eeh? Come ya!" He yanked her out of the shower by her hair and hauled her into the bedroom.

She screamed and immediately began to beg. "Biggs, why yuh doing this to me?" She panicked even more when she realised that all the money had vanished. *Don't even try to lie Michelle. Just beg!* She followed her instincts.

"Biggs, why yuh…choking me…like that?" She tried hard to speak though short for breath. "What did I do?" The words barely escaped her mouth as she fought back the tears that would only further agitate the man that literally held her life in his hand.

"*What did you do?*" He barked in her face almost biting her nose. "*What the fuck* was Cilon doing here?" He lowered his voice but spoke sternly.

No lies Mich…Just beg! "Biggs please! I will tell you…everything! I was planning to…"

"Mi a listen! But yuh running out of time." He removed his gun from his waist and stuck it into her side.

"Biggs please…I can't breathe!" The tears flowed freely now, all beyond her control.

He loosened his grip and backed her into the corner. "Talk fast bitch! Yuh trying ma patience!"

"Cilon came here and left that money. He wanted me to set you up. I told him to leave and he threatened me. It's when he left I saw that bag over there," she gestured with her finger, "and when I emptied it, all those bills fell out. Biggs I would never betray you if that's what yuh thinking!"

He looked over at the packed bags.

She caught wind of it and offered another explanation. "I packed our stuff because I knew when I told you he came here you would come to get us. Biggs I know you don't love me anymore or even trust me, but I would never do anything to hurt the father of *my son*! Please believe me Biggs." She was sobbing now.

Biggs glared into Michelle's eyes. He was actually torn between believing her and beating the shit out of her; and not believing her, but still beating the shit out of her.

"Is only one reason why mi nah go blow a cap inna yuh forehead yuh nuh Michelle...only one reason...and yuh know it! But God help mi if mi nuh fuck yuh up inna dah house ya todeh! Yuh deserve a buss ass same way!"

With that said, he punched her in the mouth spilling blood from her lips.

Michelle wailed, but in doing so, still fought to refrain from screaming to avoid further consequences. She tried to move out of the corner, but he grabbed her by the hair and slapped the side of her head from behind.

"Shut up yuh bloodclaat and don't piss me off yuh nuh! Wha di fuck yuh a ball out so fa? Yuh did a bawl when Cilon a fling cocky unda yuh?"

"Biggs! That never happened..." She managed to say before his fist landed in the small of her back knocking the wind out of her.

She tripped over her own feet and landed on the floor, her hair still wrapped tightly around his wrist.

"Mi ask yuh nuh question? Yuh nuh hear mi seh fi shut up!" Biggs snapped and kicked her in the stomach with his sneaker-clad foot.

She howled and clutched her stomach, reflexively folding herself into a foetus. "Biggs please...no more please...I will do anything." She spoke more in whispers.

"A you dat a talk again? Yuh deaf?" He asked sarcastically, winding her hair tighter around his left wrist forcing her head to lift off the floor.

He slammed his other fist into her face. The sound of bone penetrating flesh echoed from the contact.

Michelle relinquished all fears and screamed and howled at the top of her lungs.

Biggs hauled her towards the bed though she kicked, screamed, and fought to break loose. He nuzzled her face with a huge pillow and sat on top of her.

She tussled and flailed her feet when the cold metal of his gun rested against her bare skinned vagina. As fear riddled her body overcoming her, she was more determined to leave the world fighting.

"I give you two seconds to *shut the fuck up*! Two!" He forced the nozzle between her thighs and spoke.

Michelle's body went limp below the pillow. Her sobs also subsided.

Biggs removed his gun, uncovered her face, and proudly assessed the bulk of his damage.

"Come gimme the best fuck a mi life now!" He barked, unwinding her hair from his grip. "Don't try nothing stupid either!" He perched on the bed.

Michelle tried to garner the strength to obey her commander. Her legs offered minimal support and her ribs ached with every movement. Blood continuously streamed down her face as her head throbbed to the beat of her heart. *Your time will come.* She thought to herself. *Oh God!*

"Lisa, you want the Island Grill or not?" Shane called out over his shoulder. "We don't have all night and I'm *not* walking unto the plane with food!" He joined the line of the famous Jamaican jerked food spot in the airport lounge.

Lisa walked over to him and scanned the menu board. "I'll take the number one combo. But ask for two extra festivals. Please…" She grinned at him.

"I was about to say…" He joked. "And if you still want the patties, the store's over there where that coffee dispenser is…you see it?"

She scanned the line of shops and located the landmark. "Yeah. How many should I buy?"

"As many as you're willing to hold. For the *entire* trip!" He teased with a grin.

She smacked him on the arm. "I guess you won't be eating any of the patties that *I hold* for the *entire* trip!" She walked away, of course looking back to blow him a kiss.

As Shane made much of an overzealous and evidently flustered attendant, Lisa returned to the counter.

After their previous spat in the same airport, she learned to stifle her jealously or lose her relationship. She remained silent as he marked his signature on the peak of the woman's breast, offering an extra wide grin as they walked away.

Shane had officially gotten Lisa hooked on Island Grill's irresistible jerked chicken and festivals. In addition to feeding her up to five pounds heavier, he had also ensured she enjoyed every waking moment exploring the island. He took her to Frenchmen's Cove in Portland, one of Jamaica's finest beach getaways, and to swim the dolphins at the cove in Ocho Rios. In the city, she'd been to the Quad nightclub twice, explored the cuisine of some of the finest restaurants, and most importantly dined at Hellshire for the island's finest seafood under the sunset.

"*Air Jamaica flight zero-zero-nine destination New York City is now boarding. All passengers please proceed to gate seven for boarding. Once again...*" The intercom buzzed.

Shane stood and stretched. "Alright baby, prepare yourself for flying. It'll take some getting used to."

Lisa scowled at Shane. "Baby what are you talking about? I've flown before."

He leaned over, wiped the jerk sauce from her lip, and gently touched her stomach. "And that's your mommy...she's kinda slow. That will *definitely* take some getting used to."

She pinched his neck and giggled. "You're funny!"

"I know. Good one huh?" He nodded enthusiastically trying to sway her decision.

"Good one." She confirmed with a smile.

Shane routinely dialled Regina.

CHAPTER SIXTEEN

Roxanne opened the front door to the house and was astounded to see her prized possessions sprawled throughout the hallway. *What the hell?* She thought to herself, though her anger slowly evolved into fear.

"Don't just stand there. Come on in." Regina's voice sarcastically greeted her before she could react.

She looked up and acknowledged her sister, standing at the end of the hall gleaming at her in contempt.

"Why *the hell* did you search my room?" She started to pick up Biggs' peace offerings off the floor as she restrained the urge to scream at her sister. "Why did you throw my stuff on the floor Regina? That's necessary?" She spoke more casually, trying to offset the effect of her previous outburst.

"*Your* room? *Your* stuff? Roxanne, the last time I checked you didn't pay any bills in this damn house…cause you don't even have a *damn* job! So tell me *Miss Lady*…no, please enlighten me, how is all this, *your* stuff?" She spoke with grave disdain.

"They *are* my stuff. People don't have to work to have stuff! I get gifts from friends; you know those people you don't have a lot of? What's the big deal? Why the hell did you go through my things, *and* throw them out here like this?" She subconsciously decided to fight fire with fire.

"*Roxanne Alana Mitchell*! If you know what's good for you right now, you'd better shut your *fucking* mouth and don't get under my skin! You're about a word away from being homeless. Don't *fuck* with me!" Regina walked closer towards her little - grown-up sister, but fought the urge to lounge at her and beat her to a pulp.

She continued. "This is how this situation will unfold; *I* ask the questions and *you* provide the answers. If that's *too damn hard* for you, just take all this shit, right now, and *get the fuck out of my life!*" Regina was screaming now. Her eyes even glossed with tears.

Roxanne's eyes welled with tears as well. She stared into her sister's eyes as each of her hateful words hopped smoothly off her lips. It suddenly dawned on her what she was up against for this round. She adhered to her orders and remained speechless.

"Now, which *friend*...could you *possibly* have, that can afford shit like this?" She held up the diamond earrings and the matching necklace.

Roxanne's tears spilled down her cheeks. "This guy at my school Regina...Valentine's pixie. What's there to afford? I didn't even think it was a big deal."

"*Don't stand there and lie to me Roxanne!*" Regina shouted and threw the necklace at her. "I had these appraised. They are real diamonds! *Don't tell me shit about a boy at your school*! I'm going to ask you once more; who the *fuck* gave you diamonds Roxanne?"

Roxanne was more frightened now than she had ever been before in her entire life. She had never seen her sister so irate to the point of using obscenities, or shouting at the top of her lungs. She decided to offer explanations as her steps steadily minimized the distance between them.

"Regina...please. Can you please calm down? I will tell you everything...just give me a chance to explain. *Please*, hear me out." She sobbed and tensed her body for her sister's next probable infliction.

"*Calm down?*" Regina jeered her, laughing briefly. "Calm or not, you *will* tell me everything. This is not a transaction! There's no bargaining! But I'm listening... must say I'm running out of patience though. You're one step away from swallowing your teeth!"

"Regina, there's this boy...well a guy, and he likes me a lot. And yes, he's rich so he buys me stuff...that's it. I know I should've said something to you, but you've been so busy lately and worried about other things. I was just waiting for the right time."

"*Really now*?   How conscientious of you dear Roxanne!   And this *guy*, how old is he? And what's his business liking a *school girl* like yourself? And buying you all this expensive shit? *Guys* with money don't buy gifts for free the last I heard. You must be putting out something, no?" She sneered at her.

"I know what you're thinking Regina, and it's not that. It's not about that at all. He's just a kind person...to everybody."

Regina knew the last word would have come. It was Roxanne's common excuse to pacify every situation: 'everybody'. *Everybody* was *always* doing either this or that according to her. It would always vex her, but on this occasion, it infuriated her.

"*I'm going to kick your little ass Roxanne*!   And it's not even for being lickerish and taking this stuff from some *guy*. You want to know why I'm going to kick your ass, huh? You know why I'm going to beat the shit out of you right now? For trying to make me look like a fucking ass!" With that, her hand instantly connected with Roxanne's jaw.

"Yuh think you're talking to a dummy?" She readied to vent her pent up frustrations.

Roxanne screamed, cowering under her sister's blows while trying to fight the nagging urge to retaliate. She desperately tried her best to anticipate and block the hits, but Regina was way too frisky and determined.

Furthermore, she was more focused on protecting the life that nestled within her.

When all was said and done, the two sisters were balled up on the floor bawling from physical pain and emotional turmoil.

Roxanne coiled up in the corner with her back turned to her sister, hating every bone that defined her existence.

Regina relaxed enough to speak first. "Roxanne, are you pregnant?" She looked over at her sister, silently willing an answer that would contradict the facts she already knew.

"How long?" She looked away, wiping her tears.

"Thirteen weeks." She mumbled, too exhausted to lie.

Regina mentally calculated the weeks into months and responded. "I see. So what do you plan to do?"

"Deal with the responsibility. No other choice…"

"And this *guy*…is it his?"

"Yes."

"So have you told him? What did he say?"

"He knows. He's excited, hence all the stuff."

"Hmm…I see." Regina felt a sharp pain in her chest.

"How long have you known?" Roxanne turned to face her, curious now to reveal the traitor.

"A couple days." She offered with a heavy sigh.

"How'd you find out about the guy?"

"What does it matter? You're already pregnant!"

"Why are you always so quick to protect him?" Roxanne shook her head in disbelief.

"Protect who Roxanne? What are you talking about?"

"Linton of course! He's the only one who could've said something about Andre."

"*Linton*? And who the fuck is Andre?" Regina shrieked.

Roxanne instantly realised her mistake. She contemplated backtracking her statement, but decided that *everybody* was going down. She took a deep breath before relaying the entire incident at the Hilton to her sister. She also volunteered that Michael was having an affair with some stripper that worked at *The Club*, as relayed to her by Andre.

Regina hung her head in shame and fought to control the emotions behind the tears flowing down her cheeks.

Biggs pulled into his driveway and knew almost immediately that something was wrong. His paranoia was already at its peak after leaving Michelle's, and this uneasy feeling forced him to pull out his gun and clutch it tight.

He drove around to the back of his property and inspected the grounds for anything out of place. All seemed to be in order but he still couldn't ignore the pestering gut feeling.

Deciding to sneak in through the back patio, he entered the house through the kitchen door, listening keenly as he peeped down the hallway to see into the foyer. It was dimly lit and there was nothing but dead silence.

How Toya so quiet though? He pondered as he disarmed the safety on his gun and tip-toed further. All hell broke loose when he flicked on the switch to the high-ceiling chandelier.

"*Bloodclaat*! *What the fuck*!" He screamed aloud, as he looked up at the ceiling and realised why only half of the dimly lit room had illuminated.

His one million dollar crystal chandelier dangled loosely by its electrical chord, its crystal pieces disorderly decorating the centerpiece Oriental rug.

As the light swung and brightened different angles of the foyer, Biggs mouth dropped as his inner fears morphed into extreme anger. He stepped hurriedly up the stairs, flicking on each and every light switch that he passed, still clutching his Glock tightly.

Tears slightly glossed his eyes as he caught sight of his priceless paintings with deep slashes down their centers.

Added to that, the word 'WHORE' was spray-painted all over the walls in different shapes, colors, and sizes.

Biggs burst into his master bedroom to find the mirrors and cologne bottles shattered; his clothes and personal items strewn about the floor; and the bed neatly made with a knife jammed into his favourite pillow.

"Toya mi ago kill yuh bloodclaat! Member mi tell yuh dat! Yuh fucking body ago float up in a ditch!" He snarled aloud. *"Look how the bloodclaat gyal do mi place! Jah know!"*

He shouted at the top of his lungs and made a dash for his closet, searching for anything he could salvage. A few sneakers were still in their boxes, some jeans seemed wearable, but the rest were garbage. He inspected the drawers and the bathroom and found a few useful boxers and colognes.

"Mi ago kill di bitch! Trust mi! A di wrong day she choose fi fuck wid mi! *Bloodclaat star! Toya don't mek me catch yuh a road!* From JA to NY yuh better disappear to bomboclaat! Me and yuh!" He ranted and raved throughout the house, going room to room to assess the damage.

"That's why woman...trust mi! Mi nuh trust dem a bloodclaat yuh nuh! Mi leave the dutty gyal inna mi good, good house and look wha she do! Mi ago kill yuh bitch! Wha di fuck yuh did expect? Yuh nuh want give man nuh pickney, just a fuck and fuck and fuck for nutt'n so. Pussy a di least a my concerns...can get that any time. Yuh think that can hold man again? Fuck you bitch! Mi ago kill yuh!"

Biggs found a seat and dialled the first person that came to mind. "Beverly, I know it's short notice...but yuh can meet me at my house? Just take a taxi I will pay for it!"

"What's the matter Andre? You sound upset."

"Bev yuh want see wha Toya do to the place. Bring some help if yuh can! Jah know!"

"Okay I'll be there. Don't worry. Whatever it is I will fix it. Just take it easy and calm your nerves."

"Alright Bev." He hung up.

Beverly was the childhood friend of his mother's from their inner-city neighbourhood. She had taken him under her wings at ten years old after his mother had perished in a fire that completely destroyed their home. Bev's only son had drowned at sea the previous year on a fishing trip with the neighbourhood boys. They had ultimately filled each other's void since then.

Though she was more than capable now to pay her way through life, Biggs continued to cover all her expenses by paying her handsomely whenever he used her services. Otherwise, she'd refuse his monetary handouts.

He sprawled out in his bed and contemplated his next course of action. *Fair is fair! Who God bless no man can curse. Yuh can't just a plot evil and expect seh your tings will flow smoothly. Yuh affi plan for the mishaps too cause Andre 'Biggs' Jackson is no fool. Fucking with me won't be a walk in the park. How it fi be? Fucking fools! Yuh can recruit my own woman fi fight against me? My own son's mother? She definitely have too much to lose! So oonu fuck up, so me strengthen. Payback is a motherfucker!*

He desperately tried to fight the sleep that was creeping up on him. Before he could realise it, he lost.

"So Shane, with all the terminology broken down, you do understand that my job here is to remove the obstacles from your body's own innate healing process?" Dr. LeFranc paused and waited for Shane, who seemed much more at ease than when he first entered the office.

"Yes Sir, I do. I'm ready to start." He grinned.

"Okay. I have a preliminary set of questions that will assess your Energy Anatomy. I want you to be as honest as possible, which means giving me the first answer that comes to mind. Some of the questions may seem a bit silly to you, but you'd be surprised to know how much we lie to ourselves on a daily basis."

Shane smirked. "Okay, no sweat. First question?"

"Slow down young man. I ask the questions here." The doctor joked.

"Yes sir! My apologies." He playfully retorted.

"So Shane, do you like yourself?" Dr. LeFranc looked directly into his patient's eyes.

"That's one of the questions? Oh sorry, you ask the questions. Do I like myself? Of course I do Doc."

"You see, that hesitation is a no-no. But we'll continue. Are you actively working to change anything about yourself?"

"My diet and my appreciation for life around me." He was quick on that one.

"Why is that so?"

"In case I die..." The words escaped his mouth quicker than he could stop them.

Dr. LeFranc sensed his uneasiness. "Everything we discuss is between us, Shane. We'll proceed." He scribbled notes on his clipboard nonetheless.

"Are you able to admit when you're wrong?"

"No. Not all the time; depends on the punishment."

"Are you open to feedback from other people about yourself?" He picked up the pace to fuel impulsive responses.

"Not everyone. Only those I care to have give them; the feedback that is."

"Are you honest? Do you sometimes misrepresent the truth?"

"Who doesn't? Sorry. Sometimes I alter the truth... yes."

"And why is that?"

"It depends. To avoid hurting people; to make myself look good; to get out of situations."

"Are you critical of others? Do you have to blame others as a way of making yourself feel good?"

"Guilty! Guilty! It's all a part of my line of work." Shane mused.

"I see. And the last one for today, do you feel responsible for everything and everyone? This one you can give a little thought to." Dr. LeFranc looked up from his note-taking and did his body language assessment. He already ascertained the answer to his question.

"Yes, I feel responsible for everything in my control and everyone I love. It is very important to me to ensure that my family is well taken care of, and that my career is as big as the amount of work I put in." He glanced at the charismatic man. "And now this..."

"I understand Shane. Believe me, I do. The first step is to work on your pessimism towards this *situation*." Dr. LeFranc never acknowledged 'illnesses'. He continued.

"You are the primary ingredient in the workings of your life. Whatever you say goes. You'll understand that line of thinking sooner. But for now, I want you to think more positively and begin cleaning out the *cobwebs* in your closet. You get my drift?"

"I get your drift Doc, and I've already been trying. You're not the only one who's been on my back about being positive. I *am* trying though."

"Well that's good to know. I wish you'd stop seeing it as being *on your back* though. Anyways, that's enough for today. I'll call you to schedule your next appointment for sometime next week, if that's okay?"

"Yes, that'll be fine. Thanks for the breakdown today Doc, I really appreciated it."

"That's why I'm here Shane. That's *my* sole purpose for existence; helping others to help themselves."

Shane observed his new friend and wondered what his personal story was; what would make him devote his entire life to save the living dead, or even decorate his office like he had a split personality. He decided he would save that story for a later date, and got up from the couch.

"Until next time then…" He outstretched his hand.

Dr. LeFranc shook it. "You just be positive. There is nothing you can't overcome. Nice meeting with you Shane."

"You too Doc. Take care of yourself."

"I will. And you the same."

"Sheldon are you in there?" Lisa called out from the entrance to the Macy's fitting room. "Where the hell is that boy?" She looked towards his brothers for a clue.

Steven and Simeon shrugged.

They had all been browsing the mall when Sheldon spotted one of his college sweethearts whose outfit was too inviting for him to pass up on the offer she had coyly whispered to him. In his next breath he had quickly dismissed them, promising to rendezvous in an hour by the pretzel stall.

Two hours had passed and Sheldon had still not resurfaced or answered any of their phone calls. Now Lisa, fully aware of his 'mall sessions', was busy skimming through the department stores that were reputable for their cozy and expansive fitting rooms.

"I think we should leave him." Simeon casually suggested as Lisa relaxed on an over-sized couch.

Steven smacked his little brother in the back of the head. He knew leaving Sheldon who had the car keys, would involve inviting Tina or Shane into the situation; that would not be good news for his best friend.

"Hey! We *did* try to find him!" Simeon argued. "I say we call mom, Lisa." He mockingly cheesed at Steven.

"I say we chill for a few and wait Lisa. Come on, did you see those Prada shades over there?" Steven tried to usher her out of the conversation, secretly sending Sheldon a text message in the process:

Bro, wrap that up. It's about to be 911 in this piece!

Tina sat by Shane's bedside, adoring her *baby-man* as he slept. She had administered his first intravenous chemotherapy dosage, and had given him sleep medication to spare him the nauseating side effects.

She was delighted to hear that his first session with Dr. LeFranc was successful, and that with Lisa's baby news he had decided to begin treatment until further advisement. She glanced at her watch and assessed his vitals.

Knowing that Lisa and the boys would be returning momentarily, she left his side and headed to her office to figure out the supper plans. After ordering a variety of dishes from their favourite Chinese takeout, she dialled Lisa's cell.

"We're outside Tina." Lisa answered on the first ring.

Tina peeked through the upstairs window. "Oh my, so soon? I just ordered supper. And tell those hooligans to leave the noise outside." She watched as Lisa did as instructed.

"No worries mom. We all had a hefty lunch. How's Shane doing?" Their relationship had solidified.

"Well he's asleep right now. He seems to be more optimistic about recovery after visiting with LeFranc today. I administered the chemo and we had a heart to heart before I put him out. He's trying Lisa, but you know Shane."

"Yeah. Everything at his pace." She walked into the house so they hung up.

The boys left the loudness outside as their mother had instructed but the complaining began as soon as they entered the immaculate and barren kitchen.

"Mom c'mon! We've been gone for like forever!" That was Steven, whining as always about food.

"Shut up boy. Supper is on the way; always about your belly!" Tina descended the stairs and entered the kitchen. "What did you all waste my money and buy now? You had better bought something for me!"

The trio giggled in unison.

Tina looked around at each of her three boys and smirked. "Is something funny? Cause that wasn't a joke."

"I got you something mom!" Simeon blurted and pulled out a Bath & Body Aromatherapy set. "It's lavender! Your favourite!" He smirked at his brothers.

"Oh thank you so much baby. That's why mommy loves you most and *feeds you* willingly." She looked around at the older two. "Anyone else for supper? Or will Lisa, Simeon and I be eating alone?"

Sheldon and Steven did the 'moon walk' out of the kitchen, retreating to their side of the house.

"So I thought." Tina continued to tease. "And make sure those rooms are cleaned or you two are definitely going to bed hungry!"

They chuckled and disappeared around the corner, but not before Steven slid his finger across his throat to provoke Simeon.

Simeon smirked and 'flipped him the bird', secretly.

Regina sat in the living room chair, anxiously awaiting Linton's arrival. She had allowed Roxanne to spend the night at Shari's so that she would have the empty house to devour him without distraction.

She had spent most of the day going over the details of Roxanne's testimony, and had replayed the scenario of her confrontation with Linton once or twice in her head.

None of the scripts had seemed fitting to her, so she had ultimately concluded to wing it.

As soon as Linton's keys jingled in the lock and the front door swung open, she was immediately on her feet. She was amazed by her sudden calmness and unwillingness to attack him while she stood her ground and patiently waited.   "Regina?" Linton called out when he must've seen her bags by the kitchen entrance.

"I'm in here." She called back, still more calmly than she would prefer.

He stopped in his tracks when he saw her standing in the living room with the look of doom spread across her face.

"What's the matter?" He asked casually, though terror rippled through his insides.

"Sit down. We need to talk." She replied coolly and sat back in the position she had spent most of the day in.

He was apprehensive. "What's going on with you baby? Did *I* do something?" He sat on the chair opposite her, intentionally.

She got down to business. "Tell me about that incident at the Hilton. I would choose my words very carefully going forward." She daringly eyed him.

Linton was more perturbed by her coolness than what she had just asked him. He preferred the Regina who wore her emotions on her sleeves and reacted. The silent and composed version was more threatening.

"Regina, I was going to say something to you. Believe me, it was tearing me up inside. I know you're upset right now baby, and there's nothing I can say..."

She stood. "I'll tell you what you *should* say! How about 'Regina, I know I'm a disloyal, deceitful, and selfish bastard. I know you have all reason to never trust me or have faith in me again. I know it's my fault that Roxanne is pregnant right now, because I didn't do something sooner. I know that you're thinking Michael had secrets for me too,

271

and that's why I had to keep his. And trust me *you're right*! I know I should pack my things right now and start searching for a new family because I'm no longer considered a part of this one. I don't deserve forgiveness Regina, and besides, it's not like I was prepared to support you with your move to Cayman anyway. I'll just continue to pretend like its not going to happen'." She paused, and the tears streamed down her face.

She moved closer towards him and spoke more sternly. "I want you out of here Linton! Take all your *shit* and *don't* look back! And you'd better talk to Natalie before I do! I hate everything that *is you* and *yours*!"

She stopped for a minute, entranced by his deep brown eyes that seemed to penetrate her soul.

"Be gone before I return!" She firmly demanded and stormed past him toward the front door.

Linton sat motionless as he absorbed the shock. Suddenly, he jumped up and sprinted toward the door. *Oh shit! Oh shit!* His thoughts tried to motivate him to act.

"Oh shit!" He screamed, as the sound of metal on metal echoed before he made it to the driveway.

Regina sped off down the hill with her rear bumper dangling from its rightful place. She reflexively dialled her best friend and waited anxiously for him to pick up.

"Hey..." Shane answered, sounding half asleep.

She immediately broke into sobs.

"What's the matter Gina?" He garnered more energy. "Is everything okay?"

"Shane, I've had the worst day of my entire life!" She tried to explain but her temper wouldn't permit thinking.

As the roadway became a blur, she instinctively pulled over to safety.

"Regina, calm down and talk to me. Are you hurt? What happened?" He was growing anxious.

"Shane, Roxanne's pregnant...for a *fucking man*! But that's not the worst. Linton, all this *fucking* time under my nose knew of this *man*...and he hid it from me Shane. How could he be so stupid? I can never forgive him!"

Shane listened in silence.

"Oh and did I mention that he concealed it because he's keeping secrets for his philandering brother? Yeah! Michael's cheating on Natalie with some stripper whore!" She cried even more at the mess that became her life.

"Damn! Sounds like a fucked up day alright."

Regina couldn't help but chuckle. "Tell me about it! I could've killed him Shane, but I was so calm. I'm so angry at myself for being so calm! Oh man..."

He laughed. "Well, I'm glad you were calm Gina. You can't call cell phones collect you know that?" They both laughed and he continued. "Look, I know you're pissed. But take it easy and think this through. Did you talk to Roxanne?"

"Yeah! I confronted her about being pregnant, and she told me about everything else. A house full of secrets Shane. Where the fuck have I been?"

"Working your ass off and doing your best! Just relax with the self-blame. So what now? What have you done? Or what do you plan to do?"

"Roxanne and I worked it out. I'm surprised she actually has her head clear about all this. Says she's prepared to handle it. As for Linton, I'd put up my entire savings to get him..."

"Hey!" Shane interjected. "We're taking it easy remember? Stop talking crazy like that. And Roxanne's dude?"

"Some guy name Andre, a deejay she said."

"Andre?" He flipped through his mental list of government names for popular entertainers. "Rass! *Biggs*? I mean, really?"

"You know that fool?"

"Don't we all?" He decided to drop the topic to avoid getting her agitated again. "But he's cool about it?"

"That's what *she* said! I should have him locked up for statutory rape! You should see all the expensive shit he bought her Shane. Damn! Nobody ever gave me diamonds before."

"You're not one for jewellery Gina. You leave them in the boxes to gather dust, remember? I can get you some bling though, no sweat."

She chuckled. "I miss you Shane. Times like these I realise I can't go to no damn Cayman. I can't live so far away from you." She started to cry again.

"Gina...see what you get for sleeping through five years of Geography? Cayman...far? Don't use me as an excuse to thwart your dreams and then later down the road when we're old and wobbly you call me the biggest mistake of your life. I nuh tink so my fren." His alter ego came to life, though faintly.

Regina laughed heartily. That accent could always bring a smile to her face. But this time, she was more pleased to hear Shane refer to life down the road. She suddenly felt glum.

"How are you doing by the way? I didn't even ask. Tina told me about the chemo..."

"So...so. It was bad, but not the worst. I think I slept through the roughest part. Anyways, don't worry about me. I'm in good hands. Wish you were here though. Oh, and I have other news unless big mouth already spilled. Lisa's pregnant."

"What!" Regina shrieked, temporarily deafening him. Not that she was entirely surprised based on the events of her last encounter with Lisa, but the confirmation made it more of a reality. "For whom?" She teased, chuckling.

"Ha! Funny! Don't hate, appreciate. Yeah, she told me two nights ago. It knocked the wind right out of me. But what can I tell you? That's my girl."

"Congrats Shane. Lisa's a lovely girl. I hope you'll do the right thing."

He knew exactly what she implied. "One thing at a time Gina, please. You can't expect me to give up *all* my bachelorhood cold turkey. I'd be like a fiend for crack!"

They both laughed.

Regina could hear Tina in the background encouraging him to have his supper.

"Anyways my love, I'm about to go into the grocery store. I'll check up on you later..." She fought back sobs, though her tears spilled freely.

"Alright baby girl. You take it easy and think on your feet. Call me if you need me. Mom says hello. Love you."

"Tell her hi. Love you too Shane. Take care." She hung up and her sorrows engulfed her.

Somewhere along her journey, she had apparently strayed from her usual path of ultimate control. Her work environment with Stacy was extremely uncomfortable; her relationship with Linton was now officially a mess; she had failed at protecting Roxanne from the world as she had planned; and now she wasn't there as she'd like to be to support her best friend.

Regina sobbed uncontrollably, relinquishing all her fears, insecure feelings, and pent up anger.

Linton sat on the sidewalk in front of the neighbour's house, rubbing his temple as he barked into his cell.

"*Wait*! Didn't you hear what I said? Regina knows everything! She's going to talk to Natalie! You're *fucked*!

We're *fucked*! *Fuck*! You should see how she fucked up my car man! And kicked me out! This shit is all your fault! Meet me at the Hilton ASAP! And don't *fuck* with me Michael!"

He disconnected the line and walked back to the foot of the hill. He shook his head in disbelief as he gawked at his Evolution mingling with the mango tree in the groves.

"*Fuck*! *Fuck*! *Fuck*!" He cursed as he kicked the tree, his voice echoing for miles throughout the hillside shrubs. "Why the fuck did I park behind her? Damn..."

CHAPTER SEVENTEEN

Michael strolled into work at eight thirty looking more haggard than a homeless bum.

His secretary routinely greeted him with enthusiasm and held out the morning's newspaper which he snatched from her grip, growling gibberish in response.

"Should I hold your calls Sir?" Antoinette asked, not exactly expecting a response.

Barely making it to his office, he plopped his husky frame into his oversized leather chair. He blinked for an extra long minute to rest his burning eyes, but the sunlight beaming through the sparkling French windows irritated him. He wheeled the chair over to the window and blindly fumbled to close the shutters. Sleep deprived for going on three days, he was officially exhausted.

The previous day had been nothing short of a disaster. He had fled court prematurely per Linton's demand then fed Natalie an award-winning reason he would not be home for the evening; of course, not without some chastising and insinuating of her own. His nerves had churned his insides the entire evening, with thoughts of leaving her home alone at the disposal of a raging Regina.

Added to that, he had spent the night being chastised for his 'loose' lifestyle, and his influence on everything that was presently wrong with the world. It was three in the morning when Linton had proposed the 'what now' plan.

Hmm! I could stay like this forever. Sleep my sorrows away. His thoughts raced. *Man oh man, what a night! What a day...what a life! I've dug a deep hole for myself, my career, and my family. And for what? For a fat ass and some plump lips around my dick! Goddamn it...*

men are so cheap and pathetic! How could I let this bitch come between me and my Natalie? I'm such a damn fool! Now I've pulled Linton and his family into my mess just like old times. So many years and not a damn thing changed but the expensive suits I wear!

Natalie will never forgive me! How could I possibly explain this to her? Oh God...and with the baby coming, I'm going to lose everything! Who was I fooling to think I could get away with all this? I'm such a fool...a damn educated fool! Now what? Can't see nothing but downhill from here...

The piercing sound of his private phone line penetrated his thoughts, giving him an instant migraine. "And the bullshit begins..." He murmured aloud, deciding to ignore the call.

His cell phone instantly vibrated under his butt as the desk phone stopped ringing. *Jesus! Go away! I'm not available people...please! Give me a moment.* He cursed mentally. The phone continued to vibrate without cessation, until it irritated him enough to retrieve it. With his eyes still closed, he took a deep breath and answered.

"Michael Simmons." He was barely audible.

"Yuh neva see mi calling yuh all this time? What the hell yuh so busy doing?"

"Law! You know that thing I get paid for?"

"I'm not in the mood for your attitude yuh nuh Michael. Don't get smart with me!" Caramel's words sliced the stiff air.

"*You're* not in the mood?" He chuckled. "My apologies dear Demon. How the *fuck* may I help you?"

"*Chocolate Thunder*, I think you know how *the fuck* you may help me! But first let me say this, if you fuck Anne-Gina *one more time* behind my back I'm going to *fuck yuh up! Yuh hear me?*" She screamed without mercy.

"Stop fucking screaming!" He barked. "I don't know what the hell you're talking about. And when did you determine who I fuck? You better stop calling me and riding my nerves! *You hear me*?" He barked in the same manner.

"I *better* stop? Or what *married* Michael? You're going to do what? *Not a god-damn-thing*! How's the wife's pregnancy coming along? Huh? I can bet Natalie's in her best moods these days. Would you agree?"

"*Fuck you*! Don't speak her name! Fuck you, and all the bitches that are *just like you*! Fucking home-wrecking, gold-digging…hmm!" He growled.

"Bitches? So *I'm* a bitch now? *I'm* the home wrecker Michael? Okay. I can fix that…"

Michael sat forward. "Listen, right now I'm just tired 'shitless'. I didn't mean to get upset, or get you upset. Let's start over. Where do you want to meet?"

"Come to *The Club*. I have something special for you." Her voice revealed no sign of their previous argument.

How unfortunate…He mused inwardly. "Okay, I'll meet you there before your set. Is that all?"

"Well, I went to the doctor yesterday and I got some interesting news. I'll just tell you when I see you."

He was not enthused. "Good news or bad news?"

"Depends on who you ask. I'll see yuh later *baby*. Chow!" She giggled and hung up.

Michael sat with the phone to his ear, mentally trying to pinpoint the exact reason his nausea returned. *Is it that sheepish giggle? Or that emphasis on 'baby'? Or that enthusiastic 'chow' at the end of a heated argument? And my dumb-ass asking 'good news or bad news' as if the devil ever has good news…Fuck me!*

He immediately snatched up the desk phone.

"Roxanne Mitchell, some of us work you know? I don't have all day to frolic." Regina turned and stared pointedly at her sister, who was unhurriedly pacing behind as always.

Though she made a conscious effort to be more understanding of her sister's 'snail's pace' approach to life, sometimes Roxanne would simply abuse her privileges.

They began to bicker in the parking lot of Medical Associates on their way to Roxanne's first appointment with the obstetrician gynaecologist. Since she had made the decision to be responsible, and Regina didn't have a choice but to support her, they agreed to live in harmony with the facts than at odds with each other. After all, they were the bulk of the only family they had.

Regina took a deep breath and continued ahead of her sister, entering the doctor's office long before her.

"Good morning. Roxanne Mitchell for nine o'clock..." She greeted the front desk attendant who barely looked up before responding.

"Are *you* Roxanne?"

"No. She's on her way in. I'm her sister, Regina."

"I see. Well you can have a seat, and one of you can fill out these forms. The doctor will call you by name." The middle-aged woman handed her the usual clipboard with the pen dangling from the chain.

Regina was not in the mood to lounge around, and did not like the idea of 'having a seat' five minutes past their scheduled appointment.

"I'm sorry, Mary is it?" She tried to read the name on the woman's breast tag. "Will there be much of a wait? It's already five past nine." She offered a smile.

"Miss, just have a seat please and the doctor will call you shortly." That was all Mary had to say before she returned her attention to her computer screen.

Regina scathingly eyed the callous woman before taking refuge in a seat close by. When Roxanne finally entered the office, she immediately tossed the clipboard into her lap.

"Fill those out while we *have a seat*!" She snapped.

Roxanne flipped through the pages and decided it was too much. "I don't know what to write."

"You can read can't you? Figure it out Roxanne! I'm not doing it." Regina snapped without even looking in her direction, and took out her cell to dial Shane.

As she pressed the send button and brought the phone to her ear, Mary's rigid voice pierced the silence.

"No cell phones in the office Miss." She pointed to the sign on the wall to emphasize her point.

Regina dropped the phone in her bag and was about to attack, when the doctor stepped into the waiting area.

"Mitchell, Roxanne." He called out, continuing as they approached him. "Sorry about the delay. I'm Doctor Smith. Which of you is Roxanne?" He flashed a million-dollar smile.

Regina was completely flustered by the man's charming, good looks. "She is." She replied faintly, pointing at Roxanne.

"And you are?" Dr. Smith's held her gaze.

"Regina, the *older* sister." She smiled sheepishly.

"Well then, I'm pleased to meet you both. Follow me."

The two got comfortable in the office as Dr. Smith completed the questionnaire with his patient.

"Is there a restroom I can use back here?" Roxanne shifted in her seat then stood.

"Yes there is." Dr. Smith replied, a little distracted. "But we're going to need a full bladder for the ultrasound. Can you hold it for just a tad bit longer? Please?" He looked up at her and asked sincerely.

She blushed at his enchanting smile and nodded in agreement, before retreating to the examination room as he instructed.

Regina had not anticipated, the full effect, that sitting in on this appointment would have on her emotions. Hearing the intricate details of her seventeen year old sister's sex life

281

and the accuracy with which she recalled the information, made her uneasy and in some way embarrassed.

"Ready!" Roxanne impatiently shouted from the examination room, disturbing the peaceful ambiance.

"There's my call." Dr. Smith eyed Regina and smiled, breaking the awkward silence between them. "I'm going to do a vaginal inspection first. Do you want to be present for the entire examination, or just the ultra sound?"

Regina's eyes hadn't exactly followed his face as he stood, leaving her awkwardly staring at his crotch. Unconsciously, she nibbled on her bottom lip and zoned out to the tune of her dirty thoughts.

"Regina!" He repeated, smirking at her facial expression as she zoomed out of the *Matrix*.

"Uhm…I'll just join you…after." She cleared her throat and spoke airily.

"Okay. Listen for my call then." He instructed before vanishing behind the curtain.

A cloud of embarrassment instantly overshadowed her. *What the hell was that?* She mentally chastised herself. *Regina Alicia Mitchell, you're a hot mess! Goddamn he's so fine though…hmm. My body's on heat right now. Haven't felt like this for another in years. Bless that chocolate skin and those glistening pearly whites! He's perfection! What am I thinking? This is crazy! I can't lust at my sister's doctor!* She smiled at the thought. *But then again, why not?*

The doctor's raspy voice called out for her, caressing her ears like a melodious tune. She stood and focused hard on composing herself, before joining them behind the curtain.

"Oh my God!" The words escaped as she suddenly felt faint. "This is real!" Her hand covered her mouth reflexively.

Real it was; on the screen, right before her eyes.

Dr. Smith steadily manoeuvred the transducer and explained the continuous image. "Yes Regina, Roxanne's around thirteen weeks progressed; just about the end of her first trimester. Everything seems to be in order for her *and* the baby. Come closer, you'll hear the heartbeat."

Regina's eyes filled with tears. Coincidentally, so did her sister's. She listened, in amazement, on the sounds of a new life after zooming in on the less powerful thump.

"This is amazing!" She blurted. "I don't know what else to say. I guess congrats to you Roxanne."

Roxanne was unsure how to interpret those words. She smiled nonetheless, though discomfort riddled her expression.

"What's the matter?" Regina urgently asked.

Dr. Smith sent the image to the printer and switched off the machine. "She just needs to release." He chuckled and pointed Roxanne to the restroom before leaving.

Regina stood motionless. She tried to mentally digest that her baby sister was no longer a baby, but having one.

"Regina, I'm sorry!" Roxanne immediately blurted when she returned from the toilet. "I know this is all awkward for you...to drag you through all this. It wasn't intentional."

She knew better than anybody else that this situation manifested her sister's deepest fear.

"There is nothing to apologize for Roxanne. I'm proud of the way you chose to handle this...taking responsibility for your actions. At least you learned *something* from me."

"I've learned *many* things from you sis. I just do a good job at pretending otherwise." She grinned.

"I can *attest to that*!" Regina affirmed, jokingly.

"Ladies..." Dr. Smith called out from his office where he patiently waited.

He handed the ultrasound pictures to Roxanne as the two emerged from the back room arm in arm.

"Please see Mary on the way out." He relayed his final instructions. "She will schedule your next appointment.

If you have any questions or problems before then, please don't hesitate to contact the office or me personally. You have all my numbers." He shook her hand and smiled.

"Thanks for making me so comfortable Doctor Smith. The experience was cooler than I imagined." Roxanne smiled appreciatively.

"The pleasure was all mine Roxanne. And Miss *Older* Sister, it was a pleasure meeting you as well."

"Same here..." Regina gazed at the man lustfully. *I'll definitely be calling you per-son-ally Doctor...Hmm!* She mused inwardly.

Natalie slammed the phone into its cradle and screamed.

"Where the hell are you Michael Simmons? I've been trying to reach you all morning!"

She flipped through her agenda and reasoned inwardly. *Hmm! You'd better not forget our appointment today Mr. Unavailable...and I'm not calling you again to remind you. Whatever you're busy doing...well. Can't believe you've been on my ass all these years about having a baby...starting a family...and now this shit! You're more unavailable than ever before. I swear Michael! Don't think it's too late!*

Hmm...I should call and check in on Shane. Ensure things are going well with him. Oh! I should call the contractor and make sure we're still on target for our May 15th opening. I have no time for these people and their everlasting stories. The Hope and Cope center will finally be realised. Wow! My dream is finally a reality!

The intercom buzzed, interrupting her planning session. Tameka informed that her ten o'clock had arrived.

"Thanks Tameka. Please send her in." Natalie closed the agenda and leaned into the comfort of her new massage chair. "Come in." She called out with her eyes half closed as she heard the light tap on the door.

"Hey Natalie!" Stacy exclaimed the minute she entered the office. "How's it going today? You look comfy!" She admired the doctor's growing bulge.

"I'm great!" She tried to maintain the same level of enthusiasm. "You're obviously in a good mood today." She smiled and shook her hand. "Please, have a seat."

Stacy smiled, nodding her head in affirmation. "I'm in a great place Doc! I think…no, I *know* I'm ready to get my life back on track. I'm ready to do right by myself and my son."

"And that, I'm glad to hear! Where's this inspiration coming from? If I may enquire…" Natalie teased.

She blushed. "Well, apart from *your* straightforward advice, I met this guy. Before you say anything Doc, please hear me out. He's not into the shit that all the others are into; he's an upstanding citizen. I've been seeing him for a while now, on and off. But it suddenly dawned on me how much I love him Doc. How much I care about what he thinks of me. I find myself feeling guilty for leading this double life; for not being completely honest with him." She paused as if reminiscing then concluded with a grin. "He's so protective of me too; in a good way."

"As long as *you* have it together, I'm glad. But remember, you came to me seeking advice on *you* bettering *your* life; not some *man*." Natalie chastised her out of sheer concern.

"I know Natalie. But don't worry I'm still doing this for me. The bad part is figuring out how to break all this to my son's father; that won't be so easy!"

"Well take it to the police then…" The suggestion came from an honest, naïve place.

"The *police*! If it were only that easy. They're on his payroll too. I'll have to come up with another way; have to fight fire with fire for this one!"

Natalie listened in amazement to the dilemmas of a beautiful woman. In her opinion, she could've easily been sitting in her place had she been given a better opportunity. She realised how privileged her own life had been growing up; with her parents always guaranteeing and providing the best of everything. She deeply sympathised with Stacy.

"Stacy, you're a smart woman. Whatever you decide, do it with utmost caution. Anything you can't solve, take it to God in prayer. *He* never sleeps."

"I know. And that's what makes this so bad too. Because my guy...well, there's something else..." Stacy leaned back in the chair and sighed.

"I knew you were holding out on me. Go ahead." Natalie urged her with a slight chuckle.

"The thing is...he's kind of not *my* man alone."

"Kind of?" She repeated rhetorically.

Stacy smiled. "Yeah, he's married."

Regina sat at her desk, vividly fantasizing about Dr. Smith. Smiling to herself, she wondered what mysteries hid beneath his poise. *Would you be Mr. Traditional with the flowers, champagne, and slow jams? Or are you the contemporary, cut to the chase playboy? Hmm, I saw those nasty looks you gave me under the quiet. Wonder what you'd be like in my bedroom...Regina Mitchell!* She giggled childishly.

I know...naughty. But still I wonder. Mister and Misses Smith. She chuckled at the irony of her insinuation. *I'd be lying if I said I didn't like the sound of that right now. Why can't I remember if he had a ring on his finger? Probably. Oh Lord!*

She sorted through her client's portfolios and put them in order of priority. As she slipped through the Rolodex, she sighed and rested her head on the desk.

Who am I fooling that I can pack my stuff and move to Cayman in four months? Nobody but my damn myself! No wonder Linton didn't take me seriously to begin with. He knew I wouldn't walk away from him, much less Shane, and now Roxanne. How could Linton deceive me like this? How could he look me in the eye and tell me he loves me, hiding secrets and lies like this? Men are definitely a different breed! Especially this fool who got my baby sister pregnant!

Pregnant! Roxanne's going to be a mom? I never saw this one coming. Portfolio definitely mismanaged! What am I going to do with her? I can't expect that she'll just up and leave with me; and I definitely can't force her. I'll have to prepare my heart for the worst. As if anything could be worse in my life right now! And that cheating son of a bitch Michael...ooh I can't wait until Natalie finds out about him! I'll definitely help her to kick his dumb ass! I should tell her my damn self. But I'll take the back seat on this one. I'll observe the ride...but not for too long!

Glancing over at Stacy's empty desk, she grew even more irritated. *And what the hell are you up to now Ms. Thing?*

With that thought in mind, she impulsively reached for the phone and dialled Michael's office number.

"Thank you for calling Clark and Simmons, this is Antoinette speaking, how may I direct your call?"His secretary's chirpy voice filled the line.

"Good morning Antoinette, this is Regina Mitchell calling for Mr. Simmons."

"I'm sorry Ms. Mitchell, Mr. Simmons is currently unavailable. Would you like to leave a message for him?"

Regina glanced at her watch and shrewdly replied. "Please tell Mr. Simmons that he should *sensibly* get in touch with me before I have to call him again. He knows where to find me." She had enough of playing phone tag with him.

"I'll ensure to relay your..."

Regina slammed the phone into the cradle. "Argh!" She screamed aloud, dying to confess Michael's transgressions to Natalie. She got comfortable in her chair and dialled her confidante instead.

"House of pain! What's your pleasure?" Shane laughed at his own one-liner.

Regina laughed too, though tears welled in her eyes.

"Watch dem bloodclaat to nuh!" Biggs stared in amazement as his best friend wilfully climbed into the passenger side of his main arch nemesis.

He had spent all day trailing Cilon after learning that he was aware that Michelle and the money were gone. The worst punch to his stomach only came five minutes ago, when he trailed him unto Benji's street. He leaned back in the seat of his rental, spying on the conspirators to his slated demise.

"Mi can't believe seh Benji woulda really betray mi like this yo!" He contemplated aloud to plug the unusual silence. "After all the shit I do for him? All the things we've been through together? Bloodclaat star! This hurt mi more than Michelle iyah! A wha mi do this man though Fatha God? A wha Cilon coulda really tell Benji bout mi?"

Continuing the pursuit, he slowed the car at the top of the dead-end street that was all too familiar to him. He watched as Cilon parked in front of his baby's mother's gate. There was no immediate action as per the zoom of his camera lens.

A moment passed before the front grill of the house opened, and a woman stepped into the yard. The four car doors instantly swung open as if choreographed, and four men emerged, walking hurriedly.

"A wha kinda meeting this man?" Biggs commented aloud as he snapped pictures of the men in motion. "Cilon, Benji...yes Julian yuh a move heavy todeh! But who the fuck is number four?" He chuckled as the three heavier set men surrounded the younger one, all the way into the house.

"*Wow!*" He exclaimed. "Serious meeting that! All you Jules, to how mi tek care of yuh and your family...help put yuh dunce brain through school...a so yuh a move? Yuh mek *bad mind* Cilon fuck with yuh head and recruit yuh! I going *fix* yuh bloodclaat if yuh think yuh ago fuck up my life! A dat wid *'schoolas'* yuh nuh, oonu can't hold oonu mouth; always a chat! Always for sale!"

He checked in on the scene through the lens and slumped back into the chair. *A wha mi life really come to though God? How di fuck mi end up inna situation like this? Just too greedy man...never have enough! Pussy feel so good but mi still want more. How di fuck batty ting drop een? When mi get so freaky? Love batty so much mi tek it from anyone...and mi anuh battyman! Deh yah a live a lu to rahtid! Mama woulda shame a mi.*

This is it for me and dem yuh nuh! Julian and him posse can fuck off! Need to just fix this situation and tek care of my Roxie. Must can get a fresh start with she...

His cell phone vibrated on the dashboard, startling him. This call he had expected, and was anxious to accept.

"Yo!" He barked into the phone as he started the car and checked his periphery.

"What's up Biggs? I'm so sorry about the other day when you called."

"Who dis?" He played pretend.

"It's Jules. Yuh forget my voice already?"

"Who? Yuh have the wrong number yuh nuh bredrin."

"Biggs..." The line was already dead.

He powered off the phone and reversed his car back unto the main street.

Natalie spotted Michael and her mood instantly changed. "I thought you'd never get here, *husband*!" She attacked him without concern for their spectators.

"I'm not even late Natalie." He adjusted his suit to ease his embarrassment and sat. He waved to the nurse behind the desk and kissed his wife on the cheek.

"What the *hell* is with you Michael?" She wouldn't let up. "I spent the night *alone* and I've been calling you *all day* with no response! Is there something you want to tell me? Cause this is no season for your bullshit!" She sternly chided him in a hushed voice.

The nurse ushered them into the doctor's office, saving Michael from his demise.

"Hello Natalie." Dr. Patricia Jones lovingly embraced her colleague. "I'm truly happy to see you!"

"I'm happy to see you too Pat." Natalie welcomed the warmth she had been deprived of lately.

"Michael." Patricia smiled and offered her hand. "It's been ages…"

"I know right. It's nice to see you again Dr. Jones." He feigned a smile.

"So let's get down to business, shall we?" Patricia waited until everyone was seated. "Natalie, how are you feeling hun?" She asked with utmost concern.

Natalie smirked. "How am *I* feeling? Or how am I feeling with the baby? 'Cause one of those two you don't want to discuss." She sliced Michael with a hate-filled glance.

Patricia chuckled at the cynicism, but stopped when she noticed Michael's growing discomfort.

"We'll stick to you *in relation* to baby Natalie. Do I sense some moodiness?"

Michael nodded before his wife could respond.

"That's an understatement. The morning sickness is really bad Pat, but I refuse to take any drugs. Are there any *safe* home remedies you can share?"

The doctor removed her glasses and sighed. "Well, the remedies that actually work tend to vary hun. I've been told about the wonders of cucumber; others have said ginger. But you can always chew an antacid, they're not exactly drugs and they should give some sort of relief."

"I'll guess I'll try all of the above." Natalie sighed.

Patricia laughed. "Let's set you up for the ultra sound. Michael, I will call you in after the preliminary exam okay?"

"Sounds good Dr. Jones." He coolly spoke his first in the past ten minutes.

Natalie scowled at him as she followed closely behind her friend into the examination room.

"Natalie, what's this tension I sense between you two? It's not very healthy for you at this time." Patricia set up apparatus while she got comfortable on the bed.

"He gets on my nerves Pat!" She snapped. "All our years this is what he nagged for...this baby-having dream. And now that it's happening, I don't think he's so concerned."

"Wow! Natalie, you have to understand that men react differently during pregnancy. I don't doubt that Michael is concerned...and maybe that's it. He's so concerned to the point of worrying, and you know how they panic when they have to worry?" She tried to reassure her self-conscious friend.

Natalie rolled her eyes. "I guess you're right. But he still *is annoying*! Can't remember the last time he wasn't."

Patricia slapped her on the arm and re-positioned the sonogram, illuminating the screen. "Now, lie still and breathe normally." She moved the transducer about Natalie's abdomen, observing the vitals. She gasped almost immediately.

"How lovely! We should get daddy in here."

Michael impatiently tapped his foot as he contemplated leaving to attend to the issues that threatened to destroy his life. As he got up to stretch his legs, he was summoned to the back.

"Congratulations Papa!" Dr. Jones exclaimed. "Come and meet your babies!" She pointed to the screen.

"*Babies*?" Natalie and Michael blurted in unison.

"Yes! Babies! There are three heart beats. One of course belongs to the mother. Look and listen." She revelled in the privilege of being the first to know.

Michael watched the motion picture in awe, zoning out as the doctor explained the view. *Could this really be happening? Twice the blessings in one shot? Wait until mom hears this!* His face gleamed with excitement.

Dr. Young pointed to the brightest spot in the center of the image. "That's where they're nestled. Given they're about seven weeks, the peculiarities of course cannot be visualized."

Natalie was comatose from the initial shock. *I'm going to be huge! I didn't sign up for all that! Having twins at my age can't be good news. How the hell can I even be pregnant with twins?* She kept that thought to herself.

Michael clutched Natalie's hand and whispered. "Thank you". Tears welled in his eyes as the excitement overshadowed his guilt. *I need to be a better man for my wife and my kids!*

"Michael, are you crying? I hope those are happy tears." Natalie almost whispered.

He smiled and passionately kissed the love of his life. "I'm sorry baby. Of course they're happy tears."

Linton spent the entire morning at work, desperately trying to contact Regina. It was now ten o'clock in the morning, and all prior attempts since six o'clock had failed.

Accustomed to hearing only the ringtone each time he punched redial, he was caught off guard this time when she picked up on the second ring.

"Yes Linton." Her tone was stiff.

"Regina…" He fumbled for words.

"What can I do to make you stop calling?" She seemed void of any loving emotion.

Linton was insulted. "Just hear me out Regina. That's all I'm asking." He continued when she didn't comment. "You have all reason to be upset with me…but we could always talk about things, me and you."

"My sentiments exactly Linton! I'm glad you get my drift! I have things to do…"

"Regina, I'm terribly sorry for not telling you everything sooner; for not telling you what's going on. I was just confused at the time. Baby, let me come home *please*. We can talk about everything in private."

"I've said all I needed to say Linton, and I've heard all you *didn't* say! What else is there to discuss?" Her patience had worn thin.

"I love you Regina. Please give me a chance to make it right. I want to make it right between us. I want my family back!" Linton spoke from his heart.

"I'll get back to you. But if you call me again…" She didn't have to finish.

"Okay Baby. Just call me, okay?"

There was a soft click, and then the dial tone.

CHAPTER EIGHTEEN

Hurricane season was in full effect in Kingston, Jamaica. It was only mid-May, but continuous thundershowers flooded the streets causing daily traffic congestion and nightly power outages from wind-blown trees.

Natalie stepped carefully as she manoeuvred the pathway between the parking lot and her office. One of the large palm trees had uprooted overnight, and was now dangling in the electric wires it ripped from the light post.

"What a disaster!" She exclaimed to Tameka upon entering the office. "Where'd you park? I didn't see your car." She shook the excess water from her umbrella.

"Morning Doc. My boyfriend dropped me this morning. Didn't want me driving in these conditions he said…" Tameka replied casually.

Natalie felt insulted. "I see. Well good for you." She stormed into her office and slammed the door behind her.

My fucking husband allowed me to drive in these conditions! With my extreme condition! Bastard! Just another thing to piss me off! She evaluated her image in the floor-length mirror to jumpstart her daily routine that had premiered in her seventh week of pregnancy.

It had been six weeks since she had last visited with her doctor, and had not only learned that she bore twins, but had listened to their gentle heart beats. Though she wanted to doubt that she nestled two growing forms within, her thirteen-week, double-decked paunch was already protruding conspicuously.

She hoisted her dress higher and admired her handsomely enlarged breasts. *Now those I can work with!* She chuckled to herself. *Nothing like bigger tatas…I like.*

They'll definitely go well with the dress I wear tonight. But this… She gently caressed her stomach. *This will take some serious getting used to. My abs are all gone now…not cute at all. I need to sign up for a prenatal yoga class or something. Ok! I'm officially depressed. I could definitely do with a massage. Hmm! Milroy better have everything prepared for the opening.*

She referred to the contractor who was applying the final tweaks to the Hope and Cope Cancer Support Center for its grand opening ceremony that was being held on its premises that evening. The guest list was labelled with big names from all professional societies, and for safety and aesthetic reasons, everything had better be in order.

Natalie re-adjusted her clothing and decided to leave. "This place is stifling me…" She mumbled as she grabbed her belongings and headed out the door.

"Tameka, please call my lady at Jencare and get me in for a full body at around one, one thirty the latest. I'm going to step out for a while…need some air. Call me on my cell with the confirmation and if something *urgent* comes up. *Urgent*!" She reiterated and turned to leave.

"Is everything okay with you Natalie?" Her assistant hesitantly asked.

"As far as I know…why?" She curtly shot back.

Tameka seemed anxious. "There's a stain…all over the back of your dress. I think you're bleeding!"

Natalie's fears immobilised her.

Tina had volunteered to relieve Natalie of the daily oversight efforts of the opening gala. She assumed the full-time responsibility to harass Milroy the contractor, ensuring that the building was sufficiently compliant with the statutory safety code and that the preparations were falling into place as per her friend's dreams.

She stood by the grand entryway and observed the talents of the Lighting Coordinator, who had been working fervently to transform the ground floor of the building to a fairytale ripped from the pages of a classical storybook.

"This is beautiful!" Tina exclaimed. "It's absolutely marvellous what you've done with the place." She firmly believed in giving credit when it was noticeably due.

The electrician smiled. "Glad you like it mam. Let's hope the boss lady is pleased this time."

Tina laughed. "Don't mind Natalie; she's going through some changes right now. I'm sure you're used to pressure."

"That I am." He chuckled and returned to his work.

She made her way to the podium at the head of the dining room to check in with the Mic Technician.

"All is in order?" She offered a wide grin.

He responded with a mic check. "Testing; one, three." His voice ricocheted evenly throughout the room.

"Spectacular!" She gave him two thumbs up, silently wondering if he realised his mistake.

The young man jokingly saluted her.

She decided to take a break and rest her legs. To pass the time, she scrutinised the guest list. *Wow! Some of these people I haven't seen in years! I wonder if Henry knows that his ex-wife and her new husband will be in attendance...hmm! That should be interesting. Charles is still alive? I could've sworn he 'kicked the bucket'. And this better not be the same Priscilla Rowe! That brute still owes me the down payment I lent her for her house. I should've burned it to the ground before I left. And of course Barbara is still whoring her way through parliament...some things will never change. I wonder if she finally did something about that rancid breath of hers. Only God knows how those men could stand her long enough to have her exhale in their presence.* She chuckled to herself.

"Mom, are you losing it? Who are you talking to?"

The familiar voice startled Tina back to reality. She laughed in anticipation of the expression that awaited her.

"Shane! Are you trying to give me a heart attack? You're not on my will you know, so be wise!"

He laughed. "Whatever mom. Young girls like you have no use for those things, remember?"

Those were the exact words she had used when he tried to curb her latest obsession with French fries.

"How could I forget?" She cynically replied. "So why are you so previous son? The event doesn't start for another eight hours."

"What's with the cynicisms today lady? Don't let me put you over my knees! I just wanted to see how you were doing. I've been calling your cell that you never answer."

"No! It's not my fault this time. The reception isn't so keen in this room and I've been in and out of here all morning. Where's Lisa and where are you coming from?"

"Lisa's at the apartment resting. I just went for a little workout; nothing fancy." He raced through that confession and continued. "Hey I'm feeling the decorations in here. You think the caterer would mind if I scoop up some of those chocolates on the way out? The Ice Sculptor was on his way in when I parked." He gave up his distraction efforts when the unenthusiastic look on her face hadn't budged.

"Alright mom. I said it was nothing fancy. Coach wouldn't allow me to anyway. You know you paid him well..." He tightly embraced and swung her into the air. "Right? Answer me or I'll toss you like a salad."

Tina laughed. "That was so corny! Put me down! You watch yourself Shane! That's all I have to say."

"Thank God! For the beautiful day I mean..." He swiftly dodged a punch. "Anyhow, I'm outta here. I've got a lunch date with my peeps. Ensure not to nag the hell out of everyone here. Natalie wouldn't be pleased if they quit."

"Get lost!" She yelled playfully at him. "And take care of Lisa." She added, smiling at his air kisses.

"Roxanne, I swear to God!" Regina turned to locate her sister. "I'm going to sign you up for the gym or something. You are way too lousy for such a young girl man; unbelievable! And spare me with the pregnancy excuses. I knew you long enough before that sister child."

"Aren't we anxious?" Roxanne called her bluff. "Exactly who's the patient?" She was already half an hour late for her appointment with Dr. Smith.

Regina blushed. Luckily, her sister was not close enough to see. "Whatever! I don't know what you're trying to say but please remember you're not the only thing on my agenda!"

"Got that right!" Roxanne shot back. "I think you know exactly what I'm saying Regina! And I thought you said we'd go to the mall after…"

She had completely forgotten. "Right…just walk up Roxanne! You're making me tired just looking at you."

"Then close your eyes." She teased. "It's that simple."

They finally caught up with each other at the office door, and playfully saddled up to deal with 'Mary the Misery'. Barging in with wide grins, they were sourly greeted as anticipated.

Mary scowled at their see through act and grumbled under her breath. She picked up the phone and mumbled a few words into the receiver.

"Have a seat." She mentioned without looking in their direction. "Doctor Smith will be out shortly."

The two burst out in giggles. They had learned to ignore the woman's discourteous behaviour.

Dr. Smith emerged before they got comfortable in their seats. "Ladies…couldn't find the place?" He teased.

Regina turned to Roxanne, who strangely declined an explanation and shook her head at the doctor.

He smiled. "I see. Well let's not waste any more time then. How are you doing Roxanne?" He ushered them into his office and closed the door.

"Could be better; but I've heard worse." Roxanne summarised her bittersweet experience with pregnancy.

He chuckled. "I've never heard it put like that in all my years. Is it the morning sickness?"

"Actually, that's getting better. It's more like the cheerleading squad in there. Sometimes I can't even sleep." She took a deep breath and exhaled audibly.

"Well at least you're still beautiful." He volunteered. "Count that as your blessing."

She visibly blushed. "Thank you."

Dr. Smith removed a Foetal Development chart from a folder, stealing a quick glance at Regina in the process.

"I see your bump is more pronounced now. More room for that energetic baby of yours." He chuckled at Roxanne's facial expression. "You're just about entering the nineteenth week of your second trimester. I'll illustrate with the charts what's going on inside there. Please feel free to interrupt me if you have any questions." He got his papers together.

"Okay. At this stage, the foetus measures approximately fifteen centimetres…about this big." He demonstrated with his ruler. "It should weigh about nine ounces…the weight of a small breadfruit; though I'm sure it feels heavier than that to you, Roxanne." He stopped to make eye contact.

Roxanne and Regina looked on in amazement, smiling.

"Your baby should have started to swallow, and the scalp has even started to sprout hair. The kidneys have also started making urine."

Roxanne was silently crying now, though she smiled. She clung tightly to her sister's hand.

Dr. Smith smiled. "Lastly, sensory development should be at its peak. That is, its senses are now developing in the brain. It also says that for you mommy…" He looked up at Roxanne. "You should be feeling upbeat and energized, daydreaming about your baby's appearance."

She nodded in affirmation. "I do that all day Doctor Smith. It's obsessive." She confessed with much fanfare. "But I don't know about me being energized at all." She elbowed Regina who audibly grunted.

"Maybe you should start an activity. You could try swimming, yoga, or even going for walks. That should boost your energy level, given you're eating appropriately. A diet high in fats can take a toll on energy level."

"Yes, *that* Regina reminds me of daily. Do you have a remedy for overly annoying sisters?" She joked and looked over at an unusually quiet Regina.

He chuckled. "Well Roxanne, I'm sure you're the expert in that area by now. So to the examination…you may go in back and prepare as usual and call me when you're ready."

"Okay." Roxanne got up and gave her sister 'the eye' before disappearing behind the familiar doorway.

Dr. Smith lowered his voice and spoke. "And how have *you* been, *Older* Sister? I see you're a hard one to crack." He offered an easy, million-dollar smile.

Regina's entire body tingled. "And what does that mean exactly?" She coyly replied.

"I tried calling you at your office. Even left a message…" He stared directly in her eyes.

"One message? Tsk! Maybe I didn't get it." Her body was experiencing a magnetic sensation from the twinkle in his eyes. She fought to maintain her composure.

"I see." He flashed a wide grin. "And how many messages did you leave for me?"

She shrugged. "Ten! Your *wife* probably deleted them! Or Misery Mary out there…" She sheepishly smiled.

"I'm not married." He leaned back in his chair. "And Mary doesn't access my cell."

Regina shifted uneasily as his steady stare threatened to invade the thoughts of her soul.

"Do I make you nervous Regina?" He noted with enjoyment the effect he had on her.

"You'd hope!" She mustered the energy to shot back almost instantaneously.

He laughed, not expecting such a comeback.

Regina took a deep breath, exhaled loudly, and began to laugh. She relinquished her barrier with each breath.

Roxanne called out from the back and Dr. Smith rose to his business. He held Regina's gaze for another minute.

"Nice earrings." He mentioned coolly as he disappeared.

"Thanks." The word escaped in a whisper as the fingers on her free hand reflexively caressed her ear. *Nice ass!* She stared, smiling inwardly.

Michael rolled on the condom with a vengeance, fussing to himself. *I can't understand how my dick finds the will to stand so firm! I fucking hate this psycho bitch!*

"What's the hurry sexy? Slow down before you break that." Caramel giggled.

"Less talking more fucking please." He served that with a plastered grin. *The last thing I want to do is hear your voice right now! Don't make me snap your neck!* He mentally warned her.

She scrutinised him daringly then rolled onto her stomach, easing up on all fours. Sensually gyrating her heavy rear, her butt cheeks did their well-renowned dance.

Michael's frustrations were instantly subdued. *Jesus! And then she does that! I'm only human, God!* He eagerly crept up behind her and firmly spanked one cheek, almost drooling as they both jiggled back and forth in response.

"Gimme that dick *Thunder*! Rip your pussy apart!" Caramel teased in a purr, giggling.

He aggressively gripped her by the ass and without hesitation, sunk the entire length of his rigid shaft into her cushioned pinkness. He gazed as his throbbing wood disappeared entirely in her sheltered haven, like only one other person could manage without complaint.

"You love this dick?" He gripped her by the hair and yanked her head backwards.

"I love it! Fuck me harder baby! I love it!" She slithered into a perfect sideways split, leaving nothing to his imagination.

"Holy shit! Look at that *pussy*!" Michael remarked out of character, deeply concentrated on exploring her deepest regions with sturdy calculated strokes.

Yanking her closer, he pulled out of her orifice and eased his pulsating trunk into her mouth. In the heights of his eroticism, he marvelled at her expert, oral talents.

"Ready to ride this dick for me baby? Can you do that for daddy?"

"You *know* I can." She licked her lips and replied. "Assume the position lemme show yuh!" She straddled his heavily endowed cock backwards.

Caramel was prepared to do what she did best to entrap the man she was desperately trying to own. She clenched her cervical muscles to induce his usual frantic explosion, and ground her hip with a motion not easily imitable. As she felt him nearing his peak, she unsuspectingly slipped her thumb into his 'unmentionable'.

Panic button! She mused inwardly.

Michael wildly bucked beneath her as he erupted without exaggerated shudders. "What the hell...was that?" He tried to scream though his voice trembled.

"Something new. I see you loved it!" She retorted with confidence.

He instantly remembered why she irritated him so much, but forgot to comment as his cell phone sounded somewhere on the floor. He got up to search for it and glanced at his watch. *Shit! Shit! Shit!* He began to get dressed and mentally prepared for his grand exit.

"Where yuh rushing to baby? Yuh just got here!"

He stuffed his tie into his pocket. "Listen Caramel, I can't do this with you anymore. Your feelings for me kinda complicate things. To be honest, you're starting to freak me out. I'll give you money or whatever you want. But this, me and you, has to end." He spoke casually, but as a man assured.

"I already *told* you Michael! It's not about the money! It's you. *I want you for myself*! Is that so hard to understand?" Her tone ranged from loud and obnoxious to soft and sweet all in one breath.

"You're nuts! Can't you see that? You've changed man. Look, I'm going to do things differently going forward. I can't see you anymore. Do what you must! But I'd act carefully!" He checked his image in the mirror and moved to the door. "I'm out of here. Take care of yourself."

She sprang from the bed and leaped towards him. "*Don't* do this Michael! That is not what you want! And you know it! You told me you loved me, remember? And this pussy...there's no other better!"

"Not really!" He bluntly interjected. "It was fun while it lasted, but I don't love you! Don't call me anymore and don't show up *anywhere*!" He flashed his hand from her grip and stormed toward the door.

His cell phone rang in his pocket, and it must've been instinct, but he hastily retrieved it.

"*You love this pussy!*" Caramel screamed after him. "*You'll be mine Chocolate Thunder! Fuck Natalie!*"

He slammed the door behind him and hit the send button. "Hello." He held the cell tightly to his ear but there was no response. "Hello!" He looked at the screen and gasped.

Roxanne clutched her stomach and laughed hysterically at her sister's ensemble.

"Regina! That dress is hideous! What are you like sixty? Okay Misses Weatherburn."

Regina was already in tears. "Shut up! Misses Weatherburn? Who the hell is that? It *is* an ugly dress though. Oh my…" She continued to laugh at her reflection in the fitting room mirror.

They had ventured into the mall after the doctor's appointment to commence their search for Regina's perfect dress for the grand opening gala in the evening.

Regina re-emerged from the dressing room in a fuchsia, chiffon, floor-length number that seductively draped her body and accentuated her petite curves.

"Now *that's* a dress!" Roxanne exclaimed. "That's *definitely* a keeper Miss Twenty-Something Mitchell."

She twirled in front of the mirror and giggled childishly. "I really love this one…can't lie. I feel like a movie star fitting for the red carpet."

Roxanne chuckled. "Yup, and it complements your skin tone perfectly. We just need to find a *bad ass* shoes to go with it, and give you some height."

"Got *that* right! Did you find anything for yourself out there?" She always felt guilty when spending money on herself.

Roxanne scowled. "Hmm…nothing fancy. The colors are so dead. I like these tops though." She held up the selection and individually displayed them.

"That turquoise one's cute…really pretty. Well you can keep your eyes open as we walk. I'm pretty much done with this store myself." She disappeared into the room as her cell phone sounded in her handbag.

Roxanne dug it out and yelled. "It's Shane!"

"Answer it and tell him hold on." She called out.

"Hey Shane, what's up? It's Roxanne."

"Hey Roxanne! How yuh doing girl?"

"I'm good. Shopping with your bestie. And you with the cancer?" She was always blunt.

"Healing…things are looking promising. And how's your pregnancy?" Shane couldn't resist.

Roxanne grimaced. "Good. Baby and I are healthy. Nice talking to you, hold for Regina." Her response came out as one long sentence. She handed over the phone and walked away.

Regina quizzically eyed her sister. "Hey Shane. Did I just miss something?"

"What are you talking about?" He slightly chuckled.

"What's funny? Shane, did you say something stupid? Roxanne just had an attitude with me for no reason…"

"I don't know. I just asked her how the pregnancy was coming along after she asked about the cancer."

"*Shane*!" Regina knew of her sister's directness but was also aware that she was still adjusting to the 'teen mom' thing.

"*What* Regina? She *is* pregnant, no? Anyways, are we still doing lunch or what?"

"You're ridiculous sometimes! Of course lunch is on. Where are we going?" She headed to the checkout.

"I'm feeling Cabana's. It's central for everyone."

"Cool. And we're still shooting for one o'clock?"

"Yes mam. So as you go back to your spending frenzy, please note that's forty-five minutes from now. See you then. Love you honey."

Regina laughed. "Alright sir. Love you too."

She returned her attention to Roxanne. "Why are you still so sensitive about your pregnancy?" She lovingly embraced her from behind. "I know you're *pissy* cause Shane mentioned it. But you *are* pregnant you know?"

"I'm cool Regina. It was just weird at the moment. Are we still doing lunch with them?"

Regina knew where that was going. "*Why*? You don't want to now? I mean seriously…"

"I didn't say all that. I was just asking." She lied.

"Sure! You have my wallet? And please cheer up! Nothing like a fat, miserable, face!" She teased, laughing.

"Hey!" Roxanne smacked her on the arm. "I'm the only one that can call my face fat! I told you that in private Regina. *Damn*!" She had to laugh.

Regina grew to appreciate moments like this with her little-woman sister. "I love you Roxanne." She confessed.

"I love you too sis. And thanks for today."
Stacy sat at her desk playing Minesweeper on the computer. She had only been back in the office for an hour, but was already eager to leave. *Where the hell is Regina anyway? I sure wish I had a job like that…come in and out as I please. Damn!*   Her desk phone buzzed and she answered with little enthusiasm. "Thank you for calling…"

"It's me bitch!" Regina cut her off. "Save your breath. Where have you been? I called there before."

Stacy was glad to have her recently estranged friend joke with her. "I had to make a run girl. Where the hell are *you*? I'm bored as shit here by myself."

"I'm on the road with the sis…doctor's visits, errands, you name it. Anyways, I'm calling to invite you out tonight to some big shot gala. You down?"

She was hooked. "*Am I down*?" She chuckled. "I'm down, up, and around girl! What time?"

"I'll pick you up around six."

"Cool. What should I wear? Never mind…gala."

"*Exactly*! I'll call you later when I'm on my way."

"Alright girl. Thanks for the invite."

"Anytime!" Regina hung up.

Stacy leaned back in her chair and quietly screamed. She was bursting with excitement for more reasons than one. Most importantly, she was just invited to spend an evening with Jamaica's A-list money-makers at the most talked about event of the week.

It's always a pleasure to mingle with law-abiding people. She chuckled at her own wisecrack. *This should be rather eventful!* A smirk steadily graced her lips.

The honoured invitees of Hope and Cope Cancer Support Center's grand opening gala began filing into the venue at approximately five o'clock. At first contact, guests were warmly greeted by a valet parking attendant at the red-carpet drop off point. Next, each party was ushered along the well-lit runway and into the main hall by their personal concierge, who served champagne before departing.

Everyone, guests and wait-staff alike, marvelled at the immaculate, fairytale-themed décor. Above other mentions, most were extremely impressed by the level of organisation of an event of its calibre.

Tina stationed herself at the entrance of the auditorium to conduct the meet and greet. She had eagerly accepted the task when Shane had jokingly suggested it earlier, because it would provide her the perfect opportunity to be in the midst of the bourgeoisie gossip mill.

She greeted one of the former Governor Generals of Jamaica. "Welcome Sir Charles; it's an honour to have you this evening." *Boy, Charles is nowhere close to kicking that bucket. Watch him young thing nuh! Not a day over thirty! Better than fried fish!* She mused inwardly as the couple smiled and continued into the auditorium.

"Celeste Waverly!" She spotted her college-mate and good friend. "As I understand you're the new MP for St. Andrew Rural. Congratulations are in order!"

"Oh my *God*! Faustina Sinclair-Wright!" The woman joyfully exclaimed, embracing Tina. "I didn't expect to see *you* here. When did you arrive in Jamaica? She pulled away and teasingly gave her the once over. "You're looking as gorgeous as ever for a mother of four!"

Tina blushed. "Thank you darling. And as usual, so do you. We definitely have some catching up to do." She winked at her and promised to meet up later.

She returned her attention to the proceedings. *Now this is the brute I've been waiting to see*! She plastered a wide grin and greeted the Minister of Education.

"Mr. Knight, we are honoured to have you on board this evening. Where's that beautiful wife of yours?" Tina coyly asked, as if she hadn't seen who he'd arrived with.

The man smiled nervously and yanked his date forward.

"*Oh*! Barbara Nightingale, I didn't see you standing there at all. How have *you* been?" She offered a wide smile to the woman who was evidently attuned to her antics.

"Fantastic!" Barbara replied bluntly, and tugged at the Minister urging him to proceed.

Tina chuckled sheepishly. *That's a big word for a small brain! Thank the Lord that it was brief! I hope she doesn't do much exhaling inside. Lord knows the chocolates will start to melt...and that ice sculp...*

"*Henry*!" She spotted Celeste's ex-husband. "Now you, I'm genuinely happy to see."

They hugged and pecked each other's cheeks.

"Thank you for attending, and as usual for your generous donation." She eased back and offered a smile.

"Celeste is here isn't she? I gather that from your overzealous tone."

She nodded. *She's not only here Henry; she's with the new man!* "It's not the end of the world Henry. Let's just be adults and keep it civil tonight."

Henry Gore is the incumbent President of the Jamaica Water Commission, but also an avid philanthropist and activist for the Jamaica Cancer Society. He and Celeste were married for over ten years, until his extra-marital affairs with his secretary went public. Their divorce was widely publicised in the local media and the tension between them never eased.

Regina parked outside Stacy's house and announced her arrival over the speakerphone while adding the finishing touch to her make-up. She purposely left the headlights beaming so she could scrutinise the getup that emerged from the house.

"Hey girl." Stacy coolly greeted her as she closed the door. "I thought you would've been here already."

"I know girl, time and its tricks. You look glamorous!" Her words were more of a subconscious declaration than a compliment.

Stacy sensed the undertone. "Thank you Gina. And as always so do you." She smiled at her, confident that she was making the impression she had intended.

Regina's emotions stirred as she pulled unto the main street. *She did go all out for this occasion! Makeup, hair, nails, and that dress! Bad as hell! Damn she's hot! Can't lie. Well I got something for you tonight Missy.* She giggled inwardly.

"So how come you didn't invite Linton?" Stacy tried to make small talk, jolting her friend back to reality.

"That's a long story girl. But he got his own invite so I used mine to carry you. I'm sure you can imagine the root of that..." She rolled her eyes at Stacy.

"I hear yuh. But I'm glad regardless." She laughed. "I can't wait to see who attends." She winked at Regina who had impulsively looked over at her.

"I don't blame you mama. I'll be looking too; but that's all I will do, *for now!*"

They both laughed.

As the clock struck six, the MC of the evening ascended the podium, mic in tote, and stood center stage.

"Good evening ladies and gentlemen!" He spoke with much fanfare. "It is now the hour to commence the celebrations for which we have gathered." He paused until the guests settled down, somewhat. "First and foremost, my name is Jared Lee and I'll be your host for the evening." He welcomed the applause, bowing playfully.

"Secondly, I'd like to extend a warm welcome to all of you, the honoured guests, who reserved a moment of your busiest lives to attend our gala tonight." Jared paused as the audience applauded. "An extra special thank you is extended to the individuals and organisations who make it their continuous focus to donate to Cancer research, and facilitate networks of support and encouragement for our brothers and sisters that are faced with this uphill battle."

The audience applauded loudly.

He expertly continued. "Without further ado, I'd like you to join me in extending the warmest welcome to the founder of the Hope and Cope Cancer Support Center, your colleague, Doctor Natalie Carey-Simmons."

Everyone in the room mechanically rose to their feet, and choruses of distinct applause filled the air.

Natalie, elegantly adorned in a floor-length Versace couture gown, gracefully ascended the podium with confidence. Her nerves rattled as she removed her cue cards for the speech she had vehemently rehearsed for the entire week, while the audience continuously applauded.

When all was settled, and the silence fell, she opened her lips and inhaled. Offering a charming smile, she exhaled. But no words escaped. Masking the inner panic well, she scanned the crowd for a familiar face. As her eyes landed on Tina, she took a deep breath and spoke from her heart.

Roxanne rolled onto her side and caressed her rounded tummy. "Andre, what about that food? I'm starving..." She whined from behind him.

"Babes, yuh still didn't tell me what yuh want. Just look in the phonebook and pick sup'm nuh. Order whatever yuh want! I told yuh already." He spoke without looking back in her direction, fixed on his soccer match.

"God! You're *so* mean to me sometimes." She sighed heavily, though smiling.

Biggs immediately looked around for the first time in forty minutes. Just as she had intended, he was immediately suckered in by her 'puppy-dog' face.

He laughed. "Roxie, yuh good eeh man? Alright throw the phone book. I'll order and yuh just eat. And don't bother nag mi bout what yuh get either."

She didn't budge. "It's too heavy. Come get it."

"Babes, yuh a push it now! I have to come for the book *and* order the food? Yuh serious?"

She nodded in affirmation.

"Oh! I know this game..." He got up from the chair and climbed into the bed. "Romp yuh a look?" He grinned.

Roxanne smiled and leaned in for a kiss. "That's what I wanted! Now aren't you glad you came?" She giggled, gazing into the bright eyes that lingered above hers.

Biggs smiled and kissed her on the forehead. He was continuously amazed by the new-found boldness of his woman.

"Why yuh staring at me like that?" She teased. "The *food* babes! *We* are starving. Work with *us* here."

"Alright. I'll get Chinese and the regular. You can just eat whatever yuh feel like."

He couldn't stop smiling as he flipped through the yellow pages and dialled a couple restaurants.

"All set. *Now* can I watch my sports, *in peace*?" His eyes widened as Roxanne negated with a nod. "Why not? Babes…" It was his turn to 'puppy-face' her.

"Andre it's *me* time now. You've been watching sports all night. TIVO allows you to see those *anytime*!"

He caved. "Bwoy, mi ago run weh before yuh hit the third trimester. Cause trust mi babes…"

"*What*?" She shrieked playfully. "Okay forget it. Watch the sports!" She folded into a foetus-like position in the middle of the bed, which consequently made her scantily clad butt the object of Biggs' fixation.

"My Roxie is something else." He pinched her on the butt and got up to join her.

"*Ouch*!" She shrieked from under the pillow.

"Ouch what? Yuh think yuh see ouch? Watch me and yuh!" He switched off the television and dimmed the bedroom lights. Scooping her into his arms, he gently pulled her to his side of the bed while she clung tightly to the pillow.

"Why yuh being so spoilt Misses Jackson? Oh! A cause yuh soon have big-shot last name?" He laughed when she did. "Now that you have *all* my attention, mi sorry fi yuh! *War* mi seh!" He poked her in the side and she flinched, but remained buried. "Oy! A you me a talk to yuh nuh Miss!"

Roxanne burst out laughing. She couldn't contain her giggles any longer, especially now that he had his finger by her armpit. She tossed the pillow and began to plead.

"Alright! Alright! I'm not vex! See..." She offered a cheesy grin.

Biggs maintained his grip, furring his bushy eyebrows at her. "What? Repeat! I didn't catch that."

She laughed uncontrollably. "I'll do anything babes!" She clutched her stomach as a ploy. "Just please stop! I'm sorry." Her laughter disrupted all attempts at making 'the pout'.

"*Anything*? How about one more of those kisses?" He slowly loosened his grip, but didn't release her.

"As you wish..." She blushed, and straddled his lap.

Biggs gently stroked her back as their tongues intertwined feverishly. Resisting the urge to squeeze her tightly as her erect nipples brushed against the well-defined muscles of his bare chest, he allowed her complete control of the moment.

"Baby...I want you inside." Roxanne whispered between breaths. "I need you so bad Andre."

He responded to her urgency by easing out of his sweat pants and holding his turgid wood in place.

"Mmm...mmm" The moans escaped her as she easily welcomed his entire length. "I love you Andre."

"I love you more Roxanne Jackson." He meant that.

CHAPTER NINETEEN

Natalie had concluded her speech with a memorable quote by Steven Gilman; 'Success is *not* to be measured by income, but by *influence*; not by *power* but by personality; not by capital, but by *character*.'

The audience had eagerly praised her with a standing ovation, and whistles had emanated from the younger guests throughout the auditorium.

Regina and Stacy had arrived just in time to hear Natalie profess that giving back to the community is one of the most effective ways to measure true success.

As the audience settled, the two made their way towards the table where Shane and the gang were seated.

Natalie gracefully made her celebratory walk from the podium down the center isle, running into the duo at the bar.

"Regina Mitchell! I thought I saw you come in... *late*!" She teasingly chastised her friend.

Regina smiled apologetically and embraced the lady of the hour. "I caught the most moving part of the speech though. Made me realise I've been leading a selfish life."

Natalie scowled. "Hey, you do your share in giving back. You're the mother *and* sister of a teenager, young lady. Take some credit for that!"

She smiled in appreciation of her outlook, and pulled Stacy, who had been scrutinising the 'big shots', closer.

"Look who I brought with me." She offered a wide grin.

"*Stacy*! What a pleasant surprise! I didn't even recognise you standing there. Girl, you look absolutely stunning!" Natalie warmly embraced her troubled client.

"I'm glad to be here Natalie." She revelled in the feedback. *Though I didn't personally receive an invite...* She mumbled internally before adding. "Your closing remark really moved me. It was very motivating."

"Thank you darling. *Oh*! Before I forget, I'd like you to meet someone. Come." She gently tugged her along.

All three ladies moved stylishly through the crowd, stealing the attention from a few wives.

"*Honey*!" Natalie called out as soon as she got within ear shot of her table. "I'd like to introduce you to someone." She tapped Michael on the shoulder when she got closer.

Michael was still immersed in his conversation when he stood and put his best face forward to acknowledge his wife's companion. A placid expression instantly wiped the already fake smile from his face.

Regina mused inwardly. *I caught that! I so caught that you sneaky little bastard! This should be great!*

Natalie continued, unaware. "Stacy Jones, this is..."

"Michael, your husband." Stacy interjected, outstretching her perfectly manicured hand. "It's a pleasure to *finally* meet you Mr. Simmons."

As Michael fumbled with his response, Regina eagerly interjected. "You two know each other?"

Natalie quizzically looked back and forth between the two people she had supposedly just introduced.

Stacy gently withdrew her hand from Michael's and innocently replied. "*Not formally*! But Natalie's descriptions were definitely on target. Tall, dark, and handsome; wasn't it Doc?" She glanced at her and smiled.

Natalie mentally skipped through their inter-office 'man' talks and was somewhat satisfied with her explanation. She still didn't appreciate the way she had briskly cut her off or familiarly mentioned her husband on a first-name basis. She faintly smiled however, and coolly replied.

"Yes...that sounds like *my* Michael alright. Am I the only one who's starving? Let's eat!" She curtly dropped the issue to avoid any further discomfort.

Michael was evidently not amused.

Regina made a mental note of Michael's awkward behaviour and laughed to herself. She also caught on to Stacy's overly exaggerated and confident response to her knowledge of her friend's husband. Nevertheless, she led the way to their designated table without any further comments.

As Stacy was being welcomed by the overzealous men fixating on her beauty, Regina glimpsed Linton's phone blinking brightly on the table beside him.

I'd bet my next pay cheque I know exactly who that is! She sneered inwardly, and slipped the phone under the table to retrieve the text message. *Told you to put a password on this thing slow poke! Hmm!* She scanned the words.

Just as I fucking thought! I knew it! Too many coincidences...had to mean something! She deleted the message, cleared the screen, and glanced over her shoulder to get a glimpse of Michael. It disgusted her how he appeared to be coolly involved in his conversation.

"Regina!" Shane called out, startling her. "What took you and your *beautiful* friend so long to get here? Your invite didn't have a time?" He had directed the attention to her on purpose, having witnessed her foul-play.

Tina slapped him on the arm as she picked up on his emphasis and felt embarrassed for Lisa.

"Baby, you almost spilt your water on this." Regina hurriedly whispered and handed Linton the phone before she acknowledged Shane with a smirk.

"Thanks babes." Linton answered, but subtly glanced at his phone screen as she spoke.

"Actually Shane..." She feigned a smile. "I had to make a stop to visit your *pregnant* woman. I see she didn't make it after all?" She wittingly slammed him, knowing exactly where he was headed with his insinuations. "Besides, you're not married!" She coolly added, and dug into her meal.

Stacy smiled in her heart. Admittedly, she was enjoying how the events of the evening were fluidly unfolding.

I knew you invited me here for a reason Regina. There's never smoke without fire! But don't think you're going to humiliate me tonight. You should've collected all your facts before you came head on into this one. One more comment like that and this little gala will be upside down! Her inward smile steadily graced her sultry, red lips.

Linton squirmed inwardly from the sexual energy that effortlessly oozed from Stacy's body. Thoughts of burying his wood in the folds of her over-spilling breasts swirled in his head, igniting him.

It's been years since I've felt such an attraction to another woman! He admitted inwardly. *Goddamn that Stacy's fine! Hmm! Hmm! On the other hand, what the fuck are you up to Regina Mitchell? I know when you're scheming better than anyone sitting here! Something's not right with you! And that random 'married' remark to Shane...you're up to something!*

He was sure too that she had purposely showed up late with Stacy for reasons that have yet to be exposed, but will be damaging. His suspicions heightened with each moment that she was friendlier to him than she had been in the weeks since she'd allowed him to return home. As he toyed with his food, another of her *caring* questions penetrated his daze.

"Baby, you've barely touched your food." Regina looked from him to his entrée. "What's on your mind? You don't like it? I find it's delicious!"

Why do you even care? He wanted to ask. "Yeah babes, it's great. Just have a lot on my mind…think I need to go to the restroom too. Where is it anyway? You know?"

"Through the main door and to the right." She eyed him casually, though seething on the inside. *Sibling's intuition huh Linton? You look so damn guilty!*

Linton stood and excused himself from the table, but not before stumbling into a misplaced chair.

Regina snickered inwardly. *Well aren't we clumsy tonight? Nervous much? I'm on to you two like white on rice!* She looked over at Stacy. *And don't think I don't notice you revelling in all of this…like it's a fucking masquerade! Just wait, I will personally fix your ass!* She chuckled to herself.

Just as that thought manifested, Stacy moved into Linton's seat beside her. She began to blabber about the delicacy of the food and how unfortunate it was that every sexy guy in attendance had a lady on his arm.

Shut up slut! You know that's how you like them! Regina mentally rebuked her *friend*, but continued to listen absently as she pondered her next move.

Shane watched his best friend keenly.

Michael looked up from his un-engaging conversation and noticed his brother moving through the crowd. He immediately stood and excused himself from the table.

Natalie looked on as her husband hurriedly walked away. *What the hell is going on with you Michael? You've barely spoken a word since we sat. Too busy 'texting' away! Why would you go to such extremes to send a message…and to whom when everyone important is seated in this room!*

Something real fishy is going on...stinking up your already sour behaviour! This better be nothing when I get to the bottom of it! But I'm on to you husband!

"Natalie darling, you did an excellent job up there this evening." The President of Jamaica's biggest bank approached on her blind side and politely interrupted. "I've been waiting for an opportune moment to congratulate you, but I was too anxious." Mr. Carter had always had a 'thing' for her.

"Oh please Andrew." She smiled. "Have a drink with me...sit." She gestured towards Michael's empty seat.

Linton almost jumped back into the toilet when he opened the bathroom stall to see his wide-eyed brother standing directly in front of him.

"What the hell man? You scared *the shit* out of me!" He snapped as he pushed him out of his way.

"Question is, what the hell took *you* so long?" Michael completely disregarded his comment.

"Took me so long to do what? Take a piss? There *are* other stalls!" He pointed to the doors on the left and right of where he stood.

"Don't *fuck* with me bro! Didn't you get my text?"

"Fuck with *you*?" Linton asked derisively. "Wait, what text? Oh! Regina..." He mumbled his own response.

"Regina what? Forget her!" Michael grew erratic. *"The bitch is here bro! This can't be fucking happening! My worst nightmare Linton!"* He toned down. "That's *her* that Regina's with! Stacy...*that's* Caramel!"

Linton's jaws dropped. *Ding fucking ding!* His eyes widened, somewhat mimicking those of his brother's.

"Are you fucking serious? Tell me you're joking!" He chuckled nervously.

Michael tightened his jaw, almost gritting his teeth, as he stared at his brother in silence.

"You're *not* joking! This *cannot* be good. *This can't be fucking happening either*! Regina will *kill me* if this blows up tonight! She's definitely already onto it!" He clutched his head then massaged his eyes.

"I can't believe you're thinking of yourself right now…" Michael carelessly uttered.

Linton hastily moved in inches away from his face. *"Who the fuck am I supposed to be thinking of Michael?"* He lowered his voice as someone entered the restroom. "You got yourself into this mess and you have to get yourself out! Were you thinking about me when you had your dick buried inside the pussy of that black, Jessica Rabbit looking babe? Did you put in a round especially for me, since thanks to you, Regina won't give me none? I don't think so! Right now, this is as fucked up for me as it can possibly be for you! Regina is already *at her end* with me! I didn't even *do anything*!"

Michael mused inwardly at his subtle confession that Caramel was gorgeous, and indeed thought provoking. In his second breath, he realised that he was sailing a ship that was about to sink; his lifelong scapegoat was bailing on him.

"Listen man, I don't know what you're going to do, but you *better* do it soon." Linton warned in a hushed, but rage-filled tone. "I've had enough of taking shit from people just for you Michael. My whole *life* is falling apart because of this!"

"Oh please!" He uncaringly exasperated. "Your life was already falling apart *before* all this…with that whole moving to Cayman bullshit. Don't try to put all that on me!" He tried to evade the blame as always.

Linton stared at his brother in disgust, and seriously contemplated knocking him out. "Whatever you say man. Either way, I'm out of here." He walked away instead, but stopped in his tracks at the doorway. "By the way, what exactly did that text message say?"

Michael caught wind of the added predicament and looked down at his feet. "Too much."

Regina glanced over at Natalie's table and noticed that an unfamiliar gentleman was seated in Michael's previous place. She quickly scanned the area and realised the man himself was nowhere in sight. *Bastards! The shit must be heating up fast!*

She held the thought and turned to face the photographer who was requesting a shot with her and Stacy.

One picture became two as the overzealous man seemed obsessed with their dissimilar beauty. Before he could be tempered, the session turned into a photo shoot and heads now turned in their direction.

With Linton somehow sandwiched between the two as they posed by a beautiful floral arrangement, Regina spotted Natalie and demanded that the 'lady of hour' joined them.

"Natalie, who was that hunk-of-a-man that was sitting in Michael's place earlier?" She asked as she got closer. "Please spill the beans cause Miss Stacy here is looking for a *man*...a *single* one of course."

Stacy wanted to blast her for putting her on the spot, but playfully tapped her on the arm instead.

Natalie seemed surprised. "Stacy doesn't *need* a man...she met a *wonderful* guy. Haven't *you* heard?" She teased, arching her delicate brows and looking back and forth between the two.

Haven't you? Regina grinned. "Is the guy single or what Natalie? Stop holding out! A man like that...so scrumptious, and am sure established, should never have to venture out to an event like this alone. Mmm..." She moaned jokingly, ruffling Linton's feathers as she had intended.

Natalie laughed. *"Actually*, I think he's presently going through a divorce. May I say single-in-training? I guess I could put in a word...but for whom?" She quizzically eyed the ladies.

The three women laughed, much to the discomfort of the fourth wheel who audibly cleared his throat.

Regina wasn't finished. "And where's that husband of yours anyway? I want to get a group shot of all of us."

Natalie looked towards her table and signalled Michael when he finally glanced in their direction.

Stacy was fully attuned to the game Regina was *trying* to strategize, but had to admit she was enjoying every moment of it. She also noted too that Linton was overbearingly more handsome and rugged than his uptight brother, and wondered if he was anything like him in bed.

Linton quickly broke Stacy's entrancing stare, trying to avoid her venomous spell. *Michael was right! This chic must be the daughter of a voodoo priest or something. Shit, I've seen beautiful women before...but goddamn! I can't shake the thought of those lips around my...Linton! What the fuck are you thinking? Focus! Cause this is about to get real ugly!*

Michael finally arrived - after much delay - and stood his place beside his wife. He lovingly rested his hand on the small of her back and pecked her on the cheek.

"You look ravishing darling. Can't wait to get you out of here..." He whispered in Natalie's ear, implementing the making-up before the war.

Natalie giggled but mentally scowled at his transparent phoniness.

Regina signalled the photographer, who seemed more than eager to relinquish his present duties.

The scene was set for lights-camera-action.

The starring line up for the drama included Michael, Natalie, Stacy, Linton, and Regina; in that order. Before the posing could begin, Regina stepped forward to tweak the script.

"Hold on, something is off balance here. Michael, you should move between Stacy and Natalie to even out the coordination of this line up." She grinned at his expression.

Natalie flashed Regina a quick glance, but voluntarily moved to Michael's left instead, leaving him standing rigidly beside the woman he'd spent many a nights with.

"Now everyone come closer!" The photographer called out. "This will be beautiful!"

Regina shuffled closer towards Linton, forcing him to bridge the gap between him, Stacy, and Michael. She could feel his tension in her arms, but he was the least of her concerns at the moment.

Unknowing to her, Natalie was experiencing the same reaction though smiling effortlessly.

The scent of Stacy's Chanel No 9 tickled the nostrils - among other things - of the two *taken* men. The temptress herself revelled in the sensual feedback to the point of arousal.

"Smile!" The photographer shouted as the flash blared.

Before the moment was captured, one member went down with a thud.

Natalie's eyelids fluttered as she steadily regained consciousness. Reflexively, she sat forward as her vision cleared and tried to identify her surroundings.

"Natalie it's okay...you're in the hospital." The voice came from behind her.

She whisked her head around and came face to face with Shane. With a deep sigh, she released the breath she had held.

Shane gently held her by the shoulder and eased her back unto the bed. "You're not alone, don't worry."

A faint smile graced her lips as tears involuntarily glistened her cheeks. "What happened to me?" She whispered, suddenly realising her throat felt parched.

"Well, you pulled an Australia on us...tried to one up on me." He teased, referring to his own previous ordeal.

She started to smile, but gradually remembered the moments before her blackout.

"What's the matter?" Shane asked, moving closer to her side. "That look just now...it was all over your face, even in your sleep. Care to share?" He watched her in silence, waiting.

Natalie broke his gaze and looked up at the ceiling. "Is there any water in here? I'm thirsty." She fought to control the emotions that hurtfully tilled her soul.

He quickly filled some tap water into a paper cup and watched as she swallowed every drop.

"Thank you." She whispered, handing the cup back to him. "Where's that wretched husband of mine anyway? Fucking that bitch while I'm unconscious?" She averted eye contact and reclined onto the pillow.

Shane was lost for words. "Uhm...well Michael stayed back to wrap up things with my mom. I volunteered to come...is there something you want to talk about Nat?" He couldn't ask that question fast enough. "Fucking what bitch? Wow!" He had never heard her use such foul language.

She focused on the tube protruding from the bandage on her forearm. "What's all this for? People can't just faint anymore without all this excitement?" She grew irritable.

"I'm no genius Doc, but I think that's for the baby... or should I say babies?" He tried to joke. "I didn't even know...congrats!"

Of course...the babies. She smiled and turned to Shane. "Twins huh? Sounds like a complete nightmare." She confessed her innermost fear.

"*Easy*...my grandmother made it a sweet dream with my dad and his brother. And might I add, *alone*. You're lucky you have Michael."

Natalie pondered the thought of 'having' Michael, but only for a split second. *That couldn't be! It would depend...Oh no! It cannot be!* She cleared her throat and spoke.

"You know what's weird?" She nervously glanced at him. "There are no twins in either of our families."

"Impossible!" Shane quickly sat forward sporting the same troubled expression. *No way! It cannot be.*

Michael relinquished his post by the doorway and barged into the room. He had heard more than enough.

CHAPTER TWENTY

Shane parked in front of Simone's box-sized residence and eagerly walked the few steps to her front door. He had just wrapped up a light workout session at Sullivan, and had decided to take a detour from the slow lane that had steadily devoured his life. On a whim, he had dialled Simone and coerced her to see him.

He had already begun to accept that with Lisa bringing his first official child into the world - Amanda had sacrificed the first two - his womanizing and philandering days were soon behind him. Soon, would not be today however. He needed a release from the stress of sharing his bachelor pad with his pregnant woman for going on three weeks, catering to her every whim. His 'husband' tolerance had worn thin.

Simone stood in the doorway, arms tightly folded. "Bway Shane, yuh a *fuckry*! I have to find out all about yuh life from the news? A so we live now? Like mi a yuh groupie or sup'm?" She rolled her eyes at him.

"I'm sorry babes. Like I was telling yuh on the phone, I called as soon as my time freed up babes. Can yuh just forgive me? Please?" He grinned and made his puppy face that would usually penetrate her rigid barrier.

She didn't budge. "Yuh not funny Shane! Da face deh nah go work fi yuh! After how we have so much fun the last time we link, and yuh tell me one bag a foolishness. Then I have to hear that yuh sick from TVJ? Dat's unforgiveable!" Tears trickled down her cheeks.

"I'm sorry Sim…" He tried to embrace her.

"I was so worried about yuh Shane, worried sick!" She cut him off. "I even tried calling yuh one time! I know I

326

don't mean much to yuh, but at least a likkle phone call? Just nutt'n so?" Her body jerked as her sobs fuelled her temper. "Yuh really break ma spirit dis time."

"Simone, of course you mean something to me babes. I'm here now aren't I? But I understand what yuh mean. I'm sorry babes. And I don't want yuh to worry. That's why I didn't tell anybody in the first place. I've *been* ill Simone. I just didn't talk about it until now."

Shane was moved as his self-titled 'ghetto love' sobbed. Though he wasn't one for unnecessary female emotions, he held her close as her barriers collapsed and she broke down.

"Babes, please…I will tell you everything you want to know. But can you stop crying? Please, you're making me feel real bad. You want me to start crying with you?"

Simone awarded him a giggle for that attempt. She slowly released him and tried to compose herself.

"Please don't! But not because a laugh yuh off the hook!" She wiped at her tear-puffed eyes.

He chuckled. "I didn't expect *all* that now."

She held his hand and led him through the tightly crowded hallway of her mother's two bedroom house.

He had only visited her place once before and he suddenly remembered why he hadn't returned. He made a mental note to 'upgrade' her lifestyle as he observed the well kept, but impoverished surroundings in transit.

"Did yuh eat?" She asked him somewhat testily, as they finally took a seat on the congested back patio.

Shane smiled, not surprised by her usual concern for his stomach. "Not since breakfast…did you?"

"Not yet, but I was about to make something."

"Don't bother. I'll take you out after."

She drummed her fingers on the rusted, three-legged - should've been four - iron table and pointedly eyed him.

"How bad is it? The cancer…and *don't lie to me*!"

"It's not that bad Simone, *really*. I've started treatment...feeling much better already." He truthfully testified for the first time.

"So if yuh doing the treatment how come yuh hair don't fall out? I read somewhere dat should happen."

It touched him that she had actually researched his predicament. "Guess I'm just lucky!" He shrugged, tousling his low cut, curly hair.

His attention soon turned to her skin-tight dress that perfectly hugged her tall but curvy frame, and flaunted her hefty breasts. As his hormones leaped into overdrive, he tried to wrap up the bulk of the deficient conversations.

"Babes, just know that I'm okay, and I *will* be okay. I promise to keep you informed from now on. Cool?" He reached over and slipped his hand under her dress.

"But Shane, can you?" She seemed genuinely concerned.

"Ask him!" He looked down at the tent that now pitched in his lap and grinned.

Simone blushed and got up from her position with his hand still fondling her treasures. She slowly eased her weight unto his lap and locked her legs around him.

"Shane I really missed yuh..." She clutched his face and fervently kissed him, raking his tongue with her teeth.

"Ride ma cocky for mi babes. Gimme all...yuh have...bottled up inside." His words barely escaped.

As per his directions, Simone freed his monster and anxiously straddled him. She rhythmically rotated her hips forcing herself deeper and deeper onto his unsheathed, turgid cock. Her voluptuous breasts sparingly caressed the sides of his face as he nestled his head in her chest.

Shane met her intense movements with urgent thrusts of his own, maintaining a firm grip on the bare flesh of her ass. His mouth busied with her bouncing nipples, as his erotic sensations heightened. Feeling much too restricted for his satisfaction, he hoisted her into the air and switched position.

"Babes I can't fuck yuh like I want to out here! Yuh feel so good on my dick yo! We have to go inside!"

Simone's body instinctively tensed in his arms, but he completely disregarded her concerns and marched them into the house. Never allowing any space between them, he rested her on the bed nearest to the bedroom door and spread her legs wide. Without thought or mercy, he sunk the entire length of his shaft deeper into her warmth.

"Lawd Shane yuh ago kill mi! Woi! Fuck mi harda!" Simone screamed as his motion rippled sharp but pleasant pains throughout her abdomen.

He revelled in her vulgarity and the way her orifice skilfully managed his well-endowed cock. She was the only girl he had met to date who could do that without complaint. He leaned in closer and aggressively massaged her breasts, shortening his strokes as his climax neared.

Simone twitched with her third orgasm. "Fuck yuh pussy Shane! Fuck mi!" The foul words fluidly escaped her mouth as she wildly rubbed her pearl. "Lawd yuh a kill mi! But mi love it! Mi love it!"

He quickly removed his throbbing dick as his explosion neared its peak. "Where yuh want it babes? Talk quick!" He panted heavily, stroking himself.

She welcomed his entire length with her mouth, eagerly milking his eruption to the last drop. Without further hesitation, she teasingly licked her lips then swallowed.

Dr. Smith had been seated at a corner table in the Hotpot restaurant for over ten minutes. He anxiously willed his guest to arrive as his eyes wandered, scoping the room.

As disappointment began to seep in, he checked his watch one last time then looked up. He smiled from within as his eyes landed on the object of his anxiety standing across the room. He stood and waved her over, sharing a brief embrace before sitting.

"I'm happy you finally made it, *Older Sister*. Had me worried there for a sec..." He winked at her, grinning.

"I'm glad I did William..." Regina replied coolly, though her cheeks slowly reddened. "Glad I had you *worried*, that is!" She tried to stabilize her own hyperactive emotions.

He laughed. "Oh, I see. You did that on purpose? Nice to know." He couldn't stop smiling. "I took the luxury of ordering your tea...chamomile?" He watched her intently.

Regina was already impressed. "Right on point actually..." She cleared her throat as a warning to the panic within that threatened to frazzle her mind.

"Is everything okay with you? You seem pretty tense. Can't relax?" A teasing smirk settled on his lips.

"Please!" She arched her freshly-groomed brows and snapped. "Any more relaxed and I'd be naked!"

That's not exactly what she had intended to say; *that* was the workings of her inner self.

"I see. Well then..." William chuckled, unusually lost for words.

As if orchestrated, they spontaneously erupted in laughter. They laughed away the awkwardness that tightened the air between them and settled in for some one on one.

Regina decided to grasp the reigns in her least powerful moment. "So Doctor William Smith, how did you convince Misery Mary to allow you out *with me* for breakfast? No appointments? Or she didn't know?"

"Well Miss Regina Mitchell..." He tried to reply in the same tone but couldn't stop laughing. "I'll have you know that I *did* have appointments this morning. Mary and I just agreed I could re-schedule them to take a beautiful woman to breakfast." He casually assessed her reaction and continued. "Yeah, but then I couldn't seem to find one of those so I was forced to call yours truly." He chuckled.

"Ha! Ha! Ha!" Regina tossed a packet of sugar at him and playfully scowled. "You're *very* funny today Mr. Smith. I'm sure your wife appreciates your humour..."

"Who's that? Mrs. Smith? That's just in the movies darling. I already told you, I'm not married." He confidently held her gaze as if trying to read the words that were scribbled on her soul.

She effortlessly returned his engaging smile and took a sip of her tea. "Well, there's only one thing left to ask; what's your story? *You*, William dearest, can't possibly be *just* single! What's the catch?" She gave him 'the eye'.

"Very funny!" He returned 'the eye', chuckled at her bluntly expressed presumptions, and coolly replied. "Is that so? First of all, thank you for that subtle yet very sweet complement...means a lot coming from *you*. I'm wondering though why it should matter if I'm single, widowed, or forever engaged...this is simply a *just-friends* breakfast remember?" He teasingly repeated the exact words she had used earlier when he had called to invite her out.

"Forget that I asked." She bluntly replied, clearly misinterpreting his remark.

"Regina, I was only joking with you. Are you planning to relax? I mean seriously...are you sure everything else is okay?" He quizzically eyed her, waiting for a response.

Not wanting to completely ruin this otherwise refreshing occasion, Regina sighed and put her best self forward.

"I'm sorry William. I really didn't mean to come at you like that. Forgive me?" She was flustered, but struggled to maintain eye contact.

"Forgive you for what darling? I just want to ensure everything's cool with you, that's all." His smile genuinely revealed the workings of his heart.

Regina was entranced, hooked even, as she relaxed and allowed his warming demeanour to penetrate and caress every groove in her soul. She silently revelled in the essence of meeting a man that seemed to be such a treasure amidst all her current drama.

God really works mysteriously...right in the knick of time! But Lord, please tell me exactly what you want me to do with this wonderful creation of yours... She unknowingly smiled.

William held her gaze and grinned at the very moment her lustful thought had actualized. "*Now* what's funny?" He asked, chuckling. "From one extreme to the other Regina...what's really going on in that head of yours?" He dug for a confession.

She leaned in closer. "Let's get out of here William. Go somewhere, more pri..." Her words tangled with his warm breath that eagerly filled her mouth.

"Are you...sure?" He tried to speak with his bottom lip still caught between her teeth.

"Mmm." She moaned appreciatively, afraid to speak.

This moment would count as the first time in seven years that she had anything to do with another man, besides her *beloved* Linton. She had had the gut feeling the very instant she first laid eyes on the man, that he would be *trouble in paradise*. In the previous weeks she had spent avoiding him, she had put a lot of thought into the workings of her attraction. Without settling on any one thing, she determined that something about his aura and subtle advances tilled her thirsty soil.

Without further delay, William had hastily paid the tab for their uneaten meal, decided they would leave in his car, and even buckled her seatbelt.

"One last chance..." He teased as he climbed into the driver's seat and started the engine.

Regina got comfortable in the plush leather seat of his Infiniti and lustfully eyed him. Undoing the top button of her shirt, that until now had been doing a fine job covering her fully laced breasts, she turned up the heat instantly.

"Luckily, you have the ticket." She mentioned coolly.

William grinned. "Oh! Then I *must win*! One dollar will surely turn my life around." He joked while he carefully backed out of the tight parking space.

As he sped toward the main gate too small for two-way traffic, the driver of an incoming Lexus truck stopped to allow him passage.

He honked him a thank you and sped off.

The sound of a tremor-like horn jolted Roxanne out of her slumber, and she eased up from her reclined position to observe the happenings. She instantly gawked at the image that settled on her steadying vision.

Hmmm! She thought to herself, but incidentally mumbled aloud.

Biggs looked over at her. "What?"

"I can smell the food from here babes. Lawd, hurry up!" She offered to side track him.

He chuckled at the heightened sensory development of his ever-hungry pregnant woman.

"I'm going babes! Can't scratch up mi truck!"

She smiled and leaned back in her seat. It wasn't the champagne-coloured FX35 or its sparkling clean Giovanni rims that caught her eye; nor was it that she immediately recognised the handsome driver. More so, it was the overly relaxed passenger who bore a striking resemblance to her.

You are so wrong Regina! So nasty! Ha! I was so unto you. Oh my God! I mean Dr. Smith is hot as hell. She giggled inwardly, shaking her head in disbelief.

Natalie had begun her morning screening applicants for positions at the Hope and Cope Cancer Center. Without any job specific requirements in mind, she worked backwards from her vision of a unified environment to determine the personalities and qualifications that would set that tone. Her medical practice had been closed for the last two days as she worked continuously to get this process done, after much delay.

She scanned points of interest on the résumé of her tenth interviewee then paged Tameka to send her in.

When the soft tap came at the door, she stood and walked half the distance to greet her visitor. She offered a genuine smile when she recognised the young lady, from the day she personally delivered her resume.

"I see we meet again Doctor Natalie. I'm Alesha Taylor." The upbeat young woman greeted her with a firm handshake and a wide, natural smile.

Natalie was immediately captivated. "It's a pleasure to meet *you*, Ms. Taylor." She returned her enthusiasm.

"Please, call me Alesha." She offered, smiling.

"Alesha it is." Natalie remarked as she instructed her to sit wherever she felt comfortable. "So Alesha, first I'd like to thank you for giving us your time this morning. I see you're in your final year at UWI majoring in Psychology, with a minor in Social Work. What, if any, were the motivations behind your choice of studies?"

"My degree focus was heavily influenced by me having adoptive parents." Alesha got straight to the point. "I've never met my mom or dad. And though there are stereotypical stories surrounding adoptive kids, I personally don't have one. My parents provided me with the love and support to live and appreciate life as I do now. My focus was, and still is, to assist children in those differing circumstances, affording them the same nurture that I was blessed with growing up."

Natalie admired her eloquent response, and poise while sharing such a story. "I couldn't think of a better motivation myself..." She remarked truthfully.

Alesha chuckled.

"Now that I know what drives you, I wont even ask why you chose to volunteer with Father Ho Long Ministries. But tell me Alesha, what is the most important value you've learned from that experience?"

She briefly pondered then replied confidently. "The most important value would be acknowledging the powers of the mind...I will elaborate. I worked with people of all ages, with the simplest to the most extreme cases of physical and mental infirmities, including terminal illnesses. I observed how the ones who were bubbling with hope, continuously used their God-like abilities each day to powerfully heal themselves. It was truly a moving experience."

"I understand exactly what you're saying." Natalie was excited now. "The power of the mind goes far beyond the instances recounted in tales my dear..." She decided to curb her lecture on the topic behind her own personal motivations.

With her keen motivations, charisma, and overall genuineness, this applicant was already on board at the Center in one way or another.

"Alesha, are you presently employed?"

"Yes. I work part-time at the commercial bank. However I'd much prefer an opportunity to do something more in my field and that's why I applied here."

"Okay. So you would prefer a paid position then?"

"Yes Doctor Simmons. Though I could still volunteer off the clock if the need arises."

"Please, call me Natalie." She smiled proudly with that. "You're definitely on board Alesha!" She was truly excited to work with her. *Woman after my own heart...* She mused.

Linton went into work seemingly for no other reason than to haunt Regina. After spending most of the morning trying to contact her by phone to no avail, he sat at his desk during lunch hour trying to communicate his thoughts via email.

He drummed his fingers on the keyboard as he encountered writer's block. *Fuck! I mean, what else is there to say at this point?* He mentally voiced his frustrations.

Regina was already aware that he refused to end their seven-year relationship and that he wanted his family back. He had made it crystal clear that he wasn't bitter in any way that she had completely humiliated him in front of over a hundred high society people at the gala; and that he too was extremely furious with his brother, was nothing like him, and wanted nothing more than to strangle him.

Nonetheless, he was void of any further explanations why she should forgive him so they can move forward.

Fucking Michael man! I should've knocked your dumb ass out right there in that damn bathroom! Always pulling me into your web of shit when the ride gets bitter and the lights get dim. Dad was so right about you and your everlasting selfishness. You are indeed like mom...I was just too ignorant to accept it. I should've listened...should've kept you at arm's length...then I wouldn't be caught in all this shit! He grabbed the desk phone and slammed the redial button.

"Hello." Michael answered with a cautious tone on the fourth ring.

"*You fucked up my life bro!*" Linton snapped. "*And I mean that this time! You really fucked me over with this one!*"

He took a deep-breath, remembered where he sat, and lowered his voice. "Michael, you're my brother and all, but it's the least I could do to strangle you right now. Nobody would even care...but mom. Please tell me your shit is *fucking* sorted out! Cause you're *really fucking* with my patience! You're taking this loyalty shit *way* too far!"

Michael sighed, as if he deserved to be frustrated. "Linton, I really hope you're not at work carrying on like this…next thing I hear I'm the reason you lost your job!" He paused, but quickly continued when Linton grunted.

"Bro, I'm going to fix this! I already told you. My plan has officially been put into action. This too, shall pass." He was cool as a cucumber and spoke as if he meant it.

"Put into action?" Linton barked. "Fool the shit should've *been* put into action, *executed* and *sealed* by now! Yuh think you're planning a *fucking* vacation? Wait, why am I even arguing with you? I'm calling Natalie *today!*"

He slammed the desk phone unto its cradle, knowing it would ring back almost instantly. *Fuck this man!* He exhaled with a grunt.

Regina stirred, took a deep breath, and laughed as she exhaled. Having just climaxed with her fifth orgasm, she had good reason.

Moaning appreciatively, she nestled her nude body against an over-sized cashmere pillow.

William turned towards her, ruffling the sheets as he did so. He propped his head against his arm and lustfully admired the way his bed mate's velvety-skin reflected the sunlight filtering through the roof.

"You're so beautiful Regina." He declared, using his fingers to outline her profile.

"William! Are you trying to kill me?" She tried to sound serious but her voice failed to contain her excitement.

He chuckled. *"What*? I'm not even doing anything!" He rebutted, knowing well that teasing her lower back had been the official kick off to their last round.

She turned to face him, snuggling into his embrace. "I'm sore as hell! I don't think I can manage another session and walk straight for the rest of this week." She laughed at her honest confession.

"Well hey! I *am* the *vaggie* specialist around these parts. If it's *that* sore, I got the remedy!"

Regina giggled at his quick comeback. "I don't like the sound of that *remedy* at all...think I'll pass *Doctor*!" She playfully chided him.

"How about I give you a *sample*?" He couldn't forfeit the challenge. "Then we can decide if you will indeed pass?" With that, he made his way to the foot of the bed.

"Where are you *going*?" She whined. "Come back to me..." She pretended to beg, before the cold trail of his tongue moistened the back of her rump. "William!" Her eyes sprung open, the sunlight temporarily blinding her.

"No need to panic baby." He moved in closer between her thighs and pinned her to the bed. "Relax..."

The situation escalated with slick, swift motions under William's complete control.

"William..." Regina barely managed to speak as she bucked under the pressure. "Mmm." Her body trembled beneath his firm grip. "Oh God! I'm coming!" She exclaimed between gasps. "I'm coming!"

Almost reflexively, her legs clenched as tightly as he'd allow while she ground her crotch wildly on his face.

William resurfaced with a wide grin, chuckling almost mockingly. "Was that your first darling?" He kissed her on the neck. "There's more where that came from, *and* more, if you allow me..." He stopped just shy of saying too much and playfully poked her in the side.

Regina stared deeply into his eyes. "That was absolutely amazing! I won't lie...it was indeed my first." She looked away. "This entire morning has been nothing but amazing William, and so refreshing. But I need you to understand..."

"Darling, please..." He immediately interjected. "It's not that serious. I mean, not that this morning *wasn't* serious...that was serious. I just mean there's no pressure." He fumbled more than he'd like for the right words.

She looked up at him and smiled. "No pressure huh? But you stare at me with those intense eyes, trying to dig into my soul! I'd say that's a lot of pressure Mr. Smith. And you're good, I'll admit that."

"I'm *good*? As in, I could've been better? Hmm! I'd be careful what I wish for in this territory if I were you."

They both erupted in laughter.

Regina pinched him on the arm and rolled her eyes. *Once again you're on target William Smith! You're absolutely, mind-bogglingly, erotically, fantastic! But will I admit to all that? Oh no! Too grown to be sprung on some dick!* She mused inwardly and smiled.

Michael wallowed in his frustrations as he shuffled papers about his desk. *My world has completely fallen apart! If this shit lands on the wrong ears, I could make the front page of the news! My career, my family, my friends...Linton is surely going to strangle me as he promised. How could one fuck just ruin my entire life? Men have got to be the dumbest species in existence! It's a wonder we've avoided extinction!*

Natalie hates my guts and I know she's onto me... being so damn bold and prissy all of a sudden. Turn down my lunch invite? As if she has anything better to do! God knows she's busy fishing. And just my luck, it's fishing season. I'm fucked! Backed against the wall! Nobody to take care of this...what now? He grabbed the desk phone from its cradle and angrily dialled a familiar number.

"Always a pleasure baby, how can I fuck you today?" The familiar voice purred over the phone.

He forced himself to remain calm. "Listen. I need to see you tonight! What time are you free?"

Caramel giggled with an air of vindication. "Changed your mind so soon? I thought we broke up."

"No games! No more games! I'm ready to be whatever you want! But this *must* be between us for now; until I find a cheap way to divorce the wife."

Her excitement instantly softened her heart. "Ok baby. I completely understand. You know your secret's safe with me. I've missed you so much Michael. I think about you around the clock." She truthfully confessed.

He chuckled out of sheer nervousness. "I've missed you too sexy. After seeing you at the gala, I realised my mistake! I'd be dumb to let you go. My dick is so hard right now. I just wish you were right here." He lied.

"This must be destiny baby, 'cause I had the same thoughts in mind." Her wretched, sexually under-toned voice re-surfaced. "I woke up this morning in the middle of dreaming about you; about *us*. My pussy ached for you *Thunder*! And after three orgasms with my toy, I still longed for you. I knew if I called you…"

The line suddenly fell quiet.

"Hello?" Michael checked if they were still connected.

"Yeah, I'm here. Sorry about that. I knew if I called, you might not pick up or you wouldn't come to me. So guess what baby? I brought the pussy to you!"

On that note, his office door swung open. He sprang forward out of his chair, his jaws immediately dropping along with his phone.

Stacy stood in the hallway of his firm, fully nude except for a mesh garter and a button-down white dress that was now wide open. Evidently uncaring that she could be spotted by anyone that stepped foot into the hallway, she ran her fingers along the opening of her pinkness and chuckled eerily.

"Your pussy is fully marinated *Thunder*!"

CHAPTER TWENTY-ONE

Lisa manoeuvred through the bustling travellers of the airport lobby with caution. She was desperately trying to make it to the book shop that seemed far beyond her reach.

She had ventured off without Shane when her tolerance for his incessant phone calls, text messages, autographs, and photo-ops had depleted. Added to that, their flight had already been delayed for over an hour, and there were no recent updates on the status of its departure.

As she browsed the fiction rack for an interesting Jamaican-based read, she flinched when her name bellowed from the storefront. Reluctantly, she turned to acknowledge her man and frowned.

"Babes, why would you step off and not say anything to me? You can't just wander off like that." Shane chastised her as he got closer.

She impulsively rolled her eyes. "I cannot *wander* in an enclosed airport Shane! Besides, you *obviously* saw where I went. Done with your phone calls?" She sparingly scanned the summary on the back of a novel.

"Is that what this is about? Lisa please…" He opted to defer another of their recurring arguments.

"*Please* what?" She chose to proceed. "Please sit there and stare into space while you spill the stories of your life to the world? *You please!*"

Shane scowled and shook his head in disbelief. "You really want to argue in the middle of this *very* crowded store huh? What's gotten into you Lisa? Please tell me it's this pregnancy thing."

"This *pregnancy, is not a thing* Shane! You'd better realise that and get with the program! You're the one with the problems so don't blame this on my *thing*!" She marched a few steps away from him.

Shane nervously smiled and waved at a bunch of curious onlookers. He moved in closer to his unruly woman instead of just walking away.

"Lisa, what did I do now?" He lowered his voice but spoke sternly. "What's my problem? Please, enlighten me!"

"Enlighten you? I think you've already *enlightened* yourself Mr. Wright. Don't think I'm dumb because I'm quiet eh! I've been in Jamaica for almost a month, and where have we gone? I've been stashed like a hermit for the *entire trip*!"

This argument was going in all sorts of directions in the most inappropriate place.

He snapped. "First of all woman, *lower your damn voice*! Second of all, you're the one that's *always tired*! Always needing *a nap*! And haven't I been *stashed* in the house with you for most of the trip? Lisa, *relax* yuhself man! Cut out di fuckry now! Yuh really been pissing mi off!" He couldn't maintain his composure. "Matter of fact…"

"What?" She shot back, pissed that he reverted to speaking patois to intimidate her. "Whatever Shane! Please leave me in peace to buy my book." She dropped the issue and gingerly strolled away.

Shane was about to go after her, when his cell phone loudly chirped 'New Message'. He walked in the opposite direction, eager to see the response to message he sent. Subconsciously, he stopped in his tracks and read:

Safe flight babes! Of course yuh pussy still sore! So addicted to dat dick…hurry back! Miss yuh areddi…and no gifts! Kisses.

"What the *fuck* is that Shane?" Lisa carelessly shrieked over his right shoulder, fully alerting the entire store and few passersby to look in their direction.

Shane's face reddened with embarrassment. "You have got to be kidding me." He mumbled more to himself than her, and stormed straight out of the store.

Michael dimmed the lights on his Mercedes CL 500 as he discreetly pulled in behind the cluttered shrubs. Reclining in his seat, he gently massaged his head and pondered his next course of action.

Here's to the grand finale of Michael 'the Adulterer'! No more Caramel...Stacy...whatever the fuck she calls herself...and as hard is it will be, no more Anne-Gina. I have to live right by Natalie and our kids. Have to restore the peace in Linton's life. This is the final hour!

He climbed out of the car, activated the alarm, and made his way down the hidden path towards the beach front house. He redialled the last number in his cell.

"You here baby?" The raspy voice eagerly enquired.

"Yeah. Let me in through the patio." He decided to use the first entrance he encountered.

When the door swung open, Anne-Gina appeared in her birthday suit and a pair of red, four-inched stilettos.

"I was anxious..." She teasingly offered as he gawked at her from head to toe.

Michael snatched her impossibly curved waist and eagerly kissed her glossed, plumped lips. He was instantly aroused, his throbbing shaft forcing against its restraint.

"Let me get that for you baby." She seductively purred while unbuckling his belt. "*All that* for me? I'm one lucky girl." She gently stroked him as she teased.

He bit down on his lip to relieve the rising pressure.

In one smooth motion, she buried his entire length inside her handsome mouth, skilfully and effortlessly leaving none of his nine inches unattended.

"Jesus Christ sexy! Take it easy on me! Mmm." He groaned, enforcing her by the hair and thrusting his groin.

Anne freed herself from his restraints and broke the momentum. She walked over to the living room couch, urging him to follow with every swing of her hip. As she rested her voluptuous butt against the back of the chair and sensually raised her right leg, she tucked it behind her head to form a perfect standing split.

Michael shuddered at the sight of her fully exposed pinkness and entered her with a firm thrust.

"Oh-my-fucking-God!" He blasphemed, as he mercilessly pummelled her orifice and groped her heavy breasts. "I love this pussy so much Anne-Gina! It's a damn shame!" He passionately kissed her yearning lips. "I'm going to miss you." He whispered in her mouth, causing her body to shudder perfectly in sync with his.

Biggs and his four-member posse boastfully made their way toward the entrance of the Asylum night club. He briefly acknowledged the security attendant, eased his way through the crowded lounge, and headed for the V.I.P area.

The club manager immediately discharged his most beautiful and scantily-clad female servers, to attend to the 'high-profile' client and his accompanying guests.

It was a typical, overcrowded Friday night affair at Kingston's most recognised hot spot.

Though Biggs had recently forsaken the club scene, he had ventured out tonight to see the performance of an up-and-coming female artist whose talent he admired, among other things. He leaned by the V.I.P balcony to watch the crowd in action, as the deejay blasted his newest record through the speakers and alerted the audience that he was 'in the house'.

The lights on the disco ball suddenly turned off, leaving the room dark except for the spotlight that dimly illuminated the stage. The reputable *Dem Gyal Sittin' Riddim* blasted from the speakers, thoroughly exciting the crowd for the main event.

"Which part di good up good up gyal dem deh?" The raspy voice of dancehall diva Timberlee bombarded the microphone before the artist came into sight. Stylishly dressed in Dior couture, the unusually beautiful woman emerged unto the stage with utmost confidence. She immediately delved into her performance and expertly engaged the audience to recount her newest single *Stress Free* - ode to the God-blessed divas.

Biggs and his friends looked on with zeal, fully enjoying her delivery and expert control of the stage.

"Yeah man, she wicked…" He replied to Screwface's enquiry. "She definitely deh bout fi top the charts fi a while."

Screwface nodded in approval as he focused more on the woman's voluptuous frame, accentuated by her body-hugging mini-dress.

The star delivered her internationally known single *Bubble Like Soup* to wrap up her segment, and literally bring the house down. Men and women alike jointly sang along, respective of the female-empowered lyrics. When her set was complete, she thanked her fans as usual for their continuous support and informed on upcoming events.

Biggs was now ready to take the party to the 'big man' club - the strip joint. He made the first move, and the rest of the men automatically followed suit.

As the herd got to the doorway leading to the backstage area, Screwface tapped Biggs on the arm and leaned in closer.

Not surprised by what he heard, he shook his head and smiled. "Do yuh ting rude bway. Just link mi pon di cellie when yuh rally...if so!"

They laughed and boomed fists.

Natalie jumped out of her sleep as the bedroom door screeched open. "You have a fucking nerve Michael!" She shouted into the dark, unleashing the anger she had fallen asleep with.

She fumbled for the switch on her bedside lamp when there was no response, though she felt a presence.

"Michael?" She grew nervous as footsteps steadily approached her, but she failed to locate the light switch.

Before she could defensively react, a firm hand gently gripped her flailing arm and the room illuminated.

"I didn't mean to startle you baby..." Michael barely muttered, using her hand to caress the side of his face. He was kneeling by the bedside, eyes closed.

She fumbled for a minute, but was not about to let him off the hook that easily. "Where the hell have you been Michael? Waltzing up in here like it's sunny outside!" She yanked her hand away from his.

"I've had the worst day baby...the worst day of my life!" Tears seeped from his tightly-shut eyes.

Natalie's defence was fully penetrated. She sat forward and embraced the first love of her life.

"What's the matter baby? Did something happen? Talk to me Michael...you're scaring me." She nestled his head into her bosom and held him tightly. "Michael..."

"Natalie...everything that's happened to us is my fault! I'm so sorry for doing you wrong! So sorry for messing things up between us! You're such a good woman...a great wife. I messed up baby...really bad. I hope you can forgive me. And no matter what, just know that I'm truly mortified and I'm terribly sorry for everything."

She steadily released him, bracing herself for whatever revelation came next. Though she had been searching for evidence of his adulterous affairs, even having confirmations, she had never expected or braced for an outright confession.

Michael stared into the eyes of his woman of fifteen years. "Baby, I've betrayed you. I've betrayed what we've built our love upon. I had an affair Natalie. But I'm begging you not to hate me. Be mad baby...but please don't leave me!" He began to sob. "I'm so sorry Natalie. I swear on *my life* that it will never happen again. Just please find it in your heart to forgive me this once. Please!"

Tears streamed down her cheeks as the ugly truth massaged the temples of her mind. She refused the hand that reached out to touch her, and moved to the center of the bed.

He panicked. "Talk to me Natalie!" He stood and climbed into the bed beside her. "Say something baby... anything! Please..." He scrutinised her every motion for any sign of what was to come.

"I've known all along Michael." Her lips trembled as she spoke amidst hushed cries. "I've known since the very first time, believe me. There's nothing like the energy that two people share when they've lived as one for fifteen years." She paused for a moment.

"When one of those people falter Michael, it naturally puts a drag on the other. I haven't even had the energy to enjoy my pregnancy. Even regretted it for a while..." She paused, allowing her confession to resonate. "Michael, how did we get to this point? What really happened to us? To our love?"

"Baby nothing happened to us; it was me! I was dumb Natalie! So foolish!" He clutched both her hands in his. "I'll make it up to you baby. I'll do whatever it takes! Name it..."

"No. Something happened to *us* Michael. It's not just you. Something changed between us, at some unrecognised time. I don't know how this is going to turn out..." She paused to deliberate her next words.

Michael didn't like the sound of anything she had just said, or where the conversation was headed. "Natalie, please don't talk like that baby. It's going to work I promise. I'll do what it takes. I take full blame." He was sobbing now.

CHAPTER TWENTY-TWO

Roxanne jolted out of her sleep, startled by her chiming cell phone. She wearily swatted the bed to locate the disturbance, trying her best not to shift an inch.

"Hello." She mumbled into the phone while trying to balance it on the side of her face.

"Wha kind a 'Birthday' voice *dat*?" Biggs teased with much enthusiasm. "The day break already yuh nuh babes! A time fi get up and tek in some of God's beautiful sunshine!" He chuckled at the thought of waking her.

"Thanks baby. What yuh doing up so early and yuh went out last night?" She rolled unto her back and got comfortable for a longer conversation.

"Look through the window and find out for yuhself."

She immediately struggled to sit up, climb out of the bed, and walk briskly towards the window. *Oh my God!* She exclaimed inwardly.

"Oh my God!" She screamed into the phone. "Andre yuh didn't!" She couldn't find her slippers fast enough.

He laughed. "So yuh up or what babes?" He continued to tease. "A birthday time or sleep time? Alright call me…"

"Stop playing!" Roxanne bolted out the room and through the front door, still wearing her pyjamas and clutching the cell to her ear.

She stopped in the middle of the driveway to gawk at the sparkling new 2008 Lexus IS, custom-painted in her favourite cherry red, adorned with a big red bow.

"*Oh-my-God*! Oh my God! Oh my God! Andre! I can't even drive!" She grinned and ran towards the end of the driveway where he sat in his Lexus truck. "Baby…" She started to express her enthusiasm, but opted to kiss him instead.

After a prolonged heated session that churned Screwface's stomach as he lounged nearby, their lips finally unlocked and they both spoke at the same time.

"You go first." Roxanne laughed, blushing atop her natural glow.

Biggs kissed her on the forehead. "Is there a better way to kick off your eighteenth year on this earth? Tell me, who loves yuh?"

"His Excellency, Sir Andre 'Biggs' Jackson. *But* who loves him more?"

"Roxanne Mitchell?" He quizzically eyed her.

She slapped him on the arm and pouted. "Actually, that's half the answer. It's Roxanne *and* Adrian!" She playfully massaged her protruding, five-month tummy and grinned.

"It's a boy babes?" He shrieked with excitement. "When yuh find out? How yuh jus a tell mi? For real?" The questions rambled on.

Roxanne smiled and teased. "I'm full of surprises too yuh nuh? Wha yuh feel?"

"Yuh sure are babes! Wow! Adrian Jackson...it have a nice 'bad man' buzz to it." He dodged her fist.

"He wont be no bad man so whatever!"

He laughed, clutching her violent hands. "That reminds me..." He reached over to the back seat and retrieved a large gift bag. "This is for *both* of you."

"What more could you possibly buy babe? Have mercy..." She eagerly welcomed his spontaneous lips.

"Roxie, I have to run now." He kissed her on the cheek then on the tummy. "Call mi when yuh decide what yuh want to do later, cool? And tell your sis I said waddup. Screwface!"

His friend walked around to the passenger side of the truck and hastily hopped in.

"Call mi babes!" He called out to her as he slowly pulled away from the house.

Roxanne anxiously made her way to her birthday ride to check out the features. As if having the full option package wasn't enough, her initials were imprinted in gold on the head rest of each seat and the floor mats.

"This is *way too cool*!" She shrieked as she adjusted the driver's seat and cranked the engine.

Regina appeared at the front door and immediately screamed. "Roxanne! What the hell is going on?" She ran out to her sister with much excitement.

"Regina, you wouldn't believe! Andre got this for my birthday! Isn't it super?" She grinned, looking back and forth from her sister's awestruck face to the new ride.

"Hop on in!" She exclaimed, enjoying the idea of having her usual chauffeur as a passenger.

Regina chuckled when she caught on to the mockery, but hopped into the back seat. "This thing *is* off the chain! What kind of car is this anyway?"

Roxanne burst out a sarcastic laugh. "This isn't a *thing* or a *car* sis! It's a *Lexus IS* and it's an *automobile*!" She always pitied her don't-really-care-for-cars or 'guy stuff' sister.

They laughed in unison.

"I need to meet this Andre yuh nuh." Regina finally admitted. "I would say it's about time. We should all have dinner tonight. How does that sound? Let me know and I'll make the reservations..."

"That sounds great!" Roxanne was naturally excited about this progression. "I'll call and tell him! Oh, and he did say to tell you hi."

"Cool. Anyways I'm going to start your birthday breakfast cause *I'm* starving. My less-expensive gift is upstairs in my closet. You can go take a look when you're done." She smiled teasingly and kissed her on the cheek.

"Happy Birthday hun! It'll be a great one! Love you tonnes."

"Love you too sis! Wait, I was thinking…could we invite Linton to breakfast? I kind of miss him!" She truthfully confessed with a cheesy grin.

Regina loved the idea but didn't dare reveal it. "You just want to *show off*! Invite him if you want. *Obviously* you're calling." She turned to conceal the smile that threatened to grace her lips.

"Stop acting like you're too *distracted* to miss him!" Roxanne called out to her, laughing vulgarly. "I can see right through you!"

She immediately dialled Linton as her sister, without looking back, flipped her 'the bird'.

Natalie got warped in a moment, admiring an artistic fruit display on a corner stall at the market.

"Mom, you wanted ripe bananas?" She called out to an equally distracted Cecile as she walked over to join her.

"No, that's too much fibre." She airily replied while inspecting some oranges. "How much is it per dozen for these?" She looked up at the heavy set woman, who irritably repeated the price.

"Hmm! You watch that attitude with me you hear?" Cecile abruptly chastised the vendor, ready for a death match.

"How do you sell the melons?" Natalie immediately asked the woman to ease the tension.

"You better listen to her well because it's a difficult task for her to repeat." Cecile had to interject, eyeing the woman scathingly.

"Fawty a pound miss." The vendor shrewdly replied ignoring the middle-aged woman. "How much yuh want?"

Natalie chuckled at the ensuing friction between her usually troublesome mother and the burly woman. "I'll take that half." She pointed to the reddest piece. "And I'll take two bags of those pineapples." She hugged her mother and sighed.

"Do you have to be a brute everywhere you go? My God, give the woman a break mom. You already paid for those?" She referred to the bags she had in hand.

"You give *too much* breaks, then wonder why you're in the situation you are in! No I didn't pay anything!" Cecile snapped, her words piercing.

Natalie cringed at her mother's insinuation that she was to be blamed for her broken marriage. She was also embarrassed, and rightfully so. It was time to scrap.

"Oh *really* mom? Just like that you out my business and ridicule me?" She visibly seethed. "You're the last person to be nudging anyone about breaks! How close did your *non-breaks* with dad keep him? Huh? What's my illegitimate *brother's* name again?"

She referred to her parent's tumultuous and abusive marriage of twenty five tears that birthed an unofficial child, of which her mother is still masking the pain.

"I'm sorry Natalie. I didn't mean for it to sound like that. My sincerest apologies, I'll be in the car." She paid the woman and walked away.

"Mom..." She hadn't meant to take it that far herself. "Mom, I'm sorry...come back."

Cecile maintained her pace, much to the vendor's amusement who enjoyed her daughter's admonishment.

As soon as Regina stepped into the kitchen, the house phone rang. Without checking the call display, she answered with much enthusiasm.

"Good Morning."

"Sis, you should've heard how excited Linton sounded! Oh God please be nice, just this once, for me?" Roxanne dramatically recounted her tale from the driveway. "Oh! And I kind of told him about Doctor…"

"Roxanne you didn't!" She cut her off. "Why would you do that? I should poison both your breakfasts! Goodbye!" She hung up and went into the refrigerator to retrieve the ingredients for the birthday edition of her regular Saturday morning feasts.

She decided to make her sister's favourites: ackee and salt fish, brown-stewed liver, fried dumplings, and plantains. She set up to knead the dough for the dumplings, but as she sunk her hand into the flour, the phone rang again.

Roxanne enough now! She mentally chastised, seeing her through the window on her cell.

"Yes?" She bluntly answered.

"Well, a *pleasant* good morning to you too *Rudeness*! What's your early morning dilemma?" Shane's sarcasm spilled through the line.

Regina laughed. "My bad! No dilemmas; just Roxanne and her dumbness." She turned on the speaker phone and rested the handset on the counter. "*Good morning* sunshine! How art thou?" She smiled in anticipation of his response.

"*Good morning* my ass! Thou art great, but peeved! Before I lament, isn't it Roxanne's b-day today? Tell her I said waddup. Gina, I need your unbiased, neutra-gendered advice right now." He paused, then laughed when she did.

"Well Shane, I don't know much about neutra-genderism, but I'll try my best. Continue…" She worked to perfectly separate and mould the dough.

"Lisa and I have been arguing like crazy. She's just been acting up Gina. Man, we got into it bad at the airport last night before we left. She totally embarrassed me in front of millions of *Jamaican* people!"

Regina chuckled at Shane's usual, over-dramatic recount of his predicaments.

"You'd better not be laughing at me Gina…this is serious! I don't know if I can take this misery anymore my friend. Not saying that I want to break up; but maybe *disappear* for a while. You know?"

She knew exactly what Shane's 'disappearances' were like, and also knew that she was in no mood to be harassed by a raging, pregnant Lisa.

"Shane, I see what you're saying but I would also have to hear Lisa's version. However, my unbiased opinion is this; talk to her about it and see where this is suddenly coming from. Unless she's losing her mind, or this is *not so sudden*, she should have a reason. I'd bet my next pay check on a little insecurity, mixed with the natal mood swings. I have my bouts with Roxanne too."

Shane sighed loudly on purpose. "I hope you're right, or I'll have your head! By the way I can smell what you're cooking from here; mail me some! Remember to hail Roxanne for me. Gotta run again. Love you sis."

"Love you too Shane, and take a deep breath!"

Regina hung up and added the finishing spices to the liver and the ackee, and removed the last batch of dumplings from the pot. She sliced oranges and prepared to make fresh juice, when the loud roar of Linton's V12 engine - evidently newly repaired, hummed its way up the main street.

She quickly dropped everything into the sink, turned off the stove, and made a dash for the stairs.

Can't be caught dead looking like this! Have him think I miss him…or I'm here worrying or something… please! She made a quick stop in the bedroom, grabbed some clothes from her closet, and disappeared into the bathroom.

Shane drove south on the I-87 at unbelievable speeds, cutting the one hour journey from White Plains to Fort Lee, New Jersey to forty minutes.

Sheldon followed in his car closely, as the family headed to Lisa's parents' house for a barbecue.

Tina had worked fervently to prepare a few of hers and the boys' favourite recipes, ensuring to bake a macaroni casserole for Simeon who travelled with a finicky appetite.

As they pulled up to the expansive property and Shane pushed the security intercom, the large brass gates automatically slid open revealing the immaculate grounds. They drove the distance along the winding path, sandwiched by the fairy-tale garden, to the parking area.

"This place is awesome!" Simeon exclaimed, as he hopped out Sheldon's car and joined his mom.

"Now *that's* what you call a garden!" Tina marvelled at the brightly-coloured array of tulips, roses, and petunias encircling the stone-carved angels that were tip-toeing in the enormous water fountain.

Lisa's parents emerged from the side of the house, visibly excited by the arrival of their special guests.

"Welcome to our home!" They greeted them in unison.

Lisa's mother warmly hugged Tina. "You *must* be Shane's mother, because I *know* there's no *younger sister*!" She remarked with much fanfare. "I'm Linda Artuso. Please, call me Linda."

Tina laughed, blushing at her pleasantries. "I'm the mother Linda, Faustina Wright. You may call me Tina. It's a pleasure to finally meet you." She consciously offered her marital name despite the gruelling divorce.

Linda smiled and continued. "Same here Tina. And let's not forget this hefty hunk beside me...my Alessandro, Lisa's father. He's the boss around these parts."

They all laughed. The man's rigid stature made her statement believable.

Alessandro firmly shook Tina's hand and pecked her on each cheek. "It's a pleasure to meet you Tina, and thanks for making the trip with the boys." His stern, raspy voice was contradicted by his warm, gentle grin.

"The pleasure is mine Alessandro. This trip was indeed overdue." She subtly acknowledged the handsomely preserved face and stature of the man she knew was over sixty, seemingly going on sixteen.

"Where's my darling daughter?" Linda hurriedly walked away. "Shane, you look as ravishing as always... decadently dipped in that Gucci Rush fragrance I see." She gave him the tightest hug. "Lisa baby, why are we so sluggish? Aren't you happy to see your mother? Let me get a look at that bump! My word, you're almost huge!" She laughed at her self-conscious only child. "I'm only teasing baby, you look adorable! Are these the handsome brothers? How I wished I had more girls. This one here would definitely be a catch! How old are you sweety?" She gently embraced Sheldon.

"Twenty-two...going on thirty." He flirted with the overzealous woman. "I'm Sheldon by the way. Nice to meet you Mrs. Artuso. You have a lovely house."

"Thank the mister over there, sweety." She pointed toward Alessandro and truthfully confessed. "This mom only twiddles her thumbs and spends! And who is *this* charming Casanova-in-training?"

Simeon visibly blushed and shyly replied. "I'm Simeon and I'm fifteen." He grinned widely.

She smiled. "You're so precious. Well I guess that leaves Steven, which must be you." She playfully pointed at the last of the trio.

Steven, who was generally more reserved, coolly replied. "That's me. Nice to meet you Mrs. Artuso." He firmly shook her hand.

"Everyone, *please* call me Linda." She spontaneously declared as if begging, much to everyone's amusement.

"Shall we proceed?" Alessandro enquired of his guests. "Everyone in back must be wondering what's taking so long." He walked off ahead of the pack.

The music and chatter grew more audible as they neared the entrance to the backyard. There were about sixty people in attendance for the *family* gathering.

Children were busy playing by the pool while their unconcerned parents sipped wine and tanned. Other adults were circled around board games or near the extensive dining table that stretched comfortably to accommodate each person.

"*Yuh-mmy!*" Simeon excitedly belted when his eyes friskily scanned the table and landed on 'dessert paradise'. "Chocolate fudge brownies? This must be heaven mom!" He watched without care as the others laughed.

"Go and help yourself Simeon…don't be shy!" Linda encouraged him and turned to the others. "First we'll introduce the who's who. The rest you'll get to know as the day goes by." She casually informed Tina, provoking a chuckle from her otherwise serious husband.

The introductions were extensive nonetheless, but they eventually got through with it and settled down for brunch.

As the festivities reigned with loud chatter and laughter, Alessandro indicated he would make a toast.

Silence instantly befell the mass.

"I just want to thank everyone here today, for joining in on our families' celebrations. I'd like to also offer a special welcome to the Wright clan, my extended family. Shane, though we've had our differences, I respect you as an ambitious and upright man, and I love what you do for my daughter." He tilted his glass towards him and continued.

"Lisa baby, you've grown into such a beautiful young woman. Daddy's very proud of you and I'm *always* here whenever you need me." He paused to acknowledge his daughter, and everyone used the opportunity to clap and cheer.

Shane flinched inwardly at Alessandro's emphasis on 'always'. He silently wondered if Lisa had been discussing their recent squabbles with her very robust and intimidating father; the idea admittedly ruffled his nerves.

Alessandro continued. "Now, there's enough of everything here to enjoy! So please, eat!"

Unsuspectingly, Shane stood to make a toast of his own. Almost regretting the move the second he received everyone's undivided attention, he composed his thoughts and smiled.

"Good afternoon everyone. Some of you may know me, but for those who don't, I'm Shane Wright." He paused for their simultaneous greetings. "I just want to personally thank the Artuso family for hosting this lovely gathering and for the warm welcome they've extended to my family."

"Secondly, I want to toast Lisa for being a breath of fresh air in my otherwise congested life. Baby..." He turned to face his visibly nervous woman.

"I'm so blessed to have you in my life. I thank God for each day he gives me to spend with you, to love you, to build memories with you, and most importantly, to start my family with you. But something is still missing..."

There were mixed reactions from the audience at his choice of words. Lisa too, seemed tensed and puzzled.

Shane smiled inwardly and removed a fortune cookie from its wrapper; it was Lisa's new favourite snack.

Handing it to her, he got down on one knee as she hastily cracked it open.

"There's only one right way to start *our* family baby." He continued as the diamond embellished platinum band fell into her lap. "Lisa Arianna Artuso, I need you and our baby to spend the rest of your lives with me..."

Regina insisted on arriving at the Star Apple's Restaurant ten minutes ahead of the scheduled time in order to prepay the tab.

The waiter eventually directed them to their private booth on the terrace, where Kingston's cool evening winds appreciatively greeted them.

Roxanne was visibly nervous as she sat across from her sister, tapping a melody with her fingers on the table.

"Calm your nerves Roxanne! You're making me nervous just looking at you!" Regina quizzically eyed her.

"Stop look den! I can't help it!" She bluntly replied, wondering if Andre would show up on time, among other things, that could turn this celebration into a nightmare.

Before Roxanne could utter another word, she spotted him in the distance scanning the restaurant. She flinched with excitement, alerting Regina to look in his direction.

"Good evening ladies." Biggs, handsomely dressed head to toe in Armani spoke as he neared the table. "I hope I didn't keep you two waiting long." He gently shook Regina's hand and offered her a rose. "Nice to finally meet you Regina, I'm Andre Jackson." He added his charming smile.

Regina noticeably blushed. "Nice to finally meet you too, Andre. Please, have a seat." She noted he was nothing like she'd anticipated, beginning with his strikingly handsome face.

"Roxanne, you look beautiful." Biggs took his place beside her. "Happy Birthday again babes." He handed her the second rose, and consciously refrained from kissing her.

Roxanne was already smiling from within. "Thank you Andre. And you look quite dapper yourself...as always." She elbowed him, giggling childishly.

Regina acknowledged and admired her sister's visible glow, and the couple's disposition towards each other. It became more apparent to her now, that their relationship was truly genuine.

The trio sat in silence while they individually scanned the menu. After they had placed their orders, with Roxanne pointedly reminding Andre that he was allergic to shrimp - much to the amazement of a bewildered Regina - the moment had surfaced for the anticipated 'discussion'.

"So Andre, now that we've settled. First I'd like to get it out there that I don't think a seventeen year old schoolgirl and a twenty eight year old man should be having intimate relations."

She acknowledged the morbid look on Roxanne's face and continued. "But before we all get frazzled, I'd also like to add that I respect your decision to accept the responsibility to raise this child with my sister. It is rather evident that you two genuinely respect each other, and I must admit it is quite admirable." She glimpsed Roxanne's nervous smile at that admission, but left the floor open and leaned back in her seat.

"Regina, I perfectly understand your position. I'm not going to sit here and pretend that what Roxanne and I share is traditionally acceptable. What I will say is that I not only respect your sister, but I truly love her. I would never do anything to intentionally harm her, or you guys relationship. Accepting the responsibility to care for Roxanne *and* the baby wasn't an option to me Regina; it was an obligation." He stopped there when Roxanne gently stroked his thigh.

Regina was already moved by his sensitivity towards the age disparity. She appreciated his honesty, sincerity, and overall genuineness with respect to their familial unit. She also took her sister' s contentment into consideration.

"I understand you more vividly Mr. Jackson. Whether or not it was your intention, I'm truly impressed." She offered a warm smile, sealing the deal on her acceptance.

Michael sat on his front porch anxiously awaiting his brother who had already postponed on him three times throughout the day. He quickly sprang to his feet when the hum of his racing engine pierced the silence, before the car came into view.

Linton backed into the driveway, almost running over his raging brother.

"What part of urgent didn't you understand man?" Michael irritably snarled, staring him down.

His brother unenthusiastically looked up at him. "Don't fuck with me Michael! I had shit to take care of! What's up?" He decided to remain in the car.

"You wouldn't believe the night I had bro!" His attitude quickly adjusted. "I spilled my guts to Natalie man...told her everything! Every single thing!"

"Well that's good news! Must be part of the reason I got invited to breakfast at Regina's this morning. So what the hell was so *urgent* then?"

Michael flinched. "*That's* the reason you ditched me this morning? To have breakfast at Regina's? That's foul brother. I'm always there for you when you call!"

"Foul? I'm fucking homeless and loveless from *being there for you* lest we forget! Now get to the urgent part! I don't want to be here longer than I need to!"

"Alright, alright! Would you believe that after all I went through to confess my spoils to Natalie, even bawling and shit, she turns around and admits to fucking on *me*?" He shook his head in disbelief as Linton's jaws instantly dropped.

"Yeah, confessed without a *drop* of remorse! I've been feeling guilty and paranoid for stepping out on my *good wife*...going through all sorts of *shit* to fix things, and this?" He paused to collect himself as grief and anger riddled him.

"I mean, damn! Did she say with whom...when?" Linton asked the first thing that came to his mind, despite the irrelevance.

"I couldn't tell you bro..." He sighed. "I passed out."

With that confession, Linton was almost floored. He laughed uncontrollably until his eyes welled with tears.

"Well...at least it's *all* in the air now. What can I say? You win some, and you lose some! Karma's a bitch." He tried to stifle his amusement but failed miserably.

"Would you like some popcorn to go with your entertainment?" Michael was annoyed. "A cocktail maybe? Aint shit fucking funny Linton! At least now you can finally get off my damn back about me ruining your life!"

"Tell me one more thing dear brother, how *exactly* did you *fix* that *situation* of yours? You killed that psycho goddess?" He smiled teasingly.

Michael frowned and looked off into the distance. "That's not relevant now, is it? Fact is it's done with! As you were..." He left it at that.

Linton nodded approvingly. "I really hope so man. But hey, I gotta get going." He finally stepped out of the car, stretched, and gripped his brother's rigid shoulders. "Just take it easy bro. It can only get better from here. Call me if anything..." He climbed back into the car. "Or don't..." He mumbled audibly.

"Screw you!" Michael curtly shot back.

Linton smiled. "You've done enough screwing my brother. Try praying!" He waved goodbye as he sped off.

Regina made it inside the house just in time to catch the evening news. She glided into the kitchen to put on the kettle, and turned on the television.

Perched on the kitchen counter, she skimmed the developing headlines before the firm voice of the news correspondent belted out the leading story of the evening.

"The body of a thirty year old woman washed up on the shores of Lime Cay this morning and was found by two local fishermen. The woman has been identified as Stacy Jones, a local resident of the Grant's Pen vicinity. Maurice Channer is on the scene to further report." The screen switched from the newsroom to the shores of the secluded, off shore beach.

The tea mug slipped from Regina's grip as she gawked at the picture of Stacy on the corner of the television screen. Tears immediately welled in her eyes as mixed emotions overwhelmed her.

Maurice, the news correspondent, reported. "The body of Stacy Jones showed signs of severe strangulation and heavy bludgeoning to the head that could've ultimately resulted in her death. Charlie here, is one of the fishermen that first discovered the body. Tell us what you know Charlie…"

"Well, me and mi bredrin just did a do we work when wi boat lick pon sup'm inna di water. Mi look inna di water but mi neva see nutt'n right aweh. So wi decide fi use the net and see wha wi bring up. When wi drag it uppa shore, wi see di body and mi bredrin call di police. But mi know her man. She's a stripper over *The Club*…Caramel she name. Mi know har tattoo caw mi used to love her off! Jah know star…"

Charlie's best recount of the incident wrapped up the segment on the story.

As usual, the police were asking the public to come forward with any information that may lead to an arrest.

Linton had let himself into the house using the key that Roxanne had slipped him at breakfast. He had strolled into the kitchen just as the last part of the news broadcasted. He silently wished he hadn't showed up, and braced for the unexpected.

Regina turned to see who was standing so closely behind her. If she was shocked to see Linton, it didn't show through the look she already held.

"Do you know anything about that?" She bluntly asked him as tears spilled down her cheeks.

"Nothing! Why would I?" He quickly responded.

"Whatever reason, you better not! What are you doing here anyhow? How did you get in?" She wiped the tears from her cheeks. "Answer me!"

He shifted uneasily. "Roxanne. I thought…"

"I told him to come!" Roxanne took over the situation. "You need to forgive him for what he did Gina. You would've done the same thing for me! Besides, what's the point of all this quarrelling if you're going to get back together eventually? It's all just a waste of time if you ask me!" She shrugged and walked away.

Linton spoke first. "Regina, I want you to know that I know *nothing* about that! I know I've hurt you babe, and given you tonnes of reasons not to trust me. But you should know me better than that!" He pointed to the television and held her gaze.

Regina broke down. "Linton, promise me you have nothing to do with that murder. Promise me, on everything that you have!" She pleaded between sobs.

He tightly embraced the love of his life. "I had *nothing* to do with it Regina! I promise you on my life! I had nothing at all to do with it!" He allowed her to cry.

Nestling in the firm embrace of the only man she'd ever know until recently, she appreciated his warmth and comfort. *What am I going to do with you William?*

CHAPTER TWENTY-THREE

Biggs stirred in the bed and glanced at the clock out of sheer instinct. "Babes, yuh nuh plan fi get up? It's after ten yuh nuh." He mumbled to his bed mate who slightly shifted but didn't respond.

He turned to face her and spoke firmly. "Roxanne! Yuh have to get up so I can drop yuh home. How you one so tired babes?" He teased laughing, fully aware that his late night antics were the primary reason.

Roxanne irritably sucked her teeth. "Andre, leave me nuh! Give me ten more minutes, *please*!" She rambled in an impatient whisper.

In one smooth motion, he carefully scooped her over to his side of the bed. "Babes, no more sleeping." HE spoke directly in her ear.

"Jesus! Alright I'm up! What a way yuh want get rid of me eeh...yuh have plans?" She tried to irritate him.

"Dat nah go work! My *plan* is to get your ass home so that yuh won't miss that flight! I don't want to hear Regina's mouth for something I had *no* part in!" He bit her on the shoulder and got up to use the bathroom.

Her sister's birthday gift included a two-week stay in New York City, for which they were scheduled to leave in less than four hours.

Roxanne grumbled and tried desperately to blink the sleep from her eyes. Her lids got half way up, but quickly shut when stung by the morning rays.

"Andre! Lock the blinds please. It's too bright in here! I'm going to get up this time I promise!" She covered her face with a pillow.

"Babes, the blinds *are* closed! It's just extremely bright outside! Early morning blessings yuh nuh…can't complain." He stood by the bedside and admired her womanly form outspread in the middle of his bed.

Her wavy locks spilled wildly across the pillows, and her shiny bump stubbornly protruded from her tank top. He climbed into the bed and joined her under the pillow.

"Babes…" He poked her in the side.

She giggled childishly. "I'm up! I still have five minutes though." She chuckled.

"Not *that* babes! I mean, *babes*…"

Roxanne laughed, instantly understanding the difference in his tones. She turned to face him in their dark cocoon and welcomed his eager kisses.

"I love yuh yuh see Roxie." He whispered as he massaged her tummy. "Head ago hurt me when yuh gone."

They both laughed.

"So come with me then…" She made another attempt to tag him along; the previous ones had failed.

"Babes, that's time for you and your sis…can't violate di ting." He peeped over at the clock. "It's eleven now, we have to get going. Plus I need to make a stop and get yuh some US." He slipped from her warm embrace and climbed out of the bed. "Get up babes!" He stopped in his tracks to ensure that she did. "Go cook yuh man some breakfast!" He teased.

"Yeah right!" She chuckled and unwillingly stood, following closely on his heels into the bathroom.

"Cilon wha yuh deh pon? Go is the word yuh nuh!" Benji impatiently barked into the phone. "Look from when mi call yuh and yuh fi call mi back! Wha u really deh pon?"

"Sorry big man! Got a little tied up yuh nuh? Go is the word man! Anything a anything still. Yuh ting done sort out, yuh zimme?" Cilon preferred not to upset him.

"The whole ting, or the *ting, ting*? 'Cause the way how mi feel yah now, is a all the way *ting*! Mi fed up a di situation, yuh zimme? Mi nuh like have fed up tings round me too long, yuh hear dat? Only a *ting, ting* me deh pon right now! Yuh zimme?"

Cilon understood precisely. "Alright then. Deal wid it big man! Mek sure it clean a way, yuh zimme?"

"Dat a di least! Likkle more." Benji hastily disconnected the line and tossed the cell phone through the car window.

Go is the word! A pussy duppy todeh! He glanced at his watch. *Eleven thirty and people still a sleep? Don't mek me affi come in deh fi yuh yuh nuh batty bway...mek a move!*

Cilon walked into his studio and plopped his robust frame into a large, swivel chair. He turned on his laptop then flicked on the wall-mounted TV in search of something to fill the void that hovered throughout the room. He settled on a porn channel and mused at the ill-treatment of the female.

When the computer loaded, he immediately signed into his email account to clear all the new messages that recently came in on his cell phone. He was surprised to see that the top two emails were from Biggs, who hadn't contacted him since he had stolen his money.

Pussy catch him fraid! He mused inwardly as he opened the first one. His amusement was short-lived.

Loading right before his eyes were pictures of him beating his 'wife' on the front lawn of their home, and sexually violating her in the process. The caption after the last of fifteen images read:

Rape is still a crime inna Jamaica yuh nuh faggot! Watch yuhself pussy!

Cilon jolted out of his gawking slumber when the woman on the TV screamed 'Help! Help!' incidentally portraying a rape scene. He muted the sound and quickly returned to his inbox to retrieve the second message; a third email had since arrived.

As a throbbing pain made its way up his spine, his heart stopped when images showing him, Julian, and Benji walking arm-in-arm in front of his house, studio, and his woman's house flooded his screen. *How the fuck him do that? These scenarios don't even add up!* He felt stifled.

He scrolled through the rest of the photos that blasphemously showed Benji and one of his personal handymen leaving Michelle's house with three duffle bags.

A Benji really thief mi bloodclaat money? "A wha di fuck really a gwan?"

The third email summed up his position:

Know the company yuh keep uptown batty bway! Yuh tink yuh can come between years of friendship? Rid yuhself of the likkle bitch! Yuh tink gangsta life is a dolly house pussyhole? Mi have a bullet with yuh name pon it! PS: video to mi ting this time!

Benji's adrenaline went into overdrive as the front door to the expansive mansion opened. Knowing the premises all too well, he sneaked in and dipped behind the thick trunk of a mango tree that shaded the gate post. Gun on cock, he patiently waited for the occupants to make their way down the driveway.

As he had anticipated, the Lexus truck came to a complete halt with the driver's door in exact alignment with his hiding place. In one swift motion, he lounged in the direction of the vehicle and opened the driver's door.

"Don't move a muscle pussy!" He warned Biggs who instinctively reached for his own gun, as expected.

Benji's mental plan dismantled immediately.

Standing there motionless, speechless even, he had not expected to see Roxanne.

Eyes wide open, she fearfully shielded her protruding tummy as she clung tightly to Biggs' protective arm.

"Benji, whatever it is…we can work this out." Biggs tried to reason with his friend. "What is this about? You see Roxie here, and she's pregnant. Don't do this in front of her. At least let me send her home in a cab. Benji, for all the years…" Knowing his friend's ruthlessness, he was determined to beg.

Roxanne silently began to cry upon hearing Biggs' sacrificial suggestion.

In an unsuspecting move, by some twist of fate, Benji slowly backed away though cautiously maintaining his aim at Biggs' head. His face still reflected his initial shock, but his eyes now glistened with tears for reasons only he could know.

In the same hurried manner in which he had pounced on them, he vanished from the property.

Roxanne instantly began to sob. She was stricken with not only relief, but anger.

"*What the fuck was that about Andre?*" She screamed. "*Why the hell did Benji come to kill you? Huh? What the hell was that?*" Her body trembled with rage.

Remembering her present state, she tried to compose herself. "I can't live like this Andre. This life is not safe for me *or* Adrian." She reclined in the seat and wailed.

Biggs tried to embrace her, touch her even. With each defensive shrug, his tears of relief surfaced.

"Babes, I really don't know what's going on." He tried to temper himself as his emotions threatened to frazzle him. "If I knew I had heat…" He couldn't finish.

His cell phone buzzed in the cup holder, startling both of them in the midst of their dilemma.

"*Pussy!* A you bring threat to *my wife*? To *my seed*? Right in front of mi *fucking* face?" Biggs barked into the phone as soon as the line connected.

"That was all Benji, Biggs!" Cilon hurriedly offered. "The man gone mad iyah! Dat mi a call yuh fi tell yuh right now! Mi done deal with the ting and a send the video to yuh as we speak! Believe me Biggs, that's all Benji!"

Biggs wasn't buying it. "Convenient seh yuh call me as soon as him leave! Seeing *is* believing! Mi nuh have *nuh otha words* fi you!" He disconnected the line and immediately dialled Screwface to meet him at the house.

He determined it was imperative to have a protective escort to take Roxanne home, and also ensure that she and her sister arrived at the airport safely.

"Stop at the Money Shoppe on yuh way up and buy three thousand US." He wrapped up his list of instructions and returned his attention to a weeping Roxanne.

Mi know seh a get the pussy get the email yuh nuh! And send Benji fi clean up him dutty work. Den a call man like me a ediat a gimme bag a story! Yuh life just end pussy! Girl a leave town so mi time free up now! I going show yuh how real bad do work! Pussyhole, uptown, batty bloodclaat bway! All you Benji? Mad yuh mus a mad to rass…you fi know betta!

He made another attempt to get close to Roxanne, but she wasn't having it.

"Babes, I love yuh. I don't know what else to seh! I'm really sorry about that…terribly sorry! Forgive me…" He sighed and wiped the tear that made its way down his cheek.

"Mister Kong, what's the reason for your visit today?" The voluptuous nurse seductively purred at her client, instantly arousing him.

"Well, I have sharp chest pains, excruciating groin pains, and sometimes a feverish temperature…among other *minor* ailments." He confessed, smiling.

Resting her hand by the nook of his neck, she nodded in affirmation. "Indeed; you're slightly warmer than normal. And those groin pains, are they onset by anything in particular?"

He grinned. "Honestly, the pain continuously lingers. But it does get worse when I'm…you know?"

She bashfully giggled. "I understand what you mean Mr. Kong. And the chest pains?"

"That's definitely from heartbreaks. I've had to make some restrictive choices lately in my life and I find myself dwelling on the regret."

"I have the exact remedy for you my heartbroken pony." She playfully winked at him.

"Yeah?" A rigid tent formed at his crotch.

"Mmm. Starting with here…" She eagerly freed his pulsing cock from its realms and effortlessly devoured his entire length with her mouth.

"Mmm!" He appreciatively grunted. "Come closer…" The words faintly escaped his mouth.

He firmly groped her impossibly-sized butt, thrusting his groin in an upward motion. His eroticism peaked to new heights as he observed the way her beautiful mouth expertly accommodated his enormous, pulsing member.

"Yuh want my sweet wetness Mister Kong? Can your heart manage all that?" She teasingly giggled.

"I'm always ready Anne-Gina…I mean Nurse Anne. Okay…I'm done with the role play! Put that leg up here baby! You wouldn't believe how I've missed that pussy!" Mr. Kong excitedly shuddered when she hoisted her leg to an otherwise impossible height, and leaned over the bed.

Unimaginable to him, and all the morals he once stood for, he got down on his knees and eagerly tasted the love juices that glistened her inner thighs. He ran his fully extended tongue from her enlarged clit to the depths of her moisture.

"Ooh!" She purred, as his tongue slipped into her ass and lingered there. "Gimme that dick Donkey Kong! Come fuck your pussy good!" She vulgarly pressured him.

He stood and aggressively plunged his unsheathed cock into her gaping orifice, gripping her hair for leverage. He revelled in the pleasure of watching her ass cheeks gyrate as he forcefully smacked them around and clenched them.

Remembering a story she had once told him, he surprised himself by pulling out of his comfort zone to treasure-hunt a cave he had determined never to explore.

"Fuck!" He screamed upon entry, as he quickly withdrew his damaged member and plopped down on the bed.

"Are you okay Michael?" Anne worriedly asked, turning around to assess the damage. "You should've warned me. I'm so sorry." Her large, bright eyes weighed with remorse.

"It's not your fault!" Michael smiled embarrassingly. "Rookie's eagerness…my bad!"

Anne-Gina crawled between his legs and dutifully used her mouth, tongue, and hands to remedy the situation until his phallus unfettered its bottled up gems.

Roxanne scowled at the extremely long line up at the taxi stand outside the JFK International Airport.

"Regina, how exactly are we getting to the hotel? We're *not* taking one of *those*, are we?" She pointedly eyed her sister who glanced at the cab stand and laughed.

"Thank heavens, no! That shit looks like the lotto line when they up the jackpot!"

They both laughed at that fact.

"Oh, so Shane's coming to get us?" Roxanne was confused now, but more so tired and eager to get going.

"Lawd misses! You're a reporter? Question after question…just easy yuhself nuh!" Regina tried the technique that usually intimidated her inquisitive little sister.

But 'Little Sister' was all grown up. "Lawd, what's the big secret? I hope is not somebody like mommy or anyone weird yuh nuh! That would just ruin my birthday! For real!"

Regina quickly spun around, shocked to hear her sister mention 'the unmentionable' with such nonchalance. She couldn't help but to laugh at her facial expression.

"You're actually serious right now? She couldn't stop laughing. "First of all, your birthday has long gone Diva. And second of all, who *the hell* would recognise your mother even if she looked identical to you? Shut up Roxanne!"

Roxanne had long stopped listening to her to admire the dark red, Lexus LS 470 - the matriarch to her birthday car - as it came to a complete stop right in front of them.

"Now that's a *fine* automobile! Customised color… Giovanni rims…must be a drug dealer!" She scrutinised the vehicle but couldn't see through its heavily-tinted windows.

Regina smiled from her heart as the trunk popped open. *I beg to differ.* She mused inwardly when the occupant climbed out, and walked around the front of the vehicle.

"*Doctor Smith*? What the hell is *he* doing here?" The real Roxanne stood up. "So *that's* why we're here Regina?

And to think...*great*! My *vaggie* doctor has front row seats to my birthday trip! That was a good one sister...who would've thought? Should I get naked now, or later?" The cynicisms rolled fluidly off her tongue, even as he handed her a large bouquet of flowers.

"You must be the *beautiful* little sister." He coolly offered. "It's nice to finally meet you. I'm William, a friend of Regina's." He smirked and shook her unintended hand.

Regina eyed her unusually silent sister, dreading the response she seemed anxious to deliver.

"Cool. Since you're *William*, the *friend* of my sister's; I guess I'm Roxanne, the less uptight, less secretive, and more upstanding *sister* who happens to think your LS 470 is a *fine automobile* that goes perfectly well with your extremely handsome face and your *fine* taste in fashion; those *are* Prada loafers?" She daringly glanced from his feet to his face, acknowledging her man's favourite footwear.

Before he could reply, she added. "Since we're done with the pleasantries, William, *will* you attend to my luggage? It's kind of heavy." She uncaringly stepped off the curb and climbed into the backseat of the car, firmly shutting the door.

Regina's face flushed with embarrassment, underlined with a dose of jealousy. She imagined that William overly appreciated Roxanne's blunt compliments, and realised that she had never been so kind with words to a man. She barely glanced in his direction, but smiled when he looked up at her.

"Relax Regina...we talked about this remember?" He flashed his enchanting grin. "Besides, I didn't even find it all that bad. I think I got away clean." He chuckled and opened her door. "Get in lady..." He winked before sealing her in.

After saddling up for the journey ahead, William looked at Roxanne through the rear-view mirror.

"By the way Roxanne, I don't know what kind of trips you and your sister are used to taking, but there's *no* getting naked on this one!"

His words lingered briefly before fully resonating with his passengers who blurted out laughing simultaneously.

The joke prolonged, serving as their entertainment for the bustle through the airport traffic.

"Michael, where the hell have you been all day? And why are you walking like that?" Natalie immediately attacked her husband as he stepped foot into the house. "Answer me!"

He was visibly irritated. "What? You haven't acknowledged my presence in the past three days, and now you want to know where I've been? Irrelevant!"

She was enraged. "*Excuse you*? Have you said anything to me since the night *you passed the fuck out*? Uh, let me think...*No*! Don't come in here walking like a dick is *stuck in your ass*, and tell me about *irrelevant*! I'm really up to here with you Mister!" She demonstrated with her hand atop her head. "I'm really worried about where this *entire shit* is going! Don't put me in the position to make that choice Michael! God knows why my fucking husband has to be roaming the streets all kinds of hours! Come let me smell that dick!" She pointedly eyed him.

Michael was astonished. "Excuse me? Are you hearing yourself?" He teasingly asked and chuckled. "You've definitely lost your fucking mind talking to me like that! Screw you Natalie! Do whatever the *fuck* you want!" He started to make his way up the stairs, but stopped in his tracks when the TV remote connected with his spine.

He made an about turn and forcefully grabbed her by the shoulders. "*Natalie Celia Carey*, I've never *once* put my hand on you in any forceful way...but *don't push me*! I'm a far cry from the man you *used* to know; hear me when I *tell you*! You want some dick? Dick got you mad? Cause I'll give you dick! But you don't need to *smell shit* if you not *sucking it*!"

He gripped her arm and yanked her towards the couch.

Caught off guard by his response, Natalie was too distracted to defend herself as he ripped her shorts from her body with one firm grip. Before her mind caught up with the present moment, she was butt-naked and pinned to the couch.

"What the hell has gotten into you?" She whispered from beneath him, tears flowing down her cheeks. "You're going to *rape me*? Rape *your pregnant wife*? *Get the hell off me Michael*! Don't make me scream! I swear to God!"

Michael didn't budge. "How can I *rape* my wife? You swore your *life* away to me, forgot? You argued for the dick, so dick you shall have!" He used his hips to force her legs apart.

Natalie was crying now.

"What's with the resistance?" He callously snapped. "I'm not in the mood for games woman, open up! Make this easier for yourself! You're already too tight to be so tense."

He referred to the fact that after fifteen years of intimacy she still couldn't accommodate the entire length of his shaft.

"Is this what you did to her?" The question came out of nowhere. "Is this the way her life ended?"

"What the fuck are you talking about Natalie?" Michael barked without flinching. "Whose life ended?"

"Your little *slut*...Stacy; or did you prefer Caramel?" She had longed to confront her wretched husband on his deceitful activities, but never could have imagined the present circumstances.

Her conscience had been gnawing at her since seeing the headline of Stacy's death on the prime time news. She found it too coincidental that she had been reported missing the same night that he showed up late, confessing his transgressions. It didn't help that *The Club*'s name was all over the story, and she was aware that he had been frequenting the strip joint.

"I don't know what the hell you're talking about." He snarled. *"You don't even know what the hell you're talking about!* Whatever!" He forcefully sank his entire manhood into the depths of his wife.

The scream she had been desperately trying to stifle, succeeding until now, rippled through her body and escaped from her mouth.

"Michael! The babies..." Natalie tried speaking directly to the soul of the man who once loved and adored her.

He eerily chuckled. *"That's* definitely not my problem!"

How the fuck mi life really come to this though God? Benji sat in the darkened living room of his brother's apartment and blasphemously deliberated his premature mid-life crisis. *How the fuck mi lef Biggs yard todeh and nuh blow off him head? When conscience drop in pon mi ting? Set mi definitely set up myself fi turn duppy ya now! Just true mi did always check fi Roxie yuh nuh...she all pregnant ya now to bloodclaat! Cyan trust nuhbody afta dis! Mi nuh affi ask if Biggs a plot the payback as mi siddung ya suh.*

All you Biggs, just mash up wi bloodlcaat friendship ova fuckry! How yuh can have all a di gyal dem inna di world and still fuck my Cindy? All subject her to bare fuckry star...Jah know! A my fault still. Shoulda never show yuh certain vibes 'bout her...chat mi chat too much!

He began to sob. *Mi can't believe mi flip out and kill mi own gyal to rass...fucking ignorant! Wha di fuck she a* *do a breed fi my best friend? How she manage do dat? But she still neva deserve fi dead! I shoulda stopped! I'm so sorry babes. It really went too far...*He wiped his tears.

The battybway now, mi nuh regret that! All a dem kind deh fi dead! All you too yuh nuh Biggs...no exemption to di batty-fucking. If yuh just never fuck up shit and breed mi gyal...shit woulda arite ya now. So much backstabbing and blood shed...cyan even sleep a night time!

Thirty two years on this earth, and wha mi have fi show fi it? Not a fucking ting but grief and sins! Can't afford fi live my life inna paranoia though...not me! Since Biggs money much bigga dan mine, mi shit outta luck now. Mi nah go mek nuh man bloody mi up or torture mi! Nah go out like nuh pussy...not me Benjamin Barkley!

He silenced his thoughts when he heard hurried footsteps lining the corridor in front of the apartment. *As quick as that eeh...* He nervously chuckled. *Well I have a grand surprise for those that hope to surprise me.*

In his paranoia, he had not heard the key being inserted into the lock before the door slowly creaked open.

As the streetlights spilled into the room, temporarily blinding his visual, he fired one round from his Glock 9mm semi-automatic pistol.

Roxanne stood on the balcony of the penthouse suite admiring the New York City skyline. She had been standing in the exact same position since they had checked into the room, going on twenty minutes.

This view is absolutely amazing! She mused inwardly. *So many lights...so much life. I only wish Andre was here to share this moment with me. This would definitely make for romantic. Hmm, we should take a trip out here together! Especially with his birthday coming up...*

Inside the bathroom, Regina sat on the edge of the bathtub and exhaled loudly into the phone.

"Listen, how many times do I have to answer that question? I forgot to turn my cell phone on when we landed! What's the big deal?" She was about ready to hang up on Linton who had called as soon as they had got into the room.

He wasn't accepting her reasons for not receiving his numerous, frantic phone calls; and she was in no mood to explain any further.

"Linton, I'm exhausted. I already apologised. We'll continue this pointless argument later...if ever." She hung up without further consideration.

When did we flip the script though? I must've missed that memo! She quickly brushed her teeth and went back into the bedroom.

"Yuh sure yuh done talk? We have thirteen more days yuh nuh...don't rush on my account." Roxanne, sprawled half naked on the spacious bed, cynically teased.

Regina half smiled, and plopped herself unto the bed beside her. "Don't start with me please! It's all your fault anyway...inviting him over for breakfast. Now he thinks he's back on a throne! Whatever! So what's the first thing on the agenda tomorrow? And I mean besides *eating*!" She mocked her sister's increasing appetite.

"Shop! Duh! What else could be more important *than eating*? Isn't that the *only* other reason to come to New York City?" She playfully rolled her eyes.

"Not really...but I get your drift. I'm so glad we're here though Roxanne; just me and you. It's good to just get away sometimes. I'll admit it's been *kind of* cool bonding with you these past couple of weeks." She consciously poked at her ego.

"*Kind of*? Without me, you'd be a hot mess these past couple of weeks! If it wasn't for Roxanne Mitchell, you wouldn't be all kissy-kissy in the back of a Manhattan restaurant. Don't think for *one minute*, I didn't see that!"

Regina pleaded guilty with a heartfelt, guttural laugh. "How could I, Inspector Gadget?"

Roxanne fell quiet. She had spent the last two days contemplating whether or not she should disclose the disturbing details of Linton's conversation she had overheard on the night of her birthday. Biggs had already warned her of the repercussions of her actions, and the mental tug-of-war had subsequently ensued.

"Regina..." She started to speak but paused.

"Hmm?"

She bit the bullet and continued. "How would you feel if something *really, really* terrible should happen in your life, and you found out that *I* knew about it but I didn't say anything?" That was the best introduction she could find to set the platform for Linton's pending demise.

Regina had already begun to seethe inside, knowing well enough that this could only be about Linton.

"Just say what you're saying Roxanne. You don't have to tell me *how long* you've known."

Roxanne acknowledged where her loyalty lied. "So I *kind of* overheard Linton talking on his cell outside...on my birthday night. I don't know exactly to whom. Let's just say that when he told you in the kitchen that he didn't know anything about that murder, he wasn't lying; *at the time*! But I will say that he *personally* or *physically* had *nothing* to do with it! Take that how you want to."

Regina was fuming. "That *dirty bastard*! I knew it was too good to be true...I *fucking* knew it! I don't care what you say Roxanne..."

"Uhm, what part of *nothing* to do with it did you *not* understand?" Roxanne hastily interjected in his defence. "You're so quick to jump on his back these days, Regina. You clearly need to decide where your loyalty lies, *soon*!"

She left it at that, not wanting to fuel her own anger.

No other man could ever replace her love, care. and respect for Linton; ever.

CHAPTER TWENTY-FOUR

egina and Roxanne had kick-started their first day in
the City as planned. In the early morning, they had
enjoyed full body spa treatments in their suite, including
manicures and pedicures. With a refreshing pep to their
steps, they had worked their fashionable wardrobe for an
early date with William.

By eight o'clock, he had picked up the 'Cover Girls'
from the hotel and had taken them for an exotic breakfast at
the well-known Sara Beth's. They had feasted on the famous
fruit-stuffed crepes - drizzled in vanilla and chocolate sauce;
and omelettes made-to-order with a variety of fillings.

After breakfast they had ventured on a mini tour of
the Boardwalk in downtown Manhattan, and had visited the
famous Madame Tussauds' museum.

By the time they made the journey to Shane's
Brooklyn loft, it was twelve o'clock.

Regina had conducted the necessary introductions,
and had reluctantly bid William farewell for the now.

"So, William huh?" Shane got right to teasing as he
closed the front door. "Who? When? Where? And what's
with that cheesy ass grin?" He made a sarcastic frown, much
to Lisa's and Roxanne's amusement.

"*That* my dear, was Doctor William Smith, my
vaggie specialist." Roxanne couldn't resist. "And now, your
bestie's new *spoogie*!" She arched her newly-trimmed
brows at her seemingly discontented sister.

"Excuse me! *Nobody* asked you anything Roxanne!
Damn you for being so scandalous!" Regina was not about
to be served by the two most sarcastic brutes of the bunch.

"Well who he asked was all tongue-tied, so I figured I'd do the honours!" She curtsied.

Everyone laughed, at Regina's expense.

"Take it easy Gina. We won't pry since you mind." Shane knew better than to push the envelope. "And Roxanne, I see we're bulging." He smiled and glanced at Lisa.

"Hun, at least you've got some *real* company for a few days." He teased both women. "Anyways, I have to make my appointment with the Doc. Regina, you're rolling with me or them?" He looked back and forth between the ladies, grinning at their expressions.

Roxanne and Lisa had already determined their train was headed straight to Fashion district; no stops.

"*Definitely* you!" Regina smirked and shot Roxanne a glance, playfully sneering at her. "Besides, we have some catching up to do." She looked down at Lisa's sparkling engagement diamond and winked at Shane.

Lisa caught on and instantly blushed. She playfully twiddled her fingers to show off her prized possession.

"You like?" She teased, grinning ear to ear as Roxanne quickly snatched her arm.

Regina sighed. "Do I? *Like*, my dear, would be a serious understatement. I'm overly jealous!"

They all laughed.

Shane grew antsy. "Well we should all get going then before the lunch traffic builds up. Babe, make sure you keep your cell close. You know how you get when you hit the mall with company. Roxanne, please behave!" He kissed Lisa on her cheek and headed for the door.

"Roxanne, remember that we're here for two weeks. You don't have to spend *all* your money in one day." Regina, attuned to her sister's newly-discovered spendthrift shopping style, forewarned her.

"That's why they made telephones sis. There is no *need* that can't be *filled*; or *re*-filled rather." There was no subtly in reminding her sister that she had a boyfriend who easily solved such problems.

"Whatever!" Regina replied without looking back and exited behind Shane.

Biggs turned off the main street and ascended the hilly terrain leading to one of his secluded lofts. His cell phone sounded, blasting his hit song that Roxanne had blue-toothed to his phone before she had left.

"Hello." He answered coolly, knowing it was someone from the studio.

"Biggs, its Lorna. Am I disturbing you?"

"No man, I can talk. Whagwan Lorna?" He inwardly hoped she didn't want another personal favour.

"I just wanted to know if you heard about Benji. I mean I know you guys were on the rocks, but you've been friends for so long yuh nuh?"

Biggs grew more alert when he acknowledged the strain in her voice, and soon realised she was crying. He pulled over to the side of the road.

"Heard *what* about Benji? Wha yuh a talk bout Lorna?" His emotions went haywire.

"Benji is dead Biggs. Apparently suicide…his brother saw the whole thing." She began to sob. "Everyone is down here talking about it. I didn't see you around, that's why I called. Now Warrior a cuss seh is a set up, and him plan to get to the bottom of it."

Warrior, another iconic and notoriously feared Dancehall artist in Jamaica, is Benji's eldest brother.

Biggs was instantly overcome with remorse. Though he should've been inclined to feel relief that Benji was one less person hot on his tail, he could only dwell on the fact that his best friend of eighteen years had died.

"Thanks for calling Lorna. I'll swing by the studio as soon as I can."

They disconnected.

He resumed his journey on autopilot, and let himself into the loft. He thoughtlessly acknowledged the maid, who quickly disappeared, shouting lunch orders to the chef.

As he walked down the expansive hallway of the one-tiered bungalow, he dismissed his security guard with a nod and unlocked the bedroom door.

Subconsciously, he took a deep breath.

"Suffice to say Shane..." Dr. LeFranc concluded his observations. "The cancer frequencies have receded. Now, like I've continuously repeated, this is not to say that your cancer is cured. I don't..."

"Diagnose or heal diseases." Shane was too anxious to sit in silence. "Trust me, I remember. But in a short breath, you've healed me? *You've healed my cancer*!" He jumped up and shrieked. "You hear that sis?"

Regina's eyes were already brimming with tears since the moment she had met the doctor, and he had mentioned her very own frequency imbalances. As Shane's emotions overwhelmed her, she cried tears of joy.

"So this means I can stop doing the chemo, right?" Shane anxiously enquired, pacing the room.

"Shane, you know that..."

"Without the B.S Doc! No mumbo jumbo for real!"

Though unruffled by his brutal frankness, Dr. LeFranc voluntarily obliged him. "It would be safe to say so, yes. Of course I should note that I had disagreed with it in the first place." He truthfully reminded his overzealous patient then added.

"But I wouldn't let your mother in on that fact just yet though...should you decide to do so that is."

Regina nodded in consent with his suggestion.

Shane chuckled at the effect his mother had on people of all calibers. "You have my word Doc...scout's honour!" He mockingly saluted.

"Very funny!" The middle-aged man shot back. "Don't force me to manipulate your mother's energetic frustrations and direct them towards you." He grinned.

Shane quizzically eyed him, wondering if what he said was indeed possible. "You wouldn't dare! Would you?" He smirked and remarked.

They all laughed simultaneously.

Lisa and Roxanne had spent a total of five thousand dollars between them, in under two hours. They had taken the Fashion District of Manhattan by storm; without limitations.

Having indulged in the best of maternity wears, perfumes, jewellery, and trendy baby clothing, they were now seeking their most-prized purchases in the trendy and upscale Stuart Weitzman shoe boutique.

Roxanne was overwhelmed that every style she tried on fit like a glove. In a perfect world, she wished to purchase one of each pair, and had already called Biggs to wire more money to Lisa's account so that her pockets would be replenished by the time she left the store.

She enthusiastically identified another five-inched heel, four-hundred dollar pair of 'must have'.

"Lisa! Did you see these? I mean, I'm *definitely* not a pink girl, but *damn*! I'm not leaving without these."

Lisa chuckled, fully enjoying Roxanne's company and her like passion for shoes.

"Those are hot for real. But kind of high, no? You're not going to be able to wear those much longer."

Roxanne quizzically eyed her new shopping pal. "That's what *you* think! Didn't you see Jenny rock them high ass Louboutin's in her last trimester *with twins*? She wasn't half as small as I am, but she sure did work them!" She laughed at Lisa's cynical expression.

"Indeed. But Jen *is* a pro at stilettos sweety. Just try them on…that's all I'm saying."

Roxanne summoned the store attendant with much excitement. Her grin instantly morphed when she noticed the woman scowling at her protruding five and a half month bump, seemingly unwilling to retrieve the size six she requested.

She scrutinised the woman with grave disdain then turned to look at Lisa.

Lisa had noticed the prolonged scrutiny and hadn't appreciated it either. "Yeah, I saw that. But don't pay her any mind! It must be tough working here and even with an employee discount, still can't afford to shop here! Welcome to New York sweetie; the city of attitudes!"

They both laughed heartily, especially when the lady returned with the shoes.

Roxanne snatched the box from her grip and gingerly sat beside Lisa on the plush leather chair. "These *are* the bomb though! You should get one Lisa. They don't feel as high as they look and they're comfortable! Hmm! Hmm!"

She paraded in front of the mirror, pretending to pose for a photo shoot much to the amusement of Lisa and a few of the other shoppers. She got so carried away with the attention that she failed to notice the shoes that were lying displaced on the floor behind her; until she was already tripping over them.

The speed with which the entire situation unfolded prevented anyone from cushioning the impact. She landed in the aisle with a loud thud, after slamming into a shoe rack.

Lisa had initially risen to her feet when she had realised Roxanne's predicament, but she wasn't close or swift enough to prevent the happening.

Some patrons rushed to Roxanne's aid, though she frantically waved them away while fearfully clutching her stomach. She desperately tried to get up on her own, but it was evident that she was in tremendous pain.

She panted heavily and whispered. "Lisa…get help! Mmm!" She groaned. "*Get help! Get help!*" She screamed repeatedly, with the little energy she could muster.

Though everyone in the store froze in their panic, the *feisty* sales attendant dialled 9-1-1.

Natalie stared at her pocket mirror, desperately trying to identify the woman in the reflection. She had come a far way from the driven, patient, and gregarious young lady whose destiny was written in the stars and divinely aligned. She was slowly losing zeal and her strides were out of sync.

Stroking her swollen eye lids, she feigned a smile though tears welled in her eyes again.

She had spent the entire morning locked up in her office after dismissing Tameka with a paid vacation day. Besides feeling like a failure, she contemplated reporting Michael's sexual violation to the police.

Raped by my husband? Who'd actually give a shit? Probably would laugh in my fucking face! When did my life make a turn for the worse? I know…when I waited seven years for Michael to propose then actually said yes. I should've read between the lines before I allowed him to shackle me…even recruiting my own mother against me.

'He's a good man Natalie!'; 'He's going to be a lawyer Natalie!'; 'There's no better than him!'; 'You're lucky that he has his act together and wants to make you his wife!'…Shut the fuck up! That's what I should've said. How lucky was I to take sobriety advice from a crack head?

She leaned back in the chair and allowed her tears to fall. *Marriage…it did more to slow me down than uplift me.*

By far the best way to lose your divine focus and drain your God-given energy is to vow your years to a human being; an ungrateful man at that! Thirty six years old and I'm already going through mid-life crisis. I desperately need to make some changes. I need to live for me now. I don't give a fuck how selfish anybody perceives that! I must do what's best for Natalie Carey.

She got up, retrieved her belongings, and flung the mirror at the wall across the room. *Just go home, pack my shit, and do it like Lot! Just like that.* She smiled, loving the thought of that plan.

Biggs dialled Roxanne's cell for the fourth time as he walked into the building that housed the Reggae Entertainment television studio. He had been trying to call her to no avail, since he had wired the money she had requested. He was now more worried than upset, if anything.

He stopped in the lobby and scrolled through his phonebook to see if he had a number for Regina. *Only the house number...Roxie, call me nuh man! Yuh a freak me out!* His nerves grew hyper as the front desk secretary gleefully acknowledged his presence.

"What's up Dre? You're looking as dapper as ever!" She informally greeted him while lustfully staring and licking her lips.

He chuckled at her efforts, but dryly responded. "Where's Amanda? I don't have all day."

The woman defiantly eyed him and snapped. "Yuh lost your manners? What happen to Good Afternoon Renee, where's Amanda?" Led by her emotions, she folded her arms across her chest in defiance.

Biggs smiled. *Today of all days...okay.* He leaned in closer and cleared his throat. "I'm sorry. Good Afternoon Miss Boring-Pussy, Stop-Call-Off-Mi-Fucking-Phone,

Renee! Where *the fuck* is Amanda?" He was devoid of all patience.

Visibly flustered, she pointed him in his intended direction; not a single word escaped her.

"Thank you. And have yourself a *great* day!" He wittingly remarked, smirking as he stepped away.

Amanda Fox spotted him from a distance and enthusiastically greeted him. "Biggs, it's a pleasure to finally meet you." She was visibly enamoured with his boyish good looks up close.

Biggs' usually rigid public demeanour dissolved when he met the charismatic woman. "The pleasure is all mine Miss Beautiful Fox." He grinned as he slightly lingered on the handshake, turning up the charm.

She blushed at his flattery but fought to maintain the professionalism. "I've prepared a list of the questions beforehand. You may look them over." She smiled and nervously handed him the sheet of paper.

He quickly scanned the questions and handed the sheet back to her. "Cool. Let's do it." He gawked at her voluptuous derriere as she walked away. *Damn white girl, yuh batty fat though! Yuh nah ramp...*

She turned in time to catch the lust in his smile, and fumbled for the words to instruct him on the setup for the interview. Eventually, they settled into their positions and the program director rolled the cameras.

Amanda cheerfully introduced the segment and thanked her weekly audience for tuning in. She introduced her guest artist of the week and proceeded with the interview.

"Andre Jackson, do inform our listeners on the origination of the stage name 'Biggs'." She smiled inwardly, already privy to one particular reason.

Biggs chuckled, wondering which of his many stories would be most appropriate. "Well, as a little yute ma friends nick named mi 'Big Head' still...for reasons unknown to me cause my head was smaller than all of them put together." He paused as she giggled.

"But then, as I got older and became popular amongst the respected men in my community, they named me 'Little Big Man'...a big man young boy yuh nuh. And then to make a long story short, the ladies started spreading *big* news on their own..." He grinned and concluded. "Then it was just 'Biggs'."

Amanda composed herself enough to continue. "Wow! Biggs it is then. So how does it feel to have the number one song in the country for the past twelve weeks?"

He visibly blushed. "I'm just the boss! A joke...well I just feel blessed that people are ready for what I have to offer yuh nuh. I've been 'deejaying' for a while now, but people weren't ready to hear what I had to say...or didn't want to hear it from me. Then thanks to LJ I got my first boom riddim. With that, I just tweaked a few things about my act and worked hard to get my music some air play. So how it feels? It feels like hard work pays off...even though it took a while. Of course I have to thank all my devoted fans for their support as well. Nuff respect to them!"

"Well said." She couldn't stop smiling. "So when will Biggs perform live in Jamaica again? All we've been getting is televised performances of you entertaining the rest of the world. What's with that? Should we take it personal?"

Biggs erupted with laughter. "No man! But you know I have to cater to my fans all over yuh nuh! Big up to Trinidad for their love last week at my show! But yeah, the next big thing I'm scheduled for here is Reggae Sumfest in July. Make sure *you all come out* and support the event too!" He pointed at the camera and jokingly demanded.

"July it is then." Amanda's blood was boiling. "That's all we have for you today Biggs. Thanks again for having your first sit down of the year with RE TV; any final thoughts?"

"Yeah, definitely want to thank the fans again for their undying support. Big up to LJ for being a creative producer. And I want to say rest in peace to my bredrin Benji; gone but never forgotten my brother. Big up Warrior! R.E! Over and out..." He threw up the peace sign and smiled.

The cameras signed off just as his cell phone vibrated on his hip. Thinking it was Roxanne, he quickly answered the call and walked to the corner of the room.

"Babes, where yuh been?" He anxiously asked.

"This is Regina, Andre. I saw that you had been calling but I couldn't pick up before. Roxanne's in the hospital. She had a bad accident today..."

Biggs instantly made a dash for the exit.

Michael pulled into his driveway and instantly flinched at the site of his wife's car. *What the hell is she doing home already? Fuck! So much for going in and coming right back* out...He switched off the ignition and mentally prepared for another of their routine showdowns.

As he stepped foot into the house, he intuitively knew something was out order amidst the dead silence.

Not even the TV's on? Natalie hates silence! What the hell is she up to now? He proceeded without announcing his presence, thinking it would be better to catch her red-handed.

After inspecting the entire downstairs area, he tip-toed up the stairs and checked their bathroom first.

*Hmmm...*He mused, as he made his way to the study but stopped dead in his tracks.

"Natalie! Natalie, what are you doing?" Michael screamed, rushing to her side. "Natalie!"

Her naked body splayed lifelessly in the hallway.

In the next few moments that mimicked a disastrous tornado, Michael scooped her limp frame into his arms; grabbed her robe from the bathroom door; placed her on the back seat of his car; and sped off down the driveway.

Fifteen minutes later, he sped up to the emergency area of the Nuttall Hospital.

There were three nurses stationed to meet him with the stretcher and oxygen tanks in tote, as they had promised when he had called ahead.

"How long has she been out?" One of them asked as they moved hastily to connect Natalie to the temporary IV and secure her oxygen mask.

"*Mr. Simmons*!" The head nursed shouted, jolting him out of his stupor as he fixated on their busy hands.

"I'm not sure...I mean I wouldn't know. I got home and found her like this about ten-fifteen minutes ago." He watched the action in dismay.

They rushed into the emergency room, relaying instructions back and forth in jargons only they could understand.

Michael followed closely behind the entourage for as long as he was allowed then retreated to the waiting area.

Roughly thirty minutes had passed, when the doctor returned with an update.

"Hello Mister Simmons, I'm Doctor Walter Jackson." The stoic man curtly introduced himself and proceeded. "Natalie's unconsciousness was onset by her diabetes; possibly a dizzy spell as her insulin levels are extremely low." He paused when he acknowledged the man's quizzical expression. "You didn't know your wife has diabetes?"

Michael shook his head in negation and averted the doctor's chastising stare.

"Okay then. The diabetes was originally onset by her over-active gestational activities during pregnancy. This condition could worsen as the pregnancy progresses resulting in more incidents such as this especially since Natalie is carrying twins. I've estimated that she's been unconscious for roughly thirty minutes which substantially reduced her heart rate and breathing, and consequently that of the babies. As of now, we haven't ascertained the extent, if any, of such damages. We may be at that point Mr. Simmons, where you may have to choose between your wife and your babies."

The doctor allowed that thought to resonate before he added. "I should also make mention that her cervix shows signs of *forced entry*. The scar tissue present indicates that the bruises are a day or two old. We'll have to wait until Natalie is conscious to deduce any further information. In the meantime, the nurse will inform you when it's okay to visit." Dr. Jackson nodded and quickly disappearing behind the closed doors.

Michael buried his face and cried.

Linton relaxed in the living room couch, watching the sports highlights he had recorded with TIVO while browsing the Internet on his laptop. He had spent most of the day obsessing over the fact that Regina had not called him since their spat.

You're not taking my phone calls and you're not calling me! When we do speak it's all about attitudes and proving...getting disrespectful on some new levels. Something's just not right with you Miss Mitchell. There's another version to this story that I'm missing.

With that, he logged into her email account using the information stored by the KeyStrokes software he had discreetly installed on all the computers in the house.

He filtered her messages to display by order of sender, instantly acknowledging a familiar name. *William Smith?* He pondered. *That should be Roxanne's doctor! What the hell does he have to say so often?* He opened the latest of six emails, dated the day before.

Regina,
I'm anxiously looking forward to spending these
two weeks with you. I'm so glad you encouraged
me to take the time off. I can't wait to continue
my exploration of your tightly shielded soul. I am
not HIM!   I WILL make you my everything
darling, and I'll prove that with actions...

Voyaging to your heart,
William

Linton's jaws dropped. Rage instantly welled within him, amidst disbelief. He switched to the outbox and opened her reply to the message. This he read aloud.

"I know you're not HIM sweetheart, but everything takes time. I anxiously look forward to our vacay in the Big Apple as well. Kisses..." He continuously repeated the words to himself, allowing the anger to consume him.

Before he processed another thought, he sailed his laptop across the room and sprang off the couch.

"Everything takes time huh?" He barked aloud. *"Everything takes time! What the fuck is that supposed to mean Regina? You deceitful bitch! When were you going to notify me of this time? And who the fuck is HIM? Is that all I am to you now...HIM?"*

He barked his frustrations aloud, erratically smashing household items in the process; his plasma television excluded.

As he headed to the upstairs bedroom, he noticed an envelope sitting in the exact spot he had retrieved the TV remote earlier. He stretched over the banister and grabbed it.

It was clearly addressed to him, and formally signed Regina A. Mitchell.

Biggs hastily moved through the crowded terminal of the Norman Manley International Airport. One of his previous 'flings' who worked with the airlines had used her rank to boot a first class passenger to the economy section, and had gotten him unto the five o'clock flight to New York.

After all that, he was still late in arriving at the airport as always. This had left him little time to find a parking space, check in, clear his carryon luggage with security, and make it to the departure gate even though he was escorted through most of the process.

He reclined in his spacious first class seat and finally released the breath he had been holding since Regina had called. *I'm coming Roxie. Just hold tight babes. Life can surely throw yuh some curve balls eeh...first Benji tek him life, now Roxie and the baby. I really hope bad things nuh come inna threes fi real. Father God, please mi a beg yuh! Not when mi a start a clean slate. Not ma Roxie and little Adrian!*

He looked off into the clouds as the plane levelled at its cruising altitude. Whispering a silent prayer, he fought back the tears that had already brimmed his eyelids.

After two hours of lounging around the waiting area, Michael was escorted by a nurse to visit Natalie. He hastily kept up with her hurried pace, anxious to see what had happened behind closed doors.

"She's still asleep, so you'll have to be quiet." The nurse quietly informed him before leaving the room.

Walking over to Natalie's bedside, remorse instantly overcame him. He stared in disbelief at his wife's pallid face, semi-covered by the oxygen mask. Gently caressing her four-month bulge, he easily tuned out the world except for the intermittent beeping of the heart monitor.

Your worlds are so sheltered…yet so vulnerable; still nothing like it is here on the outside. He allowed himself to cry. *I wasn't a good man to your mother, and I must accept that fact. I was selfish, and most times unsupportive. You guys probably wouldn't have liked me anyway…*

"I became a monster." He began to whisper. "Got too caught up to remember what was real anymore. And now, because of me, everything is at stake; my career, my marriage, your mother's health, and now your health." Michael was sobbing now. "I really hope your mother awakes in time to make this decision on her own. If we never see each other again, I want you to know that I'm so so sorry about everything…all the pain…all the jeopardy!"

He looked up at the love of his life and pierced the silence. "I'm so sorry Natalie! I love you so much! God knows you deserve better than me!" He sobbed. "You always deserved better than me! I know I will pay for all that I've done to you. God always protects His angels." He anxiously caressed her hand that housed the IV, and thought he felt a slight twitch.

He moved in closer to her ear and spoke softly. "Natalie, can you hear me? If you can, move your arm again…please." He remained still and waited; there was nothing.

"If you can hear me Natalie, I want you to know that whatever you decide from hereon, you'll forever be the love of my life! I don't deserve you so I'm leaving baby…for good. Your mom is already on her way here. You'll be in good hands." He lovingly kissed her on the cheek, his tears trickling unto her face.

"If this is really it for us, just know that I love you with all my heart. Take good care of yourself Natalie Carey. I will forever miss you." He stood to walk out of her life forever, but stopped when she faintly squeezed his hand.

CHAPTER TWENTY-FIVE

In the blink of an eye, two months had passed branding August as the month of life-altering decisions.

Regina drove her car onto the deck of the Old Harbour shipping wharf and scanned the interior once more for any personal items. Though her new boss had included an automobile compensation package, she had stubbornly decided to keep her Camry for 'sentimental reasons'.

She planted a kiss on the steering wheel before getting out and handing the key to the Shipping Clerk.

Roxanne strolled towards her sister and laughed. "Regina, yuh have to be kidding me! Two weeks! Are you seriously crying? At least you get to drive around in luxury for the meantime." She dangled the keys to Screwface's BMW M3 that Biggs had volunteered for her remaining two weeks in Jamaica. "And my dear, did I add that your ish is a *drop top*?"

Regina grinned and anxiously snatched the keys. "Crying? What's that? Don't be silly…" She playfully rolled her eyes and walked briskly to 'her' luxury convertible.

"Babes, are you guys going straight to the house?" Biggs called out to Roxanne as she checked out the car's impressive features with her sister.

"We're going to the embassy first to pick up the passports, and then the house." She shouted above the wind. "I can call you when we're on the way there if you want to go ahead." She knew he had other business to attend to.

Biggs waited for the wind to subside and coolly replied. "Alright babes. Put on your seatbelt and tell your sis to drive safely. That's a powerful machine."

"We will Andre. I love you!" She cautiously climbed into the low-suspended car and forcefully slammed the door before opening the window.

He smiled. "I love you too Roxie. Call me after."

It had become a habit for the two to express their love for each other at every opportunity, ever since Roxanne's incident in New York. That had also caused him to be more protective of her than ever before, sometimes even to her own annoyance.

Regina busied herself with adjusting the seat and mirrors, prepping their driving music, and dropping the top off the car. Even if she wanted to, she couldn't stop cheesing at her sister while driving the distance towards the exit.

Biggs followed closely behind the duo on the premises, but turned in the opposite direction at the main street. He mumbled a short prayer, another of his new habits.

Bad luck had unfortunately come in threes for him this year. While he was away in New York attending to Roxanne, his beloved mother Beverly had died in a car accident on the busy Spanish Town Road.

Of the five passengers in the vehicle that day, none had sustained injuries. Unfortunately, Beverly was crushed when their vehicle had overturned unto the sidewalk.

Natalie outstretched in her queen-sized bed, watching the blades of the ceiling fan dutifully do their rounds. She clung tightly to the gold card that cordially invited her to the place she had spent the last three months trying to bury. She acknowledged, even before opening the envelope that it was silly to believe moving back to Brooklyn was the solution to dismissing her past.

I've turned my back on so many people...so many things. Ugh! How could I go back at this point? For a fact

I'm not ready to face the emotions…the embarrassment. She deliberated with herself. *But then…what's so new? I haven't been through anything that women before me haven't, or women behind me won't!* She took a deep breath.

Shit does hurt like hell though! In the blink of an eye, my life as I knew it for fifteen years deceitfully restructured without my consent. Everything I worked for…all the sacrifices I made to build something concrete! Hmm, at least Hope and Cope is doing a swell job without me. Always knew I had a leader in Tameka. Such a driven young woman…

One thing's for sure, I definitely don't want to see him again! Him, I could die without ever seeing again! Lord knows I'm not ready to forgive! But could I do this for Shane? For Tina even? She sighed and returned her gaze to the ceiling.

Waited so long to open the goddamn envelope, I don't even have time to think about it… She glanced at the clock on the night stand and wiped the tears from her cheeks. *Well, the jury's still out of the court on this one.* She walked over to her closet to do stocktaking.

"Natalie!" The husky voice almost startled her. "I'm going to need a towel babe."

Shit! Thomas…almost forgot you were in there. A towel…hmm…yes, here. "I'm coming dear."

Shane had commenced his early morning workout with the usual, forty-minute warm up laps. He deeply inhaled the crisp August air, fully appreciating how his life had made a turn for the better.

Life is definitely on my side again, thank God. I'm healthy, training, baby on the way…Hmm, couldn't ask to be any happier right now.

He had decided on his own to stop the chemotherapy treatments after Dr. LeFranc had 'cured' him.

Surprisingly to everyone when his mother had found out, she had agreed without commentary.

Where business was concerned, he was still unofficially banned from competition for the remainder of the season. Most important to him however, is that Coach Sullivan allowed him to train with his teammates. They were busy preparing to create havoc at the 2008 Beijing Olympics.

Shane completed his final lap and ran off the field, headed for the weights room. He spotted Kendra in the distance and willed her to turn in the opposite direction soon enough.

"Shane!" She called out to him, waving frantically. "Where've you been? I heard that you were back, but I *never* see you. Yuh couldn't give me a call or something? Lawks..." She subtly snarled.

He smiled and pretended to be out of breath to stall time. "My bad Kay. I've been so caught up...trying to get back out there yuh nuh? But I *did* ask the guys for you though, 'cause you're never here when I'm around either."

"Yeah, well chatty mouth Nicholas had mentioned something of the sort. But my phone still works..." She read his eyes and moved forward with the topic. "He also said something about you doing some big things this year. Are you back for competition?"

Shane almost choked on his breath. "Ahm, not for competition but I'm allowed to train with you guys for the rest of the season." He noticed that revelation was not about to hold its own. "Maybe he was talking about my cancer recession?" He offered a half smile.

Kendra shrieked and used the opportunity to hop into his arms. "Are you for real Shane? How? I mean when? I'm so glad for you! Not that I doubted it..." She hugged him tightly as if she had been yearning to do so for many lifetimes.

Before he could reply, an overpowering, familiar voice came from behind them.

"What the hell is this frolicking?" Nicholas grinned from ear to ear. "I've been here all this time with my ball sack drying out, and pretty boy comes back for one day and gets the action? Fuck you Kendra! And besides..." He acknowledged Shane's chastising stare and zipped it.

Kendra, attuned to the awkwardness, slowly slid from Shane's embrace and scowled.

"Besides what, big mouth? Finish the sentence!" She repeatedly looked back and forth between the two.

Shane hastily interjected. "Besides, weight training has officially begun. We're late people...chop, chop! He hurriedly strolled away with Nicholas in tow laughing uncontrollably.

He playfully punched him on the arm as they got into the gym. "She doesn't know, Shane?"

"Why yuh have to be an ass *all the time* Nick? Seriously...sometimes you need to shut the fuck up!"

"*No*! Sometimes *you* need to open the fuck up and free up these ladies so I can get some *puss-seh*! All these chics strolling around here, saving their virginity for lover boy Shane, and lover boy's busy putting a clamp on his future! If you get what I'm saying..."

"Watch it! Aint no damn *clamp* on anything! Don't be fooled huh! You'll *always* call me daddy!" They both laughed heartily at that mutually accepted fact.

"What the hell's so funny you two?" Sean caught wind of their antics and strolled over to get in on the action. "Who fucked who this time?"

They all broke out laughing.

Shane smirked at his usually inquisitive friend. "Why does *everything* have to be about sex with you? Can't two friends just share a regular joke?"

"Shane, aint *shit* regular about you and 'Dumb Dumb' over here! Now that that chemo's done melting your dick, don't tell me you don't have a juicy fuck story to share." He pointedly eyed his usually adventurous best friend.

"First of all, I'll have you know that my dick has been in perfect order *during* and *after* my chemo; thank you very much! And for the last time, we were *not* talking about sex! What's with you? Your girl's got it on lock again? Need me to *talk* to her?" He winked at him.

Nicholas was dying with laughter.

Sean was not amused or convinced. "Whatever Shane; keep playing. You know Nicholas will spill his beans before the day darkens. Another thing; how come Kendra's not up to date on your happenings? She was asking me all sorts of questions outside...like I was on trial or I'm Nicholas. What the fuck?" He quizzically glanced at Shane, who in turn looked to Nicholas.

The two laughed boisterously, continuing in their previous private amusement.

Sean sucked his teeth and threw his sweaty towel in Nicholas' face. "Dumb asses!"

He left the two suspicious hyenas to enjoy their secret conversation, and walked over to Coach Sullivan for the workout program.

Linton sat in the parking lot of the Cayman Embassy, staring at the newly issued visa in his passport. *I can't believe I actually did this! Some foreign force must be compelling me to act a damn fool! After all the unnecessary shit that Regina put me through...messing with my sanity so she could fuck around guilt free! Can't believe she let another man fuck my pussy! Don't even know when she got so damn bold! Three months I've been single to do whatever the fuck I want, but still I can't fuck no other! Un-fucking-real!*

He stashed the documents in his glove compartment and prepared to make his way back to work. *That's just to keep my options open anyhow…nobody says I have to use it! Some fucking year this has turned out to be…Damn it!*

He sped towards the main gate, only stopping at the intersection to await an opening in the busy flow of traffic. As he checked his left, his eyes landed on the fiercest looking automobile that expertly hugged the curve as it entered the Embassy parking lot.

Now that is fucking breathtaking! Being a die-hard car fanatic, he immediately recognised the 2009 BMW M3 convertible he had recently drooled over in the July issue of *AutoMags* magazine.

Which lucky mothafucka already has the M3 fully customised, paint job and all? Somebody with a bag of money for damn sure! He admired the car, as did other passer-bys as it seemingly glided right by.

What the fuck? The thought screamed in his head. *I'll be damned if that's not Regina and Roxanne Mitchell.* Without further thought, he did the unimaginable.

Biggs sped his truck out of the Devon Court townhouse complex, and made a sharp right unto Waterloo Road. He repeatedly checked his reflection in the rear view mirror, looking for any indications of infidelity.

How the fuck mi feel so nervous? A wha do mi? He mused to himself and took a deep breath. *Roxie really have mi in a frenzy these days to rass! But the damn white gyal was so persistent! Woman a real crassis yuh nuh…can get man fi do anything!* He chuckled aloud.

Nah go lie, dem uptown gyal yah freaky nuh bloodclaat! Jah know! Bway babes, mi really sorry…and mi really a try fi easy; but the temptation is oh so overwhelming! He turned unto the main street leading to Roxanne's house.

Somehow finding the free time in his jam-packed schedule for infidelity, he had only made dash from Amanda's condo when Roxanne had threatened to turn his special 'Twenty-ninth' upside down.

He made the forty-five minute drive in less than twenty minutes, coming to a screeching halt at the top of the driveway.

Two hours after telling his woman he was on his way, he readied for the interrogation.

Roxanne yanked the front door open before he touched the buzzer. "What was taking yuh so long?" She carefully scrutinised him from head to toe.

"Babes, yuh forget seh mi a keep session tonight?" He replied with a straight face. "Wha yuh mean what took me so long? Stuff!" He stepped past her and playfully pinched her on the nipple. "Yuh sis done pack yet? Yuh talk to her bout the stuff we discussed?"

Biggs stopped in his tracks when he got to the living room and realised she had not followed him into the house. In his heart he already felt busted, but wasn't about to reveal that. He turned and saw her lingering by the doorway.

"What?" He asked, mustering a chuckle.

"What *what*?" Roxanne replied dryly. "You tell me what's so funny!"

"The way yuh staring at me babes. Wha mi do now?"

"It's more like what you *were* doing *then*! Why is your pants on the wrong side Andre? And tell mi that's how it mek."

He didn't even bother to look down. "Babes..." He started but couldn't finish.

Roxanne made her up the stairs, completely ignoring his apology. Though she had begun to conceive that her man may sleep around because she wasn't able to please him sexually, she was more aggravated that he had found the time to do so amidst all the other things he had planned.

Hushed communication could be heard at the top of the stairs then Regina came into view.

Biggs anxiously rose to his feet, smiling. "Hey Regina! All's well?" He wondered what Roxanne had already revealed upstairs.

"Hey Andre!" Regina grinned. "Everything is going well so far. Thanks a lot for the car, man! I really love it!" She gave him a high-five. "So Roxanne said you wanted to talk to me about something?" She plopped down on the couch beside him and offered her undivided attention.

Thanks for the heads up Roxie! He mused inwardly and audibly cleared his throat. "Yes. I just wanted to see how you felt about Roxanne staying behind until after the baby."

Regina sighed. "First, thanks for even caring how I feel. But to be honest with you, I saw this coming. I didn't expect Roxanne to just up and move with me and leave you here. Things have changed, and my lil' sis has her own family now."

"Thanks for understanding Regina. I promise you it was never my intention to tear your baby away from you."

They shared a laugh before he continued.

"Seriously though, your approval means so much to Roxanne's happiness; and of course my peace of mind. I'm just glad we can all get along at this stage. Besides, there's something else I wanted to ask you." He removed a black, suede ring box from his side pocket.

Regina shrieked loudly and snatched the box from his grip. "Oh my God!" She gawked at the penny-sized diamond that pretty much sheltered what hid beneath it.

She quickly returned the box to Biggs as she heard Roxanne's footsteps thudding across the ceiling.

"Of course!" She whispered to him. "But no more *messing around*! I'm serious!" She gave him 'the eye'.

He replied by drawing a cross on his chest over his heart, silently embarrassed that she was onto his antics.

"Oh my God what?" Roxanne called out while trying to get to the bottom of the stairs. "Hello!" Patience was not one of her prominent virtues.

Biggs got down on one knee as she appeared on the last stair. "Roxanne Alana Mitchell, A. K. A. 'Babes', A. K. A 'Roxie', 'Misery', 'Adrian's Mother', 'Greedy', and 'Sleepy'..." He paused, allowing the two to scream and laugh at his intended senselessness. "Babes, I need you to be my Mrs. Jackson. Allow me..." He confidently slipped the band onto her finger. "Perfect fit for a perfect woman. What yuh seh?"

"Well done!" The sisters responded in unison, tightly clinging to each other and laughing.

CHAPTER TWENTY SIX

Earth's globe seemingly spun at light speed on Saturday, August thirtieth two thousand and eight. The bright and sunny morning had quickly warped into early afternoon, tempering the parching heat with clear clouds and winds.

Without warning, Nicholas and Sean barged into Shane's dressing room, chatting at the top of their voices. Despite noticing that he was undressed, they got comfortable regardless, fully immersed in their conversation.

"And what the fuck is *he* doing in boxers and socks gazing through the window?" Nick eventually blurted, looking in Shane's direction.

"Don't tell me..." Sean chimed in, looking over at his best friend who continued to ignore their presence.

Nicholas scowled at Sean then turned back to Shane. "Don't tell you what?" He suddenly understood the implication. "Ohhhhh! You mean *that* don't tell you! Oh dear..." He removed his bow tie, loosened the top button of his shirt, and sat on the bed beside Sean.

There was a prolonged and unusual period of silence among the three, until Nicholas elected himself the official spokesperson of the moment.

"Shane man, I won't even say I know what you're going through right now. Fuck it! I most *definitely* don't! But you know, I can say honestly that I've never seen you happier than that day you broke your intentions to us. Well, *us* being everyone except Kendra." He paused to allow the snickers that escaped from his two best friends, then continued.

"I definitely won't lie that I was pissed as hell too! You know, with you being my official pussy magnet and all. But you know what made me feel better after thinking about the whole thing?"

Sean chuckled in anticipation of the punch line.

Shane looked over at the two for the first time since they had entered the room.

"I felt better when I realised that no matter what that pretty motherfucker decides, as long as he's Shane Wright and physically around, there will *always* be chicks...and pussy...*for me*! Bam!"

They all busted out laughing.

"No, seriously." Nick continued. "And as a consolation to you my friend..." He looked directly at Shane. "I'll remind you that looking is not cheating! Scouts honour!" He saluted him. "Jokes aside though, Lisa's a great girl Shane...I was actually surprised. You know how good *you are* at choosing them!" He couldn't help but join in on the laughter he was inducing. "Anyways, that's my piece... hope it helps."

Shane couldn't stop laughing. Standing by the floor-length window, he had spent hours channelling the serenity from the expansive view of Strawberry Hill. But in all honesty, peace of mind came just now from the company of his boys.

"I don't know what happened to me all of a sudden." He spoke for the first time since they had entered. "I was so pumped all morning...couldn't be more excited. But then I checked into the room, got up here, and I'm the only one here. Can't find my brothers anywhere...or you bums for that matter. Then I started to wonder all sorts of crazy shit."

"Do I have to give up time with my friends? Change everything in my life as I know it? Give up my freedom? Then I just lost it..." He turned to face his best friends and smirked. "I completely lost it, man."

"But you said one right thing Nick, for the *first* in your useless life. I'll *always* be Shane Wright and that won't ever change! Ever!"

"Who the fuck else you thought you'd be? John the Baptist?" Sean couldn't forsake the slot to inject his piece.

They all collapsed unto the bed laughing hysterically.

One by one the men repeatedly took turns congratulating Sean for a joke well-timed, a fact they rarely admitted.

Of course, it didn't take long for the attention to get to his head. "Guys please...Shane, you need to get dressed! Stop acting like it's the first I've ever made a joke." He teasingly looked back and forth between the two.

The usual suspects glanced at each other, failed miserably at stifling their grins, and unanimously professed.

"No, but it's the first *funny* one!"

They resumed their infectious cackling despite Sean's cynical frown.

Most importantly, the groom hastily got dressed and mentally re-vamped.

There was never any doubt that an event celebrating the nuptials of Jamaica's most popular and glorified athlete would be bombarded by uninvited individuals - professionals and fanatics alike.

Despite Shane shelling out millions to conceal the prominent details of his special day, the outside sources proved to be well-informed and more resourceful.

Curious onlookers enthusiastically hoarded the streets leading to the entrance of the venue, evidently unworried about disturbing the peace. The few individuals who had used their professional credentials to bully their way beyond the initial security checkpoint, lingered in the grand parking area in front of the main entrance.

At two o'clock, the honoured guests began filing into the main garden after successfully navigating the tightest security point. They were all suited in their ivory colours as requested, lending the atmosphere an angelic glow.

Tina played the usual host and welcomed as many people as she could by name. One hour and eighty five guests later, she solemnly relinquished her post but not before strictly cautioning the usher. She confidently strutted into the well-manicured garden, smiling and briefly acknowledging extended family members and acquaintances. Eventually making it to her row, she sat between Regina and Simeon.

"How are you feeling?" She leaned in closer and asked Regina as the organist melodiously signalled the arrival of the groom and his party.

"Honestly…" Regina smiled and gently grasped her hand. "I'm okay. It's not as bad as I had always imagined."

Tina gave her the sarcastic scowl.

"Tina, I'm serious. Really, I'm okay."

"I'm only teasing Regina." She smiled and patted the hand that lovingly covered hers. "But you already know my greatest desire. You see my handsome boys over there?"

She switched the topic to admire the interaction among her three young men. Tears welled in her eyes as she bashfully returned their airborne kisses.

In the midst of engaging in her 'mom's proudest' moment, an usher approached on the sidelines requesting her presence in the back.

"As in right now?" Tina asked with a dreaded look. "Is this *really* urgent?" She looked over at Regina as the nervous young man affirmed with a nod.

Though unwilling, she rose and rested her belongings in Regina's lap. As she made her way to the back of the garden, adrenalin quickened her steps as the face in the distance came into closer view.

"Natalie!" She called out in somewhat of a hushed tone. "Natalie, it's you!" She ran the remaining distance and eagerly embraced her friend as the tears she'd been fighting back spilled down her cheeks.

"I thought for a minute…it doesn't even matter! I'm so glad you made it!" They held each other tightly.

Natalie tears also flowed freely. "Oh Tina…I couldn't miss this for the world. I'm so glad to be here!" She clung tightly to the woman who had spent every waking moment emailing words of encouragement during her meltdown.

"This place is gorgeous Tina! I know this is *all* you!"

Tina loosened her grip and grinned. "*Damn right*! I'm joking. Natalie, you look *amazing*! You've cut your hair…*all of it*! And forgive my insolence, but who's this handsome *hunk* of yours?" She composed her emotions to be introduced to the man who had been quietly allowing them their moment.

Natalie blushed, smiling from within. "This *hunk* is Thomas Delmar. Thomas, this is my very close friend Tina Sinclair…"

Thomas chuckled, visibly flustered by the pleasantries. "It's a pleasure to finally meet you Madame. I've heard great things in abundance. "

Tina melted at the sound of his colloquial British accent. She teasingly smiled at Natalie and winked. "Hun, we *must* catch up!"

"Indeed." Natalie laughed, revelling in the moment.

Shane stood confidently in his place at the altar, sharing a few laughs with his favourite boys. He looked strikingly handsome in a black, well-tailored, three-piece Armani suit; his shoes also by the same designer. His only accessory, the turquoise triangle peeking from his jacket pocket, was just the cherry on top to complement his incredible features.

The six groomsmen, similarly suited except for their ivory-coloured shirts, further added to the levels of sex appeal steaming up the environment.

Headlining the pack were Shane's brothers Sheldon and Steven, who found it entertaining to flirt with the 'thirsty' females - as per Sheldon - ogling from the pew.

Sean and Nicholas, with their athletic bods stuffed neatly into their tuxedos, were busy making small talk with the older 'honeys' allowing no time to be wasted.

The final two, Lisa's cousins, were gorgeous in their individual ways. It seemed they either travelled with their own fan base, or made acquaintances quickly.

Amidst all the chatter and frolicking, the organist sounded the bride's arrival.

Everyone immediately stood and faced the rear, anxious to see what 'the star' of the moment had in store.

Shane grinned as his woman came into view.

Alessandro and Linda Artuso stood confidently by their daughter's side, exuding great joy and pride as they readied to escort her.

Lisa was nothing but stunning in a four-tiered, customized Roberto Cavalli gown, accentuated with shimmering pearls and stints of turquoise about the hem of each layer. Beyond its sample beauty, it effortlessly disguised her seven-month paunch with utmost grace and flawlessness.

Accessorised in the finest cut diamonds, complements of her mom, the bride's modest up-do created an elegant finish.

The bridal party refined the classical fairytale imagery. Preceding Lisa, the four year old flower girl resembled a porcelain keepsake, curtsying and waving queen-like to her mesmerised admirers. Her handsomely dressed ring-bearer, only three years old, orderly followed suit but took the humble route to get to his place.

The seven bridesmaids were timeless beauties in their one-shoulder, toga-style, body-hugging numbers; primarily ivory, the cinched waists boasted hues of turquoise and pearl-shaped diamond gems. Their neat up-dos, pearl earrings, and incredible stilettos perfectly enhanced their statuesque frames.

As Lisa glided to the organist's rendition of NSync's *This I Promise You*, she acknowledged familiar faces with a proud but bashful grin and a subtle wave.

The guests audibly marvelled at her ornately designed, ivory-coloured masterpiece, especially at its twenty-foot train.

When the parties eventually settled into their places, the pastor instructed everyone to bow their heads in prayer.

That's when drama ensued from all angles.

Regina had been laughing continuously while enjoying the entrance spectacle. But somewhere between sharing that silent conversation with Shane as he waited for his bride; and acknowledging the light in Lisa's eyes as she eagerly made haste to be by his side; she began to cry.

She turned to retrieve another sheet of Kleenex from her purse, and gasped - almost too loud. She spun right back around, seething on the inside.

"Regina, we need to talk." Linton spoke closely by her ear. "Regina, I know it's been difficult, but I want to work this out." He adamantly pursued the conversation though she shrugged him away. "I'm willing to forgive you so we can move past this!"

A chuckle involuntarily escaped her mouth. Unfortunately, it was loud enough to interrupt the pastor's proceedings. She quickly looked down at her feet as Reverend Chung eased his reading glasses unto his nose, looked up from his Bible, and glanced over at their section.

"*Listen!*" She quietly snapped as soon as the coast was clear. "I'm kinda *busy* right now! You realise why we were all, *except you* invited here? I'm at my best friend's *wedding!*" Her tone was sharp enough to slice ice. *And damn you for wearing that cologne that turns me on!* She admitted inwardly.

Michael repeatedly checked his tail to get a visual on the two men who had boldly followed him into the private venue.

He pulled his chair as close as he could get to his target, in almost three months.

"You look good." He whispered in her ear, skipping the usual conversation openers.

He himself had not only made it pass security, but had somehow forced his way into the seat directly behind Natalie.

"I see." He chuckled when she moved closer towards her gentleman. "*That's* the reason you haven't called me back? The reason you don't reply to my emails? Because some white boy lousily tickles your fancy? Please!" He piercingly eyed Thomas as he turned and their eyes made four.

"You and me...we had a good thing Natalie." He continued, not feeling threatened. "Fifteen years...and just like that? There was a point when I was ready to be a better husband to you. I was ready to do things the right way. And don't kid yourself for a minute that you didn't want to make it right with me!" He stopped himself when he noticed that she was laughing, evident by the movement of her shoulders.

"You think this is *funny?*" The words escaped his mouth at a disruptive pitch. He played nonchalant as Reverend Chung looked towards their penny section, this time evidently a bit more irritated.

Other guests glanced in their as well, with nothing but perturbed and repulsed expressions.

Michael leaned back in his seat, deciding to ease up for the moment.

Shane cringed as the Reverend opened the floor to the moment he silently wished could've been skipped altogether.

"If there is anyone who believes that Shane Wright and Lisa Artuso should not join forces under God, please speak now or forever hold your peace." Reverend Chung closed his Bible and removed his glasses.

There was an awkward moment where the 'people in the know' reflexively turned towards Amanda Fox.

In what seemed like a prolonged moment, Shane skimmed the masses and wondered who, outside of the obvious, could object. *Amanda! How the fu...church! Sorry God. Rich girls and their powerful daddies! I dare your spiteful and deceitful self to say something! Oh today would just be your lucky day for a one on one with Shane Wright. Somewhere in your warped mind, you know better!*

Simone, ma likkle ghetto princess...you wanted to be a part of my big day, so you're here! And rocking the hell outta dat BCBG dress! You care for me too much to ruin this for me! Kendra, my forever crush...we were not aligned in the stars as you'd perfectly imagined it. You're here because my cover was blown. He briefly glanced at

Nicholas in light of that fact, and gave him a nod when he acknowledged him.

His eyes then averted to the section seating his family members and closest friends. *Regina, my forever sweetheart...God knows it was you...it was always you. The world and everyone in it knows that. Twenty two years of friendship...ride or die. Your objection I could live with.* His inner smile immediately diminished.

Linton! Michael! What the hell are they doing here? How much does one have to pay security for a job well done? Ridiculous! You two better sit still and not embarrass me in front of the Artusos!

He returned his gaze to his groomsmen, and smiled at their contorted expressions. *Wish one of you jerks would step to the plate! Throw a fellow brother a life vest? No? Just leave me hanging like that huh? Cool...*He silently grunted as the pastor continued the proceedings.

It was time to seal the deal with a kiss.

The newlyweds jumped the broom and proudly sauntered down the aisle as Mr. and Mrs. Wright.

Shane had pleasantly acknowledged his friends, Simone and Kendra among them, on his way out. On the contrary, he had rolled his eyes at Amanda as he acknowledged her rebellious stance when he strolled by.

As the guests cheered on with laughter, applauses, and a few chorused whistles, Tina jumped up and pulled Simeon along to join the Artuso clan behind the wedding party.

Natalie intended to follow in Tina's hurried footsteps, but Michael firmly gripped her by the elbow and promised he would cause a scene. She reluctantly asked Thomas to go ahead without her, assuring him that she would be fine.

Regina's attempt at exodus proved to be more successful. She hurriedly made her way to the back of the garden, with Linton desperately chasing behind.

Roxanne tried to keep up with her sister, but she could barely manage her weight through the tight crowd.

Biggs dutifully kept pace behind his woman, but spotted Amanda in the distance oozing lust in his direction. He instantly tensed and tried to walk wide of where she stood, praying that she would not acknowledge him in public.

As soon as Roxanne's feet made it past her, leaving Biggs one step behind, Amanda zoomed in.

"You dropped this at my place." She teased with a sly grin, dangling his wallet high in midair. "It's yours if you promise to fuck me like that again!" She returned the shrewd stare of a few guests who had overheard her vulgarity. "What can I say? Best dick since Shane."

Biggs nervously chuckled. "Stop playing." He tried to grab the wallet but failed. "Listen! We can't do this *here*, or *now*!" He snarled, snatching it from her loosened grip.

Shoving 'the demon' out of his way, he walked out with a group of people and caught up with Roxanne by the exit to the parking area.

"Babes, what happened with your sis?" He asked, trying to seem cool as he neared her.

Roxanne miserably snapped. "What happened with *that* bitch? What the fu...what was that about Andre? Sleeping with the enemy now?"

"*What*? Babes, Amanda works for RE TV. I did an interview there today and I must've dropped my wallet at the studio. What?" He scowled, shaking his head in disbelief. "Yuh just leave church babes. Wha kinda argument dat now?"

"*Another* interview? I swear to God, don't let me find yuh out!" She rolled her eyes and walked away.

Michael brazenly held Natalie's repugnant stare while he clutched tightly to her elbow. He realised in this moment, more than ever before, that everything they once had was now gone.

She forcefully yanked her arm away from him, breaking his gaze in the process. "Why are you here Michael?" She sneered at the shell of the man she once loved.

"Why the hell are you showing off in front of your little boy toy? Are you still mad?"

"Oh no! Why would I be mad? You *only* disrupted an important ceremony of a very close friend of mine... embarrassing me in the process! Not that it matters right?"

"Oh! We both know that he is *more* than a *friend* Natalie! Listen, I didn't come here to argue with you or cause you any worries. I just wanted to apologize for all the pain that I've caused you, and to let you know that I've signed the divorce papers that you served me!"

"So there, you're free as a bird now. Free to pretend to love your little white boy over there, but give his pussy away to some stallion! Take care of yourself!" He stepped aside and allowed her to storm past him.

Michael dreadfully watched as the two men who were tailing him all day, made their approach now that he was alone.

He instinctively rubbed his head. "Can we do this without the cuffs Sarge? I'm no threat." He casually addressed the one who held the warrant.

"I'm sorry it had to go down like this Michael...but we're shot for time. We should've picked you up on sight as per orders. We gave you as long as we could." Sergeant McKenzie coolly informed his friend though completely regretting the circumstance.

"I understand Dalton. You have to do your job. I'm ready anyhow." Michael truthfully admitted, as he hung his head in preparation for the walk of shame.

Regina sat in the driver's seat of her car, staring straight ahead while Linton professed his love and desire to rekindle their relationship. Though she admittedly missed him and wanted to repair their broken ties, she wasn't willing to let him off the hook that easily.

"I want to make us work Regina." He persisted. "I got all the documents together babe, *on my own*, to move to Cayman with you. I've been missing us babes...a lot!"

She finally glanced in his direction, giving him her undivided attention.

His eyes welled with tears. "I can't go another day without hearing your voice or sleeping next to you. I want you to be my wife Regina! Grow old together you know? Even Roxanne, I miss being around to help her out. We can do this as a family babe. I know it!"

Regina chuckled. "Roxanne has her *own* family now; she's engaged." She sighed, soaking in that fact. "I've missed you too Linton...home is never the same. I tried my best to get over you, to move on with my life without you." She paused and looked directly in his eyes. "But..."

She was caught off guard by his spontaneous lip-lock, but welcomed it earnestly.

"Baby just please..." Linton was prepared to beg.

"Just let me finish!" She instantly cut him off. "Linton, the truth is nobody can replace you in my heart! Nobody can fill your shoes in my life. I love loving only you...and that's the plain truth."

"I love you more Regina!" He anxiously professed. "You are my everything!"

Biggs nestled his face in Roxanne's neck and playfully bit her. "Babes, cheer up nuh! How long yuh ago vex ova di white gyal?" He lovingly caressed her tummy then leaned his *lenky* frame over her, looking down into her eyes.

"Andre, leave me alone please. I'm not vex!" She instinctively rolled her eyes with that confession, but giggled when he pinched her on the nipple. "*Alright*! *Stop it*! Yuh can't behave? We're in public!" She tried to chastise him between laughs but he completely disregarded her concerns. "I said *stop*! I'm not vex babes…for real. You just don't understand the history with that bitch! She really did Shane bad back in the day."

"*Shane*!" He almost shrieked, but continued more coolly. "Amanda messed with Shane babes?" He had thought that's what she had said before he snatched his wallet.

"Messed *up* Shane is more accurate. They dated a while back for a *really long* time. But not only did she cheat on him and embarrass him in front of the whole Jamaica, she fucked his father! I didn't tell you all that." She pointedly eyed him.

Biggs sealed the zipper across his lips. "All of *that*?"

"Hmm…*and* more. But anyways, I'm starving. What are these people really up to though?" She scanned the surrounding area and spotted Regina necking with Linton. That made her smile inside.

"Andre, I'm seriously starving! What the hell?"

"Babes what yuh want mi to do? You want to go buy something and come back?"

"*Buy* something? As in there's a place that sells personalised *backshots*? That's what I'm starving for!"

He blurted out a laugh. "Babes, yuh wicked eeh man! I thought we were talking about food! All of a sudden you have a sex drive? Hold on let me take this…"

He retrieved his vibrating cell phone from his pocket.

"Hey Michelle. What's up?"

"Biggs, sorry to bother yuh but it's urgent." She only contacted him when necessary since they had ended their intimate relationship.

"No it's cool Mich. Is something wrong?" He watched as Roxanne struggled to climb into his truck.

"Biggs, *we're* pregnant!"

Natalie tightly embraced Tina and wiped the last of her tears from her cheeks.

"I just didn't visualize it to be like this you know?" She continued to vent in between sobs as Thomas lovingly caressed her back. "I've went over this day so many times in my head…what I'd do, what I'd say. I just didn't expect it to be so soon. He even looks so different now Tina…"

Tina held her friend. "Darling, you know better than anyone that nothing ever goes as planned! I'd say you did pretty well for someone who was caught off guard; right Thomas?" She intentionally included the gentleman who was evidently out of his element.

"That's right!" Thomas hastily offered.

Natalie took a deep breath and chuckled. "Thank you both so much. I couldn't have done it without you two." She turned to face an empathetic Thomas.

"As for you, I'm so glad that you're in my life…that you chose to be here with me…and you want to love me at my weakest and meanest moments. I thank God for you." She pecked him on the cheek.

As Tina admired the two love birds, she caught on to some excitement in the distant plane. Her wide grin instantly changed into a grimace.

"Linton, *look*!" Regina shouted as she pointed to the commotion stirring in the distance. "It's Michael! Should we go?" She seemed genuinely concerned.

Linton looked in the direction that was quickly becoming the center of attention for the guests and frenzied media. He consciously remained in his position.

"Stay where you are babes." He airily replied without any further explanation.

Though he had mentally prepared for this moment since the day Michael had confessed his transgressions, nothing could have prepared him for the emotional pain that was now racing through his veins. He fought to stifle the emotions that welled within his chest.

Shane looked beyond the photographer's lens and tried to observe the disruption at the exit to the parking area. He entirely disregarded the repeated directions to 'smile for the big one'. *What the hell is this now?* He pondered as he scanned the grounds to locate his mother.

"Sheldon, go see if mom is onto that!" He sternly ordered his brother.

"What's wrong Shane?" Lisa worriedly eyed him then quickly looked in the direction he was pointing. "Shane what's going on? This day cannot be ruined!"

"I know babe. I'm sorry. Look, stay here and take more pics with your girls. I'll take care of it okay?" He lovingly kissed her and smiled.

"Okay baby." She was her usual understanding self.

Biggs clutched his head and massaged his face, all in one motion. *Mi tink dem seh crassis come inna threes! Why the fuck mi get brawta? How mi ago explain this shit to Roxie now? Mi cyan kill none of my yutes!*

"What's the matter babes?" Roxanne called out from behind him. "Andre!" She shouted, growing impatient when his response delayed.

"Roxanne!" He reflexively snapped back and turned to face her. "Gimme a minute nuh! Nothing's the matter babes." He looked beyond her and caught on to the happenings ahead of them.

"Whatever!" Roxanne shot back. "How yuh so lie sometimes? If nothing's the matter then why yuh rubbing yuh head like that? Andre, I'm talking to yuh. What yuh staring at like that?" She looked to see what was causing his distraction.

"What the hell?" She unconsciously remarked. "Isn't that Michael babe?"

Michael Simmons used his arm to shield his face from the media photographers who worked fervently to gather their 'Breaking News'.

Though he had been obliged his request to withhold the handcuffs, the two plain-clothed police officers were now joined by four of their uniformed squadron as they escorted him to an unmarked vehicle.

Everything about the situation screamed drama, and there was no diverting the attention of the masses.

As soon as he got closer to the car, Natalie tried to approach him but was prohibited from penetrating the protective barrier by one of the uniformed officers.

Dalton quickly overrode the decision. "Let her through." He sternly instructed his partner.

"Michael, what's going on here?" She asked, tears glistening her eyes. "Why are the cops taking you…and where? What's happening?" She desperately searched his rigid expression for any clues.

Michael stared into the eyes of the woman he would always love and never forget. *What happened? Where should I start?* A smile barely curled the side of his lips as the memories of their happier moments flooded his mind. He looked up and briefly scanned the faces surrounding him, carefully noting the expressions on the few that were familiar. *Yes, I know I've let you all down. I love you too brother.* He noticed that Linton was missing. *Natalie, what didn't happen?* He determined to offer the safest response he could conjure when Dalton audibly cleared his throat.

"Natalie Carey, *life* happened."

Grandpa Harry Young:
"You fell asleep for eternity on my ninth birthday, hours after we hugged. Thank you for life lesson number one; Resilience. I love you. R.I.P"

Shawn Thompson:
"I lived vicariously with you through Shane Wright. God knows I wish the fates were reversed. I release you. I'll forever miss you. R.I.P my parrie."

Horace L. Murphy:
"You were what many men strive to be daily; a provider, professor, and protector. You're an irreplaceable dad. Miss you tonnes! R.I.P"

Guy Jones:
"Tears…that's the 'last' thought I had. Jah must've had a better plan for your beautiful soul. You're forever missed during basketball playoffs. R.I.P"

"Many are the afflictions of the righteous; but the LORD delivereth him out of them all." – Psalm 34:19

ABOUT THE AUTHOR

On September 28th, Libra celebrates the birthday of a few greats: Confucius, Amelie of Orleans, Immanuel Wallerstein, and Janeane Garofalo, to list a few. In keeping with its tradition, Libra also claimed the child born **Damali A. Henry**.

Born and raised in Kingston Jamaica, this colourful debut writer has always found herself in search of knowledge and self-enrichment through culture and the arts. In less than three decades, Damali has undertaken a vibrant life, enjoying her own quasi-anthropological observations of her hometown, fitting in a constant flow of energy and voracity for life. On her quest for fulfillment, she ventured to reside in the city of Havana, Cuba, where she perfected her second tongue Spanish. As if achieving bilingualism wasn't satisfying, she went on to tackle a third language, French, in the city of Montreal, Quebec where she currently resides.

Damali is an Honorary Graduate of Concordia University in the field of Accounting. She too had found herself TAUNTED By Choice…, attempting to fulfil as many aspects of her dynamism by deciding between pursuing her C.P.A designation and presenting to you this, her magnetic and entertaining novel.

This "young, gifted, and black" unstoppable woman brings to the world of literature, a taste of the island life that you don't get hints of by listening to Bob Marley's *One Love*. She keeps her readers intrigued by using unique ways to relate to each one of us through her characters, who like the rest of us, in one way or another, have found themselves **TAUNTED By Choice…**